THE KING'S MISTRESS

Clyve Rose

PRAISE FOR
Always A Princess

"I CAN RECOMMEND THIS BOOK TO "EVERYONE!! TRUE HISTORICAL .... AND AUTHENTIC CHARACTERS!!! HEART ❤ GRIPPING SCENES .... Absolutely .... Wonderful. TRULY A MUST READ!!" ~Veronica Martinez

"*Always a Princess was the story I didn't know I needed right now - and Wil and Syeira are magic! Rose's writing is beautiful and dialogue so vivid, placing me easily in Regency times. I love their dynamic -- two strong fierce spirits, whose connection is palpable -- and the world in which they move, not heightened by the fluff of aristocracy, but real movement in the times in which they lived. I also loved the focus on the Romany peoples. A refreshing change from typical "royal stories." Rose is knowledgeable on not only the time period, but the different groups - from outside to inside perspectives. And how this is conveyed through the story to the reader is seamless. Master Class."* ~Bay Reader

"I love immersing myself in another period, and it's a bonus when I can discover more about a place and culture. The author doesn't rely on tired stereotypes of a people, but strives to reveal the nature of noble and royal families within the predominate English society. The clash of cultures is unavoidable to heighten the story's tension that leads Captain Clifton and Princess Syeira closer. Their sweet romance is a slow burn of sexual tension until the satisfying end." ~Pax

www.BOROUGHSPUBLISHINGGROUP.com

THE KING'S MISTRESS
Copyright © 2023 Clyve Rose

ISBN 978-1-957295-26-8

For Beautiful Bella, who always belongs to herself

ACKNOWLEDGMENTS

For mum, Dad, Danni, Julie, Sara, Gavin & Alon – all the ones who encourage me to keep writing are in these pages somehow.

A special thank you to Jack, my editor, who made me a better writer with each draft.

AUTHOR'S NOTE

It is not feasible to summarize an ancient and noble culture in a short a note. Instead, I offer some of the research and insights from which I've been fortunate to benefit.

The arrival of the Romany people in continental Europe dates from much earlier than the Regency period, and the traditions of various tribes or houses vary with the geographic region in which they travelled. I concerned myself with the UK Romany only.

Romany people have been present in England since the 1500s. The first record of arrivals began in Scotland in 1505, and in England from 1513. In 1530 Parliament passed "The Egyptians Act," establishing the foundation for a prejudice that still exists today. Some readers may recall the manner in which the Romany people are portrayed in Austen's *Emma*, where they're termed "gypsies."

The term "Romani" is more popularly used today than "Romany," though in the Regency period "gypsy" would have been correct among the English. However, in today's world, the term "gypsy" is often considered a slight, which is why I altered it in my story.

The King's Mistress (and *Always a Princess*) include some anachronisms, which I've detailed below:

Romany caravans: The covered wagons now so popularly identified with the Romany people were not commonly used in England until the 1850s. They were found on the continent a little earlier. The word *vardo* is used more often than *covo*, but both are accurate.

Romany royalty: The title "King of the Gypsies" has existed in England since at least the 1600s. It may be inherited, or bestowed, and sometimes simply claimed. One of the most famous royal Romany families of England were the Boswells. They were large in number and often negotiated between the English and the Romany, which is how their reputation grew. I debated a great deal as to Valkin's "title," and agreed with my authenticity reader on the slightly awkward English translation of his Romany *krallis* to Romany King. It's slightly anachronistic, because Regency Englishmen would undoubtedly have called him a gypsy to his face, and gypsy king when they felt it necessary. I have explained my reasoning for not preferring a pejorative term.

Romany Language: Much of my information comes from a Romany-English manuscript I discovered, dated from about 1865.

Further Reading:
These are a few of the available resources, for those readers who are interested:
Smart, B. C.; Croften, H T (1875) *The Dialect of the English Gypsies*
MacRitchie, David (1894) *Scottish Gypsies under the Stewarts*
Acton, Thomas Alan; Mundy, Gary (1997) *Romani culture and Gypsy identity*

With thanks to the University of Hertfordshire Romani Studies Unit, my own family history, and the inspiring Roma who have shared their stories with me.

GLOSSARY OF ROMANY TERMS

Bebee – aunt

Bengako – a place belonging to devils (hell), and is used as a curse word

Boronashemeskrutan – references the Epsom race course, where the derby is still held today

Boshta – saddle

Bostaris – bastard

Brishen – born during a rainstorm

Cana – now

Covo – caravan

Dosta – enough

Gadje – a non-Romany woman

Gadjo – a non-Romany man

Gare – to hide or conceal, or to take care

Gry – horse – *gry* pens refers to the horse enclosures

Gry-engros – horsemen, horse-fellows

Kek cana – not now

Ker– home though it's sometimes mistaken to mean camp, or campsite

Koshti sarla – good evening

Kosko – good

Krallis – king

Kris-tan – the tent in which the kris is held

Levinor – a type of ale in the Regency era that likely contained wormwood

Mi Dubblesky – for god's sake

Miro – my or mine

Muscro – constable

Paracrow – thanks or to thank

Paracrow tute – I thank you

Pireni – sweetheart

Rak – beware

Rak tute –take care of yourself

Ratfelo fakement – precious scoundrel

Sarishan – a greeting – how are you or peace to you

Shan – you

Sher-engro – Head man – every Romany house (or tribe) has one

Sherro dukkers – head aches – commonly refers to a hangover

Shuvvali – with child, pregnant

Syeira – princess as well as a girl's name

Tatchipen si – it is truth

Vardo – caravan

Yag-engri – gun

THE KING'S MISTRESS

Romany Rhyme *(trans. c. 1625)*
Lavender's blue, dilly dilly
Lavender's green;
While I am king, dilly dilly
You shall be queen.

Who told you so, dilly dilly?
Who told you so?
'Twas mine own heart, dilly dilly
That told me so.

PROLOGUE

1 November 1820

Fosse Way, Lancashire

Lydia

"Ouf." Martha winced as she slammed against the unpadded carriage seat.

"M-*Martha*." Lydia grabbed her maid's flailing hands. "Are you h-hurt?"

"No, my lady," her maid replied stoutly, though it was clear she'd felt the jolt.

"This c-curricle is n-not suff-fficient to c-carry our party and so m-many bandboxes. I d-did request the London c-carriage." Lydia's stammer grew worse when she remembered her father's response. "Are you m-much bruised?"

Martha muttered something under her breath and frowned, though whether in answer to Lydia's inquiry or the duke's—her *father's*—refusal to grant them his carriage, Lydia could only guess. Martha grabbed the side of the vehicle to steady her seat. Lydia did the same, wishing she'd brought her travelling herbs.

"Have a care, Young Yates," she called out.

Her driver barely turned his head. "I'm tryin', my lady."

"It's this stretch of run-down road, my lady," Martha soothed, arm firmly around Lydia's trembling shoulders.

By the time the curricle sped up the drive to Clifton Hall, Lydia was certain her bones rattled right out of her skin. Young Yates drew up before the door and leapt down to assist them. Lydia expelled a slow breath, gazing at browning fields and fallowed farmland. A crispness to the air signalled the onset of winter. Soon, she'd be free to wander Clifton Woods, her dog by her side and room to ramble about in peace. Bruised in pride as well as body, Lydia shivered as she looked around. The countryside might be enough to shake off the pain of a second lacklustre Season.

"It's good to be home." She smiled at the heavy oak door, keeping an ear out for her little dog. Bony usually bounded into sight at the first sound of her voice. Stretching inelegantly in a manner that would have scandalised her governesses, Lydia's smile fell away as the door opened. Instead of the usual coterie of footmen, Mrs Edwards appeared. The duke's housekeeper brandished a paper in her hand, lips forming a sorrowful frown. Her paper bore the duke's seal. *What now?*

"G-good a-aftern-noon, Eddy. Is s-someth-thing amiss?"

"Begging your pardon, Lady Lydia. I've just this hour received His Grace's instruction, sent express." She paused as though preparing to deliver a blow of some sort.

Lydia raised her eyebrows, held her breath, and waited.

"You're bid to Davenport Manor for their Bonfire Night. Your hosts offer a house party run on from Michaelmas. The carriage is to convey you directly, in a manner befitting the duchy." She took a breath, releasing her words like pepperbox bullets. "You—you are not to stay at the Hall tonight."

Martha gasped, and Young Yates let out a cough.

"We've been nearly three weeks on the road." Martha's tone bridled. "Mrs Edwards—"

Lydia placed a hand on Martha's arm; *steady, steadying, steadiest.* "Hush, M-Martha. This is n-not Eddy's d-doing, and Davenport M-manor is n-not so far. Another n-night or two b-before we m-may rest, is all." She dug her nails into the palm of her hand, hoping her voice sounded less pained than the housekeeper's. "I suppose I m-mayn't take Bony?"

Atop the ancient stone steps, the housekeeper tightened her lips.

"Eddy?" she repeated. "D-did Papa say I c-could n-not?"

"He did not, my lady." Eddy's voice quavered.

"H-have Young Yates fetch him to the c-carriage, then."

"I cannot, Lady Lydia," Eddy replied. "Your little dog isn't here. His Grace—"

"—G-gave h-him away." Lydia forced herself to meet Eddy's limpid gaze. "I see." She faced away from the Hall, staring at the lowering sun. *Was this how Mama felt?*

Swallowing a ball of hurt, Lydia stifled the urge to dissolve into tears beneath the ancient stone lintel. Crying solved nothing and trials must be faced. She turned back to the others, holding herself ramrod straight.

"We're for the D-Davenports', then. The c-carriage c-cannot be readied in less than an hour. D-do g-go in and refresh yourself, M-Martha, and remember to pack my calming herbs. I've a feeling I shall need those." She hoped she sounded as brisk addressing her coachman. "You'll wish to visit your family b-before staying away again, Young Yates. Please, c-convey m-my c-compliments to your m-mother b-before removing our b-belongings to the c-carriage."

"Thank you, m'lady." Young Yates's face filled with something suspiciously akin to pity.

Lydia eyed all three members of the duke's household. "There's n-nothing else to b-be d-done," she said bleakly. "Is there?"

"At least you'll not trouble yourself with much preparation," Eddy replied.

"Oh?" Lydia tried a smile that didn't hurt too much.

"His Grace sent new gowns ahead of you, direct from France. They'll await you at Davenport Manor. Will you sit by the fireside now, my lady?" Eddy's request sounded more like a plea.

Lydia pretended not to hear, walking slowly towards the stables. Between pity and solitude, she preferred solitude.

"Hello?" she called out. The grooms were gone to their dinnertime. Approaching the stall at the back, Lydia dug in her travelling cloak for the apple she'd saved since the last hostelry. The handsome hunter she'd inherited from her eldest brother nosed his way above the stall door, whinnying in welcome.

"Yes, Stammer, it's m-me." She fed him the fruit and stroked his long nose with a sigh. "I'm n-not able to stay, boy. I'm to go westward." The Irish Sea lay to the west, leading to the channel, to France, and her brother. Lord Clifton hadn't returned for her second Season. It didn't matter. Not really. *Then why am I crying?*

"I'm not," she whispered into Stammer's warm, powerful neck, before opening the lower door and leading the gelding to the tack room. She didn't see her side saddle. In any case, she needed help to mount that way. Roger's saddle sat in its bracket, leather gleaming and polished despite its owner having been absent from Clifton Hall a year to the day. Lydia fingered the stirrups. The grooms wouldn't return for at least an hour. Using both hands, she tugged at the stirrup, catching the saddle against her body with a grunt. Holding it as high as she could, she addressed the horse.

"What d-do you say, boy? Once around Clifton Park?"

Stammer clopped forward a length, shaking out his mane. Lydia took this as agreement. She hefted the device over the horse's back in a practised manner, found the rest of his tack and led him to her mounting post. Hitching up her skirts in a way that'd scandalise the ton, she lifted one thigh across the horse and sat, nodding her satisfaction.

Only a few years ago she'd been afraid of horses. Patience, persistence, and her sister-in-law's coaching by correspondence won her over in the end. Lydia was as proficient now as any lady of the ton. *More so, in this seat.* No English lady would ride astride as Lydia did—though only when no one else might notice her.

Once through the doorway, she dug in her knees and leaned forward. Excitement thrilled through her as Stammer shot rapidly across Clifton Park. A shout followed her as she passed the far wall of the carriage house. Young Yates, presumably reminding her they'd best be on the move.

Lydia shook her head as chilly air whooshed through her lungs, wind teasing her hair and cramped muscles stretching in the bracing air. If she must spend another day on the road, and weeks entombed at a house party among her father's cronies, she'd sustain herself with this moment. *I will have this.* This wildness, this drumming of hooves and breathing of air. A quarter hour, she promised herself, perhaps a half.

She smiled, bending lower over the horse's neck, breathing in oiled leather and recently worked muscle. Grinning, she whispered to the animal, urging him on, wishing to ride away and never return.

"I have to go back." She spoke into the wind. Reining in her horse, she exhaled loudly, refusing to turn it into a sob. As they reentered the stable yard, she dismounted and Young Yates took charge of the horse.

"We're past due for departure, my lady."

"Thank you, Young Yates." Accepting his arm to her carriage, Lydia stepped in, followed shortly by Martha. Somewhere, a clock tower chimed for five. They'd arrive too late for the dinner hour at any inn. Still, it wasn't as if a post house would refuse them. She was a duke's daughter, after all.

CHAPTER ONE

Lydia

The next afternoon, the duke's carriage bumped towards another of Lancashire's great houses as a slice of afternoon sun broke the trees. Lydia ran nervous fingers over the intricate filigree of her mama's jewel box. Vines and lavender flowers flashed gold, but the cameo set into the lid was Lydia's own work. She traced the shape of the late duchess's face, wondering if she could hope to match Mama's beauty.

"It's lovely work, my lady," Martha whispered, waking as the carriage lurched from paved road onto the great gravel drive of Davenport Manor. "Your mama would be proud."

Lydia smiled uncertainly. Her smile widened as Martha sat up, her curls in disarray from her unscheduled doze. Martha felt about for misplaced hairpins.

"I beg your pardon. I ought not to have nodded off like that."

"You've b-been awake since dawn, Martha. The maids at the post house were dreadful, and I'd not bear this at all without you. I insist you b-be well-rested."

"Only you would say so, my lady."

Lydia's brows rose as she bit back a retort, shaking her head.

"This invitation is very short notice, to be sure," Martha added.

"Indeed." A twinge of unease snaked down Lydia's spine. "I'm n-not sure why P-papa insists w-we a-attend."

His Grace rarely allowed his only daughter to attend mixed gatherings. This invitation seemed cajoled from Lady Davenport in a last-ditch attempt to attract a suitable match for Lydia as the duke's "unfashionable daughter." *What other reason could there be?*

"We'll be arriving shortly." Martha peered out the window.

Lydia leaned forward for her first glimpse of Davenport Manor. The house wasn't as large as Clifton Hall. No estate in Lancashire came close to eclipsing the duchy, but the manor house's gabled sandstone splendour certainly impressed. The lands were well-appointed with handsome woods running to forest. Lydia looked forward to exploring the Ribble valley on horseback, if she were allowed to ride unaccompanied.

"You'd b-best take this." Lydia handed the jewel case to Martha before adjusting her own pins. Martha stowed the box and took over Lydia's toilette. Moments later, their carriage drew up before the alabaster portico. Young Yates helped Lydia down, and she found herself curtsying awkwardly before Lord and Lady Davenport.

"Lady Lydia, we'd quite despaired of you. However, here you are, my dear, and I've never been more delighted. You're just in time for tea." Lady Davenport drew Lydia's arm into her own and escorted her into the house. Lord Davenport stood by the carriage, seemingly admiring the duke's greys. Well-trained, even-gaited, and with handsome, dappled coats, Lydia could hardly blame his lordship. She, too, preferred equine company to that of the ton.

Crack. Lydia flinched as a shot cut the air.

Lady Davenport pursed her lips a touch. "The gentlemen are out shooting while the light holds."

"I b-b-beg your p-pardon, Lady D-Daven-nport, are there *m-many* g-gentlem-men in a-tten-ndance?" Lydia tried not to sound as though this prospect was at all terrifying.

Lady Davenport glanced impatiently at her husband as they stepped into the grand hall. "Quite a number, dear, I assure you. We've an array of families staying on from Michaelmas so you'll not pine for company. Is there someone in particular to whom you wish an introduction? There are the earls, and—"

"Oh. N-n-o." Lydia blushed. She hadn't meant to interrupt. "You m-misunderstand me, Lady D-Davenp-port. I m-mean, that is, I d-do not wish to b-beg for any p-particular g-gentleman's ac-cquainttance—" she stammered, fervently hoping she didn't appear forward, or desperate, or indeed *interested*. Lydia looked down, her hands shaking slightly.

"Pray do not distress yourself, Lady Lydia. His Grace sent word that he means to escort you himself once his business in London is concluded."

Lady Davenport spoke kindly, but Lydia's insides quailed. "P-papa is c-coming *here*?" She did her best to conceal her alarm. "Wh-when d-does h-he a-arr-rrive?"

"I've not an idea, my dear. It's all been rather rushed, hasn't it? In the meantime, perhaps my daughter may do as well for your companion. You are young, beautiful, and well-dowried. You must not want for suitors. I remember my own Season like it was yesterday." Her ladyship looked up at the grand staircase as if her younger self stood there, attired in white with her tiara and tresses. "Lord Clifton was one of my first callers, you know."

Lydia forbore to mention that her brother Roger had likely called on all the attractive women who came out in her ladyship's Season. He was known for it. Indeed, the only Season he'd missed was his sister's.

"Shall we join the others?" Lady Davenport suggested. "I am in dire need of tea." Without further preamble, she led Lydia the length of the hall and into the conservatory.

"How lovely," Lydia exclaimed, the abundance of rich blooms offering a refreshing sight.

Lady Davenport inclined her gracious head, studying the plants. "I'm glad you're able to see them to advantage, dear. I hardly expected such colours. Come, there's conversation and cakes aplenty."

Most of the ladies were already seated. Lydia helped herself to fruit and tea before making her way to a solitary chaise flanked by a set of prettily screened tables. Placed well enough for the appearance of participation, the larger plants seemed to afford less expectation of conversation. Or so she thought.

"Lady Lydia?" A girlish voice breathed across her. Lydia looked up to find Miss Davenport arranging herself at the end of the chaise. Fresh from her mama's side and clearly following instructions, the girl was several years younger than herself, blonde, petite, and fair. Her blue eyes seemed very round to Lydia as the girl set down her tea.

"Mama suggested we become acquainted while you are with us, if this is agreeable?"

Lydia blinked. "Er… yes, of c-c-course, Miss D-Davenport." She flushed, recognising the startled expression on the girl's face. Clearly, Miss Davenport hadn't expected their conversation to proceed quite so painfully. Lydia bit the inside of her lips, fisting her hands in her lap. The girl glanced at her pityingly before shooting an ill-concealed glance at her mama. A moment later, she placed her teacup beside Lydia's, somewhat shame-faced.

"I beg your pardon, Lady Lydia. Mama didn't mention any impediment." Miss Davenport spoke in an undertone. "Are you quite well?"

Lydia nodded, her cheeks burning. "A n-nervous habit only, Miss Davenport, among c-crowds."

"Oh, *nerves*, is it?" The young lady's relief broadened her smile. "You need have no fears here, then. There's no ailment we understand so well as nerves." She glanced at her mama before lowering her eyes.

One or two matrons nodded, tutting in Lydia's direction. *Pity, again? Ugh.* Still, it was better than disdain. There'd be plenty of that once her father arrived.

A collective turning of beribboned heads drew Lydia's focus to Lady Davenport. She rose serenely, gliding towards a gentleman guest.

Miss Davenport seemed to deflate at this. "How long may it take to purchase a horse, indeed? He's stayed three full days already." She rattled her spoon against her saucer, plainly more irritated than good breeding allowed.

Lydia craned her neck to glimpse a dark-haired man, smiling easily as he shook Lord Davenport's hand. She sank back in her seat as a strange thrill shot through her, cheeks warming. Lydia knew this overstaying guest.

Valkin Brishen, the Romany King. As she dared another look at his face, an odd, tingling sensation teased Lydia's nerves. In the days when she'd dreamed of suitors, she'd dreamed of this man: strong, steady, and effortlessly charming, with an unyielding commitment to those he cared about. Lydia had admired Valkin ever since she'd first known him as a friend of her absent brothers. Now here he was, as handsome as she remembered.

He smiled warmly at Lady Davenport. *Hmmm*...rumours of Lord Brishen's affairs were among the most scandalous whispers each Season. Everyone knew he indulged his taste for *gadje*, or Englishwomen, among the nobility. Few ladies of the ton said anything against this. At least his affairs seemed discreet, unlike the duke's.

"Did you remark the gypsy man's arrival for All Hallow's Eve?" Lydia heard someone mutter. "It's not a gypsy occasion. I deem it odd."

"Perhaps he stays for the bonfires," another lady in pink ruffles suggested, her gaze raking over him as though he were dessert. "I've heard they make clever entertainments."

"Do those people bother to observe the Saint's Days?"

"The Romany observe them as well as the rest of us," Lydia replied clearly, aware of the scowls in her direction from several quarters. *Though I don't believe Valkin is here to attend church.*

Miss Davenport turned to her in surprise. "I understand gypsies are properly barred from your duchy." Her tone was prim and more than a little clipped, as though she knew of the connection Lord Brishen shared with her mama.

"I-it is not m-my d-duchy." Lydia was spared from further response by the reappearance of Lady Davenport.

"Enjoying yourself, my dear?" She smiled. "We repair to the music room shortly. Florence is longing to play for us. Shall we also hear you perform?"

Alarm shivered through Lydia's gut. "Oh no, please. I c-c-cannot s-s-sing before s-so many p-p-people."

"Of course she can't, Mama," Miss Davenport agreed, suddenly supportive. "I shall sing well enough for us both. The Lady Lydia may turn my pages, if she wishes." Rising, she waited to slip her arm into Lydia's, guiding her to an apartment fitted up with pastel drapes and seats patterned in violently vibrant brocades. A handsome instrument stood centre place, eliciting much admiration as the audience took their seats.

Miss Davenport performed a short medley for her mama. It was enough for Lydia to see that her talents were hardly exaggerated.

"Y-y-you sing b-b-beautifully," Lydia said as Miss Davenport accompanied her to her seat.

Miss Davenport turned on the first genuine smile Lydia had seen her display. "Thank you. As you do not sing, Lady Lydia, what is your favourite employment? Do you play at all?"

"Sketching is m-m-my *m-métier*," she replied.

"Not one of my talents, I'm afraid."

They spoke of art and music until Lady Davenport rose to leave, the faintest pink tingeing her cheeks. Miss Davenport's expression darkened as her mother left the music room. The girl looked positively thunderous.

"Miss D-Davenport? Is s-something amiss?"

She shook her head, making her way to the tea table. The pink-ruffled debutant curtsied before Lydia, slipping into the vacated seat as though invited.

"I am Miss Jessup, Lady Lydia." She offered a too-bright smile, forcing Lydia to suppress a grimace.

Miss Jessup appeared older than Miss Davenport and less blessed with her agreeable disposition. "Florence must be distressed to see *him* here," the ill-natured girl leaned in, hardly whispering. "It's not for me to repeat idle gossip, you understand, but the gypsy's attendance on our hostess was remarked upon in London. It's said her ladyship departed town on purpose to attend that fellow here."

Lydia glanced solicitously towards Miss Davenport. "Lord D-davenport keeps a fine stable," she said stoutly. "It is certainly b-business that b-brings the L-lord B-brish-shen to D-davenport Manor."

Miss Jessup recovered quickly. "This gypsy is known for attending to business. He's said to be *quite* irresistible."

Her grin faltered in the face of Lydia's stony expression. "You know this yourself?"

"Of course not." Miss Jessup huffed. "I'm not his sort. That is to say, I am not wed. Gypsies only take what belongs to others. They do not respect us."

"Perhaps respect ought to be earned, rather than demanded." Lydia cleared her throat. "Have you heard of any Englishwomen he's harmed?"

"None have said so," Miss Jessup admitted. "All who know him say he is charming."

"Then you might keep your gossip to yourself." Lydia swallowed her ire. "My mama, the duchess, considered it terribly vulgar to tattle about one's hosts." She rose, joining Miss Davenport at her pianoforte.

"I thank you, Lady Lydia," Miss Davenport whispered.

Lydia offered a half-smile. "Think nothing of it. I hear worse rumours regarding Clifton Hall. Will you have the minuet?"

Nodding, Miss Davenport gazed up at her page-turner as though she were an oracle. "It appears ill-intent is the cure for your speech."

Lydia blinked in surprise. "It s-seems you are right, Miss D-Davenport."

More curious gazes followed Lady Davenport's return, whispers swelling in her wake. Now was not the time for reflection on the power of righteous anger to drive away impediments.

Opening up the sheet music, Lydia gestured to the keys. "Shall we?"

Bending her head, the girl looked as though she might cry. *Another Season ending in tears.* Lydia sighed, grateful in this moment that these were not her own.

***

Valkin

"You'll stay to tea, at least?" Lady Davenport reached for Valkin's arm, but he shook his head. Given the subject of their conversation, she addressed him as near the open conservatory door as possible.

"I'll not place you at risk, Eliza." His low voice was as much for his protection as hers. "Your husband returns with his friends." He bowed at the Englishmen who'd grown tired of their guns and wandered in to replenish their appetites. Valkin raised his brows at the host's weaving manner.

"Brishen," Lord Davenport shouted. "My groom's taken a turn on that animal of yours. First rate, man. First rate." He warmed his hands before the grate. "Less of a gamble than I'd have thought, having seen him run."

Valkin cleared his throat, managing a smile. Now was not the time to point out the starter under discussion was a mare. Not when his lordship was on the point of agreement. He risked a glance at Liza. Warm, buxom, and generously proportioned, she was an engaging woman and an accomplished lover. Valkin turned his attention to concluding his business with her husband. No wonder his lordship's wife took her pleasures with stable boys and Romany horse traders. *You're a king*, he reminded himself as a bevy of inebriated Englishmen milled round Lord Davenport.

"I am glad you approve of the horse, my lord. As to the investment required, it is—"

Davenport waved him away. "Yes, yes. Have your agreements to my man by morning, and you'll have the guineas before you leave." He jerked his head towards the music room and held out his arm to his wife.

Liza took her place beside her husband, but not before inclining her head at his fellows. "You will join us, gentlemen?"

The Englishmen trooped past her ladyship to the music room. Liza spoke over her shoulder to Valkin. "You've not seen my daughter perform, Lord Brishen."

"Nothing would please me more." He bowed, following the sounds of a prettily played pianoforte. The music and lovely companions induced Valkin to sit a while, much to the delight of Liza and her more libertine friends. There were worse things than sipping tea while watching a pair of pretty young ladies work at their instrument. He wondered why the page turner—far fairer than the player—didn't take her turn to exhibit. She was quite the loveliest girl there. Why, if she'd been older and married…. Valkin shifted in his seat, aware of the glances many ton ladies threw his way. He'd not engage in such antics at Liza's gathering. Not while assorted *gadjos* stared threats and fury from beneath their waxed brows and overgrown moustaches.

He started as Lady Boscowan seated herself beside him, thigh tight against his. Valkin adjusted his seat again, aware the lady's husband was the most powerful lord in Derbyshire.

"Where are you for the winter, Brishen?"

"Nowhere in Derbyshire, I am sorry to say, my lady." He rose, bowing his regrets. "I am quite delighted with tea today." Valkin found it safer to collect his cup and stand nearer the performers than their audience. His gaze settled once more on the pretty page turner. She seemed familiar. His tea cooled as he studied the girl. Her lips were the kissable sort. Now where the deuce had he seen her face before?

He blinked, applauding with the rest when Miss Davenport completed her performance and led her friend to a nearby settee.

When the Earl of Basingstoke positioned himself opposite the young ladies, Valkin moved nearer. The old lech leered at Liza's daughter and her companion, despite the mourning crepe binding his upper arm. With Lord Davenport's other friends nose-deep in their wine, Valkin set down his tea as a swish of skirts announced Lady Davenport. She placed herself squarely between her daughter and the earl.

"Fetch us our tea, Florence dear." Her mother shooed her daughter towards the heavily laden table with one hand, tucking her other arm through the page turner's.

Valkin took up his cup, smiling to himself. The ton didn't deserve Liza. He edged closer, the better to eavesdrop on Miss Davenport's mysteriously familiar acquaintance.

Liza uttered a sound low in her throat. "My condolences on your countess, Lord Basingstoke."

The earl hardly glanced at her. "It is most inconvenient to lose one's wife at the end of the Season."

"It's rare to see you at a house party these days," Liza continued. "We're honoured to host you in Lancashire."

"I travel this far for *sport*." His predatory glance fixed on Miss Davenport's friend. "I am promised sport." Basingstoke's pout held an air of menace.

"I'm certain Lord Davenport's gamebirds are at your disposal, my lord." Liza remained serene.

"It wasn't Davenport who vouchsafed my amusements." The earl's tone darkened. "It was a duke."

Miss Davenport's friend ducked her head as though she'd been struck. Prickles of unease tingled low in Valkin's gut. Was she the subject of ton gossip this Season? Was this why she didn't take her turn to sing? The unlucky girl raised her chin. "Y-you ought to take c-care, m-my l-lord. N-not all game is d-defenceless."

Valkin nearly choked on his tea, more surprised by the girl's response than her stilted speech. Rapacious earls had this effect.

Basingstoke's lip curled. "The ones who fight afford the most pleasure. I take satisfaction in beating a bird."

The girl rose abruptly. "I b-b-beg you will excuse me," she whispered, following Miss Davenport to the tea table.

Valkin wondered where her male relations were. They ought not to leave so spirited a girl unprotected. *Speaking of which…* He turned as Lady Davenport introduced one of the more sober gentlemen.

"May I present Lord LeFroy? He's newly arrived from Ireland and wishes to fill his stable."

Valkin bowed. "Brishen can help you there, my lord."

The young man bowed uncertainly. "So Lady Davenport tells me." He indicated a quiet corner of the music room. "Shall we?"

Valkin nodded, smiling his thanks to Eliza. This sojourn among the English need not be a complete loss after all.

CHAPTER TWO

Lydia

Lydia accepted her third cup of tea, watching the rising steam to avoid the earl's harsh stare.

"D-does your f-family know the earl w-well, Miss D-Davenport?" Lydia ventured.

"Not at all, though his late wife was a cousin." Miss Davenport's undertone accompanied her simpering smile. "Mama was surprised when his lordship accepted our invitation. I am not yet out, you know. However, Basingstoke *is* an earl, and it's rumoured he has the favour of a duke."

"Yes, I know this of c-course," Lydia replied. "Is h-he n-not in m-mourning?"

Miss Davenport leaned in so closely, Lydia inhaled rosewater décolletage. "I've heard his late wife made him unhappy, Lady Lydia. Have you not heard the same?"

"I've n-not." Lydia remained near to the ingénue, feeling this was urgent. "M-my information says it was quite the other way around. The c-countess is the one d-dead, after all." Exhaling the tiniest fraction, Lydia glared steadily and unyieldingly at the earl. The way he stared back unnerved her. She pushed her tea away.

"My dear, are you quite well?" Lady Davenport studied her with renewed concern.

"A s-sudden h-headache, y-your ladyship." Lydia's nails scored the skin of her palms as she stared at the floor.

"Of course," Lady Davenport responded smoothly, stepping to the bell. "You've only just arrived. The housekeeper shall see you to your room. I'll have tea sent up with your maid."

"Y-your ladyship is very k-kind." Silence, tea, and Martha's comforting presence—if only her hostess knew the depths of her gratitude.

The housekeeper arrived beside Lady Davenport, whispering in her ear again. She smiled knowingly at Lydia.

"Chawton tells me a trunk has arrived for you, via Paris." She sipped her tea. "Perhaps a gift, my dear? From an admirer?"

Lydia's cheeks scorched as she hurried after Chawton. Whatever gift awaited in her rooms, it couldn't have come from a suitor. Lady Lydia Clifton, stammering veteran of two Seasons, had once again departed the capital without addresses.

Martha, of course, was already pressing Lydia's gowns. "There's a trunk from Worth's of Paris, my lady."

"My new gowns," Lydia muttered, laying the lid aside. Lifting the topmost garment from the wrappings, she held it up, staring. It was the new Parisienne style, fashioned from deeply green-dyed cloth. Beneath the gown were silk stockings and matching emerald garters, ribboned and jewelled with finely worked stitching.

Martha gasped. "That colour, my lady."

"The c-colour is lovely, Martha, but I f-fail to understand His G-grace's reasoning."

Martha tutted and shrugged. "His Grace is keen to see you married, my lady, and the colour does match your eyes. Perhaps the duke—"

Lydia glanced up sharply and her maid fell silent. *Perhaps the duke cares about his useless daughter?* Why now? She turned her attention to her new garments. The deepened bodice and the pipe-stem corsetry mocked her.

"Martha, are they not—well, a little, erm—"

"Brief?" Martha's cheeks were redder than Lydia's own.

"There's no note." Lydia shook her head. "Not a word." Nevertheless, it was clear from the timing of this arrival that the gowns and the new style of stays were to be worn immediately. The stays were stiff and seemed designed to torture Lydia's generous breasts. Martha pulled the laces as tight as she could, until Lydia noticed blood on the girl's fingers.

"That's enough, Martha," Lydia said firmly. "Find some salve as soon as you can." She pressed a palm to her side, attempting an exhalation; *impossible. Ugh.* Standing before the bevelled mirror, she reddened anew. "Is this truly all there is?"

Martha clucked her tongue, attempting to pull the bodice higher. Her tugging strained at the stays, and Lydia gasped. "No, don't, dear. I can barely breathe as it is. There's no wrap, is there?"

"No, my lady." Martha rustled the tissued papers in proof.

Lydia resisted the urge to clap her palms over her bodice. Her breasts were large for her frame and now lifted into her chin, the pipestem cords buoying them well above the edging of her bodice. French lace teased her sensitive skin to tiny pimples, as though someone touched her there. An image of Valkin Brishen flashed through her mind. Her nipples reacted too until her blush deepened.

Is this how marriageable ladies are supposed to look? Did Mama ever wear such a costume? Knowing what she did of her mother, Lydia doubted it. She doubted as well that the late duchess would have agreed to attire her daughter in so tasteless a manner.

"I appear more like Papa's whores than I do a duchess's daughter."

"I am sorry you think so, my lady."

Lydia sighed at the quaver in Martha's voice. "Never mind." She stiffened her spine. Her posture, at least, must be perfect. Her body had no other choice. "I shall wear this in to dine."

I will not cry. I will not.

***

The Earl of Basingstoke seated himself beside Lydia at dinner. She did her best to ignore his gaze slithering down her bodice. The man made no conversation, seeming more concerned in preventing her attentions to other acquaintance. After the meal, Lydia turned abruptly into the nearest room to be rid of him. Basingstoke followed her like a bird dog on point. Stationing herself on the far side of the billiards table, she gazed past him at the open door.

"I sh-shouldn't l-like to b-be accused of m-monopolising you, s-sir," she hinted politely.

The earl did not smile. "When does His Grace arrive?"

"His Grace does not discuss his plans with me."

"Very naturally not."

Basingstoke was not to be trusted. Not with her acquaintance, nor with her person—and certainly not with her dowry. While no good could come from antagonising her father's friend, Lydia's grateful smile when Lord Davenport joined them was the most heartfelt expression she'd worn all evening.

"I shall leave you gentlemen to your game." She curtsied, speaking as brightly as possible.

"Excellent notion, my dear." Lord Davenport turned to Basingstoke. "What do you say, my lord? A game before we turn in?"

Basingstoke scowled at their host racking the billiards. The look he shot Lydia was pure venom. Suppressing a shudder, she slipped quietly out of the room and glanced around the hall, seeking an exit.

She stopped a passing housemaid. "Where d-does that d-doorway lead?"

The maid curtsied. "That's the side door to the topiary walk, my lady. It's pretty by moonlight. Shall I send your lady's maid after you?"

Miss Davenport forestalled her. "There's no need, Susan. I shall accompany Lady Lydia." She curtsied, offering her arm.

Lydia smiled, allowing herself to be led.

"Oh," she breathed, taking in the attractively laid out garden, lit by several lambent sconces.

"How do you like it?"

"It's t-too lovely," Lydia breathed. "It inclines m-me to capture the d-design in a sketch, or perhaps an embroidered hanging."

Miss Davenport clapped her hands delightedly. "Mama should adore such a treasure. Do you think you may complete such during your stay with us?"

Lydia nodded. "I s-shall attempt it, at l-least. For y-you and y-your mama, who are k-kind enough to host me."

"It is our pleasure," Miss Davenport replied, shivering as they completed a turn and sat. "My wrap is forgot." She rose, turning towards the house but Lydia hesitated. Her companion seemed surprised. "Are you not cold, Lady Lydia?"

"Er—n-no, I thank you. I shall c-consider this scene a few more moments. The silvering moonlight complements the roses. Perhaps less leaves, yes, I see how I might manage it." The urge to lose herself in her design was great. It was all she could do not to turn away from her friend. "You may be sure I'll follow."

Miss Davenport curtsied and returned to the house. The last white roses of the year scented the air, set against the darker leaves one found in this part of the country. Lydia breathed deeply their sweetness, studying the intricately shaped trees placed at careful intervals along the walk. She sighed aloud as she studied the garden, tailor-made for quiet moments and lovers' trysts. Her favourite fantasy flickered a moment. The Lord Brishen…his dark eyes, black hair, strong jawline. *Until he hears you speak.*

Like ice over fire, Lydia snapped back to reality with a sigh. Tilting her head, she tried to decide which aspect offered the most charming composition. Her hands shaped the outline of her design against her skirts, her focus so fully absorbed that she hardly noticed the gradual cooling of the air. Around her, shadows deepened and the sconces burned low.

By the time evening settled, she'd sat longer than good manners allowed. Should word of her absence reach her father… Lydia's insides quailed. Shivering as she rose, she lamented her absence of mind and a warmer wrap.

Footsteps, unsteady and unwelcome, sounded behind her, someone muttering curses. The hairs on the back of Lydia's neck stood up.

Turning too late towards the dim path, her return to the house was effectively blocked—by the earl.

Basingstoke wore a lopsided leer as he staggered forwards. He was bad enough sober but worse when he drank, which was often if the rumours at Almack's held true. Looking past him, she saw no one who might assist her.

"There you are," Basingstoke snarled. "What did you sneak off for?"

"I-is there s-something y-you n-needed?"

For answer, he closed the distance between them, grabbing her wrist. "His Grace said you'd be nice to me." He leaned in, slurring with hot, fetid breath.

Lydia twisted away in disgust. "Y-you w-will please r-remember y-yourself, s-sir." She hated the pleading note in her voice. She couldn't bear to address him as "my lord." The thought of being his in any way made her sick. Basingstoke stumbled after her, gripping her arm. Lydia was no coward, but she could already tell he was too strong for her.

Seizing the front of her bodice, he tore at her buttons.

She struck his hand away with a cry and twisted again, trying to get back to the house.

"You're already mine, you know," Basingstoke sneered. "Your father consented a week ago in London."

Lydia's eyes widened with fear. He could be lying, but why would he? And it was just the sort of thing the duke would do.

"You'll be in my bed by Christmas. I say, why wait?" He made a triumphant lunge for her waist, lifting her skirts with his knee.

Lydia thrust her leg upward, connecting less solidly with his groin than she'd intended. Her nails scored his face.

"Whore," he muttered, loosening his grip.

Shoving as hard as she could, Lydia stumbled away but he grabbed her shoulder, yanking her back. She opened her mouth to scream. He squeezed her neck, pressing down hard. Lydia understood the threat in those fingers. Her cries died in her throat.

She hardly breathed. Tears welled in her eyes as Basingstoke fisted a handful of hair with his free hand, ready to rip it out by the roots if he didn't get what he wanted. Her mind dizzied as his rasp of triumph scraped her ears. He reached for her skirts again. *Oh God, please, let him kill me. I'd rather die than have him touch me.*

"I'd step away from the lady, if I were you."

Basingstoke lowered his knee from her thighs, peering across the garden. "Who's there?"

Lydia gasped for air. Basingstoke tightened his hold when he saw who it was.

"Ah, Brishen. Keep walking, will you?"

"Certainly, my lord. Once you've removed your grip from the girl's throat." Valkin's eyes glared menacing black ice. When Basingstoke made no move to comply, he stepped forward and grasped his upper arm. "Now, Basingstoke."

His grip must have been iron. Basingstoke clearly had no choice but to move or have his arm broken. He struggled briefly until Valkin's fist connected with his jaw, sending him crashing to the ground. He looked down in satisfaction before turning to address Lydia.

She stared up at him a moment before staggering away to lean against one of the topiary trees, her eyes closed. Pressing a hand to her side, Lydia attempted several slow breaths.

"What the devil business is it of yours?" Basingstoke managed to recover. "Oughta call out the law, eh, Brishen?"

"You do that," Valkin replied silkily, "and I'll have your creditors here by dawn. You may care to explain your unfortunate habit of courting girls by ambush. Isn't this how you met the late countess?"

"Damn you, Brishen. She's to be my wife, I tell you. She's lucky I bother with a defective little whore like her."

"Once she is yours, do as you wish. Until then, you'll refrain from tarnishing the good name of Lady Davenport by exposing your vices so thoroughly to her guests." His deadly tone didn't waver as Basingstoke made a half-hearted attempt to retaliate. One twitch of Valkin's shoulder sent him flat to the ground again.

CHAPTER THREE

Valkin

Valkin turned to the girl and held out his arm, surprised to find she'd disappeared. He hoped this meant she was in no danger of swooning. He had no wish to alarm her further. It was past time he took his leave in any case, especially after felling Basingstoke. He shrugged, flexing his hand as he made his way to the front entrance by another path. Bile churned through his gut. He'd never understand the way these English treated their families. He wondered why any girl of the ton would willingly enter a marriage contract with such a man—especially a girl who'd had the gumption to scratch the earl's face, and he thought he'd seen her kick him in the balls.

He smiled grimly. At least the girl showed courage—she'd need it to marry a reputed sadist like Basingstoke. If he spoke the truth, which Valkin took leave to doubt, and the girl had already lost her innocence, her family may feel they didn't have any choice. They lacked honour then. She was their blood and they ought to support her, especially if she'd been the victim of one of Basingstoke's "seductions." A pang of pity moved him. If the girl had been *his* sister, the earl would no longer be able to walk. Or breathe. He clenched his fist as he strode around to the front of the house where Lady Davenport's man held his horse. The butler glanced warily at the animal's flattened ears. Bavol was known to bite the English.

Valkin grinned as he approached his mount. He'd parlayed two of his best mares for this handsome fellow. The stallion was not quite a full Romany horse. Something about the lines of the beast's haunches suggested thoroughbred blood as well. While the Romany didn't have as ready access to thoroughbred bloodlines as the

English, Valkin's popularity with the *gadjos* had seen this become less of a hurdle in recent years. This coal-black beast was the fastest so far in his sprints, though he remained half-tamed.

The House of Brishen was known throughout England for its fine showing of racehorses. The training program begun by Valkin and his *gadjo* friends last spring would soon be tested at track. Bavol tossed his mane, stamping his impatience and yanking the reins from the butler's grip.

"I beg your pardon, sir."

"That's quite all right, Rawlins." Running his hand down Bavol's sleek nose, Valkin unbuckled the stallion's headgear.

"I thank you." He shook the man's hand before removing the borrowed bridle, smiling faintly at the *gadjo*'s expression. "He'll not bite as long as I hold his head. A Romany-trained horse does not need such tack." Valkin gathered the black mane to mount up. He stopped, turning back to the butler. "Before I go, there is a guest. A young lady—" He wondered if Rawlins had passed the girl on her return indoors.

"There are many young ladies in attendance for the Bonfire Night." The butler paused meaningfully, lowering his voice. "I passed a lass in a torn gown on the servant's stairs. I've alerted her ladyship."

"Good." Valkin mounted his horse, hesitating. There was little else he could do. While both he and Basingstoke were invited guests, Valkin was aware most of the ton saw him as nothing more than an expert trader in horseflesh and silks. Basingstoke was a peer and a *gadjo*. Should he bring complaints against Valkin under English law, the Romany would not fare well.

"The lighting in the topiary garden is poor," Rawlins continued. "Lady Davenport is aware of this. A guest may fall too easily on the paving and—ah—bruise his face."

Valkin snorted. "Just so, Rawlins. I thank you." Clicking his tongue at Bavol, he walked his horse sedately down Lord Davenport's famous gravel drive. The assault on Basingstoke aside, this house party was not nearly as amusing as Valkin had hoped. With most of his trades concluded and rumours of a duke en route, the decent thing to do was return to *ker* as discreetly as possible, foregoing further acquaintance with Liza and her friends.

He was impatient to be among his family, missing the openness of the Romany manner. Valkin smiled as he thought of his sisters, all of whom raised frankness of feminine speech to an art form. He frowned at the road running counter to his homeward route. He'd be two days on horseback unless he rode steeplechase through the woods. It was dangerous to ride over lands owned by so many *gadjos* without asking their leave, but a rapid steeplechase ride was an indulgence rarely afforded the *krallis*. Valkin halted a moment, considering.

He turned Bavol's head towards the boundary wall. "*Ja.*"

With a bit of luck, he'd be with Brishen by sunset tomorrow. He trusted his family completely, but only he was the *krallis*, or Romany king, as well as *sher-engro* of House Brishen. Overseeing the myriad dealings between his Romany and the English was serious business. More serious than lingering memories of smooth, milk-white skin and chestnut curls gleaming under moonlight. *Defective? Hardly.*

Valkin hoped the girl had the good sense to stay inside and lock her door this night. Basingstoke wouldn't behave any better once all the guests were abed: he'd likely grow worse. It was a pity the lovely young thing he'd glimpsed at the manor house had no brothers like the men of Brishen.

***

Lydia

Lydia's limbs quivered as though she were ill, her legs so inadequate to her support she hardly gained the house. Once the wooden door stood between herself and the earl, she took a breath, slowing her heart rate with an effort—until she spied her reflection in the gilded mirror opposite. *My gown.*

Worth's green silk ripped ragged. Martha's clever mending couldn't salvage this travesty. Scowling at her pale face, Lydia tore off the remains of her sleeves. Velvet ribbons alone held her bodice in place. Spying a staircase so narrow it could only be for those belowstairs, she hurried into the dim opening. Surely Basingstoke wouldn't seek her via a servant's route? Nevertheless, she dared not pause until she emerged on the upper landing.

"My dear."

Lydia fairly leaped out of her skin as she ran bodily into Lady Davenport, who seemed to take her in with one glance. "The earl?"

Lydia gasped. "H-how d-did y-you—"

"Rawlins saw you come in. No matter, I shall make your excuses at supper. The headache, should anyone inquire. You must be well by tomorrow evening."

"T-tomorrow evening?" Hopes of an early departure vanished before her.

"His Grace is joining us. Did he not—" Her ladyship shook her head, sighing a little. "I beg your pardon, my dear. We must proceed as best we're able." She hailed a passing maid. "See Lady Lydia to her room."

As the servant took Lydia's arm, Lady Davenport squeezed her hand. "You're not—hurt? I mean by *him*, dear?"

The way she asked alerted Lydia to her true concern. Mutely, she shook her head.

Lady Davenport exhaled in relief. "Then the only injuries are to your gown. This we may remedy before the duke arrives. I'll have it seen to first thing in the morning." She nodded at them both and bustled away, her posture rigid with restraint. Only her reddened cheeks gave any hint of her true sentiments. Good breeding simply didn't allow for any outcry. This, Lydia already knew.

"If you'd be so kind as to send Martha up, I shall be all right now." She dismissed the Davenports' housemaid at the door to her bedchamber. Once inside, she locked the door before tossing the remains of her sleeves aside. Leaning into the wall beside the empty fireplace, she covered her eyes with her hands. Tears threatened, and Lydia blinked hard until the pricking sensation behind her eyelids receded.

Fumbling among her belongings, she located an old letter with an enclosure of dried herbs for "nervous complaints." Crushing a withered leaf in her palm, Lydia inhaled the scent of laurel…*better*. Tears were useless. Therefore she would not cry. She had to *think*, damn it. There must be a way out of this. The duke had no interest in her except as a pawn he may marry off to his advantage, but that he hadn't told her—her cheeks burned with humiliation. She'd once cherished a tiny hope of gaining her father's affection, but this was the end to such foolishness. An icy lump settled inside her. His Grace didn't care about his useless daughter. Lord Roger Clifton, the duke's heir, was the only child her father acknowledged.

Of her other brother, Wil, no one at Clifton Hall was permitted to speak. He'd run off with Valkin's sister over eight years ago, and the duke didn't suffer his name to be mentioned. Wil was Consort to the Romany Princess now and thoroughly embraced his Romany family.

Lydia understood his satisfaction. Her memories of Brishen were warm, close, and kind. Everything Clifton Hall was not. She clutched her letter, glancing over the well-worn paper written in a small, neat hand detailing clear instructions for steeping a calming tea. Over the page she scanned a stepped-out list of recommendations for mounting a racehorse astride while gowned. Signed by the Romany Princess Syeira and dated a year ago, this remained the last correspondence she'd received from Wil and his wife: their congratulations on her coming out. Lydia exhaled harshly, gulping down the wave of sadness threatening to engulf her.

Valkin once lost to Wil in a duel. How strange it was to see him here, admiring Florence and Liza Davenport. He hadn't recognised Lady Lydia Clifton. Why would he remember her? The little girl who'd looked up to her brothers and admired their handsome friends was long gone. She was grown up now, and Romany were not permitted at Clifton Hall. It was Roger who'd told Lydia that Wil was a father—that she was an aunt. She longed to meet her niece and nephews. She wished she'd thought to ask Valkin if such were possible. Most of all, she wished with all her heart that both her brothers were here to help her now.

A soft tap came at the door. Lydia turned the key again the moment her maid stepped inside with her scuttle of coal. Martha busied herself with laying the fire. A warm blaze drove most of the cold from the chamber and Lydia tugged at her clothes. Her maid hurried to help. Lydia exhaled deeply once her laces were loosed, flinching as Martha gingerly probed the bruises on her skin, clucking softly.

"And the Earl of Basingstoke's valet came in not two minutes past. Said his master's all bruised and bleeding like he's been in a fight," Martha went on. "Serves him right, from what the butler saw. Tried to take liberties, he did, but the gypsy gentleman got to him first." She drew the ties on Lydia's nightgown. "He's a bad lot, that earl, and no mistake. Why his last wife's not been laid longer than three months. Why what's—what's the matter, my lady?"

Lydia's shivering worsened until she couldn't hold back the avalanche of sobs any longer. Between choking gasps, she explained what happened in the garden. Martha pulled Lydia to her again. "Why that good-for-nothing blackguard." She examined the marks on Lydia's neck more closely. "Did he—my lady? He didn't—?"

Lydia shook her head. "N-no. Lord Brishen m-made sure of that."

"Well, thank goodness for him, then. Don't fret now, my lady, if it's only the torn gown. You'll get your pretty eyes all puffed up. I'll make up some salve soon as I go down. I'm afraid they've no stillroom."

Lydia sniffed, drying her eyes on Martha's handkerchief. "B-basingstoke's abominable, and it's worse. Papa has b-betrothed m-me to h-him."

Martha's shocked gasp nearly started Lydia's tears again, but the maid took her hand. "There's no point crying over this, my lady. Write to your brother, his lordship, in France. Ask him to come back and front the duke. Lord Clifton won't want you to—to be given to such a man. Why, the earl's far too old, and that's not all," Martha whispered, looking hurriedly away, but Lydia caught the fear in her eyes.

Taking a breath, Lydia smiled tightly and nodded. Then she set to and wrote a letter to Roger. It was short and to the point, imploring him to return and help her. She directed it to the last address she had for him, sealing it with her mother's ring. Lydia didn't remember her mama very well, but she knew the duchess had been kind, and beautiful. She was certain her mother would have been appalled by Basingstoke. Wil always said Lydia was the very image of their mother. Oh, how she missed him.

"How long d-do letters take to reach France, Martha?" Lydia asked as her maid came back in with a tea tray and more coal. She couldn't stop her voice from sounding sad and hopeless. There was little chance Roger could return in time, and the last direction she held for him was old. "The earl claims we're to wed by Christmas."

Martha placed the note in her apron pocket. "I'll make sure Mr Rawlins posts it first class tomorrow. Lord Clifton is a good man, my lady. He will not fail you."

Once the maid left, Lydia ran across and locked the door. Returning to bed, she poured herself a cup of tea, limbs still trembling. She shuddered to think what might have happened if Valkin hadn't appeared. Again, she wished she'd had the courage to speak up, but his appearance had taken her so entirely by surprise.

He was broader and more powerful than Lydia remembered. With his square jaw, wide chest, black hair and eyes, he was a man who banished all thoughts of the lecherous earl. She thought back to his calm, hard voice, and the ease with which he'd felled her attacker. Lydia didn't suppose she'd get the chance to thank him for giving her one bright, warm moment in the icy coldness that had become her life.

CHAPTER FOUR

Valkin

After slowing Bavol to a walk, Valkin extracted a small green leaf from the slit in his vest. He placed the leaf on his tongue with a sigh. An overnight ride on top of too much brandy had not been wise, and it wasn't the first time he was extremely grateful for Brishen's familiarity with healing herbs. Despite his delicate temples, early mornings were the Romany way. He dismounted, seeking the signs on the forest floor marking the boundaries of *ker*.

A loud whacking noise to his left led him towards his youngest brother, Chal. At sixteen, he'd recently betrothed himself to a girl from another Romany house. An accomplishment that filled Valkin with pride.

"*Sarishan*, Chal." He turned towards the scent of woodsmoke and breakfast.

His brother fell into step beside him. "Welcome home, my *prala*, my brother. We did not expect your return so soon."

Valkin shrugged, leading Bavol by a hand beneath his head. "Not all my parlay with the *gadjos* is successful. Is Janfri returned?"

"Not yet, but we hear rumours of a fast new filly."

Valkin frowned. "Our preparations for the West Lancashire Cup are nearly complete." A flicker of doubt skittered through him. "Find out all you can and let me know."

Chal rolled his eyes. "I have the *patrin* to set out first and this day's hunt to lead, *sher-engro*."

"Of course, but it is important we make a good showing. There is time to adjust our training if Janfri can report back on our competition. We must use every resource to prepare for the main purse."

Chal shrugged. Valkin roped in his annoyance to explain to his brother—once again—that while money held little standing with the Romany, it was the opposite with the *gadjos*.

"We've not survived so long by being impractical," he pointed out.

Chal shrugged again but this time he nodded. "I know it is important to depend on more than our goods. Your horses serve the Romany well in this."

Valkin inclined his head in accord. "It is the work of us all. Race meets are also about goodwill. Maintaining our relations among the *gadjos* is important. *Gadjo* law is not known for its understanding of the Romany."

"Your strategy proves sound so far."

"If it proves otherwise, I shall adjust it." Valkin clapped his brother on the back so heartily, Chal flinched, and they both laughed. They made their way across the camp, Valkin stopping to shake hands and embrace his cousins and friends as the rest of Brishen welcomed him home.

He watched Chal out of the corner of his eye. While their Romany benefited from Valkin's *gadjo* friendships, the weight of maintaining beneficial relations for all the Romany of England pressed heavily this morning. So much depended upon the favour of his English friends and their lady wives. Unease prickled low in his gut as he recalled the incident with Basingstoke. Coming between a depraved English peer and his quarry may not have been wise.

Valkin wondered how much more difficult his English connections might become if he married. He'd not dally among the likes of Lady Davenport once he had a wife, and it was well past time if he listened to his family. Their calls for his coupling grew louder with each new Brishen match or birth. Valkin didn't know what stopped him other than a feeling, deep down, that something was missing in his relations with women. Something he'd witnessed as a boy, in the way his papa looked at his mama when they sat beside each other, or sang together, or when they danced. *Oh, when they danced.*

Valkin's first Romany dance had been with his parents, giggling that he'd been allowed to stay late into the night with the adults. His mama twirling him in her arms, placing him on his father's boots to dance together to fiddles and flutes and chanting songs. He'd looked into his mama's face, seen his father pull her close into his strong arms, and it was as if no one else was there. As though the stars shone only for his parents in that moment and even he—their son, their eldest, their "brightest one"—had somehow been eclipsed, leaving them in a sort of separate place, a place of love. The feeling in that moment had been golden, powerful, and precious. Valkin had never forgotten it. He'd not wed without it.

His younger brothers were all betrothed before age sixteen, except Culvato. Sweet, romantic Culvato, who'd loved a *gadje* and believed she loved him too. Such careless affections had seen his younger brother dead at fifteen. It was a lesson in betrayal Valkin never forgot. It reminded him love ought not to be rushed, and he'd no intention of marrying for obligation as the *gadjos* did. The *krallis* may well be the last man of his house to wed, but Valkin was in no hurry. Whenever his siblings asked when he was likely to settle down, his patient reply was always the same: *When it feels right.*

He pretended to ignore their muttering about wasting his time among *gadje* women. Valkin enjoyed an informality in his liaisons with Englishwomen that would never be permitted among his own people. He freely admitted this was not the most moral course of action, but another famous Romany precept was recognising the power of the moment. It was his good fortune that seizing the moment often meant taking a heady plunge into the sensual delights of a *gadje*'s bed. In any case, at present there was a distinct lack of women among his Romany. Valkin wished, for the good of his house, to ensure as many Brishen men were wed while he was *krallis.* If seeing his people flourish meant he waited longer for a bride, then so be it.

He straightened as he returned to the *gry* pens, nodding to his cousins waiting nearby. Valkin indicated the three horses they would be working with first.

"Not Bavol?" Chal asked.

Valkin shook his head.

"We must complete his training if you wish to start him at track next year. He remains half-broken," Chal pointed out.

"Let him rest," Valkin demurred. *Let his spirit run a while longer.*

Taking out a pocket watch, he led the way to the clearing outside *ker*, where his makeshift track was already marked out.

"A fine watch, *sher-engro*," Dela said. "It does not bear the Brishen seal."

"It does not," Valkin agreed. "This watch belongs to the consort. Mount up, please."

Signalling with a raised finger to the small boys stationed at the other end of the track, he squinted into the mist. The four youngsters all raised their hands in recognition.

"*Ja.*" Valkin watched the starters closely.

With his training program under way, Valkin left his men to it, mentally ticking off his first task for the day. His sisters and cousins set off for the woods with large, empty bushel baskets. Gathered herbs were bundled and dried for use once the snows came. What little fruit they found needed preserving into jams or liquor. The women of Brishen had this well in hand.

Chal's men were hunting game for stewing. What his Romany didn't eat tonight could be dried or jugged for the coming winter. Brishen travelled with their own goats and chickens, but while they had permission to camp and hunt in the Forest of Bowland, they gathered all they could for the long, lean weeks ahead. Chal's hunting parties were invariably successful, and Valkin looked forward to seeing them return with their usual trophies of hare and fowl. There were few sports he enjoyed more than a good Romany hunt, but he had no time today. In truth, he barely recalled when he'd last joined in this. Time was one thing for which the *krallis* could not trade.

"Ah, there you are, *sher-engro*."

Valkin suppressed a yawn as one of the elder women, Cin, hailed him.

"I am here, *Bebee* Cin." Cin held her tent flap open, awaiting his presence at *kris*, the meeting where Romany disputes were heard. "Who is first?"

"There is a dispute over ownership," announced Dela, holding a mewling pup in both hands.

"Of the dog?" Valkin settled himself down to listen to both sides. "Go on."

"The bitch is one of my finest hunters," began Dela. "And I am a cousin of the *krallis*." He stepped to one side of the tent space.

"The sire is one of mine." Artáros, an older Brishen man, took his place opposite Dela and the dog. "Though he seems not to know it, and *I* am a cousin of the *krallis*."

Valkin bit back a smile. "You are both my cousins, which means little when a dispute reaches *kris*. As cousins of the *krallis*, I assume you're both aware of this."

He eyed the shamefaced lurcher seated by the tent flap. *Satisfied, are you, Chore? At least one of us has sired offspring.* He could have sworn the animal smirked. Valkin scowled, turning his gaze on Artáros.

"How many is the litter?"

"Only five, *sher-engro*. Three bitches and two males."

"Very well, you may each take a breeding pair." He paused. "The remaining bitch pup you may either sell at the West Lancashire fair, or gift to the House of Beti, who has not had good luck this season. Beti shall join us for Christmas, so there is time to choose and let pup's eyes be open before the trade is made."

"Yes, *sher-engro*," his cousins answered in unison.

"You may go." Valkin turned to his aunt with a sigh. "Is there coffee, *Bebee* Cin?" Adjudicating disagreements among the families of Brishen was a task unique to their *sher-engro*. He couldn't delegate it to anyone else, no matter how much he wished it. Accepting his cup, Valkin tipped a little between his lips, grinning at the strength of the brew. "I thank you. Allow me another cup before whomever is next."

***

The winter sun rose higher by the time Valkin stood to stretch. *Bebee* Cin rose beside him.

"Shall we break our fast, *sher-engro*?"

Valkin waved his hand towards the tent aperture. "Close the flap if you please, *Bebee* Cin. There is no other matter that cannot wait until we've taken refreshment." He smiled winningly at his aunt as he bowed her from the *kris*.

Cin laughed, studying him seriously for a moment. "Take your rest on horseback if you wish, nephew, but do not forget to eat."

"Bavol needs no more riding this day, and I will not forget." He kissed her wrinkled cheek before leaving to walk the boundaries of *ker*. Taking a slow patrol around the entire perimeter, Valkin checked Chal's *patrin* remained in place. These signposts warned other houses that the royal Romany were present, and not to encroach on their site without asking leave of the *krallis*.

Valkin visited Bavol in his own *gry* pen, the prolific Chore at his heels.

"Get away from the hooves, you old rascal," he muttered as the dog snapped at his horse. Bavol stamped at the lurcher, thrusting his nose into Valkin's outstretched palm.

"We'll head out tomorrow," he promised his horse, making a mental note to find some carrots or apples before then. "What do you say to a ride by the river?"

Bavol harrumphed and shook his mane. Valkin laughed, patting the animal's sleek neck. "It is a trade, Bavol."

"*Sher-engro,*" a young voice called from behind him.

"What is it, Cato?"

"*Bebee* Cin said to find you. The *kris* resumes shortly, and I wish to be spared patrol this night."

His cousin's face seemed etched with permanent worry. His wife expected their first child any day.

"How is your wife, cousin?"

Cato shrugged. "I do not know, *sher-engro*. She is not sleeping well, and—"

"And neither are you?" Valkin guessed.

His cousin's weary nod confirmed this.

"Then find another to replace you tonight. If you cannot, meet me after *kris,* and I will take your place. Is your wife at rest now?"

Another nod.

"Then take your rest with her now and forego our hunt today. You may tell Chal it is so."

"Yes, *sher-engro*. Thank you, *sher-engro*." Cato smiled as he visibly relaxed his shoulders and turned away towards his tent.

Valkin felt as if Cato's tensions had merely transferred to his own shoulders. He ran a hand through his hair as he turned towards the central cooking fire. He'd best find some food before returning to *kris*. Then he'd review the timed trials from his *gry-engros*.

After a long day of adjudication and horses, Valkin sank into his bed with a heartfelt sigh. Relaxing back into silk cushions, he considered all that remained to be done at *ker* before Christmas. He'd best rise earlier than usual if he wished to enjoy his ride. Fortunately, there was nothing more magical than the turn of forest leaves at dawn.

CHAPTER FIVE

Lydia

Lydia uttered a cry of pain, tears starting in her eyes as Martha tightened the laces on the new stays one more time, wincing in sympathy. The Worth's tea gown seemed designed for an opera girl, with the bodice cut lower and tighter than Lydia's damaged evening costume. There was nothing for it but to be cinched into the pipestem corset again. English stays simply wouldn't fit beneath such French gowns. Lydia scowled at her elevated breasts.

"I'm certain I may scent my décolletage, Martha."

"I beg your pardon, my lady." The maid knotted the lacing several times over. "His Grace's orders are that you wear this costume to tea."

The duke wanted Lydia on display like a sacrifice. To disobey him now could not help her cause. He'd arrived to a late breakfast and was likely travel-worn. At least he'd agreed to her request for interview. Lydia tried drawing a deep breath—*impossible*. Her stays were as stiff as iron. She felt a momentary affinity with grouse.

The bruises on her neck stood out clearly. Good: Lydia wanted her father aware of them. She had to believe he'd not want her married to a man so cruel as this. Lydia could not think what else to do, unless Roger returned in time. Her brother wouldn't think twice about breaking off such an alliance, whatever the law said. He'd find a way to keep her safe, from the earl and—she closed her eyes against the pain of it—from their father.

Moving gingerly in the tightened stays, Lydia made her way downstairs, stepping pointedly past Basingstoke. She noted the livid scratches on his lordship's cheek with satisfaction. She also admired the purplish bruise on his jaw where her Romany lord had struck him. *Her Romany lord?* She wasn't likely to see Valkin again.

Basingstoke accosted her in the dining room, brandishing his overfull liquor glass. "I'm to escort you to table."

"I am p-perfectly c-capable of f-finding m-my way," she responded stiffly. "And I've w-written to L-lord Clifton."

He shrugged. "You've not heard the channel's impassable, then. No packets may leave port."

Lydia's blood seemed frozen in her veins. Her fingernails scored her palms. *This can't be true...it just can't.* Basingstoke lurched towards her again, retreating only when the sounds of tittering laughter and many slippers announced the ladies' arrival. Falling in with the group as best she could, Lydia stationed herself close by Lady Davenport, who slipped her arm through Lydia's, shooting a dark glance at the earl.

"Lady Lydia, my dear, I've been meaning to inquire where *did* you find that fascinating costume?" Lowering her head, she whispered, "I must beg your pardon. Lord Davenport insists the earl remain with the duke." She patted Lydia's arm as the group of ladies rustled in to dine. Holding her ladyship's elbow like a lifeline, Lydia attempted a smile.

Her smile fell off immediately she took her seat between her father and the earl. The moment Basingstoke sat beside her, his hefty paw clamped her knee and began moving higher. Lydia swallowed, forcing her features to stillness as she tried to pry his filthy fingers from her thigh. Finally, drawing her butter knife into her hand, she stabbed blindly downward, gratified to hear her nauseating suitor grunt in pain. Her father, seated to her right, remained silent, though he must have noticed. The first course was placed before them. Lydia's stomach roiled, not that she'd be able to eat in this gown. Her nerves drew tight as a bowstring as she mentally rehearsed her arguments for His Grace.

***

Lydia put her case in the Davenport library, before His Grace and numerous portraits of Lord Davenport's forebears. Their sombre faces were enough to quash any hope of success, or perhaps the duke's presence made it seem this way.

"I'll not hear another word about it, girl. The earl's offered. I have accepted him. What has it to do with you?" Her father imbued his tone with the usual impatience when it came to addressing her.

"B-but, Y-your G-grace, the earl m-may not b-be…. He is n-not the m-man y-you think he is." She was desperate to make him listen. "I w-will m-marry anyone else y-you c-choose. Anyone a-at a-all but p-please, sir, *not him*." She hated the way her voice shook. Hated the splinters of fear in her belly and the icy coldness in her heart. Hated most of all the indifference in her father's eyes.

"There is no other alliance that suits me so well." The duke spoke flatly, as if the whole conversation bored him. "And you'd best avoid spreading slanders like that, girl. It's not every man who makes good his promise after what transpired last night."

Lydia's mouth fell open, her knees buckling. She grabbed at the chair back in front of her. Had the earl been spreading rumours to force her submission?

"Y-you are m-m-misinformed, Your G-Grace," Lydia said hollowly. Swallowing hard to keep back her bile, she lifted her chin. "I—I assure y-you th-that y-your assumption is q-quite f-false." She leaned forward to show him her bruises and describe what happened in the garden.

Whack!

Her father's open hand across her face rendered her mute.

"Will that teach you?" He hardly glanced at his handiwork. "I'm certain Basingstoke knows when he has—and when he hasn't— taken a girl." The duke sniffed as his tone coarsened. "I told you to further gentlemanly acquaintance this Season, not to embrace dishonour. It seems you can't help yourself. You're too small and sickly to make a fashionable wife. If only you had brains, girl, a little wit, or could *speak* in a manner to be borne—ah, but there again, you fail."

Lydia blinked back pain, both her pride and her left cheek smarting. *I will not cry.*

"Your second Season has been as unprofitable as your first. You cannot blame me for consenting to the only proposal you've received. You will accept this betrothal and be grateful there is one man in the ton who can bring himself to take you at all." The duke stared somewhere over Lydia's left shoulder, his face stony. "I will not countenance another scandal in this family, so you'll do as you're told."

His tone struck Lydia like a fist. She curtsied once, blinking back the throb of his strike. Without lifting her head, she hurried from the room, mind whirring in the face of this latest blow. By next week the earl's rumour would be all over the ton, and Lydia would be trapped. Forced into this betrothal as surely as she'd been trussed into Worth's expensive stays. She could no longer wait for word from her brother.

Pausing outside the tearoom to compose herself, Lydia breathed as deeply as possible before entering with a brisk step and hoping for friendlier acquaintance. Miss Davenport was playing as diligently as always, under the benevolent gaze of her mama. Lydia stepped up to turn a page for her, leaning in to whisper. "Miss D-davenport, I am aware you d-do not approve of h-him, but I wish an audience with Lord Brishen."

The girl's fingers stumbled over her keys. "Lady Lydia, you cannot be serious?"

Lydia's cheeks flamed scarlet. "I must speak with him."

"Then I am sorry for you," replied Miss Davenport, resuming her nocturne. "The gypsy left us yesterday, not long after the earl was injured." The girl seemed to know her piece by heart because she turned her gaze to Lydia without pausing her fingers on the keys. "Thank you for your assistance, but I need no page turning today."

She smiled tightly, turning back to her pianoforte. "You ought not to have been in the topiary garden with the earl, you know. The other young ladies are already speaking of it. Is this why the duke is come?" The younger girl's cheeks glowed pink as she angled her posture away.

Lydia stepped back in shock, staring around for a chair. All the seats appeared to be occupied or reserved with reticules. In Miss Jessup's case, the company of two pugs seemed preferable to her own. The coldness within her set like granite. Swallowing bile, ire, and every epithet she'd heard her brothers utter, she stumbled from the room, barely acknowledging Lady Davenport's signal. That Basingstoke's rumour was untrue made no difference. If her father refused to support her, no one would take her part. After all, how did someone prove they hadn't lost their innocence? Lydia didn't intend to find out.

She rang for Martha as soon as she gained her bed chamber, gathering what valuables she could. *Leave my gowns. Take only my jewels. Do I have enough sovereigns to reach the coast?* Once there, she'd trade her jewels for passage to France. A knock at the door drew her attention. To her surprise, Martha wasn't alone. Lady Davenport entered immediately behind her.

"I see you waste little time, Lady Lydia." She nodded approvingly. "Very well, let us get organised. You are attempting to reach Lord Clifton, I presume?"

Lydia stared. "M-my lady," she stammered. "What—I mean, h-how—I d-do not understand."

Her ladyship smiled tightly. "Rawlins and Martha here have been very astute. I understand your father wishes you to marry the Earl of Basingstoke?"

Lydia nodded.

"And being a girl of sense and reputation, not to mention your highly developed instinct for self-preservation, you do not wish this marriage?"

Lydia shook her head, unable to repress the shiver of disgust creeping through her. She thought she saw a more subtle shudder move through Lady Davenport.

"His late wife was a distant relation of mine. A silly girl, it is true," Lady Davenport admitted, "but she didn't deserve the life he tricked her into. Now, you must be careful, and you must wait until tonight. If you leave now, you will certainly be pursued."

"P-pursued?" Lydia hadn't considered such a thing.

"Basingstoke will not give up your dowry without a fight." Lady Davenport smiled gently. "I was—very fond of Lord Clifton. He spoke of you to me often. I would help you in any case, but especially for his sake. Do you know where he is?"

"I b-believe h-him to be in Paris."

"The bonfire works take place tonight on the back lawn. Remain here until then—and keep your door locked. Once attentions are on our excellent display, Rawlins shall assist you by the servants' door. I regret I cannot offer you the carriage. My husband would notice, but I can help you to the coast. From there, you will have to trust to luck. You must reach the Forest of Bowland before dawn. Then ride west for Morecambe Bay." She pressed a purse of sovereigns into Lydia's hands.

"I shall do what I'm able to quash the rumour I heard at dinner." She gazed steadily at Lydia. "No one who knows you, my dear, would believe such scandalous falsehood." She patted Lydia's hand. "Take care on the road. A woman travelling alone is at great risk. I truly wish I could send someone with you, but it wouldn't be safe. Your father is a powerful man."

Tears of gratitude streaming her cheeks, Lydia embraced her ladyship. Then she looked at Martha. Her young maid looked terrified. Once the duke found his daughter gone, Martha's life in service would be over.

"Your ladyship, about M-martha—" she began.

Lady Davenport squeezed Lydia's hands tight. "Martha shall remain here. I will protect her as best I can." Her expression remained solemn. "Florence comes out next Season and is in need of a lady's maid. You should be aware, my dear, that all who assist you will find themselves falling foul of both the duke and the earl, and possibly the law, which neither gentleman will hesitate to call out in force, I shouldn't wonder." She paused. "If Martha has no objection, I suggest you travel under her name."

Martha smiled through her tears and hugged Lydia. "May it bring you luck, my lady."

Lady Davenport left, and Martha unbuttoned Lydia's gown in silence.

"You'd best leave the stays," Lydia remarked. "There's not time to undo all that lacing and prepare your own things. See to yourself now, Martha. I must learn to do the same." Her brisk tone faltered. They both knew there was a chance Martha, too, may need to flee. The breadth of the duke's rage was unpredictable, but that he would unleash fury was in no doubt. With one final, shaking embrace, Martha kissed her cheek and left Lydia alone.

As soon as she'd locked the door, Lydia opened the false bottom of her jewel case, staring at Wil's service pistol. He'd taught her to shoot it as a child. Her aim had always been sharp. She carried his weapon more as a memento of her absent brother than anything else, but it might prove useful now. Whether she'd have the courage to use it at need was another matter. Clenching her teeth, she remembered the earl. *I will do what I must.*

Lydia took as deep a breath as she was able, weighing the pistol in her hands. It wasn't terribly heavy. A paper fluttered out from beneath it. Lydia caught it up and unravelled one of her old charcoal portraits in the hesitant strokes of an uncertain artist. The black curl above his brow, the line of his jaw, those jet-black lashes closed in sleep. Capturing Valkin's likeness while he slept the day away at Clifton Hall had been a joke between his sister and herself. *The Romany Prince, as he was then.*

She'd been so young, all those years ago. *Young and almost happy, as I was then.* Lydia shook her head as though dislodging another memory she needed to leave behind. She crumpled the paper in one shaking fist, before tossing it into the flames with a shiver. Once she'd sorted through her jewels, she pulled out the meagre pile of letters she kept in the golden case. One by one, she read them for the last time, dwelling on every affectionate expression from her absent brother and his good-hearted wife.

Wil's letters were full of stories about evening meals all together, his new family sharing songs and tales from the day's hunt, clever trades among each other, or their business with the English. Syeira's letters were more fragrant. The Romany princess sent dried leaves and seeds with directions as to their correct preparation "to support your nerves," Syeira's notes said, as though she knew of the anxious struggles plaguing Lydia. What she wouldn't give to belong to a family like Brishen... Her resolve stiffened as she fed her papers into the fire. Memories were burdens she could no longer afford.

Managing to don the Worth's riding habit over her rigorous corsetry, she studied her reflection again. Her habit fit too snugly but at least she exposed less flesh. Stowing the damaged green gown in her largest reticule, she considered the rest of her belongings.

Only carry what you're likely to need. Her pistol was about protection. She tucked the weapon into her garter and took out her workbox to begin the painstaking task of stitching jewellery into the lining of her riding bonnet. A moment's panic flared...*am I truly doing this?* Running away from her home and her family? Her throat constricted. *What family?*

Lady Davenport's words echoed in her mind. *Your father is a powerful man.* She was right. Anyone aiding Lydia's escape from a legally binding arrangement placed themselves in a dangerous position. Her nerves drew tighter at the thought of Miss Martha Dale—a woman, alone and with very little aid—pitting her wits and meagre resources against the combined means of the Duke of Carston and the Earl of Basingstoke. *What chance do I have?*

The clock showed less than an hour to sunset. Lying back on her bed, Lydia tried resting. The corset dug mercilessly into her flesh, her discomfort made worse by the stiff, snug fit of her bodice. She sat up and crossed to her glass, donning her bonnet. Was it obvious where she'd stowed Mama's gems? She didn't think so. The French-cut riding jacket made her generous breasts seem larger than ever. She looked like an expensively dressed whore, or someone's mistress. Perhaps she'd be safer if people believed she travelled under the protection of a man they'd not wish to cross. She couldn't use the duke's name of course, and it was known that Roger was out of the country. Whose protection might she claim?

She thought again of Lord Brishen, her cheeks flushing brilliantly. Would Valkin object to her using his title to gain safe passage as she tried reaching her brother? Would he have any occasion to find out? It was well known that Valkin and her brothers were acquainted. A liaison between him and Lydia's "friend" Martha Dale might be credible. *Do I dare?*

Everyone knew the Romany took their responsibilities to their women seriously, but did that extend to their—Lydia swallowed—mistresses? She didn't know, but it was only another risk among all the others she was taking tonight. Warmth spread through her as the idea took hold. Valkin's mistress wouldn't have to flee from anyone or fend off any attacker. She'd be safe.

***

As Lady Davenport had promised, by sunset the house was as shadowed as possible. Loud bangs and gasps sounded near the north wing. The sky lit briefly with flowering lights, but Lydia didn't look up. Keeping her firm hold on Rawlins's arm, they stole quietly out the servants' door. Once out of sight of the manor, the butler explained his preparations.

"I've saddled Miss Davenport's grey for you, my lady. Her name's Lady Queen. She's a fast little thing and easy to manage once you've the hang of her. I've packed food and a water flask into her saddlebags, but if you'll take my advice, you'll not keep anything too valuable in the bags. There's thieves on the roads, and if the horse gets pinched, you'll at least not lose it all."

Lydia swallowed hard and nodded, barely breathing past the hammering of her heart. Stepping nearer to the horse, she ran her palm firmly down the mare's curious nose. The animal stamped a hoof in the cold night air, apparently sensing her anxiety. Lydia thought of the gems sewn into her bonnet. The comforting weight of Wil's pistol pressed into her thigh.

"I'll d-do j-just as you s-suggest, Rawlins, th-thank you." She shivered, but not from cold. Her warmest cloak did nothing to stop the dread coursing through her blood. "I wish I h-had something to g-give you," she stammered. "I d-don't know h-how to repay your kindness."

The man smiled and kindness shone in his eyes. "There's no need, my lady. Best wait to canter 'til you reach the road proper. The noise. You find Lord Clifton, my lady, and take care on the roads."

Lydia nodded again, allowing him to lift her into the sidesaddle. She walked the mare to the stable exit and continued sedately down the drive. Halting briefly by the gates, she stared back at Davenport Manor. Somewhere within, the duke and the earl planned her betrothal announcement.

Bang. Lydia flinched as a yellow firework bloomed above the gabled facade. She shook herself hard. *You are not the Lady Lydia anymore. You're Martha Dale, mistress to the Romany king.* Patting the neck of the little mare, she urged her to canter as soon as they cleared the gates. Lydia dared not gallop—not in the dark, and not with a sidesaddle. There was no hope at all should she fall.

***

As dawn rose, Lydia found herself deep within the Forest of Bowland, doubting whether she'd remained on course. It was difficult to follow any path through the mist, and the all-night ride did not help her wits. Yawning, she kept the mare to a cautious walk, wondering how far it was to the coast and whether she ought to ration her food. Unable to dismount without aid, she'd eaten nothing as yet. In any case, she couldn't stomach a meal with her insides tied in such knots. The result was a light-headed nausea and a desperate desire for sleep.

This fraught-with-peril feeling didn't surprise Lydia. Her situation was desperate enough. She hadn't expected the thrill of release as complete freedom washed over her. Here she was, heavy-limbed, entirely alone and in danger, and a part of her was not cast down. She wasn't safe, not remotely, but for the first time, Lydia—no, *Martha*—was completely in control of herself and her life. Blinking in astonishment, Lydia clicked her tongue at Lady Queen, nudging the little horse up a pace. Lifting her gaze, she watched the sun rise, singing softly to the breaking of the new day:

> *A young man stands, stands and ponders;*
> *He ponders and ponders all night long:*
> *Whom to choose and not offend?*
> *Whom to choose and not offend?*
> *Maiden, maiden, can I ask you?:*
> *What can burn, burn and not stop?*
> *What can cry, cry without tears?*
> *Foolish young man, what are you asking?*
> *Love can burn, burn and not stop;*
> *A heart can cry, cry without tears.*

It was an old melody, one her mama had imparted to Lydia along with all the high hopes the duchess cherished for her daughter. Lydia sobered, knowing she'd already disappointed all the earnest wishes of her gentle mama.

As one after another of Lydia's acquaintances announced their excellent matches—often after their first Season—she'd honestly felt relieved. She feared binding herself for life to a man who may treat her unkindly. Certainly, kindness had not been her mother's experience. She'd gathered this much from the dark hints dropped by servants at the Hall.

As the morning drew on, she kept up her singing, moving westwards through the woodland. She remembered her old nursery rhymes along with some of the ballads her governesses insisted she play and sing. Despite her flagging energy, singing buoyed her spirits, leaving her less cold and alone, until she noticed rainclouds glowering ahead. Lydia's voice faltered, a dull throb taking up residence at her temples. Halting her horse a moment, she took an extra breath and drew herself up in her saddle, ignoring her tired limbs and the acute pain of her stays biting into flesh. She was riding right into a storm. Behind her lay the earl. There was no sign of Morecambe Bay yet. She shook her foggy head, wincing as her headache worsened. She'd no time for illness.

She quickened the pace of her little horse, beginning an old Scots folk song she'd heard from one of the stable boys at Clifton Hall. The ditty was both jolly and somewhat vulgar. She felt better immediately, resolving not to think about her father, her family, or Clifton Hall for the rest of the day. Defiance was a great deal better than despair.

CHAPTER SIX

Valkin

Valkin rose with the dawn, lamenting that dried clover grasses were the best he could offer his horse. Fortunately, Bavol seemed to consider his treat a fair trade as he walked placidly enough to the western boundary of *ker*. After twisting his fingers into the horse's mane, Valkin swung himself up and across the animal's back. He straightened, tapping the firm flanks with his heels. Bavol trotted a short distance before increasing his pace without being urged. Valkin grinned into the wind as he leaned forward, whispering words of encouragement to his mount.

He slowed by the riverbank, allowing Bavol to pick his way down to drink. When the stallion had had his fill, Valkin walked his mount into the woods, circling the camp and checking the *patrin*. The sky lowered, a sharp breeze coming up as he made his way back. Valkin tilted his head, listening. Was that a girl, singing? He listened a moment longer, admiring the sweet voice. There were few folk songs Valkin couldn't recognise with ease. The ballad was Scots, so his singer likely wasn't Romany. He grinned as he caught a few ribald words. The singer's accents were distinctly aristocratic, piquing his curiosity. He drew up his horse's head and held the animal motionless, listening intently.

No sound came from any other party. He nudged Bavol silently onward. At this distance he couldn't see more than a mounted figure in a hooded cloak, moving through mist. Might she be lost? Halting in the nearest copse, he noted Chal's hunting party surrounding the rider. The group of hard-eyed young men carried smallish boughs. A few had rifles and their dogs too: several whippets and Chore,

Brishen's sire-of-many-pups. Valkin's mouth quirked as the enormous lurcher circled the mounted *gadje*. The beast's continual growl echoed ominously in the forest.

Could the girl know their *ker* was close by? Valkin hoped not. He peered into the mist, inching Bavol closer through the trees. What was the girl doing here? Drawing her cloak more tightly about her, she appeared to be shivering.

"G-good m-morning, sirs." She lowered her head, disturbing the hood she wore as some of his men eyed her up and down. "Could you tell m-me if I am h-heading w-west?"

Chal stepped forward. "First you will tell us what you are doing in these woods, *gadje*. Are you here by leave of the Lord of Bowland? We patrol this forest under oath to him."

The girl tugged her hood forward over her face. "I b-beg your p-pardon. I d-did not kn-now these are private lands. I am—I am an *intimate* friend of y-your L-lord B-brishen." She cleared her throat again, speaking slowly and, it seemed, with great effort. "That is, I am h-here to seek the assistance of your Romany King."

Valkin's gut tightened with fury. How dare this chit claim his protection? He studied her as best he could, though her face remained hidden. He could already tell, with an eye that paid intimate attention to many women over many years, that her cloak hid curves he wouldn't object to learning. There was something familiar about her, but he was nearly certain he hadn't been to her bed. *Nearly certain?* His face twisted in chagrin. He never claimed to be a saint, but if his lifestyle had reached the point where he couldn't remember a woman he'd bedded, perhaps it was time to reevaluate. Yet he knew this girl was not one of his lovers. Therefore she was lying.

He couldn't for the life of him fathom why an English girl, clearly a lady by her dress and manners, wished to masquerade as anything else—unless she intended a liaison? She wouldn't be the first Englishwoman who wished to sample a Romany lover, far from it. In point of fact, his *gadje* lovers usually sought him out, rather than requiring pursuit on his part. It was safer for all parties to conduct their affairs so. This *gadje* was going about it with some nerve, though. Perhaps he ought to let her. At least until he knew what trade might be made of it.

Quietly, he eased his mount forward, nodding to his brother. His men retreated in silence as Valkin rode up behind the grey. The *gadje* gasped as his thigh nudged tightly against her shins, her English horse skittering sideways. Without a word, Valkin dismounted and lifted the girl down. Her animal shifted again, stamped and stilled. The *gadje* staggered against the horse as Valkin set her on her feet. Her hand gripped the mare's bridle, seemingly for support.

He drew back her cowl, barely pausing in surprise at the chestnut curls framing a pretty heart-shaped face, with large eyes and a delectably sensual mouth. Staring into her widening eyes, his first thought was that Liza had sent her daughter's friend as consolation for their failed tryst. *I admire her ladyship's taste.*

"I—" The girl's speech seemed stuck.

"Tell me what it is you want." Touching her ear with his lips, he caught the shiver of breath beneath flesh. She quivered against his mouth for an instant before jerking away. He waited until it seemed she refused to speak.

"There is a price to pay for your desires, *gadje*." He pulled her swiftly towards him.

His lips claimed hers without a single sound, hand firm against the softness of her nape, holding her tightly in place. Teasing her mouth open, he tasted her muted sigh, his tongue moving against hers. She gripped his hair, tugging him closer. Her kiss turned hotter, hungrier, and she strained towards him.

What the devil?

Valkin let go abruptly, his breaths coming short and sharp as he struggled against his rising heat. The girl's hold on him slackened, her body slumping downward. He caught her as she swooned, dropping to his knees and laying her partway across his thigh. He stared down at her unconscious form in alarm. He hadn't meant to frighten her. Well, yes, he had, but only enough to teach her a lesson. Touching a hand to her cheek, he started. *Far too warm.*

"I know the *gadje* fall over themselves to lie with you, my *prala*, my brother, but don't you think you're carrying this a little far?" Chal appeared from the copse, laughing.

Valkin glared at him. "This isn't funny, Chal. The girl is ill."

His brother spoke carefully. "You heard what she said? What she claimed?" Glancing at the generous curves her riding habit could not flatten, Chal looked away. Pausing, Chal turned his gaze back. Valkin cleared his throat loudly and impatiently, fixating on the girl's face. An ugly bruise marked her cheek, the wound recent. He flinched reflexively. Anger stirred. Anger, and recollection.

"Who is she?" Chal demanded.

"A guest from the *gadjo* house party. Some friend of the daughter's, but where is her escort? To ride so far in that sidesaddle… it makes no sense, unless her ladyship suggested this as amusement."

"How is a *gadje* accosting you at *ker* amusing? Who should find it so?" intoned Chal.

Valkin flushed. *Damn.* He never flushed. He had too much dignity.

"The amusements of English ton ladies are difficult to fathom. I left the manor early, unable to see Lady Davenport—Liza that is, she…er…" He mounted his horse, staring down at the girl. "I do not recollect her name."

Chal scowled at him. "So, this is one of your—"

"Of course not," Valkin shot back. "I would never allow one of them at *ker*. But we can't leave her here. An English girl alone in the woods is at great risk."

Without another word, Chal lifted the *gadje*, calling Dela, to assist in placing the girl across the *krallis*'s lap. Valkin tightened his arms protectively, wondering at himself: his second act of disinterested chivalry for the week. Perhaps he was learning to behave like a gentleman after all. His glance strayed to those elevated curves. Maybe not that disinterested.

He mentally kicked himself. He'd already frightened her once—a sick, scared young girl who'd sought his aid. She didn't seem a threat to him or his house. He'd behaved like a brute. He wracked his brains to recall if anyone at the Davenports had mentioned her connections or her estate. There'd been much talk of horseflesh and whores, but not one gentleman had mentioned this beauty. He wondered how old she was. She was out, certainly, or Basingstoke could not have claimed her.

Chal examined the mare. Glancing up at Valkin, he shook his head. "I can't ride her like this." He looked disgustedly at the sidesaddle and unbuckled the girth. The little thoroughbred snorted appreciatively. "Whoever she is, she's taken better care of her horse than she has herself. The animal looks well despite having been ridden through the night."

Valkin agreed. "She'll need watering. Walk her back along the river and set her up in the *gry* pens. Find her some good grain and a brush-down."

"I'll see you at *ker*." Chal headed off, leading the little mare through the forest.

Valkin urged his mount to a steady canter, his gaze on the ruddy cheeks of the woman who'd claimed to be his "intimate friend." Who'd sought his protection. She looked awfully young and helpless in his arms.

***

Bavol knew his way to *ker* without direction. Once there, Valkin summoned more cousins and rode straight to his *covo*. As *sher-engro* of the royal House of Brishen, Valkin's *covo* was the largest dwelling at *ker*. Quite ten feet long and adorned with the proud equine symbols of House Brishen, it was drawn by two massive Romany-bred horses when mobile. His sister Reyna ran up as he arrived, having been forewarned of his "guest." She hurried inside to light his stove.

Dela held Bavol, while Valkin handed his charge carefully down to Cato before dismounting. He took the girl back into his arms and without a word to either cousin strode into his *covo*, laying the *gadje* among his silk pillows just as the first drops of heavy rain came splashing down.

Reyna untied the girl's bonnet, before touching a palm to her pale forehead. She pressed the back of her other hand to the undamaged of those too-pink cheeks, wincing at the mark on the girl's face.

She glanced at Valkin impatiently. "Who is she?"

Valkin didn't answer, guilt tearing at his gut while his sister's tutting gave way to an uneasy silence. A queer ache invaded his chest. He sighed, wondering what it was about the girl that made him feel responsible. Was it because she seemed so damned familiar, though he didn't know her name? Or because he'd already hurt her without meaning to? Or was it because she'd pretended to be his *gadje* mistress, and he wanted this to be true?

"Well?" Valkin demanded in Romany. "What the devil's the matter with her?"

Reyna shot him a fierce glare. "How should I know? The *gadje* are not strong folk. She is exhausted, certainly. She needs rest, and food and water." His sister paused, eyeing Valkin with a severe stare. "*Shuvvali* perhaps?"

The girl from the Davenport's garden, Basingstoke's intended victim—pregnant? Valkin blanched visibly, biting his lip. "Not by me," he said quickly, his voice higher than any *krallis*'s ought to be.

"Are you certain?" His sister's gaze didn't waver.

"Of course I'm certain." Doubt flickered as Valkin regarded her in silence, rain drumming ominously on his *covo* roof. He held his breath as Reyna examined the girl's abdomen, honing her point.

"Did she not claim to be your mist—"

"She isn't."

Reyna widened her eyes. "All right, *sher-engro*. There's no need to shout."

"I—I did not." It seemed prudent to close his mouth at this point and avoid glancing at the lovely woman in his bed who'd kissed him back. Who might be with child, and who was not his mistress. *Dear God.*

Valkin's hands shook, and he felt a powerful urge to disgorge his breakfast. With a determined effort, he forced himself to calm down. When his sister finally shook her head, Valkin sank onto a chair with a moan. Reyna looked up, cocking an eyebrow as she opened her mouth. He flung up his hand.

"Don't." He gave a short head shake. "Just—don't." He was in no humour for a lecture on mending his behaviour among the *gadje*. "And thank you," he continued more gently. His kettle bubbled and hissed on the stove, so he busied himself filling the herb bowls for his sister. Reyna dropped dried leaves into them, arranging them around the bed. A refreshing scent stole through the *covo*. The woman on the bed murmured something but her eyes remained closed. Valkin watched the rapid rise and fall of her chest. She was breathing unnaturally fast, lungs struggling for air.

"What on earth did you do to her?" Reyna asked.

"Kissed her," he muttered, pretending not to notice his sister's stifled laugh.

"This is something I do not understand," Reyna said. "I wish Syeira were here. She is better at healing."

"Is there any word from Wil?"

Reyna nodded. "They will travel from Scotland once the new babe is born. That may be a week or so and—well, I do not like to wait so long." Touching the girl's forehead again, she looked at Valkin. "Do you wish me to nurse her?"

Reyna was overseeing much of the winter store preparation, and she had Christmas to organise as well. In Syeira's absence, she was also responsible for the welfare of their younger brothers and sisters and various other family members. It wasn't fair to ask her to take on anything else. Valkin shook his head, sighing.

"I can manage for now. Just tell me what to do."

She searched through his cupboards. "I'm not certain what ails her. Keep her warm. I will prepare some relief tea. If she has truly been riding for hours, she will be in some pain later. Stay with her until she wakes. She may be frightened to find herself among strangers."

He nodded, leaning over to draw up the covers. The girl was shivering. He warmed her hands with his larger ones, rubbing them absently. Bruises coated her neck and he winced. Had he done that when he grabbed her? The thought horrified him. Valkin traced the bruise on her cheek, her skin silk under his fingers. Something stirred deep inside him. Something he couldn't quite name.

"Her breathing seems difficult, and her face is far too warm. I can't think what might be causing it." Reyna lifted her shawl to cover her hair and left.

Valkin widened his eyes in sudden realisation. Stepping to the door, he called Reyna back, shouting to be heard over the pounding rain.

"Unhook her gown," he ordered as she rushed back in.

Reyna stared at him, shaking her head in shocked disbelief. Valkin let out an impatient breath. "Please, Reyna."

"You will please not watch, then, my brother, my *prala*."

Valkin turned his back.

A few moments later, she gasped. "What in God's name *is* that thing?"

He bit back a smile. "Her stays," he replied without turning around. "Some of the *gadje* tie them very tight."

Reyna snorted in disgust. "Why do their women consent to such a torment? The laces look difficult to manage. It does not appear comfortable in the least."

"Comfort is not the intention," Valkin said. "It is to give her a certain appearance. I have heard it is a reason the *gadjes* swoon so often."

She snorted again. "If a *gadjo* must truss up his woman as though she were a gamebird, she is likely to suffer by it."

Valkin nodded. "I shall wait outside while you remove it." He stepped to the *covo* door, already ducking his head against the rain.

"I wouldn't know where to begin." Reyna cast a look of cool deliberation at Valkin. "Do you? Of course you do," she answered herself as he turned to face her.

Valkin glanced at the bed, raising his eyebrows. The girl's corset was in the new style, and it was certainly the most unfriendly undergarment he'd ever seen. His fingers twitched; he wanted, badly, to get to work on those laces. To free this beautiful *gadje* who wasn't his mistress…*yet*. Valkin gazed at Reyna, how she rested her hands lightly on the girl's skin. His palms itched, and his mouth. Not to mention the rest of him.

"Hmm. Do you take care of that, then. I shall make the relief tea." Reyna spared him an arch look as she gathered her shawl again, making a concerted effort to hide her expression. "I will be back *very* soon."

Is that a warning? Valkin scowled at his *covo* door, then checked himself. His sister was right. There was no one in the whole camp who knew how to unlace an Englishwoman's undergarments better than he.

Rain drummed heavily over his *covo* roof as he turned back to the unconscious woman in his bed, suddenly nervous. *What, exactly, do you have to be nervous about?* Valkin didn't know, but his hands were far from steady as he leaned over the girl, fumbling clumsily in the dim light from his stove. This was not the first time he'd done this, for God's sake.

Valkin set his jaw and concentrated on his fingers, making a determined effort not to stare at the generous curves of her breasts. He forced himself not to remember the way she'd responded to the pressure of his lips on hers—*before she lost consciousness*. He mentally slapped himself, focusing on reversing some maid's expertly tied knots. His ruthless attempt at control merely made the hot pounding of his blood more noticeable, the urgent heat of his body more painful. Valkin grimaced, telling himself he deserved it, waiting for some part of him to disagree. It didn't.

He lifted her gently, noticing how his hands fit neatly around her waist. He wondered why the girl wore her stays so tight in the first place. She was a tiny little thing, really. Petite, though buxom… and he'd best keep his eyes on his hands. Leaning her forehead against his shoulder, Valkin concentrated on unwinding her spiral lacing, resting his chin on a bed of the softest chestnut curls. When a loud thunderclap crashed overhead, he realised he was holding his breath again.

He exhaled slowly, working from eyelet to hook, and right to left. He breathed in again, savouring the scent of woodland and lavender, biting down on his tongue to keep his attention on the job at hand. If he allowed his thoughts to wander… Right eyelet, left hook, left eyelet, right hook… *halfway and she's too lovely. Those curves…* Steadying his breaths, he continued. Left eyelet, right hook… *her untamed kiss… Three-quarters now… this is impossible…*

A moment later the girl sprang up, shoving him violently aside, before backing against the wall. Her eyes held a wild, unfocused look. Valkin was too stunned to do anything but stare open-mouthed as the *gadje* grabbed desperately beneath her skirts, lifting her gown in the French manner. *What the devil?*

"It's all right. I wasn't—that is, you need have no fear of me. You could not breathe, and—" His words died on his lips as she drew a pistol from beneath her petticoats and levelled it at him. Despite using both hands to hold it, the barrel shook—not that it mattered. She could hardly miss at this distance. Valkin froze as he heard the weapon cock. His thoughts stilled and he was cool-headed once more. *Romany chivalry does not extend to assassins.*

"You are my guest, and this is my *ker*." His voice was steady, but his eyes never strayed from her pistol. He held out his hand for the weapon. "You are in a Romany camp full of women and children. You will not discharge that weapon here. You will not endanger my people." *Or yourself.*

He dared not blink. He did not like the glazed look in her wide green eyes. The *gadje* glanced at the pistol as though she wasn't sure where it came from. Shaking her head, she blinked a few times. Looking down at her partially opened stays, she tightened her grip on her weapon and steadied her arms, affixing a glare.

"Why?" she demanded. "Why were you undressing me?"

"You were ill. I thought your stays were making it difficult for you to breathe." He paused, giving her a moment to absorb his words. "Can you breathe more easily now?" He softened his tone further. She was pale as a ghost; she looked scared to death. God alone knew what she'd been through. *Before you scared the daylights out of her in the woods.* A muscle jumped in his jaw. His focus locked on that pistol. The rain outside seemed twice as loud.

The girl drew in a deep breath and let it out again. The action seemed to calm her. His guest gazed slowly around the *covo*, taking in the healing herbs steaming gently on either side of her, the embroidered silken bedding, the carved and painted images of horses and flowers around his wooden walls. Dropping her hands, she sagged back into the cushions, huddling against the wall.

"That's right." Valkin did not exhale until he saw her fingers ease off the trigger. He stepped slowly forward and relieved her of the pistol. She let go of it easily, as though she barely had the strength to hold it any longer. He turned the weapon over in his hands. A military pistol, correctly loaded and fully cocked. Valkin shook his head. His *gadje* was full of surprises. *His?* Surprising, indeed.

CHAPTER SEVEN

Lydia

"You—you k-k-kissed me." Lydia did her best to still her shaking limbs. *Dear God, what had happened to her?*

"I did," Valkin answered quietly. "And if I may be so bold, my lady, you kissed me back."

"I—I d-did?" Her brow furrowed. She remembered his *kiss*. Not much else. She breathed out slowly. Breathed in again. She'd been riding in the woods.

"You swooned." He spoke in that same gentle voice. "I brought you here, to my camp. I do not pretend to be familiar with all *gadjo* customs, but I believe covering one's host with a pistol verges on discourteous."

Lydia flung a hand to her mouth in horror. She'd pointed her weapon—had threatened—the very man she'd dreamed about since she was a girl. This was Valkin, the man who'd been nothing but kind to her in her life. Oh Lord, what if Wil were already in the camp? *He can't be.* Syeira was Brishen's healer. She'd have been summoned in the first instance. Neither her brother nor the Romany princess would have failed to recognise her, but Lydia refused to relax entirely. Lady Davenport's words echoed in her mind. *Your father is a powerful man.*

Valkin had already protected her from the earl... *Dear Lord—the earl.* Recalling everything at once, she shifted uncomfortably. She'd claimed to be Valkin's mistress. He'd been angry and said his protection came at a price.

"I d-do b-beg your pardon," she whispered. "I d-did n-not m-mean to… I was f-frightened when I woke, y-your f-f-face in the sh-shadows. I d-didn't know where I w-was. Please, forgive m-me."

Valkin smiled wryly. "I will, if you promise to forgive me for alarming you in the first place, my lady." He drew back the bedclothes and motioned for her to get in, carefully averting his eyes. "It is important that you keep warm."

Lydia flinched as he raised his hand to her bodice.

He saw it, pausing. "I beg your pardon in my turn. There is no one else who knows how your undergarments work. Have you no maid?"

Lydia swallowed. He'd afforded her an opening. *Tell him. Now. Tell him who you are. Ask him to send for Wil*…and then what? Watch while the duke and the earl disrupt the lives of these good people? Destroy Wil and his young family? Ruin this man who'd already aided her at Davenport Manor?

I will not do it. Lord Brishen's two most powerful enemies were connected to her. Revealing her identity now placed them all at risk. Besides, her cheeks burned at the thought of detailing her circumstances. Could any man begin to understand it? Clutching her loosened gown over her chest, Lydia moved slowly towards Valkin.

"I have no maid," she replied, staring at her hands. "I'm quite alone, you see."

"Then I must finish your laces, if you will permit me."

She couldn't tell if he believed her or not. Her whole body blushed when she bent her head before him, his strong, warm hands moving across her back. Truly, breathing may have been easier if she'd stayed laced up—and away from Valkin Brishen.

"Your garter is a most unsafe place for your *yag-engri*," he said. "This is the word for pistol in Romany."

Lydia shrugged lightly. "Where do you suggest I keep it? It ought to be handy, if I'm to defend myself at all." She couldn't repress her shudder, as though the cold weather crept beneath her covers. Valkin tightened his hold, drawing her closer. Her next shiver had nothing to do with any chill.

"You must be in some sort of danger, or why the weapon?" The weight behind his words at odds with warm hands stilled at her waist, one palm curved over her hip.

"N-Not yet. Please." Lydia's voice shook and she couldn't steady it.

Valkin sat her up, studying her face intently. "We will talk more of this when you are rested."

Gratitude glistened in her eyes. She spoke again, softly. "I th-thank you, L-lord—er—how ought I to address you?"

"I beg your pardon?"

"Do I address you as Lord Brishen?"

"Oh, I see." He smiled at her again. "My true title is *krallis*, though I am used to being called Lord Brishen or the Romany King among the English. You may call me either, if you wish, but my name is Valkin." He paused. "How may I address you, my lady?"

The heartbeat of silence only emphasised her hesitation. "M-miss Dale. Martha Dale." She shivered before him.

Valkin cupped her face, lifting it so she looked directly into his dark eyes. He ran his thumb softly over her unmarked cheek, biting his lip. Lydia flinched at his touch, fear flaring in her chest.

"I shall call you this if you wish, *Miss Dale*," he replied. "But do not lie to me again."

Jerking away from his touch, Lydia glared coldly at Valkin, shoulders quivering, chin lifting.

His gaze flicked to the bruise on her face. "Does that hurt?" His tone was oddly gentle.

Lydia turned away from him, closing her eyes as a few slow tears slid over her cheek.

"Will you trust me, Miss Dale? Here, now, in this moment alone?"

Lydia sniffled, turning to look into his face. Lord Brishen didn't know who Lydia was. Those she ran from had no idea of her whereabouts. Right here, right now, she was protected. *In this moment alone...* How many moments alone had she spent? How many since she felt safe? Staring into Valkin's warm eyes, Lydia struggled with herself, remembering Brishen at Clifton Hall all those years ago. She wanted to trust him, to know him now, to learn something of an honourable man.

"All right," she whispered. A brighter sensation invaded her chest, warmer and softer than anything she'd felt since Wil left her behind. This is Brishen. This is Valkin. *In this moment alone, I am safe.*

Seating herself before him, she bowed her head, then leaned forward, lightly resting against Valkin's upper arm. Lydia closed her eyes, releasing a breath she'd held too long. "Thank you for your help," she whispered.

Valkin settled her forehead more snugly against his shoulder, returning to her stays. "*Pireni,*" he murmured.

The rhythmic rain soothed the frantic whirling of Lydia's thoughts. Valkin's hard, warm hands moved over her again, his heart beating fast against her ear. As he removed the last of her lacings, she pulled herself free, giving a small celebratory shake. Lydia released a slow sigh, surprised to catch Valkin exhaling in a similar manner.

"How do you feel now, Miss Dale?"

"As though I've b-been let out of a c-cage. Thank you. It is such a blessing to be able to b-breathe." She glanced at the corset with distaste before drawing up the Romany coverlet like a shawl.

"May I ask why you find it necessary to wear them at all?"

Lydia arched a brow. "It is not modest *not* to wear them. Surely you've met other Englishwomen who—" She stopped, blushed, and lowered her gaze.

Valkin's wry smile warmed his black eyes. "I see my reputation has not improved any." He chuckled and shrugged. "Very well, yes, I've had occasion to familiarise myself with the intricate undergarments of your countrywomen. Is it not usual to wear such a device only in cases where a woman, well, exceeds the expected shape?"

Lydia worked hard to hide her amusement. "What sort of gentleman discusses undergarments with a lady?"

"You are not exactly large," he pointed out, without apologising.

"M-my father ordered m-me to wear them," Lydia said quietly. There were no polite phrases in *The Young Lady's Book* for explaining that your sire insists you display yourself as a whore for his friends. She closed her eyes against the needles of shame pricking her skin. When she continued, her voice was barely audible. "H-he g-gave m-me to understand that I d-do n-not h-have a f-fashionable shape w-without aids like the one h-he provided. H-he is eager to see m-me m-married, and—"

"I'll bet." Valkin spoke under his breath, sounding savage. He clenched his other fist. "*Bostaris.*"

Lydia started at his tone and his deadly expression, schooling her face to indifference. Catching her look, he seemed to steady but his gentle inquiries were effective. To speak aloud what the duke thought of her hurt more than Lydia ever imagined. Did Valkin notice the old bruises beneath her chemise? She shivered as the icy sensation in her belly set like stone.

"H-he believes m-me d-defective."

"I noticed no defect."

"M-my m-manner of speech." Lydia shrugged wearily.

"A silent wife is much prized by many wedded gentlemen." Valkin lifted one ironic brow.

She smiled weakly. "Is this why you're n-not w-wed yourself, then?"

"How could you know that?"

Lydia fixed him with a mock-glare. "N-neither an English w-wife, nor a Romany one, will allow h-her h-husband to place another woman in her marital bed."

"Common ground at last." Valkin inclined his head smilingly. "You are correct in my case at least."

"You c-cannot find a w-woman silent enough to wed you?" Lydia gazed up at him, wondering if she dared laugh.

He did it for her, laughing and shaking his head. "I should consider such a companion remarkably dull. I do not seek silence in my wife, Miss Dale, which is just as well. I have four outspoken sisters, but they are not the reason I remain unmarried."

"What is the reason?"

"The wrong kind of love can be dangerous," he replied quietly, as though he hoped the conversation closed.

He did not know Lydia. "In what way d-dangerous?"

Valkin gazed at her for a long time, his eyes soft when he spoke. "There were four Brishen brothers once, Miss Dale. Culvato was my third youngest sibling."

"I-is he…is he no longer w-with you?" She matched his solemn tone, thinking of her own absent brothers.

"Culvato died for the wrong sort of love," Valkin explained. "He loved an English girl, a *gadje*, like you. She loved him too, or so she said."

Lydia blinked. "You doubt her loyalty?"

Valkin's laugh was bittersweet. "I did not know her well enough. All I do know is my brother gained my agreement to wed and rode out to meet his betrothed. He never returned." His voice turned harsh. "We found him in the woods at sunset. Beaten."

Lydia gasped. "Th-they b-beat your b-brother?"

"To death," Valkin replied flatly. "It is what happens to Romany who meet the English alone in the woods." He glanced at her, adjusting his tone.

"You b-believe she l-lured him there? She may h-have been unaware—"

Valkin shrugged, offering half a nod. "She never inquired after him. I do not believe she loved him, and Culvato was the sort of boy who—" He smiled suddenly, his face suffused in memories. "He was what you English call an optimist."

"I am sure he was a good brother," she said gently. "He sounds romantic."

Valkin seemed to shake off his nostalgia. "All Romany men are romantic, Miss Dale. Our way of life lends itself to sensibility." His smile faded. "As for me, I seek a certain kind of love. Something I saw once, long ago. Special, and so very beautiful. It was golden, magical." His voice deepened and the wistful cast to his eyes made Lydia's breath hitch. "What I seek is rare, I believe."

"And if you d-do not find it?"

"Then I will not wed." He sighed again, shrugging. "I do not speak of it often at *ker*. It is a source of great frustration to my family, especially my sisters."

"Then they b-believe you will marry eventually." She tried to keep the sadness from her voice. "M-my p-papa has n-no such h-hopes for m-me." Lifting one hand to her damaged cheek, she winced.

"Leave it, *pireni*. Let yourself heal."

"H-he says I h-have l-litt-ttle to att-ttract a g-good m-man," she stammered.

"Your father told you this?" Valkin watched her restive hands attacking each other. She flinched as he reached towards her, and his hand fell to his side.

"Would you believe me if I told you your father was wrong?"

An odd warmth moved through her skin at his words. She pressed her lips closed, staring back at him. "H-he isn't. I h-have b-been out for two entire Seasons n-now. No d-decent m-man has c-come n-near m-me."

"No man?" He smiled all the way up to his eyes.

Lydia shivered with something other than cold, remembering *he* had been near her. He'd been about as close to her in the woods as he was now, and coming closer. He didn't touch her; merely stood close, staring down at her mouth. She blushed furiously under the intensity of his stare. His warmth was palpable.

Valkin's gaze held her fast, seemingly reading her every thought. Lydia stared back, entranced with this heat, this burning... The nearness of his body to hers affected her breathing, her pulse, her ability to think and move. She sat motionless, watching Valkin Brishen lean in close enough to lick her lips. He traced the pout of her lower lip with his gaze, learning the shape of her mouth. His tongue flickered over his own... *close, closer, closest.*

A loud knock sounded from the door, a voice calling for Valkin, and Lydia leapt back, gasping as she yanked the coverlet over her shoulders, pulse racing as her heartbeat thrummed beneath her skin. Staring at Valkin, she opened her mouth to speak, but her voice stalled.

"Reyna," he murmured, not answering the impatient knocking of this Reyna while his gaze stayed hot on hers, hungry, potent, and— could he be shocked? Surely not as shocked as she. *Not this man.*

"If your Englishmen cannot see what you have to offer, then perhaps they do not deserve to know." His rasping whisper tempted her again. "It is as I have always said, Miss Dale. Most *gadjos* are fools."

***

Valkin

Valkin wasn't sure whether to bless his sister or curse her as Miss Dale sat hurriedly back in his bed and began work on the pins that bound her chestnut mane. Catching an echo of his own passion in her huge green eyes, he drew a deep breath to steady his racing pulse. Fascinated, he watched curl after glossy curl fall about her shoulders. *She is so very lovely...and she is not mine.*

He scowled at nothing and opened the door. "Miss Dale, may I present my sister, Reyna."

She smiled uncertainly at Reyna, who carried a large tray of hot liquids and a bowl of something that smelled like Heaven in gravy.

"Good. You are awake," Reyna said in English. Looking solemnly into Miss Dale's eyes, she rested a palm over her forehead, tutting to herself when she examined the welts patterned across her skin. With a black glance towards the stays, she nodded, touching her damp fingers lightly to the silken cheeks that had been too warm. "Your colour is still too high. How do you feel?"

"M-much better than I d-did, thank you." Miss Dale's flushed cheeks reddened further as her gaze remained on her lap.

"Now," Reyna said as she warmed herself by the stove. "You will please drink this, yes?" She offered a steaming cup of amber liquid from her tray. "You will start to feel pain soon, and this will help you."

"Pain?" Valkin interjected.

"From the riding," Reyna told them. "And from—that." She indicated the corset with a jerk of her head and an echo of his own dislike.

Miss Dale blew on her tea to cool it, sipping with caution. Reyna smiled approvingly, twitching her heavy braid over her shoulder. She handed some small bags to Valkin, issuing further instructions in rapid Romany. He added hot water to the herb bowls and shook out a few more leaves, then carefully folded the rest of the herb bags, stowing them in his little cupboard.

"I have prepared some remedies for you." Reyna arranged a collection of bottles and jars on a shelf by the bedhead. "And later, I will send my youngest sister to help you with a bath, when I can find one. This will heal your bruises and soothe your sore muscles as well." Her glance flicked over the purple marks on Miss Dale's neck. She shuddered as though sharing her pain. Placing the bowl of thick stew on a tray across Miss Dale's knees, Reyna added a jug of water. "I have added relief herb to your meal. You must eat. You must drink. You must rest. It is clear for you, yes?"

"Yes. I am v-very sorry to p-put you t-to such t-trouble. Is it M-miss B-brishen?"

"Reyna."

"I am M-martha. I th-thank you s-sincerely, R-reyna."

Reyna patted her shoulder and waved her words away. "It is my honour to help." Her warm, friendly smile had Miss Dale smiling back in moments. She gathered her shawl about her. "Valkin knows what to do."

"Y-you are n-not st-staying w-with m-me?" Miss Dale's smile faded. She ignored her meal, sounding panicked.

"I am needed elsewhere. Valkin shall ensure you're well cared for. Do as he tells you and you will be well. I must go." Reyna cast a long, meaningful look at Valkin. "She needs *rest*," his sister repeated in Romany.

Valkin raised his brows and glared. Reyna simply stared back, determined to make her point. He gave up, nodding. "Thank you."

She smiled at Miss Dale again and left. Apparently the rumour that he had a *gadje* mistress stowed away in his *covo* was credible enough among his own family. Valkin turned his attention to the girl in his bed. Sighing, he soaked a linen cloth in one of the healing bowls while she finished her tea. "Lie down when you've finished eating and stay under the covers."

"I'd prefer to d-dress," she countered, motioning for him to turn his back.

"It's really not my day, is it?" He caught her reluctant smile before facing away, though she was soon engaged in fitting on her habit with many gasps and whimpers of pain. Her overtaxed muscles were clearly problematic.

"Miss Dale, if I may—?"

"You m-may not," she replied resolutely. "I am p-perfectly able to c-complete m-my own d-dress."

"I did not ask with any ulterior purpose in mind," he replied.

"I d-did n-not say so." Her words slurred together as the tea and herbs took effect. "I am dressed. I shall n-not sleep if you remain." Her voice was already softening.

"I promised Reyna I'd ensure your rest." Valkin sat. "I'll not break my word to my sister, so you may as well accept it."

Her eyelids fluttered amid her futile attempts to keep them open. Brishen's healing remedies were known throughout the country for potency, and efficacy. Miss Dale snuggled into his pillows, her immense green eyes gazing up at him. Suddenly she sat bolt upright. Valkin jumped to his feet, remembering her pistol.

"M-my horse, m-my poor little horse. How c-could I h-have forgotten h-her?" She twisted her hands in agitation but made no move to do anything else.

Valkin let out a breath. "Is that all? I thought you were about to produce another deadly device from beneath your skirts."

Miss Dale reddened and lay down again, perhaps not entirely certain he'd spoken in jest. She was quite devastating enough without the pistol or anything else that might lie under her petticoat. The less he let his thoughts linger there, the better.

"Your mare is quite safe. My brothers corralled her with our own stock. She is simply worn out, like you." He drew up her covers. "Rest now, *pireni*," he whispered. "Rest."

She looked so alone beneath his enormous feather-filled quilt. Her softness called to him, reminding him his bed was made for two.

CHAPTER EIGHT

Valkin

Valkin stayed beside the *gadje* as long as he could, watching her curls drifting on sleepy sighs, her breasts rising and falling, rising, falling, rising, rising... after a quarter hour, according to the consort's pocket watch, he could no longer stand the temperature in his own *covo*. Exiting as stealthily as possible, he went in search of *Bebee* Cin.

"*Koshti Sarla Bebee*. I have a request."

The old woman nodded from her place by the fireside, sharp gaze shifting over his face. "I have heard about your guest. *Kris* is held over today. Reyna's chores will be redistributed so she may assist the *gadje*. It is time your youngest sister, Narilla, demonstrates her skill in any case. She is as adept at her silks as any Brishen woman."

"Agreed, and thank you."

"You'll not be staying in the *covo*." Cin's statement was not a query.

"I'll set up my *tan* as soon as weather allows."

"This is well done." The elder nodded at him. "Reyna says the girl is exhausted. She needs rest."

Valkin waited until the old woman turned away before scowling at her back.

"I saw that, nephew."

Valkin's scowl fell away immediately, his belly prickling guilt. "I beg your pardon, *Bebee* Cin."

"I'll no more hesitate to spank the *krallis* than I did the Romany Prince," she called over her shoulder as she hurried away. "Take care on patrol. With a *gadje* at *ker*, we must all be on our guard."

"Indeed." It was a complication Brishen could not afford. *Not just Brishen.* Valkin recalled Basingstoke's face when he'd knocked the bastard down. No Romany could hope to stand between a *gadjo* peer and his betrothed. Not even the *krallis*.

As soon as the rainstorm passed, Valkin crawled beneath his *covo* to drag out his temporary quarters. He set up his *tan* using his *covo* as a third wall, nodding to himself. Separate quarters and a greater focus on his duties at *ker* would help his guest get the rest everyone insisted upon. She need not be disturbed by his comings and goings, nor he by hers. He made up his bedroll, ordering himself to banish all images of her lovely face and arousing curves from his mind. Valkin wasn't young and foolish like Culvato. He was the *krallis*. Beautiful *gadjes* had no place in his mind, his *covo*, or his bed.

Though his temporary quarters were not large, his spare cot and bedding fitted well enough. There were a few rips—he'd not used it in years—but that wasn't important tonight. Valkin elected to join the perimeter guard's night patrol. *Bebee* Cin had a point regarding extra guards—besides, it provided an effective distraction from Miss Dale.

"For the most part," Valkin muttered as he stood shivering in his place. A light touch at his shoulder made him smile.

"*Sarishan* Reyna," he said without turning. "You ought to be at rest."

"I have hot coffee," she replied, handing him a steaming mug.

"Thank you, my sister, my *pen*." Valkin wrapped his hands gratefully around his drink. "How is the *gadje*?"

"Sleeping," Reyna replied. "There is much bruising on her back. The welts on her skin must be painful, and that mark on her face pains her." She shuddered. "Our herbs are effective. She will heal in time."

"Is she eating any better?"

"You ask me of her appetite?"

Reyna's surprise nettled him. "I simply wish to ensure—"

"You wish to ensure what, *sher-engro*?" Reyna interrupted firmly. "Our *krallis* is known for his cavalier attitude to *gadje* women, at least among our Romany. Is your behaviour so different among the English?"

"Not at all. I—" Valkin bit his lip. His infamous self-control seemed less effective than usual. Had giving up his quarters unsettled him to such a degree? "She is our guest," he said finally.

"Of course, *sher-engro*."

Valkin sipped his coffee in silence, doubly glad the night hid Reyna's expression. He didn't need to field her shrewd glances or raised brows, but her point was well-made. Since when was the *krallis* so plagued with concerns about a *gadje* he hardly knew? He shrugged inwardly, listening to his sister.

"Thank you for speaking with *Bebee* Cin regarding my duties. However, I cannot sit with Miss Dale tomorrow evening," Reyna informed him. "I have healing work in the birthing tent."

"Very well. What must I do?" He listened as Reyna ran through what was required.

"She may sleep much of the day tomorrow," his sister said. "Once she is rested, we must get her up and moving. It will be better for her healing if she takes light exercise."

Valkin drained his cup, handing it back to his sister as she returned to her *tan*.

"Sleep well." He stayed turned to the shadowed woodland. *She may sleep much of the day*, Reyna had said and perhaps, if the *gadje* did not sleep, he might learn more about this woman who'd hoped to be taken for his mistress. The woman who'd fought off Basingstoke but said not a word about it since. Might the girl be more candid once she felt safe enough? Valkin hadn't considered how to help a *gadje* feel safe before now. Safety always seemed more a Romany need than an English one.

One thing he did know: It was not safe to shelter someone for whose history the *sher-engro* could not answer. It was time to insist this *gadje* answer the most pressing question of all.

***

Returning to his *covo* before the next evening's patrol, Valkin knocked quietly on his door but gained no response. He entered silently, gazing down at his slumbering *gadje*. She lay huddled beneath the covers, looking lost and defenceless in his bed.

He couldn't shake the feeling that Miss Dale was more familiar than the girl from Davenport Manor. He'd not been to her bed (he'd never forget losing himself in those curves), but he'd seen her somewhere before, he was sure of it, and he searched his memory repeatedly for a clue. He resisted the urge to stroke her bright silken curls, heart hammering as though he'd been running. She murmured and shifted, eyelids fluttering open. Valkin immediately withdrew, seating himself in one of the chairs across the *covo*. Relief flashed through him at the sudden distance, which made sense, along with a stabbing sense of loss, which did not.

"Good evening, Miss Dale. I did not intend to disturb your rest," he said softly, smiling at her. She looked temptingly tousled against his cushions. Warm blood stirred in his veins. She sat up, clutching his coverlet like a cocoon, and blinking.

"That's quite all right. I—I think I h-have slept for long enough." The girl looked into his eyes for the briefest of moments, her gaze dropping to her hands, clasping and unclasping over and over again. "I m-must b-beg your pardon, Valkin. I understand I have c-caused you to leave your h-home. Is there n-nowhere else I may rest?"

Valkin shrugged. "It is no hardship. I am accustomed to living out of doors, though I've not used my *tan* for some time. You've afforded me an excellent opportunity to examine it for repairs. I take my turn on night patrol in any case. I merely looked in for the items I require and to see to your health, if you will permit me. How do you feel?" He rummaged through various drawers and cupboards, gathering belongings, drawing closer to the bed.

She shrank back. "I am a g-great d-deal m-more recovered," she answered, not looking at him. "I m-may b-be able to travel again t-tomorrow."

"Reyna does not think so." Valkin shook his head at her.

"I h-have very little time, and—" She pressed her lips closed, turning partly away.

Valkin pretended not to notice. "Winter travel is fraught with peril. The snows begin soon and the river will freeze. The roads deteriorate daily. It is also unsafe to travel before you recover." He took a breath and held it. "Why not stay, and heal?"

"You wish me to stay?" Green eyes faced him, weighing his words.

"I wish you recovered before travelling through such a winter. It is foolish to contemplate any other course."

"You think I am a fool?" Her voice hardened and a fierce determination crept into her eyes.

Valkin blinked at the steadiness of her words. Seating himself beside her with a sigh, he ignored her automatic recoil.

"I do not think you are a fool, Miss Dale. I think you are in trouble. I think you are running away from more than your betrothal, and I think it is time you told me your true name."

A dozen emotions moved rapidly over her face. When she turned her shimmering eyes upon him, her expression took him like a fist to his face: a determined doe facing down her hunter. Valkin recalled her struggle to stand against a topiary tree in a moonlit garden, her ripped dress and her escape. Was there anyone she trusted at all? He willed her to trust him, to tell him her name and ask for his help. He wished he could take back his demand, open his lips and ask her pardon. He wanted to show her her belief in his protection was not misplaced but he couldn't, because perhaps it was.

CHAPTER NINE

Lydia

"I'm afraid I must insist, Miss Dale." Valkin's voice pressed powerfully into Lydia's silence.

She opened and closed her lips without a sound. Swallowing, she started at a loud pop from the stove. "My true name is not safe," she whispered finally, shrinking into herself, tension travelling through her until her fingertips quivered.

Valkin watched her closely, his gaze on her anxious fingers twining over and over each other in agonised repetition. At last he stood, leaning past her to open the hangings shielding the windows above his bed. "Look out there, my lady," he said quietly. "Tell me what you see."

Clutching the silk coverlet around her, Lydia knelt and pressed her face to the glass. The Romany camp was alive with hundreds of people in brightly coloured costumes wandering through the temporary town, from the women busy around the great central cooking fire, to the men chopping wood or standing guard around their families in a wide perimeter. Children ran here and there, sometimes several in a row holding hands and led by the tallest, in a charming tableau. Lydia smiled. Warm laughter played everywhere, the press of loving families abounded. Glancing back at Valkin, Lydia's expression faltered.

"Your camp is wonderful," she said softly. "The Romany are a beautiful people. They are very kind." Her voice hitched.

"Many houses are gathering for our Romany Christmas. They are my people," he responded. "I am *sher-engro* of the House of Brishen and *krallis* of the Romany people of this land. If what you run from endangers them, I would have you tell me now." The faint edge to his voice didn't surprise her.

Lydia took a breath, turning back to the window. She must tell him something—some part of the truth. Her heart thudded against her breastbone as she faced Valkin, his keen stare burning between them.

"M-my father insists on m-my b-betrothal to the earl. A-a m-man I d-detest." She spoke slowly, her voice as lifeless and empty as Clifton Hall. "I am afraid of h-him."

"You didn't seem so afraid of bruising the earl's—"

"Pride?" A smile twitched her lips.

Valkin's gaze found the mark on her cheek. "Your father has pledged you to Basingstoke." A flicker of revulsion crossed his features. "You believe he will pursue you?" His glance shifted to the purplish bruises on her neck. Something like a killing rage flashed in his eyes.

Lydia attempted a laugh, but it came out as a choke in her throat. "P-pursuit? Not of m-me. M-merely m-my d-dowry. There is n-nothing h-he wants of m-me. Once h-he m-marries m-me, takes me, and g-gains c-control of m-my m-money, h-he—" Her words tumbled out in a rush. "When your m-men found m-me—in the w-woods, I was trav-velling to the c-coast. M-my friends g-gave m-me m-money, a h-horse. I have a b-brother in France. They thought—we all thought—if I c-can reach P-paris, h-he m-may-protect m-me. Speak for me. He is a g-good m-man. B-by n-now the b-betrothal has b-been ann-noun-nced. The earl—and m-my father—they will c-come f-for m-me. Force m-me t-to—"

She closed her eyes and told him about the rumour Basingstoke had spread.

"To g-give m-me n-no choice," she whispered, and then she sat silently for a long time, not moving at all. The smallest effort jarred too much. A single breath might send all her broken pieces spilling across Valkin's wooden floor.

Valkin said nothing. He stared out of his window, perhaps the only man she'd met who might understand her sense of helplessness. The Romany were accustomed to finding themselves out of favour with the English law, but Valkin was still a man. The law afforded every man the chance to argue his position. Without Roger's aid, Lydia was lost. She had no right to speak for herself and no one to whom she could appeal.

Lydia doubted any Romany girl need flee to protect herself. Not when those who cared about her were all around her. Their safety and security were constantly assured. She nearly wished for the long-ago times, when a Romany man might run off with any pretty *gadje* who caught his eye, adopting her as a member of his house. Wishing, however, did not make a thing so and it would not help her now.

"B-basingstoke w-will n-not allow h-himself to be th-thwarted by a m-mere g-girl," Lydia said bitterly, staring at the floor. Perhaps if she looked at it long enough, the broken pieces of her pain might dissolve and this heavy dread leave her limbs. "Y-you've n-not said anything," she added into tense, unbearable silence. "Have I sh-shocked y-you at last?"

"Your actions in this matter are the least shocking of all, Miss Dale," Valkin replied quietly. "Small wonder you've chosen to run, rather than submit to such a man. I applaud your endeavour."

Lydia glared at him. "My predicament is serious," she declared unnecessarily. "As is yours, sir." The earl would leap at the chance to avenge himself on House Brishen if he discovered her. The same thought seemed to have struck Valkin. A desperate look skittered over his face.

"I m-must leave your c-camp as soon as m-may be." Lydia's voice wavered but she pushed on. "I d-do not wish to b-bring trouble h-here. Your people—and you—have b-been kind enough to allow m-me a day's rest in s-safety. It is m-more than m-many would d-do for someone like m-me."

***

Valkin

Valkin stared at Miss Dale. The lift of her head and her steady eye told him she spoke in earnest. Her courage floored him, as a spurt of anger towards her friends burned through his gut. They'd helped her flee but had done nothing to keep her safe. If he sent her away, what might become of her? "Paris is a large city, Miss Dale, and dangerous enough."

"I b-beg you will n-not d-distress yourself on m-my account, sir. I will b-be all right once I reach m-my b-brother." She breathed deeply, slowing her words until each seemed forced from her lips. "Please tell m-me when you wish me to leave. I sh-shall do exactly as you require."

Her quiet, careful manner didn't fool him at all. Valkin read fear in her eyes as her speech grew worse. His heart clenched. He didn't have to send her away immediately, did he? His throat tightened at the thought. Reaching out, he meant to brush his knuckles feather-light across her unmarred cheek, rest his palm over the delicate curve of her shoulder, but her bruises stood out, stark and accusing. His hand fell to his side. His voice, when it came, was a low murmur, as though her wariness spilled into his speech as well.

"*Kek cana.* Not now, *pireni.*" He heard her sigh, or it may have been his. "Now, you are safc."

She shivered again, staring over his shoulder as though his *covo* wall carvings were the most interesting things she'd ever set eyes upon. "W-what is it you want of m-me?" she blurted. "What m-must I already owe you?"

Valkin swallowed slowly, suddenly gauche. "I beg your pardon?"

"I should n-not h-have pretended I was under your protection, Valkin. I-I am afraid your p-people will j-judge you p-poorly for it. I only d-did it to protect m-myself from—well, I am s-sorry for it now," she whispered.

Something flared brightly in her eyes. *Desire*... or fear? Valkin hoped he had enough sense to tell the difference. Then the moment was gone, her eyes cast down. He wanted her to look at him again, wanted to study her face and find a way to reassure her, comfort her. *Comfort her?* Liar.

"Your people will think I am... that we h-have b-been together," she said, cheeks flaming, her gaze fixing on his carved bedpost.

"The judgment of my people is not so terrible as you suppose." Valkin kept his voice hushed, raw. "The Romany respect a man who knows how to appreciate a lovely woman."

"I am n-not a d-desirable woman, Valkin," she stammered. "But you d-did say there was a price to pay for your protection." She appeared to steel herself, drawing resolve from some deep inner well. "I shall do what I must," she said quietly, her gaze meeting his at last, eyes brimming with desperation. "What c-comes n-next, p-please?" she asked in shaken accents, as though she might shatter at any moment. "T-touching?"

Never in his life had Valkin seen a woman offer herself as though it broke her. He hoped he never did again. It would be too easy to accept. To take her because he could, because she offered this—and because he wanted her. He wanted this woman who kissed him as though his lips were the last drink of water in a desert and she was dying of thirst. Blocking out his fevered imaginings that saw this woman in his arms, his lips moving over her face, her throat, his hands gripping her waist, holding her tight against him... Wild thoughts sharpened his tone.

"*Pireni*, you cannot— I will not—" There were no words in either English or Romany for this skewering agony, this all-over ache. The defeated expression on his *gadje*'s lovely face.

"I d-do n-not p-pret-tend to be able to p-please you, b-but I will d-do what I m-must," she whispered, her voice barely audible, her eyes shut tight.

"If you believe it to be so very terrible, I wonder you did not shoot me when you had the chance."

Her eyes flew open as she turned her scarlet cheeks away from him. Straightening her shoulders, she sniffed. "I must b-beg your pardon, *again*. I—I d-do not know how to speak about this but you—you will help m-me? Protect m-me, if I—I—" Her shuddering speech seemed another fraught act.

"Do you truly believe—" Valkin couldn't finish. The idea choked him silent. He shook his head harshly. "This is not the way I love, *pireni*. I'll have no more talk of it." He closed his mouth before he could say anything else.

The *gadje*'s eyes glittered when she nodded, her posture no less tense. "You d-did not ans-swer my question." Determination warred with trepidation in her eyes. "W-when d-do you n-need m-me to l-leave?"

No trace of heated overtones and no touching. *Definitely no touching.*

His voice was a growl as he returned to his seat. "You will stay here, *pireni*. You will heal. I have promised Reyna you will rest well."

She lay down obediently and turned her face to the wall. Valkin wondered at her aggrieved air. Puzzling this woman out required more wit than he possessed this day.

"There is no reason the *gadjos* will seek you among my Romany. You may rest in safety. Tomorrow you will join Brishen around our campfire." He exited the *covo*, taking up his station on the wooden steps. Chore wandered over from the fireplace with a thickish stick between his jaws.

"Chore, *besht*." The animal dropped to his haunches with a weary whine, no doubt exhausted from another canine carnal exertion. "You are lucky you are not the *krallis*," Valkin told him, taking the wood from the animal's mouth and wiping it on his breeches. He pulled out his penknife and gradually shaped a small figurine. When he was done, he'd seek out Reyna.

CHAPTER TEN

Lydia

Lydia woke to a dark, empty caravan but the fire was laid, and a cup of relief tea steamed beside the bed. She sat up against the profusion of silk pillows, sipping her tea and listening to the sounds of the bustling campsite outside. The aroma of fresh-baked bread wafted towards her as preparations began for a morning meal.

Gingerly stretching each limb, she acknowledged she was, indeed, as stiff and sore as Reyna had predicted, though this was nothing to the pricking of her pride. Such thoughts had her up and splashing herb-scented water over her face. She'd not allow another man's indifference to lay her low.

"Such sensation is hardly new," she muttered, struggling to dress. Taking up her bonnet, Lydia located her secreted jewels by feel. Now where was her pistol? She wasn't about to go through Valkin's cupboards and drawers. What if she came upon an intimate correspondence? Lydia smoothed her hair as best she could. She must look as though she'd been dragged through a hedgerow. Wondering if she may buy or borrow a hairbrush, Lydia considered the worth of her Parisienne gown. Would any Romany girl offer for it? Their dress was not nearly so immodest, stays or no.

Opening the door a crack, she peered out. It looked to be just past dawn. The great central fire was being stoked back to life by a few young girls. Groups of men were bringing wood from the forest. An older woman was already stirring her kettle, nodding as she dressed a distaff. Other men stood silently on the perimeter of the campsite, making sure everyone within was safe. They faced inwards and outwards alternately. The sight of those careful, cautious men guarding their families imbued her with a sense of calm and peace she'd not felt before. It nearly made up for being an undesirable wanton.

Shaking her head, she took a breath and stepped outside. The crisp winter air bit into her shoulders, and Lydia inhaled sharply. A series of short, hard exhalations sent her hurrying around the back of Valkin's tent. She'd put a stop to any disturbance if she could. She preferred the man remain asleep, keeping his penetrating gazes—and his prickings of her pride—to himself.

"Hush, p-please. L-lord Brishen n-needs his rest—oh." She stopped at the sight of the man himself, naked to the waist, swinging his wood axe in a heavy rhythm that rang across the campsite.

"I b-beg y-your p-pardon," she mumbled, quite certain her cheeks outflamed the dawning day. She'd best look away before Valkin noticed, then saw she'd no need.

For Valkin to see her blush, he'd have to look up, and he didn't. In fact, he seemed thoroughly disinclined to address her at all. He paused briefly in his work, black gaze flicking to a scrap of silk flung over an obliging bush. It took her a moment to recognise this as his shirt. She thought his cheeks darkened as his axe came down once more, splitting wood with a vehemence that seemed unnecessary.

"G-good m-morning," she managed, shivering in the chill air.

"You are learning to sleep like a Romany already," he said shortly.

"How does a Romany sleep?"

"Deeply. And we rise early." Valkin wedged his axe in an obliging hunk of wood and reached for his linen. "I beg your pardon." He inclined his head and kept his gaze on the ground.

Lydia did her best to look away as he adjusted his dress. "Oughtn't y-you to b-be at r-rest? Y-you m-mentioned y-you h-have a p-patrol."

"I do," Valkin agreed. "However both your *covo* stove and my *tan* require wood, Miss Dale. I shall stack it for you before I rest."

"I-I can do that." Lydia took up a smallish wedge of wood, hurrying back to chock the *covo* door open. Returning to heft a split log, she gritted her teeth, compelling stiffened muscles to labour regardless of the pain. Straightening her spine, Lydia forced herself not to wince. *I can do this.* She wasn't as strong as Valkin but she was not useless. *I must do this.*

She managed to get one piece of wood indoors, only to find Valkin taking up space in the doorway as he brought in a greater armload of fuel. Refusing to give in, Lydia stepped aside and around him before making another determined trip to the woodpile and back.

"There is no need," Valkin muttered.

"There is need," Lydia replied firmly, as much for herself as for any curious Romany who happened to pass the open doorway. "It's time I become used to helping myself." Time she remembered that relying on other people was both foolish and disappointing. It was safer all round to keep her distance from these good people. This included Valkin Brishen. Most definitely, it included him.

She dumped the last piece of wood in place, arranging the pile as neatly as possible before brushing down her hands and heading back outside to find Valkin stacking the rest beside his *tan*.

"All done inside," she replied with feigned lightness.

Valkin nodded at her before rinsing a cloth in an enamel bowl and wiping his face and hands. He hung his axe in place by his *tan*. Wet silk clung to his well-formed torso, outlining all his firm strength just as well as if he were shirtless.

"Do you not have someone to bring your wood for you?"

"I do not have servants," he answered.

"But you are Lord Brishen."

Valkin smiled patiently, relaxing against the back wall of his *covo*. "Romany houses do not work the same way as the noble families of England. I've explained this many times to my *gadjo* friends. A Romany does not serve any one man, including me. House Brishen is the oldest Romany house in the country, so we are one of the largest, the most established, and the wealthiest. I speak of wealth in the Romany tradition," he added. "Not in terms of monies or landholdings. Much of Brishen's wealth lies in our horses. Racing, breeding, training our stock. Our knowledge of special skills and craft add to our house's reputation as well."

"Skills such as healing?"

Valkin nodded. "Our coloured silks are highly prized among the modistes of London and Lancaster as well. This connection with the English helps maintain our position as the preeminent house among our Romany."

"But your men act as you direct," Lydia pointed out. "I saw them. And Reyna."

Valkin lifted one shoulder in a casual shrug. "My men and my family do as I say because I am their *sher-engro*, their Head Man. They trust me to lead them in what is right and good for Brishen." He paused. "Believe me, when they disagree, they let me know it. I am not always right," he admitted with a smile.

"As for the rest of the Romany, the head of House Brishen carries the title of *krallis* or king as a tradition only. The other Romany defer to me out of respect for Brishen's long history. They aid me because I ask them to, and some undertake an oath to do so. They may parlay their way out of their given oath if there is need. I will grant it if the trade is fair. There are many benefits to being allied to House Brishen, however. Most of the smaller houses recognise this."

"Thank you," she said at last. "I understand it all much better now. I am learning a lot here." She tipped her head to the side. "I shall have much to tell my brother." She thought his face darkened at her words, though why Valkin should frown at the idea of her departure she could not fathom. He didn't desire her. She ought not to desire him.

He was a kind man doing his duty to his guest. *He is not looking at me in any particular way that warms the skin unnaturally in November.* There, much better. *Safer, anyway.* She faced his silkshirted chest. *Oh Lord.* "It's not safe for me to remain here," she reminded them both.

"Do you truly wish to leave my *ker*?" He stared at her with an intensity that tugged at her soul.

"Valkin, I—"

"*Sarishan*, Miss Dale."

Lydia couldn't hide her relief as Reyna's voice carried across from the front of the caravan.

"I am come to inquire after your health." Reyna kissed her brother's cheek before handing him a steaming cup. "*Bebee* Cin awaits you in the *kris-tan*, Valkin."

Valkin's tight smile preceded his bow to them both. "Good morning, Miss Dale. Reyna." He seemed as relieved to leave as Lydia was to let him go, or possibly more so. She summoned a smile for his sister.

"How did you sleep?" Reyna wanted to know.

"I slept very w-well, I th-thank you." Lydia shrugged off a heaviness that settled over her as Valkin walked away. "I'm feeling a great d-deal better." *Apart from repeated prickings to my pride.*

Reyna nodded encouragingly as she drew closer, extending her arm. "This is excellent news. Perhaps you wish to break your fast outdoors with myself and my sister? Your muscles may be stiff and your movement painful, but this is indeed the best remedy."

Lydia smiled, slipping her arm into Reyna's. Narilla awaited them by the camp fireside, where she'd secured three seats and a meal of bread, honey, and berries.

Reyna wrinkled her nose, cocking a brow at her sister as they sat. She asked a question in Romany. Turning to Lydia, she said, "I beg your pardon, Miss Dale. I have asked Narilla why she selected seating so near the dye-tent." She rubbed her nose and sniffed.

"I must beg your pardon for the pungent aroma," Narilla said seriously.

Lydia pursed her lips, breathing in a scent that was at once herbal and slightly fetid. "In t-truth, I didn't notice until you m-mentioned it." She looked around, spying the nearest temporary dwelling. Many Romany women were entering and leaving, exchanging bundles of herbs and what appeared to be roots and fungi. "Is that the entrance, over th-there?"

"It is one of the busiest places in our camp," Reyna replied, nodding. "Attendance is for women only."

"You hold the s-secrets to Brishen's silk tints dear," Lydia said. "This is very wise. Many Englishwomen of my acquaintance prize your wares highly."

"You take an interest in silks, Miss Dale?"

"I devise m-my own design patterns. I have not the skill for dyeing as you do, but I enjoy linencraft. It is second only to drawing in my work at—h-home." It would not do to mention Clifton Hall.

A handsome young man passed close by their group, bowing to them all. His gaze lingered on Reyna. "*Sarishan*, Reyna."

Reyna looked round, smiled, and nodded her head. The faint blush to her cheeks made Lydia smile. "You have a suitor?"

Narilla chuckled, stopping at her sister's sharp glance.

"Sacki is my betrothed. We will wed before Lady Day." Reyna rose, gathering the remains of their meal. "I must return to my work. If you wish to see over our *ker*, Narilla is at your disposal this morning."

Lydia smiled, rising to a stiff curtsey. "I sh-should like n-nothing better."

Reyna nodded and curtsied, hurrying to catch up with her betrothed.

Narilla attempted a curtsey in her turn, overbalancing slightly. "I must attend to my work in the dye tent this morning, Miss Dale. As craftwork interests you, perhaps you wish to see this?"

"I am m-most curious." Lydia followed Narilla, grateful that the dye tent was restricted to women only. A respite from Valkin's astute observations and her own humiliation was welcome. She mentally shook herself. *I'm not a moon-eyed little girl anymore.* She didn't avoid Valkin on purpose. Of course not, but there must be some task with which she may assist this morning. This seemed important once she entered the tent behind Narilla, who was accosted with requests for assistance as soon as they stepped past the tent flap. With an apologetic expression, she squeezed Lydia's hand and joined the group clamouring for her advice. Lydia hovered nervously by the entrance as several of the women eyed her speculatively.

"*Sarishan*, Miss Dale." An elderly woman nodded at her as wrinkled palms curved round a thickish bough. The woman worked a piece of cloth suspended in liquid, her movements as continuous as her focus on Lydia.

"*Sarishan*," Lydia replied quietly.

Some of the other women glanced at her and nodded before returning to their work. Their tasks varied from stripping leaves, stirring up the ceramic vats, adding various liquids from vials kept in baskets, and checking the bolts of cloth hanging in their great tree to dry.

This tree served as the central pole for the tent, and the rest of the structure radiated out from this point. Gazing at the suspended fabric, Lydia had an idea—a *useful* idea. She glanced over at Narilla, deep in conversation with another older woman. Trembling with trepidation, she approached them. With Narilla's assistance, she gained her supplies, giving up the veil of her riding habit. Her first trade, and she was delighted with her result.

Settling on a dry patch of ground opposite the tent flap, with the great oak tree for her backrest, Lydia studied the mosses soaking against the silks. While the plants were in truth a dull brown, Narilla assured her the dye would take on a pretty leaf-green shade once the preparation process was complete. Lydia bent to her work, wrinkling her nose.

"Miss Dale?" The old woman walked towards her, unsmiling.

Lydia tensed, wondering at her offense. "I-I b-beg your p-pardon?" she whispered, laying aside her fine work. The woman merely brandished a cushion, miming the placement of it beneath her rear.

"*Besh*," she offered. "*Besh, besh.*"

Besh must mean "seat."

"Oh." Lydia smiled and stood to curtsey. "I th-thank you, ma'am." She positioned the cushion as indicated, before sitting back down and taking up the petticoats she was stitching for Reyna. She'd designed the leaf-pattern herself, years ago. There were several skirts to decorate, and Lydia hummed with the rhythm of her stitching, relaxing fully for the first time in weeks.

Reyna bustled in eventually, bearing bushels of fungi fresh from the forest. "*There* you are, Miss Dale. I might have guessed Narilla would only show you the parts of *ker* she deems important. How have you found your movement today?"

Lydia shrugged in a way that stretched the muscles of her neck and upper back. "I am not taxed unduly, I assure you, Reyna. I have a wedding petticoat for you nearly complete." Rising, she shook out the skirts, staring quizzically from Reyna to her handiwork. "H-how d-do you l-like it?"

Reyna's mouth formed a round "oh" shape as she gazed at the intricate design. "It is lovely," she exclaimed. "Truly, Miss Dale, I could not accomplish half so much as this in twice the allotted time."

Lydia knew a rush of relief. "Oh, I am so glad you are pleased. I wish to gift it to you before I leave, in gratitude for your kindness."

Reyna waved her words away. "I tell you before, it is my honour to help." Her expression changed to one of deep solemnity. "You are leaving us?"

"Yes," Lydia replied, aware of the colour rising to her cheeks.

"This is a great pity." Reyna looked at her earnestly. "I wished you to join in our Christmas. Must you really go?"

The girl's eyes were honest and warm and truly concerned. Her intense expression matched Valkin's, and Lydia sighed inwardly. The kindness here, the sense of togetherness... it called to her as it obviously had her brother Wil. Lydia wished to be part of it, too.

Valkin himself had asked her to stay, *without knowing the truth.* Could she not remain for Christmas?

By Christmas I may be wed. She shuddered, remembering the danger her presence posed for Wil and his young family. For Valkin, Reyna, and all of Brishen.

"I b-beg your pardon, Reyna." Her words sounded more clipped than she'd intended. "It is n-not possible for m-me to remain here."

"Why is this?" Reyna was clearly puzzled.

Lydia shivered, though the dye tent was warm enough. "I c-cannot," she replied. She re-threaded her needle in the pensive silence.

"Then your gift is too much," Reyna said briskly, shaking her head. "The leaf and goldenrod is so pretty. I insist you allow me to trade for it." She fingered the delicately patterned work. "There must be something you want."

Something you want. The sting of tears took Lydia by surprise. The words throbbed like a bruise on her heart. There were so many things she did want, and none of them—not one—seemed possible. Wriggling the tension from her shoulders, Lydia straightened. She could not have what she wanted, so she must accept what she could have, and bringing joy to her new friends was a gift she prized highly.

"I-I am in n-need of a sketchbook, and c-charcoal or c-chalks if this is p-possible. I also wish for a Romany gown," she replied at last. "Or at least the cloth with which to sew one. M-my English costume will not suit your camp."

Reyna nodded. "I believe Sacki's sister has something to suit. We shall go there now." She waited at the tent exit. "You'll not see my brother." Her expression softened but her smile did not return. "He is from *ker* this day."

"Oh?" Perhaps Valkin sought an assignation with a more competent—and less dangerous—*gadje* mistress in another location. One who didn't stumble in speech and was skilled at touching. Lydia blinked away the burn of jealousy in her breast. *He doesn't want you.* She turned her attention to keeping pace with Reyna, who led her between tents and myriad small groups of Romany.

"Valkin is riding our perimeter boundary today. Then he attends the Lord of Bowland at Slaidburn on business," Reyna explained.

"To consult about m-my presence here?" Lydia couldn't help asking.

"It is about horses and his lordship's health. The Lord of Bowland is unwell. I prepare his remedies and Valkin carries them to Slaidburn." Reyna shot Lydia a shrewd glance. "Do not let my brother's manner frighten you, Miss Dale. He is the *krallis* and an important Romany, but I remember when he sat his first horse."

"I suppose he rode like Romany royalty as soon as he took an equine seat?"

"Not at all. The first time Valkin sat a horse, he slid right off the other side." Reyna smiled mischievously. "It would not do to remind him of this, Miss Dale." Her smile widened. "But I remember it well."

Knowing Valkin was from *ker* on business made it easier to smile brightly at Reyna.

"No doubt that is the last time he fell."

"Truly, it was," Reyna responded. "I do not know what the *krallis* said to alarm you, but I hope you will forgive it."

"Lord Brishen has caused me no offense," Lydia replied politely. *All he did was ask my name.*

CHAPTER ELEVEN

Valkin

Slaidburn Castle was no more than a couple of hours' ride from the forest boundary. Bavol covered the distance easily enough, and Valkin left his lordship's keep earlier than expected. He made such good time that he detoured via Dunsop Bridge. While the village had no racing fraternity to speak of, the landlord at The Lancaster Inn ran one of the best-informed betting books in the country, and Valkin was in dire need of ale.

As he dismounted behind the hostelry, a young girl approached him from a side door.

"Lord Brishen?"

Valkin's brow lifted in surprise. "I am."

"My papa is landlord of The Lancaster. He bids you enter through the kitchen."

Valkin frowned. Such requests were not uncommon from the English, but he was expected. "Is Mr Baker not within?"

"He is, sir. There is a gentleman with him at present." The child flicked a look to the right. Valkin followed her gaze. A great carriage and six idled beside the hostelry. The finely dressed coachman lounged and smoked, barking orders at the inn's grooms. Few English landlords wished to mix their Romany acquaintance with those from an English noble house.

"I understand, Miss Baker." He offered the child a coin, but she shook her head. "Will you have this then, child?" A tiny wooden figurine lay on his palm, carved and polished with oil.

Miss Baker giggled, curtsied, and accepted her treasure. "Thank you, Lord Brishen."

"Thank *you*, Miss Baker." Valkin bowed. "How strange that a lord may travel so far from any of the great houses. The state of the roads alone gives most carriage-owners pause."

The girl shrugged, already focused on her toy. "I don't recognise the livery."

Valkin studied the arms blazoned across the carriage doors and his gut tightened.

Basingstoke.

Using the carriage's bulk to screen him from the coachman, he moved closer. *The better to eavesdrop, my lord.*

"Give them a good feed," the coachman was saying. "We've been at this all day, and again tomorrow." He rolled himself another cigarillo. "When his lordship gets his hands on her, it'll not be pretty."

Valkin made his way to the kitchen entrance. Pushing past the servant and several milling patrons, he stole inside the low-roofed tavern, keeping well back when his gaze found Mr Baker bowing and shaking hands with the earl.

"I'll be sure to keep my eyes open, my lord. Any whisper of a young lady's whereabouts and I'll send word."

Valkin studied Baker's blank expression. Basingstoke offered no coin, nor any reason for his pursuit. *Good.* As soon as the earl left, Valkin approached the publican.

"Well met, Lord Brishen," Baker called out. "Your discretion is appreciated. Mary, an ale for our friend here." He shoved out a chair with his foot. Valkin accepted both the seat and the drink with a smile.

"You have news, Mr Baker?"

"I've heard something regarding the new filly that left your favoured starters behind at Epsom," Baker explained.

"Do go on."

"Madam's Queen is causing quite a stir."

"I am aware she won the derby."

"I'm sure you are. Are you also aware she's expected to take the Lancashire Cup, with her sister foal as second?" Mr Baker sat back, clearly enjoying the surprise on Valkin's face. "There, you see? They've kept this close."

"They have, indeed." Valkin leaned forward and took a long swallow of his very average beer. "How is it you come by this information?"

Baker tapped the side of his nose. "I cannot reveal such," he replied. "I *can* state my source as reliable. Have you ever known me to pass along mere rumour?" At the shake of Valkin's head, he grinned in proud triumph. "This is because I don't indulge in mere gossip. I always verify my information before I sell it."

Valkin laid several coins on the table, along with a vial of syrup. "Your diligence is appreciated, Mr Baker. The syrup is for your wife's ailment, as usual."

The payment was pocketed, and Baker looked steadily at Valkin. "Will that be all? I'm pleased to stand you another ale."

"Another will be very welcome." He leaned forward again, lowering his voice. "I'm prepared to double your fee, Mr Baker, if you're able to tell me more about the owner of this filly and the sister starter. I am particularly interested in this pair's current form, and who backs them both for the cup." He fell silent as the girl delivered their beers. Taking up his tankard, he sat back, studying the *gadjo*.

Baker gazed at him with what Valkin sensed was a practised calm. He'd not missed the flicker of interest when he'd mentioned additional compensation.

"When do you pass this way again?" Baker asked.

"At least weekly while we have dealings at Slaidburn. If not I, then one of my brothers."

Baker nodded and put out his hand. "Stop in at the end of a fortnight and I may have something for you. You'll not part with a penny if I learn nothing useful. Is it a trade?"

Valkin shook his hand and smiled. "The trade is fair."

Baker accompanied Valkin to the hostelry, where he ran his gaze over Bavol.

"A fine animal. I can find you a buyer, once he's broken."

"I thank you. That won't be necessary, Mr Baker." Valkin bowed. "How is Mrs Baker?"

"Thanks to your remedies, she is much recovered. Please send my regards to the women of Brishen." Baker's face grew serious as he took Valkin by the hand once more. Clasping his shoulder, he leaned in to whisper. "I bid you take care. The law seeks a missing girl."

Valkin matched Baker's undertone. "Who is the girl?"

The innkeeper twitched one shoulder. "They'd have released her name if she were one of the greats, unless there's scandal. The seeker is a lord. An *earl*, and when the quality seek scapegoats..." He left his sentence unfinished and stood back, addressing Valkin in his usual tones. "It's always a pleasure to see you in my establishment, Lord Brishen."

Valkin's smile was brief as he mounted Bavol. The ride to the northern boundary was not long enough to gather further news. By sunset he inhaled the scent of woodsmoke and greeted his perimeter guard. Valkin dismounted and re-set the *patrin*. With all the Romany on the move at the moment, these signs between Romany houses were important. Hearing a familiar step behind him, he turned to greet Chal. His brother's eyes were stern.

"What is it, my brother, my *prala*?"

"My men say a *muscro* was in Halford, questioning the villagers about a missing girl." Chal stared steadily at him. "Is it your *gadje*?"

"She is not my *gadje*." Valkin shrugged. "It is fortunate the law seeks her on the other side of the forest. She may yet escape them." He caught Chal's glare before turning back to adjust his *patrin*. Now the sign said the law was about.

"You know how hard our winter is this year," his brother persisted.

Valkin decided not to discuss this. No one knew better than he how many months Brishen spent planning for this season. Securing a more or less permanent campsite with fresh water, ensuring the location could provide enough sustenance through the cold, frozen weeks—all this was achieved by virtue of the *krallis*'s excellent relations with the noble houses of England.

Sheltering Basingstoke's runaway betrothed could well impact this. Valkin wished Wil was at *ker*. Wil Brishen, Consort to the Princess Syeira, had once been the son of a duke. He had more insight into the *gadjos* than any other Romany. If Wil and Syeira didn't return soon, Valkin resolved to petition the Lord of Bowland for assistance. In the meanwhile, he'd ensure Miss Dale was as safe as possible.

"Take care of hiding the *gadje*'s mare by sunrise," Valkin ordered. "Keep her among your own stock once she is dyed."

Chal stared at him in alarm. "I will need more hands than just my own," he pointed out. "The dyeing we can complete by morning, but it requires many days for it to take. The men—"

"Take whomever you need. Your men may have their pick of any animal, except Bavol," Valkin offered. "This is my trade—if their work is well done, and they mention this to no one."

"It shall be as you wish, *sher-engro*." Chal turned away, soon swallowed up by the darkness between tent rows.

***

The next morning Valkin headed for the *gry* pens, eager to review his preparations for the Lancashire Cup. He worked with Bavol and another colt he'd recently acquired, studying their starts and taking detailed notes for both horses. Turning his mind to new starters seemed a better way to spend his morning than attempting to outwit Basingstoke. Besides, Romany horses made far more sense than the *gadjos*.

"See here, *sher-engro*?" Dela showed him the latest timed sprints for his stock. Valkin ran his eyes over the numbers and grinned.

"Excellent. See if Chal knows of any English filly that's making time as good as this."

"Consider it done, *sher-engro*." His cousin grinned back at him. "Your *gadje* was here earlier with Narilla. She wishes to ride, but Reyna will not hear of it today."

"She is not my *gadje*." Valkin frowned. "She attempted to mount her mare today?"

"She said something about Morecambe Bay and Paris." Dela shook his head. "She cannot be well in the head, to travel all that way—she is mad."

"Perhaps she wishes to travel before the roads worsen," Valkin countered.

"Yes, but alone? She is too pretty to travel safely on her own."

Valkin's fist clenched of its own accord. "Attractiveness, or otherwise, has nothing to do with travelling safely." He paused, attempting nonchalance. "You think she is pretty?"

"Too pretty to travel without being noticed." Dela shrugged. "For a *gadje*, I mean," he added hurriedly, possibly because the look Valkin gave him altered from merely interested to steely menace. "She is walking about *ker* with Narilla, if you wish to know of her."

"Why should I wish to know of her?" Valkin failed at disinterest.

Dela's second shrug irritated him more than the *gadje*'s determination to leave against Reyna's orders. *This is nothing but stubbornness.* He would not seek her out. He must certainly not see her today. *There is no need.* Except to tell her— firmly and unequivocally—that journeying before her recovery is complete gains her nothing. Valkin stomped off, ignoring Dela's deferential bow.

Valkin hurried to the *kris*, hoping today's hearings might be brief. Rubbing his face, he felt the familiar weariness that plagued him towards year's end. This coming winter weighed more heavily than usual, though he couldn't fathom a reason. Perhaps it had something to do with a girl travelling unescorted all the way to Paris. Stubborn *and* foolish. Miss Dale needed to see sense.

Once the *kris* was complete, he returned to his *tan* via the cooking fire, gathering a meal to eat in peace. Given he was on night patrol, he'd best rest while he was able. Not much chance of that while an abundance of feminine laughter surrounded his *tan*. Moving towards his new quarters, Valkin spied Narilla holding a hinged stepladder steady for Miss Dale, who balanced precariously atop it, leaning over the canvas of his *tan*. Valkin stilled, irritation tensing his shoulders. *Must she overtake all my homes?*

Miss Dale appeared to be stitching with something that looked like a long crochet hook, for all Valkin knew of such matters. The girl's stammer had nearly disappeared as she giggled, struggling to maintain her balance. Narilla manoeuvred the ladder into three different positions, assisting the *gadje* to mount it each time. It was only when both of them finally stepped away that he saw the repairs to his *tan* had been completed—with embroidery. *What the devil?*

"Are you certain your brother won't mind the lilac thread?" The girl climbed the ladder more nimbly than he thought her capable of, given how far she'd ridden without rest.

"This thread will close up the holes in his *tan* as effectively as any other." Narilla laughed, tightening her grip on the ladder. "Take care, Miss Dale. My sister's instruction that you 'take a little exercise' does not include falling into the *krallis*'s *tan*."

"Indeed it does not." Valkin stepped forward.

Startled, Miss Dale grabbed a tent pole in an effort to steady herself, her green eyes widening. Narilla gasped, reaching up an arm that was not nearly long enough.

"I am all right." Their guest grasped the pole tightly, wincing as she clearly wrenched her recovering muscles.

Valkin stared at them both. "What is going on here, my sister, my *pen*?"

Narilla's eyes flew to the *gadje*'s, but she whispered, "I beg your pardon, *sher-engro*."

"N-narilla m-mentioned your tent required repairs." Despite her stammer, Miss Dale's gaze didn't falter. "It is m-my doing, Valkin. Entirely my own."

Valkin sighed, staring up at her a moment before offering his hand. The *gadje* shook her head, braced herself on a tent pole, and negotiated her way to the ground without assistance, moving more stiffly than before. Had she re-wrenched a muscle? *Nothing but stubbornness.*

"The proper way to repair a *tan* is to dismantle it first, spreading the canvas over the ground," he informed her, turning to glare at Narilla. "A process of which my sister is well aware."

"Of course," Miss Dale replied evenly. "However, I could not m-manage this alone and I knew of n-no one whom I m-may ask. It was kind of Narilla to assist me, given her other duties. She t-traded for my m-materials." The *gadje* held her mending needle aloft for him to see.

Valkin blinked at the waxed yarn. "It's purple."

"Lilac, actually."

He closed his eyes slowly, drawing in a deep breath. "*Why* are the repairs to my *tan* in purple?"

"Lil—" Narilla shut her mouth at the look he levelled at her, choosing this moment to dash away. *Clever girl.*

Miss Dale stared up at him. "Is something the m-matter?"

Valkin cleared his throat, his gaze flicking over his *tan*. The rips in his canvas were sealed now, with… *Why the deuce did she have to sew* flowers?

"Embroidery?" He did his best to keep his voice light.

"I do not know any plain stitching," Miss Dale explained. "If you d-do not like it, I sh-shall ask Reyna h-how I m-may remedy this." Her stammer worsened, and Valkin realised he was glaring. Well, any Romany man might look askance at his home being sealed by needlepoint. He swallowed his irritation, releasing a heavy breath.

"There is no need to discuss this with any of my sisters," he replied, his tone clipped. *Or anyone at* ker, *ever.* "Perhaps no one will notice," he muttered. Purple flowers and vines all over his *tan*? His brothers would never keep quiet about this, and as for his sisters… He turned to his *gadje*, noting the twisting of her hands over each other as she twined the remains of the thread through slender fingers. His gaze took in her soft hands that had gone to such trouble on his account. Valkin forced himself to focus on her pretty eyes. Smiling seemed easier when he looked into her eyes.

"I thank you, Miss Dale. It is kind of you to think of me." He bowed stiffly.

"The gratitude is mine." She smiled shyly as he rose, taking her hand to kiss it.

Hmm. Valkin watched her eyes as he lifted her wrist to his lips. She flinched only once, but did not withdraw it.

Her tentative smile remained as she glanced at his *tan*. "Waxed yarn is not easy to procure. Lilac thread was all Narilla could trade for me," she explained. "I wished to do something useful." She glanced at his bowl. "May I keep you company while you eat?"

It was too tempting to watch her widening smile, to seat himself beside her and share a meal with this alluring woman. Would she tell him the truth if he broke bread with her? Would she tell him her name? Ask for his protection in truth this time? Offer herself again? *No.* Valkin was a better man than that, wasn't he? Until he knew for sure he'd not find it restful to remain with her. He glanced from the girl, to his food, to his now-pretty tent canvas, remembering Culvato.

Out of the corner of his eye, he spotted Chore slinking by his woodpile. There'd been another dispute over pups at *kris* that morning. Valkin eyed the zealous dog with envy. *Ratfelo fakement.* The *gadje* smiled guilelessly at Brishen's oversexed canine, her head tipping slightly to one side as she studied him. She was too stubborn by half, not to mention… Valkin exhaled his frustration. *Dela is right. She is far too pretty.*

"Is there any other service I may offer your Romany?" she asked.

"Indeed there is, Miss Dale." Valkin thrust his bowl of soup at her, together with a crude hunk of bread. He no longer had the stomach for food. "Eat this before it is cold. I must go."

The girl's smile disappeared but she accepted his offering. "I shall ask Reyna when I next see h-her," she said firmly, squinting as though he stood miles away. Had he hurt her feelings? This was the last thing in the world he wished to do. *Why?* Why should this concern him? Valkin didn't know, but she was his guest, had come to him for help, and he'd offended her. *Again.* He cursed inwardly, turning away with a bow.

He scowled at the other Romany tents he passed on his way to the river. Most of them were plain brown or grey. Some were sewn from sugar or flour sacks. As was the Romany custom, many were brightened with pinned shawls and tiny bells tinkling gently in the chill breezes. Not one—not a single one—sported embroidered purple flowers with exquisitely crafted little leaves. Apparently he must now accustom himself to a *tan* no self-respecting Romany man would wish on his fiercest enemy, much less his *sher-engro*.

Swearing under his breath in several languages, he whistled for Chore. The lurcher bounded over, tongue lolling in seeming sympathy.

"Come on, you precious rascal. Let's hunt some rabbit." Grabbing up a stick to pair with his rifle, Valkin strode into the woods with an oath.

CHAPTER TWELVE

Valkin

Having exhausted his hunt by the afternoon, Valkin turned in his hares and headed for the river. Stripping off his silk shirt, he sat by the riverbank, running his fingers through the water. Then he splashed icy water over his face. Once he'd shaken the drops out of his eyes, he ran wet fingers through his hair. His men stared. It wasn't usual to tip freezing water over oneself in November. The saner man would fill his pail, take it back to the fire for heating, return to *tan*, and *then* bathe. But a sane man wouldn't be afraid of entering his own home for fear of encountering a lovely woman he could not have. Valkin glared at his men, forcing himself not to shiver.

When he arrived at his *tan,* Miss Dale appeared in his *covo* doorway, moving more easily than he'd seen her do to date. His body tightened. He wanted to kiss her again. *Absolutely not.* He cleared his throat. "How are you this afternoon, Miss Dale?"

"Much improved." She broke into a smile.

"Have you any pain?"

"Only a little," she replied. "Would it be an imposition for you to take me to my mare?"

Valkin hesitated. The *gadje* may be unaware of the rumours she inspired among the Romany, but the *krallis* was not. Still, a walk in full view of his people was better than being closeted alone with her in his *covo*, wasn't it? *Was it?*

"An imposition?" Valkin looked into lovely, pensive green eyes. *This is ridiculous. This is* my ker. "Not at all. You will find she is of very different appearance." He glanced towards the lowering sun.

"Come, I will show you our *gry* pens. This is what we call the horse enclosure. I have work to do there now. Then we may eat, if you wish." He held out his arm, releasing an inheld breath when she accepted it, sliding her sleeve against his. Valkin blinked in surprise, smiling like a fool. *Ridiculous.*

"I thank you." Miss Dale looked up, sighing. "It is wonderful to be out of doors so often."

"Do you prefer the outdoors?

"I do." She shivered a little. "Though it's now full autumn."

Valkin looked round at the coloured leaves. "It's nearer winter, Miss Dale. The forest is always changing."

He forced himself to walk slowly across the camp, pretending not to notice the curious glances of his cousins. Many of his Romany were already stirring delicious-smelling kettles beside the fire, awaiting the changing of the perimeter guard.

By the time they arrived at the *gry* pens, dozens of children were collected nearby. Miss Dale stood by the fence, bemused at the collection of horses before her. Her gaze travelled from one animal to the next.

"Do you see her, Miss Dale?"

"I see an English horse," she said slowly. "But she is not a grey."

Valkin laughed. "She has been dyed."

"*Dyed?*" Her brows rose so high they disappeared beneath her hairline. "Goodness."

"It is to keep you safe," he added.

She nodded. "Yes, I u-understand. I thank you. Whom—to whom a-am I indebted for p-performing such a feat?"

"Chal and his *gry-engros*. This is the word for our horsemen." Valkin waved the little knot of men over. "They've worked through two nights in shifts to ensure the dye takes properly."

"However did you do it?" His curious *gadje* wanted all the details.

"It is vital the animal be kept on her feet," Chal said as he joined them. "She cannot roll or rub up against anything at all while the colour settles. This is why my men must work in shifts."

"Thank you," she said. "If I may be allowed to offer you—"

"No need." Chal smiled at her. "It is our honour to assist any friend of our *krallis*, Miss Dale."

Valkin let this pass. Dyeing a horse was a careful business. He repeated his commitment to the men in Romany that they were each entitled to one of his own horses and could make their choice as soon as may be. Most of Chal's men grinned; they had no intention of declining the *krallis*'s offer. Valkin's horses were among the most valuable racing stock in the country. Dela jerked his head towards the animal he had in mind, and Valkin turned his attention to his cousin.

"May I attempt to ride her today?" Miss Dale addressed Chal.

"She will not be ready to ride for several more days at least."

"Then I must try mounting another." She made her way to the smaller pen and Valkin turned back to his men.

"*Sher-engro*." Dela gripped his arm.

Valkin looked up, alarm flaring in his chest like a bird. "Miss Dale," he called. "*Not that horse.*"

The children called out warnings, and the *gry-engros* shouted at the danger. The girl either didn't hear them or didn't listen, approaching his stallion at a brisk pace. Bavol whinnied and stamped, thrusting his head over the top of his makeshift fence, already shaking his head and rolling his eyes at the Englishwoman. The animal lifted his forelegs, pawing the air. Valkin tasted fear.

"Fetch Reyna," he ordered, taking up Dela's whip and striding forwards.

"Wait," his cousin suggested. "What is she doing now?"

Miss Dale stopped a foot or so from the fence line, proffering her hand to the nervous animal. Didn't she know this was a sure way to get bit? She lifted something to the horse's nose, like a gift for a recalcitrant child. Bavol stopped rearing, pawing the ground with gradually decreasing vehemence. The half-wild animal leaned forward, sniffing curiously. His ears remained flattened to his head, but the beast snuffled large nostrils over her hand.

Pulling himself free of Dela's grip, Valkin tightened his hold on the whip as he joined Bavol and the *gadje*. The smell of apples reached him before he grew close enough to hear her speak.

"You're a fine fellow, aren't you? Is it pleasant to have your own pen, or do you miss your mares?" She waited patiently while enormous horse lips teased over her skin, gathering every skerrick of pippin. The stallion harrumphed and licked her wrist.

"You've more charm than the Lord Brishen," Miss Dale added, running her eye over the beast's lines. "You're part English too, aren't you? Oh, sir, we have much to speak of."

The determined cheek of her. Valkin's gaze homed in on the way her hands stroked his semi-wild stallion, making herself familiar to the animal. Bavol's ears relaxed, and he nudged the *gadje* with his cheek, rubbing like a cat. Inexplicable envy surged through Valkin as he watched her run both palms over his stallion's fine-boned head. *First my home, now my horse.* He ought to be angry.

His gaze ought to focus furiously on her pretty face with those damnably mysterious eyes…her hands that stitched flowers into the roof of his *tan*, now moving over flesh and sinew as his eager mount breathed hot and gustily over Miss Dale's skin, licking scraps of sweet fruit. Valkin blinked as sun dazzled his eyes. *Winter sun does not dazzle.* He cleared his throat, forcing himself not to wish for her palms on his skin, her breath against his neck as she caressed him. Never before had the *krallis* wished to change places with his horse.

"Bavol does not respond well to strangers, Miss Dale." He reached an arm over her head to pat the horse's flank. "He bites Englishmen."

Miss Dale laughed, continuing to address the horse as she fondled his ears. "I am not an Englishman." She tugged Bavol's forelock playfully. "You wouldn't bite me, would you, sir? Handsome boy like you." She glanced at Valkin. "I-I am unharmed, as you see."

"This time," Valkin countered. "But this is not a good idea, *pireni*."

"I should d-do better with a saddle." She continued fondling his mount, glancing at Valkin. "I *can* do this."

He affected a shrug, stepping back. "We have no English saddles except your own."

"Surely one may be found in a camp this size? I know your Romany do not require such tack, but—"

"Do you?" Valkin asked, very quietly and wished he'd not interrupted because her eyes grew wary. He sensed she'd stumbled into revelations she'd not intended. This girl was careful with her words, her manners, herself. So very careful. Yet she'd sought him out. Claimed his protection. *Why?*

She was already looking away, focusing on Bavol. "He is a fine horse," she commented.

"He is half-wild, unless I ride him." Valkin watched in amazement as his untamed stallion bumped his forehead against the *gadje*'s face as though intending a kiss. *Half his luck.* Valkin traced the outline of her lips with his gaze, remembering the heat and power of her mouth pressing against his.

Miss Dale pushed the horsey face aside with one palm, shaking her head and laughing. "You determined rogue," she murmured at the animal teasing between them. She glanced up, her gaze catching Valkin's. Colliding, more accurately, as he'd not hooded his expression or avoided her face. His hands stopped moving over horseflesh, his gaze focusing on Miss Dale's mouth. He forced his attention from her lips, finding heat in her eyes, desire in her gaze. Her lips again, parting, eyes widening….

Valkin swallowed loudly in a silence reserved for both of them, here in this small part of *ker*, on the edge of winter's wood that seemed too warm for the season. He held his breath. She stepped closer: one step, two steps. Three steps…

"*Sher-engro.*" Dela jogged up, panting hard.

"What?" Valkin barely kept the irritation from his voice. Seeing Dela's expression, he blinked, apologising in Romany.

"*Bebee* Cin summons you to *kris*." His cousin bowed for the *gadje*, flashing a charming smile as he retrieved his whip. "Timed trials," he explained, bowing again. "Thank you, *sher-engro*." Dela made good his escape.

Valkin turned back to Miss Dale, relief mixing with regret. Had she—had they—been about to—*what?* What did he want of this woman? That wasn't hard to decipher, but was making love to her all of it? Was it everything? Was it, indeed, enough? "Irrelevant."

"What is irrelevant?" Her voice sounded steadier than his.

God. Why had he said that aloud? "Where did you become expert with horses?" Valkin spoke quickly to cover his embarrassment. He smiled at her because he wanted to know, but also because it was difficult not to smile at this lovely woman breathing in the crisp air at the end of the year, on the edge of a fine wood, fondling his favourite stallion as though she were born to raise such stock. This was nearly as interesting as the flush moving into the girl's cheeks. Something like guilt skittered across her expression.

"M-my brother t-taught me m-most of it."

Her stammer was back. Valkin hoped this wasn't his doing because he had more questions. "Did he also teach you that my Romany do not use tack?"

"*Valkin.*" Chal's shout made them both jump.

Unmistakeable relief flashed through Miss Dale's eyes.

"On my way," Valkin called back, before bowing to the *gadje*. "This conversation isn't over, Miss Dale." He studied her face again before turning away.

CHAPTER THIRTEEN

Lydia

Lydia lay back in the hip-bath Reyna had found, sighing as the warm water soothed her muscles. Her friends had shown her how to scent the bath with distillations of herbs and grasses. She tightened and released her limbs in turn, feeling an ache of worked sinew. A just reward for a day spend out of doors, engaged in purposeful activity. *Since when is making eyes at the Romany king purposeful?*

Lydia shook her head, creating ripples that slapped deliciously against her skin. "I did no such thing," she said aloud to no one at all.

A loud knock made her jump.

"A moment." She stepped hurriedly from the tub and grabbed her chemise. If this was Valkin come to ask more questions, she'd best armour herself accordingly. She'd not seen him since the *gry* pens, though his sisters were excellent company. It wasn't as though Lydia wished him beside her or missed his handsome face at all. *Liar.*

"C-come in," she called out, then smiled with relief as Reyna and Narilla slipped inside, carrying fabrics and accessories aplenty.

"*Koshti Sarla,*" Reyna smiled back at her. "Good evening. I am glad your healing bath is complete. You will join us at the sunset fire—yes? I have here a brush and some of my hair oil. Narilla will demonstrate this for you. I have also brought you a *rivipen*. It is one of my own older gowns I think will look well." She waved a hand towards the silken fabrics and trinkets Narilla held. "It is all right for you?"

"I thank you b-both. Yes, your gown is lovely." Lydia fretted her hands again. Her Romany correspondence had not discussed etiquettes. What if she humiliated her hosts? Busy with the kettle, Reyna didn't seem to notice her tension.

"W-will the Lord Brishen be in attendance?" Lydia asked, annoyed at herself for caring.

Reyna glanced at her in surprise. "Of course. It is Valkin's duty to appear at the sunset fire before attending to his patrol." She smiled, seeming to understand Lydia's nervousness. "Do not worry, Miss Dale. You will look very pretty, I think." She handed the gown to her sister. "I shall show you how we dress without maids."

Lydia shivered a moment as the other girl's finger touched the tender places on her shoulders and back.

"Your bruises are nearly healed."

"Y-yes," Lydia replied. "I-I feel much better th-than I did."

"I am glad to hear it." Reyna removed the lid of her oil jar and brandished a stiffly bristled brush. Narilla poured them all tea and pulled out a chair.

"Come, sit, my friend. Let us smooth your hair at last." Reyna wrapped a shawl over Lydia's chilly skin and showed her how to coat the brush and smooth her tangled curls. "Do you have it?" She offered the brush to Lydia.

Lydia nodded, taking up the tool and settling to her task while Narilla arranged smaller accessories in a collection on the table. Reyna sipped her tea before speaking a few words in Romany to her sister.

"I-is your day t-terribly busy, Reyna?" Lydia asked. "M-may I a-assist in any way?"

"No one works during the sunset fire, Miss Dale, except our perimeter guards. It is our time of coming together."

Her sister spoke quickly in Romany, and Reyna nodded, turning to Lydia. "There is work for you tomorrow in the dye tent, if you are willing?"

"Your sewcraft is much admired at *ker* and we would be most grateful," Narilla added.

Lydia blushed with delight. "I am happy to be of use," she replied, and she meant it. This purposeful feeling, this joy, was worth the discomfort of Valkin's burning gaze and his frightening questions. Lydia wondered if feeling valued was anything like feeling loved. A slow smile worked its way over her face, despite the eye-watering tugging on her tangled mane. Narilla spoke something to Reyna and her sister smiled uncertainly.

"Narilla says she has never seen anyone smile while tearing her scalp at the same time," Reyna explained.

Lydia chuckled. "The pain is worthwhile if it brings me to friends like the two of you." She found herself engulfed by a brief embrace from them both. Startled, she blinked back tears. She couldn't explain how rarely she felt such warmth. Not without revealing who she was and placing her new friends in terrible danger. With such people as these at risk, Lydia was more determined than ever to keep her connections to herself.

Reyna finished her tea. "I wish I may stay here, Miss Dale, but I have much to do. Narilla will remain to help you with the Romany gown." Gathering her shawl about her, she left.

Lydia turned to find Narilla reaching for the brush. She tugged at the back of Lydia's head before tutting her satisfaction.

"It is good, Miss Dale. Now, we dress." Narilla loosed the cloth ties and held the garment open.

Lydia reached for her corset, but Narilla uttered a cry, shaking her head violently. "Reyna said on no account was I to assist you into that—garment."

"But this is dinner—" Lydia began.

"She also said I am not to be swayed by any arguments. She says it will cut your skin again." Narilla looked solemnly at the French stays. "In any case, I do not know how to secure it and it will not fit under Reyna's gown. Romany dresses are not created so." She made it clear this was the last word on the matter.

Offering Lydia a fresh chemise instead, Narilla showed her how to tie it on herself. Next, she demonstrated how to step into the silken dress, smoothing the long skirts. Lydia buttoned her bodice and looked down: the cloth was exquisite. Romany-dyed silk, in a rich burgundy that complemented her hair. A fuller effect was achieved with a layering of several golden underskirts. Reyna was taller than Lydia, her figure sparer, which made the neckline of the bodice appear lower, but it was far more modest, and far more comfortable, than the French gowns the duke insisted she wear.

"The colour suits you very well, Miss Dale." Narilla beamed at her, speaking slowly as she enunciated her English words, eyes shining with pride. "The dark red is striking against your skin."

Lydia smiled. "I thank you. Please, address m-me as M-martha."

"I address you as the *krallis* does." Narilla smiled an apology, handing Lydia a small looking glass. The burgundy fabric added a touch of colour to her still-pale cheeks. Narilla fussed round her, attempting to draw Lydia's curling chestnut mane into a proper Romany-style braid.

It took some doing, and Lydia resisted the urge to pull her head away from the determined girl. When she examined her reflection in the glass, she had to admit the effort had been worthwhile. Narilla used a square of golden silk to tie her hair back at the crown, decorating her braid with strands of tiny golden bells. As a finishing touch, she tied a silken sash in gold around Lydia's slim waist. She stood back a few steps, eyeing her work critically, then made a circular movement with her hand. Lydia obeyed, turning slowly.

"Well, m-my friend?" she asked, brows arching. "Will I d-do?"

"Reyna is right." Narilla smiled at her. "You are very pretty."

Lydia dipped her curtsey. "I thank you. It is your d-doing, not m-my own. Shall we wait for Reyna?"

A quiet knock sounded. Narilla bid their visitor enter, and Lydia wished she hadn't.

Her mouth dried at the sight of Valkin attired in full Romany regal dress. His boots gleamed in the light from the stove, his breeches outlining muscular thighs. Lydia examined the firm lines of the Romany king's chest from beneath her lashes, stopping her gaze just above his indigo sash. His finely embroidered vest and jacket couldn't conceal his pale gold linen, matching Lydia's sash and headscarf. She didn't think this was a coincidence. The woven silk clung to the hard curves of his arms and torso. She swallowed, lowering her gaze as desire sped through her.

"I am come to escort you to the sunset fire." He offered a bow.

Narilla smiled, coming at once to take her brother's arm. Valkin didn't seem to notice. He kept his gaze on the snug fit of Lydia's Romany gown, and she couldn't help her blush as his look lingered over the burgundy bodice. Was the fit immodest? Her heart hammered as she nerved herself to beg pardon.

Before she could speak, Narilla tugged impatiently on Valkin's arm. "All of Brishen awaits you, *sher-engro*." Leaning closer, she whispered something in Romany that could only mean "I'm hungry." Valkin offered his other arm but Lydia didn't move, and it was only then that he seemed to notice the stiffness of her stance, her uncertain hands clasping and unclasping before her.

"What is it, Miss Dale?"

"I b-beg your pardon. I would like to b-be sure of what to d-do."

Valkin blinked. "I beg your pardon?"

"I d-do not wish to offend your family. I wish a quick lesson in what is required of m-me." When he didn't respond immediately, Lydia lifted her eyes to his face. Narilla watched them both in open-mouthed consternation.

"I—" Valkin cleared his throat. "You must forgive *me* now, Miss Dale. I am surprised. Very much surprised." He bowed again. "I've not heard of an Englishwoman's concern for Romany sensibilities before now."

"Then I am sorry for it." She held his gaze, squaring her shoulders. "Perhaps the Englishwomen you've known do not entirely understand what it is to be treated as though one is an irrelevance." She shook off the last of her fears. "I do."

Without dropping his sister's arm, Valkin reached out to take Lydia's hand in his own. Her pulse quickened when he stroked her fingers, pressing his lips gently to her knuckles, then the inside of her wrist. He drew her smoothly to his side, slipping her arm through his own.

"You shall be quite safe," he assured her softly. "It is our dinner hour. We will eat and drink, and perhaps sing a little. It is the Romany way."

Lydia smiled tightly at Narilla as Valkin led them to the sunset fire. There were a few whispers as they joined the rest of his family, all seated on a variety of wooden furniture at one edge of the large central blaze. Lydia knew a moment's unease as so many pairs of eyes turned to watch her, but Reyna took her quickly by the hands, kissing her cheek and welcoming her to the Brishen gathering.

Lydia recognised Sacki, Reyna's betrothed, and smiled at the fond way he looked at her friend. When he stood up to offer Lydia his seat closest to the fire, she accepted with a nervous laugh and some relief. Valkin bowed before taking his ceremonial wooden seat at the head of the circle. His entire house awaited his first bite. Lydia let out a breath as he turned away to eat, the warmth in her cheeks cooling too gradually. Reyna and Narilla were her dining companions, and she turned her attention to their excellent fare.

The whole evening passed exactly as Valkin had said. There was eating, laughter, plenty of what she assumed was Romany wine, and a great deal of singing and conversation. It was very pleasant listening to the quiet voices all around her. Lydia did not understand much of what was said, but the caring and the closeness of the family was unmistakeably warm, comforting, and friendly. She relaxed more than she had in months, managing a smile at the curious questions some of the Romany asked about her *gadje* life.

"Is it true your men hunt in the forests merely for sport, Miss Dale?" Reyna asked.

Lydia nodded. "Hunting game is often done for sport. To collect trophies. I believe your men hunt as well?"

"This is true," Sacki spoke from his seat close beside Reyna. "We hunt like the *gadjos*, but it is for our food only. This is not a game to the Romany."

"And it is not merely the men who hunt," Reyna explained with pride. "All Romany women learn to hunt from a young age. I was taught to catch and kill a hare before I was eight years old."

Lydia stared at the pretty, genteel girl in surprise. "Do you truly hunt your own food, Reyna?"

Her betrothed smiled. "She has no need to hunt, Miss Dale. Reyna's brothers and I take care of hunting for House Brishen, but all Romany must know how to survive. What about your *gadje*? Do Englishwomen hunt?"

"The ladies *I* know?" Lydia pictured the ton ladies attempting to catch a hare on foot. She could not contain her laughter. "They hunt only for husbands, and this also is a matter of survival." She sobered as she spoke, but her Romany friends laughed, certain she wasn't serious.

CHAPTER FOURTEEN

Valkin

From the *krallis*'s seat at the top of the family circle, Valkin watched Miss Dale laughing with the young women of Brishen, shocked as envy spiked through him. How he wished she'd let her guard down with him as easily as she did with his sisters. Then he might finally gain the answers he sought. The desire to know this woman was nearly as great as his desire to take her beneath him and... Valkin forced his thoughts away from certain madness. It *was* madness, his desire for this *gadje*. The danger she brought to his people was reason enough to resist. *She cannot help who she is. But who is she?* Valkin exhaled carefully to avoid asking a question that might lead to Miss Dale leaving his *ker*. She couldn't go. Not yet. Not until he knew what this sensation meant.

He caught another glimpse of the *gadje*'s smile as she enjoyed his family. Her habitual wariness seemed absent this evening though she was quiet, listening to the Romany talk around her. He took in the curve of her shoulder, her elegant neck, her cheek, her mouth, her lips. *Her lips*...sighing, he commanded himself to look away. This must be the right thing to do. *Then why am I still staring?*

Staring at this woman who managed Romany horses better than any Englishman he'd met. The determined tilt to her chin as she lugged lumps of wood inside his *covo* intrigued him. She understood something of Brishen and relaxed more here than in an English house. The sense that he knew her was frustratingly close. An image of embroidered purple flowers spun through his mind.

"*Sher-engro?*" Cato passed Valkin his mandolin, an expectant smile on his lips.

Valkin shook his head, passing the instrument back, but it was no use. His Romany wanted him to sing, and he shrugged, settling the instrument on his knee.

"A song," his cousins called in Romany. "A song for the *krallis*'s *gadje*."

Miss Dale turned towards him on hearing the word, clapping her hands with the others, listening intently to hear his first note. The trinkets adorning her hair glittered by firelight and the golden, light-filled sensation took him by surprise. Valkin gazed across at her before looking down at his fingers. An old melody came to him, a memory of Papa serenading Mama as he watched from the *covo* window. A memory of love.

He looked up, strumming his instrument.

Pawnie birks,
My men-engni shall be;
Yackors my dudes,
Like ruppeney shine:
Atch meery chi.
Mā jal away:
Perhaps I may not dick tute, Kek komi.

Most of the Romany stopped speaking to listen to his song. Some of the men wandered over to play their instruments in time with his own. Valkin had several mandolins and at least two fiddles echoing his melody as he repeated the words, slower this time and more softly, watching his *gadje* across the space between them.

Her cheeks turned rose-pink as the Romany around her smiled, clapping slowly in time with his song. *Her song*, for he'd not been inspired so by other women. Certainly he'd not been so affected by the sight of one sitting here, laughing and nodding with his sisters in the firelight. The shadows on her face heightened the sense of connection, for her eyes stood out to him, light and bright. Her braid hung below her *diklo*, swaying as she clapped, shifting in her seat to the rhythm he created. *For her.*

Soon his Romany were singing in time with him, and a number of couples began to dance. Reyna and Sacki moved into the circle of firelight, swaying together. A young boy stood before Narilla, arm at the ready. Valkin frowned. Narilla was as attractive as she was resourceful, but she was young yet. Another two years, perhaps three. *What about yourself?* This voice no longer sounded like his sisters.

Valkin's attention caught his *gadje* leaving her seat, making her way deliberately towards the outside of their circle. Covering her eyes, she looked down. Something was wrong. Surely she wouldn't be so foolhardy as to depart his *ker* under cover of night? He rose in a hurry, catching her up just beyond the firelight.

"*Pireni?*"

She stopped, staring at the ground. Moonlit tears glowed over her cheeks. "I-I am all right," she sniffed. "I am only—your house, your f-family. You're all so warm and kind. I wish I—" Wiping her cheeks, she drew in a large breath as if needing strength from the air. "Music affects me d-d-deeply. I enjoyed your song."

"Thank you, but it is your song, *pireni*. Tonight, you are part of us." He bowed, seeking a way to put her at ease. "May I have this dance, Miss Dale?"

She started. "I—I do not know the dance."

Leaning in close, he whispered directly into her ear, feeling her hesitant shiver. "You do not need to know the dance. Trust me." He drew back, awaiting her choice.

The other Romany were singing her song now, chanting in time to the gentle clapping and soft music. She gazed up at him, her hand slipping into his. Valkin pulled her to his side, swaying closer until he found her, once again, within the protective circle of his arms, his mouth inches from hers.

"Do you know the way to dance a Romany dance, *pireni*? Close your eyes. Listen to the music. Feel, do not think."

She slipped as they turned, catching her foot on the hem of her dress. Valkin chose that moment to pull her tightly against him, leaning down to whisper in her ear again. She regained her balance, but he didn't draw back, his breathing shallowing, faltering, his heart hammering wildly. The press of her gently swelling curves...Heaven, light, and dangerously hot all at once.

"Close your eyes," he whispered.

She obeyed, relaxing to the rhythm of his music. It was the first time he'd seen her so at ease. He might never forget her face in this moment, all beauty, and calm, and wonder... Valkin exhaled, tightening his self-control. *She is a guest of Brishen and this is my duty.* Liar.

"Better?" He smiled, unsure whether he addressed her or himself.

"Mmmm," she murmured, swaying against him, hips shifting in time with his soft music.

"Allow me to translate," he chanted softly. "I'd choose as pillows for my head, those snow-white breasts of thine. I'd use as lamps to light my bed, those eyes of silver shine. Oh, lovely maid, disdain me not, nor leave me in my pain: Perhaps 'twill never be my lot, to see thy face again."

"So beautiful," she whispered, looking up at him.

"Beautiful," he echoed, staring back.

She seemed caught up in the magic of the night air with its slight chill. The crackling, popping sounds from the fire, flickering light playing over soft outlines of lovers all around them, her warm breath caressing his neck as though she'd forgotten all the silly English rules about maintaining a "safe and proper distance."

Whether it was the music, the food, or the quiet, melodic chanting, his *pireni* seemed more at peace than he'd yet seen her. She looked radiant, happy, and he smiled to himself, wondering how long it had been since she'd had a moment like this, or if she ever had.

"Thank you, Valkin." She spoke so softly he wasn't sure he'd heard correctly.

He took in her thoughtful expression, the wistful cast to her eyes, the calm in her soft body, so temptingly close to his own. As though she was ready to trust him completely, yield to his touch. Ready to—

He shook his head ever so slightly, releasing a carefully controlled breath. They were dancing in full view of his house. In any case, she was betrothed. *To an arse of an Englishman.* No matter, the earl was powerful enough. Valkin would not give in to the potent desire smouldering within as he breathed in her scent: elderflowers and lavender. He closed his eyes and bit his lip, hard. He hoped he'd drawn blood. He wanted to make love to her so badly, it hurt.

When the musicians finally paused to refresh themselves and the singers did the same, the dancers returned to their places. With great reluctance, Valkin pulled away from Miss Dale, tucking her arm into his as he escorted her back to her seat.

"You sing so beautifully." She smiled at him.

"Thank you. I, too, have heard you sing, when we met in the woods, *pireni.* You do not know how skilled you are."

She glowed like a dawn sky, hiding her eyes to escape his praise. He wondered when anyone had last paid her a compliment of any kind. Or told her she wasn't alone. He wanted to dance with her again, to feel her against him. Rather than return to his ceremonial chair, he seated himself with his family, chatting quietly to Chal and some of the others about his horses. He kept his hand over his *gadje*'s, gently stroking her knuckles with his thumb every so often.

Miss Dale started at first, then seemed to notice Sacki doing the same, and Narilla and her young dance partner were seated together, fingers entwined. Perhaps there was hope after all. Reyna passed Miss Dale her heavy woollen shawl and a full wine cup.

"Thank you." She drank deeply from her cup.

Valkin couldn't resist leaning down to whisper. "How do you like it?"

"It's quite the loveliest wine I've ever tasted."

He grinned. "Take care, Miss Dale. Romany spirits are served unmixed."

She eyed him as though he'd issued a challenge. Licking her lips, she refilled her cup, then drank it down by half, and smiled. When he heard her giddy giggle, he stole her cup and stood, holding out his arm once more. "Come, I shall escort you home before I take my turn on guard." He smiled, not at all sorry to share a few moments' privacy with Miss Dale.

"Oh. You ought not to disturb your evening on my account. I'm sure I know the camp well enough to find the way back." She rose quickly, tottering visibly on stiffened limbs and making a determined effort to hide her shivering.

When she raised that chin of hers, he drew her to his side, striding heavily for his *covo* without another word.

"You are the most stubborn woman I have ever met, *pireni*." His tone was curt, the heat in his blood making him sound harsher than he'd intended.

"My brother says stubbornness is merely determination," she shot back, a fierce look in her eyes.

"I doubt he'd approve of his sister risking her health." He noted her sheepish expression as they entered his *covo*. "In any case, he is not here." *As any honourable brother should be.* He kept this to himself, turning his attention to the stove. In a few moments a warm blaze chased away the cold.

"I prefer to manage on my own. I fear I put your house to too much trouble." She looked down at her hands. "I am anxious to spare you all I can. I must continue m-my journey as soon as m-may be."

She seemed oblivious to Valkin's frustrated sigh.

"Dependence is no weakness, *pireni*. Everyone in a Romany camp depends on each other. It is why no Romany feels alone." He handed her a bag of herbs. "Here is your tea. I shall leave while you change. You will please call out if there is difficulty with your dress. I will not— That is, I can find one of my sisters at need."

CHAPTER FIFTEEN

Lydia

How wonderful to wear a costume entirely under her own management. Lydia sighed at the pleasure of disrobing with ease, donning a night shift and thick shawl with equal comfort. No maids needed and no one dictating her appearance...*liberation*. She put the tea on to steep and added more wood to the stove. By the time Valkin knocked on the door again, two cups sat steaming on the table and she was already unwinding the small bells from her hair.

"Come in."

He'd brought another woollen blanket. "Thank you." She nodded at the tea. "Will you join me?"

Valkin hesitated a moment, then shrugged, removing his jacket and hanging it on the hook inside the door. When he turned back to her, he'd dispensed with his formal sash and vest, baring his neck.

"I will taste your tea and return to my *tan* until I take my place on guard. Now that you're recovered, I cannot remain here long."

Lydia straightened. "I d-do not believe you will do anything dishonourable."

Valkin smiled, that alluring mix of heated charm in his steady stare, the angle of his jaw. His eyes glinted in the glow from the stove.

"Perhaps you are learning to trust me, after all." His quiet suggestion mingled with the passion radiating from him like a mist, warming Lydia to her core.

I do trust you. She bit down on her tongue to keep her response. If she opened her mouth, she'd tell him the truth.

"You look lovely by firelight," he said softly when it seemed her silence stole too much.

"Thank you. The gown is on loan from your sister."

"A gown can only do so much," Valkin murmured. "The rest is you, *pireni*."

Lydia all but gasped. How could he say that out loud, as though passing comment on the weather? Didn't he *know?* Couldn't he *realise?* It occurred to her a moment later that the Lord Brishen, legendary seducer of legions of Englishwomen, most likely knew *and* realised what he was doing. This wasn't idle flattery. Valkin Brishen wasn't an idle man. He seemed intent on making a point, and he was going about it with the nerve and charm for which he was renowned.

Well, Lydia had nerve too, though she wondered why Valkin had grown so still and silent. Or why he stared at her in that fascinating way when he did not want her. Something glinted in his eyes, hungry and potent. Lydia didn't trust the heat humming through her as she gazed at his muscled neck. *This is foolish.*

Blinking, she realised Valkin was asking a question. "How do you like our sunset fire, Miss Dale?"

"I cannot recall when I've enjoyed an evening more," she replied earnestly.

"It's a far cry from Davenport Manor."

Lydia took refuge in a shaky laugh. Why was her throat suddenly so dry? "I prefer your fireside to theirs."

"I am gratified to hear it." He looked it too, his face relaxed as he drew out a partially carved work from a drawer, moving closer to the lit stove.

Lydia watched him at work for a while before extending her hand. "May I see it?"

He placed the wood on her palm. "It will be a gift for Reyna and Sacki. A House Brishen seal for the *covo* Sacki's family will gift them.

"Reyna will have her own *covo*?"

"It is the bride price we agreed upon. Narilla will have the *tan* to herself soon enough." He grinned. "She says her sister snores."

Lydia snorted. "Do not spread rumours, sir. Especially as regards your sister."

Valkin shrugged. "It is no rumour if it's truth. Such a noise can hardly be hidden in a *tan*. But you are right, and you are kind to speak up for Reyna."

"She is my friend." Lydia gathered up the empty cups and placed them neatly to one side.

Valkin stood to bow. "Speaking of forestalling rumours, I must leave you now."

Covering the bedclothes with one of the blankets, Lydia turned. "What sort of rumours?"

Valkin shrugged again. "This is Brishen, not the ton, but there are no secrets in a Romany camp."

Busying herself with bedclothes seemed as good a way as any to avoid discussing secrets. Lydia yawned inelegantly.

"Good night, *pireni*." He took up his carving and turned to leave.

"Sweet dreams." Her drowsy whisper followed him.

***

Valkin

Valkin stood on alert until his shift was over, swearing viciously all the way back to his *tan*. Why did his *gadje* have to mention dreams? He was having enough trouble trying not to think about her satin-soft cheeks, her wide green eyes, her delicate frame supporting generous breasts he longed to explore with his hands, his lips, his tongue. To slide his palms over her soft, sensitive mounds over and over again until she quivered with desire; to take one tight, hard nipple in his mouth until her breath jerked from her lips and she begged him to take her. To plunge deeply inside her until his love filled every part of her. Until she had no cause to doubt him. Or herself.

That's what he wanted for her. What he wanted for them both. Valkin realised with some surprise that he wanted this more than he wanted to make love to her, which he wanted far more than he'd thought it possible he could want any woman. He stopped himself there, lest he not sleep at all this night. He wasn't responsible for this *gadje*, need not make himself so, and yet, *and yet*… He pounded his pillow and swore. This woman knew so little of the dangers into which she thrust herself that she sought safety in being taken for his mistress. Safety in being with him. Valkin could barely comprehend it.

***

A loud cry jerked Valkin awake. He sat up, tumbling out of his bedroll to blink groggily at the contents of his *tan*. Now he remembered—too absorbed in the sort of heated imaginings he ought not to be thinking of, he'd drifted into a dream about Miss Dale. The sort of dream he hadn't had in years; that ache persisted. He grimaced, swearing at himself as he reached for his nearest herb bowl, splashing cool water onto his face. Another cry from his *covo*. From his *gadje*. Valkin came fully alert. He ran to the wooden door, entering without knocking.

Miss Dale twisted in his bed, her hand at her throat as she struggled to call out, sobbing. She'd all but kicked his bedclothes to the floor, her limbs flailing in violent panic. Valkin ran a hand distractedly through his hair, staring at her anguish. That odd ache invaded his chest again as he sat carefully on the bed, placing one hand on her forehead, using the other to clasp her clammy palm in his.

"*Pireni*, be calm. You are safe now. Be calm."

Her eyelids fluttered open, and he gazed down at her in silence, watching her awareness refocus. Her wary, guarded expression returned fully. She sat up, clutching at his hand. Her eyes looked huge in the dying light from his stove.

Valkin stood immediately, backing against the *covo* wall. "You've had a bad dream, *pireni*. I will make more tea. It will help you to sleep." He settled his kettle over the stove.

"I d-do not wish to sleep." The strain was evident in her voice.

He edged nearer the door. "I shall find one of my sisters to assist you further." He turned once, smiling with an effort before leaving her alone. Valkin was glad of his task—to move and think and dispel this restlessness from his body. Making his way towards a larger *tan*, he wondered what the hour might be. Wil's watch remained in his jacket, which he'd left behind in his haste. He shivered as he approached the *tan* before him. Chore sat up, issuing a sharp bark.

"*Dosta*." Valkin patted Brishen's most vigilant guardian. The animal dropped his enormous head back on his paws.

"Valkin?" Narilla's shadowed head poked out of the flap.

"I beg your pardon, my sister, my *pen*. I seek Reyna."

Narilla opened the tent flap, and Valkin ducked his head to enter, finding his youngest sister standing alone in her nightgown and shawl as she offered him a parcel and fresh water.

"From Reyna, *sher-engro*." Narilla bobbed a quick curtsey. Valkin tucked the parcel under his arm and sipped his drink, looking up when Reyna herself opened the tent flap to slip inside.

"How is your *gadje*, my *prala*, my brother?"

"She is troubled by bad dreams and needs company," he replied. *And she is not my* gadje.

"The *levinor* may affect her dreams if she's unused to strong spirits." Reyna issued a long-suffering sigh. "I am required in the birthing *tan* most of this night." The weariness in her voice matched Valkin's. "It assists Cato's wife to know I am with her, but their child is not so imminent as she believes."

"Will the birth be all right?" Valkin wished Syeira were here to assist them both. "Our cousin is most anxious."

Reyna nodded and relief washed through him. "It is their first, as you know." Her tone softened. "Another babe for Brishen."

Valkin smiled, then indicated the package. "What's this?"

Reyna lifted the canvas again as they made their way outside. "Nightwear and another gown I think Miss Dale will like. She cannot wear her French dresses here. Our brothers will not stand it."

"Agreed." Valkin laughed. It would damn near cause a riot. Besides, he stood a better chance of protecting the girl if she dressed as a Romany. "You are too good, my sister, my *pen*."

"You wish to help her." It wasn't a question. "Chal says she is not your mistress." Reyna blushed as she said the word.

Valkin shook his head, staring into the night. "I truly do not know who she is."

His sister made a noise in her throat, taking charge of the parcel in Valkin's hands. "You have known many women, my *prala*, my brother, yet you know nothing of love." She shook her head at him and knocked on the *covo* door. "Miss Dale?"

A soft voice bid her enter and Reyna did so, leaving Valkin to inhale the last vestiges of the year. Sighing, he lowered himself to the *covo* steps, watching the moon rise and glow, brightening the stars. Valkin breathed in the freedom and wonder of the Romany night flowing around him.

He must have dozed off because it seemed a mere moment later that Cato hauled him to his feet.

"Where is Reyna, *sher-engro*?" The grip on Valkin's shoulder made him wince. He stepped back, clasping his cousin's arm.

"The babe?"

Cato nodded. "*Bebee* Cin is in the birthing tent, but—"

Valkin forestalled him. "Return to your *tan*, cousin. Reyna will attend your wife and child."

Cato didn't move. "Now?"

Valkin glared. "Of course." He stepped up to his *covo* door, rapping on the wood so hard the walls shook, then stared at Cato. "Go. All will be well."

Reyna opened the door with her shawl already in place. "I heard him, my *prala*, my brother. Shall I fetch Narilla?"

Valkin recalled Narilla's sleep-filled gaze. "Ah, Reyna," he began, but Reyna's thoughts seemed aligned with his own.

"I know." She sighed. "Our youngest needs her rest this night. I must leave Miss Dale's sleep remedies undone. Will you sit with her until I return?" His sister hesitated. "You will not...?"

"I will not." Valkin heard the steel in his voice. He didn't need to see Reyna's face in the darkness to know she'd cocked a brow.

"When I return, you must sit with Cato." Gathering her shawl, his sister stepped down to his side and leaned up to kiss his cheek. "Cato's family will be well, *sher-engro*. I shall see you at his *tan* in the morning. Miss Dale will also be well." She hurried off into the night.

CHAPTER SIXTEEN

Valkin

Valkin stared at the door to his *covo*. He didn't know what he waited for, but he'd never felt so unsure of himself. It was time to see what kind of man he was. Taking a breath, he clasped his hands, breathing deeply in and out, once, twice, three times. *Why* he felt the need to do this he chose not to consider, but the practise steadied him. *As always.*

He swallowed, knocked, and waited. *Perhaps she will refuse me.*

"Please come in." A sleepy whisper.

He did, and gulped to hide his shocked gasp as he glimpsed Miss Dale's bared back. Reyna had clearly been administering a salve of some kind. Lavender and chamomile, to judge by the scent.

"I must beg your pardon again, Miss Dale," he began.

"Reyna said you would not be here for v-very long," the *gadje* replied, adjusting her chemise as she faced him.

"This is correct." He turned his attention to the bottles and jars Reyna had arranged on his bedside shelf. They were, one and all, remedies to be applied assiduously to the body. Worked into the muscles and skin gently. Soothingly. Slowly. It was all Valkin could do not to groan out loud. *God.* His body throbbed, breath quickening, pulse beating loudly beneath his skin as he fought harder for control. Reyna's words came back to him: *You will not—?*

Was he being tortured for some appalling indiscretion? His mouth twitched at the irony.

"V-Valkin?" The hesitant whisper made him turn. She'd finished her draught. "Th-thank you. The sleep remedy was working."

Valkin took a deep breath, then another.

"Do you require it completed?" he asked, sounding like a butler he'd met once.

"Reyna th-thinks so. A-are you able to—?"

"I am able to complete this," Valkin murmured. He held his breath. *She will refuse me.*

"I-if y-you'd b-be s-so k-kind." She seemed to shrink into the bedclothes.

Kindness was not the dominant sensation when Valkin sat opposite her on the bed, arranging the pillows to support those breasts he'd dreamed about.

"Turn over," he said.

She obeyed, rolling onto her stomach without a sound.

He swallowed. "I'll need to rearrange your chemise."

Her shoulders tensed.

Perhaps she will refuse me now?

His *gadje* raised her upper body onto her elbows, staring from warm, softened eyes. "*Apasavello*," she said.

His heart halted in his breast. "You speak Romany?"

"A few words only," she admitted, her green gaze fastening on his face. "It's an old memory from long ago. I was taught it means 'I trust you.' Is this right?"

Valkin couldn't breathe. No one had looked at him like this before or spoken such words to him in this way. Was this girl aware of the effect it had? Of the effect *she* had? He reached out a hand to cup her face. Her silken skin sent his control shuddering.

"It means more than that, *pireni*." Valkin licked his lips, feeling as though he'd had too much wine or slipped into some sort of dream. "It means 'I trust you, I believe in you.' It is an avowal of absolute and entire faith in another." He lifted her chin so she was looking directly into his eyes. Her cheeks flushed as she seemed to read the heated intent in his face; the desire he made no attempt to disguise. He wanted her to see it. To understand she was worth more than she'd been taught to believe.

He spoke again, very husky, very low. "It is—what lovers say."

"And I am only a pretend lover, aren't I?" That tentative smile again, so hesitant, her voice a hush.

Are you? I am not. Something like a quiet peace settled within him as he shook the bottle of oil and pointed to the bedclothes. *Sweet torment awaits.* "You will please lie still," he said quietly, his heartbeat just as low, just as quiet.

He drew her chemise lightly over her skin, until the early evening breeze raised tiny goosebumps across her bare back. He traced the welts marring her flesh, gentling his touch to feather-soft strokes.

"Mmmm," she sighed, murmured, whispered.

She breathed slowly beneath his touch, stretching, exhaling, relaxing completely. He rubbed her neck, her shoulders, her upper back, maintaining his steady, slow rhythm. If he didn't, if he listened to the rigid, painfully insistent part of himself and did what he wanted to do: run his tongue up her spine until he reached her neck, marked her there with his teeth before turning her, taking her lips, her throat, her softly rounded breasts… His sense of peace broke apart, like glass shards in his skin. This sensation defied logic. Valkin blinked, heart smarting at the pain.

He tapped a drop of oil onto his fingers before caressing the skin around one scabbed wound left by the baleen of her stays. He worked carefully around the freshly purpled bruise across her shoulder, noting other marks too, older ones so faint as to be barely visible. He tensed his shoulders in sudden anger. That her father, or Basingstoke, had hurt her—that anyone could hurt her—filled him with cold fury. Pain seemed a constant in her life.

Not in this moment, though. Right now, she'd closed her eyes and yielded herself up completely, as though accepting a precious gift: surrendering to the sensation of being cared for, healed, held, by his hands. The lavender oil was followed by elderflower cream to mend her skin, and then the oil again.

Apasavello. She'd given him her trust, had declared her absolute faith in him. Valkin couldn't help thinking she'd made a terrible mistake in doing so. He wasn't exactly known for chivalrous restraint. How could she trust him so completely? Especially now he was done with her back.

A soft sigh escaped his *gadje* as he slid one hand over her lower back, kneading the beginning of the gentle curves of her bottom. His breath hitched, and he bit his lip, clearing his throat quietly.

"Do—do you think you can manage—er—everything else?" He rested his hand on her bare skin, and it seemed her passionate response to his touch was to fall calmly asleep. Valkin suppressed a rueful laugh as he took his leave. If his siblings saw how easily he put a woman to sleep, it might do wonders for his reputation. Really, it served him right. He had no business imagining what might have happened otherwise.

***

Standing on his *covo* steps before dawn, Valkin inclined his head to the new shift of perimeter guards. Their whispers were enough to tell him that the rumour of his *gadje* mistress was spreading. He shrugged inwardly. There was, after all, nothing he could do about it. Besides, he'd left his guest alone, hadn't he? It wasn't as if he was inside his *covo* right now, taking his pleasure. He sighed; it wasn't as though he didn't want to. In truth, he wanted nothing more, but who can trust a woman who won't tell you her true name?

He reentered the *covo* as silently as possible, keeping his distance from the tempting shape curled against his pillows. He must not glance at her curls spread across his coverlet, or her softly rounded limbs twining through his bedding. He kept his focus firmly on his mental list of items required for his *tan*: linen, straight razor, healing herbs. He knelt to the cupboard with the herbs, wincing as he squeaked it open. Movement from the bed sent his heart skittering.

"V-valkin? Is it you?"

He took up a wine jar with his herbs and stood, exhaling deeply. "I beg your pardon, *pireni*. I am foraging for supplies." He indicated the herb bag. "I did not intend to disturb you."

"You did not," her soft voice assured him. "Sleep does not favour me. Please, will you stay for a little?" She sat up, the coverlet falling away.

Valkin suppressed a groan. That odd sensation of golden light crept through him again. He clenched his jaw, already aware that remaining here was a bad idea. Her eyes shimmered as she stifled a sound. The sound one makes to hold in tears. He sighed.

"Can you truly not sleep?" He wondered who'd last held her while she cried. Or if anyone ever had.

"I am afraid to s-sleep."

"Then I will stay." Valkin tore open the parcel on the table, extracting a nightrail. "If you will dress." He held out the gown.

His *gadje* took it silently as though the gift were chastisement. He turned his back, supressing a regretful sigh.

"All right," she said.

He turned to find her studying the stitching on one sleeve.

"Such fine work," she murmured, glancing up at him.

"Why can you not sleep, *pireni*?"

"My d-dreams bother me."

"Do you dream of the time in the garden?"

"N-no." She shuddered, holding his gaze.

Valkin took a breath, venturing into newly softened silence. "Is there another time?"

She nodded so slowly it seemed a statue shifted. "M-my f-father b-believes in b-beatings. W-when I t-tried to r-refuse the e-earl h-he—uh—hurt me. He a-always s-says h-he will n-not b-be d-disob-beyed—" She sat up, wiping her brimming eyes. "H-he and t-the earl, t-they are t-the s-same k-kind of m-man. He would have me wed—" Anger flashed across her face, followed closely by a sadness so deep it seemed she drowned in it.

"Don't think about it, *pireni*," he replied. "It does not do to dwell on it." Valkin dropped her shawl across her shoulders. "Stay warm. Try this, perhaps." He broke the seal on his jar and tipped the contents into two cups.

"Is that your Romany wine?"

"We call it *levinor*." He lifted his cup and stared into its depths. "I like to drink it." *Especially when there's a beautiful* gadje *in my bed, driving me to distraction.* "Have you seen what else Reyna sent for you?"

"For me?" Clutching her shawl, she seated herself at his table. Smiling, she ran her fingers over the Romany trinkets.

Valkin watched her smile, studying her face. Her colour returned to normal, and she seemed calmer.

"Your sister is very kind." She examined an emerald-green dress with matching *diklo*. "Especially as she has so much to do for everyone else. Will her wedding be a large celebration?"

"Only because Reyna and Sacki wish it so," he replied. "There is no requirement for it, but with so many Romany gathered for winter, we have much to celebrate."

Valkin talked for some time about the Romany Christmas and his sister's upcoming wedding, explaining the symbolism of the black stallion, the handfasting, and the blood bond. Miss Dale listened, a strange, wistful look in her eyes.

"Do you know Sacki well?"

"Of course," Valkin replied in surprise. "I've known him many years. Reyna and he grew up together. He is an honourable man and skilled with horses. He will provide well for Reyna and her family."

"Is she marrying for love?" Her smile flickered, sad and soft.

"All Romany marry for love." Valkin smiled. "Even if the marriage is arranged by the family, no Romany will let anyone he loves marry without it." He spoke gently, aware of how this might sound to her. She drained her cup before responding.

"It is very different to my family, then," she said in a low voice. "Love is irrelevant."

Valkin blinked, staring directly into her eyes. "You believe this is true yourself, *pireni*?" He needed her answer far too much. He didn't like it, but this was no longer only about him. *So, this is love.*

Miss Dale stared back at him, unmoving. Slowly, as if it took every ounce of her strength, she shook her head, then seemed to straighten, entirely unaware of her sadness.

"It doesn't matter," she said finally, her eyes cold and empty of expression.

"Love does not matter to you?" He was as shaken by the tonelessness of her voice as he was at her words.

His beautiful *gadje* shook her head again as she returned to the safety of the bedclothes. "You misunderstand me." She seemed to struggle with herself, twisting her lips closed over words he wanted so much to hear.

Valkin opened his lips but was arrested by the startling tears on her lashes, the rapid heave of her chest. "*Pireni,*" he whispered but could say no more. He reached for her hand, but she turned her face away, staring at his carved wooden wall.

"I think I will sleep now. Good night, Valkin."

Her quiet voice pierced him. As he bowed and took his leave, Valkin pondered what she'd left unsaid. *It doesn't matter*. The truth dawned as he began his night patrol. He drew in a breath as he realised how unimportant she seemed in her own life. The worst of it was that she believed this to be true. In her own world, her wishes and desires were placed an absolute last.

It was bad enough her father treated her like this, but that he'd taught her so well she did it to herself... His heart ached for her. Would she accept his love as anything more than what he wanted to take from her? An odd sort of pain settled in Valkin's chest, because for the first time in his life he wanted something more from a woman than to merely take his pleasure and satisfy hers. He wanted to give himself, his heart, his soul. He wanted to give this woman his love, and he wanted her love in return.

CHAPTER SEVENTEEN

Valkin

As the next day dawned, Valkin found himself balancing two bowls of food as he approached his *covo*. Miss Dale answered, looking a little pale but proffering a cup as she stood aside to allow him in.

"Good morning." Valkin swapped the bowl for the cup and bowed. "I thought to assist your breakfast this morning. Romany wine makes for a sluggish morning after."

"I believe you are right." Miss Dale's wan smile agreed with him as well. "I've attempted your coffee to compensate." She indicated his cup. "Would you give me your opinion?"

"Certainly. I thank you." He took a good swallow and made a face. "Oh."

Her pretty eyes grew wide. "I believe I've followed Reyna's directions precisely."

Valkin grinned. "The brew is fine. It is the sweetness."

She smiled back and held out her hand for his cup. "If you prefer it without honey, I shall prepare it anew." She yawned inelegantly. "I beg your pardon. I fear I am terribly slow today."

"How is your head?"

"The pain is less than I've heard from my brother," she admitted.

"I am glad to hear it." He opened a cupboard and drew out a bag of herbs. Carefully separating out a small green leaf, he placed it on his tongue. "Did you sleep at all in the end?"

"Eventually. What is that leaf?"

"For the headache," he answered, handing her one. "You have no such pain?" She ought to have done. She'd taken more *levinor* than most Romany women would drink in an evening.

"You were kind enough to leave out your tea," she assured him. "Thank you." She accepted a leaf and chewed it in any case, bobbing an awkward curtsey. "I trust you also slept well?"

Valkin chose to ignore that question. He'd barely slept at all, kept awake by the persistent ache in his groin. He certainly wasn't about to tell this to Miss Dale.

His men had informed him of a rumour that the missing girl was sighted in Dunsop Bridge. No mention of Basingstoke, or to which family the girl belonged. Nothing Valkin might deem useful. If the English continued seeking Miss Dale in this secretive manner, they may never find her at all. This thought had cheered him immensely as he stood shivering in the darkness with his perimeter guard.

He wondered if he ought to tell his *gadje* this news. Watching her smooth the green silk gown over her curves, chestnut curls falling about her face, he decided she didn't need to know these rumours immediately. It might encourage her to leave before he was ready to let her go—Valkin checked himself. Surely he meant he didn't want her to leave before the roads were safe?

"I should like to know how it looks." Miss Dale interrupted his thoughts, looking at the Romany gown.

Shrugging, Valkin opened a cupboard, revealing the three-quarter mirror fitted to the inside panel.

"How clever." His *gadje* laughed aloud. "Everything in here is so smartly done."

"It ought to be." Valkin pushed one of the bowls towards her before settling over his own. "It has been the work of many Brishen generations. Each man who lives here adds an additional comfort or decoration to make his mark, and pass something of himself on to his descendants. It is one of our oldest traditions."

"What a lovely connection to make between the generations of your house. Do you know the history of each addition?"

"I believe so." He indicated an intricate floral design on one wall. "That was carved by my father on the occasion of his marriage. Many years ago now. The flowers are all favourites of Mama's."

"Who carved this one?" She traced the skilled creation of a Brishen forebear with a delicate fingertip. A wild, rearing stallion mounting a mare, carved deeply into the Romany king's bedhead.

"My great-grandfather," Valkin replied. "He had a wicked sense of humour. My great-grandmother branded it scandalous."

"It is scandalous," she mused. "So sensual." His *gadje* studied the detailing on the carved horses, stroking the stallion, then looked across the *covo,* her gaze meeting his before flitting away. Valkin admired the colour moving over her cheeks. When she next looked at him, it was a glance only, detached politeness. He preferred her heated cheeks and tactile hands. *No.*

Valkin cleared his throat. "You have a similar tradition with your titles and landholdings, do you not?"

"I do not think it's the same," she said slowly. "Our parents and grandparents give what has always been in the family. It's not personal. It is just what is there." She fell silent a moment, rubbing her thumb over the mating horses until Valkin shifted in his seat.

"Perhaps it is a little like the jewellery," she said finally. "Each woman adds to the family jewel case and passes this collection down the ages. It is often scattered among grandchildren or great-grandchildren. I like your tradition better." She tipped her head again, smiling.

Valkin gazed back at her, watching those skilful fingers stroking his bedhead. He kept his hands in his rapidly warming lap but held his gaze on hers, a heated connection he felt in every part of him.

***

Lydia

Lydia wondered if she'd ever grow used to the way this man looked at her, then mentally scolded herself. She wasn't here to stay. She must reach France and find Roger as soon as possible. Before all of London condemned her and she had no choice but to wed the earl.

She vowed to perish at sea before she faced such a fate. Shuddering, she pushed this thought away.

She could protect herself. *From most threats.* Darting a glance at Valkin's powerful torso, Lydia tried hard to be fair. Searing kisses notwithstanding, he'd not harmed her. She glanced once more at his lean, hard physique, wishing he'd kiss her again. She flushed— where had that wanton idea come from? Not from the pragmatic part of her that said to fix her eyes on something else. Anything else; stroking the nearest carving, she coloured furiously as Valkin's gaze once again tracked her caress of the stallion claiming his mate. She hurried to fill the silence and diffuse his smouldering stare. "What will you leave for your next generation?"

"This," he said, bringing down a chess set balanced atop a cupboard. "I've been working on it for some time."

She examined the set closely, admiring the exquisite workmanship. It was a uniquely Romany set. Instead of rooks, Valkin had painstakingly carved out miniature caravans in pale wood, carefully painting each tiny figurine. The knights were not just horse heads like the chess sets she was familiar with, but full Romany horses, accurate in every detail. Each one was slightly different, clearly modelled from four actual animals. She was sure, if she went outside, she'd be able to find these mounts in the camp and recognise them with ease.

The pawns were likewise all different and appeared to be Romany children of varying ages. Instead of bishops, Valkin had fashioned four oak trees. Lydia dimly recalled hearing the oaks at Clifton Hall spoken of as Bishop's Trees by her nanny. The kings were not yet complete, but she could already see that one of them resembled Valkin himself.

"What of your queens?" She ran a delicate fingernail over the tiny wooden image of Valkin's face. "You've not carved them."

"Not yet." He touched his jaw as though he felt her fingers there. Sliding his hand around the back of his neck, Valkin released a loud sigh. He took up one of the pawns, smiling. "This is the image of one of my sisters when she was small."

"Reyna?" Lydia frowned at the tiny wooden face. It didn't look like Reyna.

"Her name is Syeira."

Lydia fumbled her touch, suddenly clumsy. The figurine fell to the floor.

"She is grown up now. In love and happy. A wife and mother." He retrieved the piece, replacing the little figure on the chessboard. "Do you play?"

Lydia nodded, setting the pieces in their correct starting positions. She paused, realising she was making a great assumption. "I beg your pardon, Valkin. Do you have the time for this?"

He laughed and nodded. "There is not much for me to do the day after a sunset fire, though we Romany prefer our games out of doors." So saying, he rose, balancing the board as he had their breakfast bowls earlier.

"Of course." Lydia smiled in response, holding the door for him as he headed outside. "Shall I bring the rest?"

He nodded, settling their game between the woodpile and the *covo* steps.

"The camp is so quiet." She returned with their bowls and looked around.

"The morning after the sunset fire is always quiet," Valkin replied. "No *kris* this morning. Too many of my Romany arc nursing their heads."

"Like us." Lydia startled at her own words. She rose abruptly, hurrying inside to retrieve their coffee, refilling both cups with utterly unnecessary concentration. On her return, she noted Valkin tidying the chess pieces with a similar focus. *There is no "us."* She took up a small stone and placed it firmly in place of the missing queen piece, nodding as though responding to a question.

"Well, if I remain abed any longer, I shall lose my wits," she added briskly. "And I shall need those. This game will help to pass the time. Are you any good?"

"We shall see." Valkin lifted his gaze to hers in an unsettling way. "I will play one game with you, if you give me your word you will eat your breakfast afterwards. Such pottage is less appetising cool."

Lydia held out her hand, nearly wishing she hadn't. When Valkin took it in his, a warm glow moved over her, as though the heat in his eyes had transferred to his palm and thence to her own skin. She remembered his hot mouth on hers, his tongue moving between her lips. Struggling to control the rising colour in her face and neck, she kept her eyes resolutely on the chessboard.

"It is a-a t-trade." She gritted her teeth at the tremor in her voice. *I cannot remain here.* She must reach her brother as soon as possible. Inhaling a deep, steadying breath, Lydia advanced her chess piece.

***

"Another game?" Lydia asked with a grin, surveying Valkin's checkmated king with a practiced eye.

Valkin looked down at the board, snorting in disgust. "Thank you, I will not. I do not think my pride will stand being vanquished by a woman four times running." He stretched and grinned at her. "Besides, you should eat. You did give me your word, *pireni.*" He frowned at her in mock-solemnity. "You are hungry—yes?"

Lydia nodded.

"How you managed to charm me into three games when I agreed to only one, I do not know."

"Perhaps it is simply your determination to win at least once," she responded, grinning back at him.

Valkin laughed. "Perhaps. Your stratagems are nearly military." His smile widened as she snorted. "Come." He slid the food over to her. "Eat and tell me where you learned to play so well."

Lydia watched his tightly muscled forearms, still smiling. "My brother taught me. We used to play a great deal."

"He must have been blinding," Valkin muttered. "Did you best him so easily?"

"Oh yes, quite often, once I learned the basics. He always said it was a man's chivalrous duty to let a lady win, so I do not think I truly won any of our games with any skill." Lydia toyed with her wooden king. *Must they discuss her brother?*

"Your judgment may be at fault then," Valkin replied. "I am not so chivalrous."

Her eyes widened. "You mean to say you did not let me win?"

"I did not. You bested me fair and square." He inclined his head towards her. "You play intelligently, with form and strategy and clever gambits. I am reckoned quite skilled in the game, but my defences proved useless. I bow to your victory."

Lydia didn't think she could blush any warmer, lips twitching with suppressed delight. Valkin appeared to study the colouring in her face with a good deal of pleasure. His jaw tightened and she stood, brushing at her skirts before gathering in their pieces.

"This pleases you?" he asked.

"Oh." One tiny figurine slipped from her hands. Her host knelt to retrieve it, then placed it in her palm. Lydia stared down at the Valkin-shaped wood as he closed her fingers over his piece, leaning towards her, *close, closer, closing.*

A charge raced all the way along her spine, igniting every nerve. She stared back at Valkin, not moving, hardly breathing. "It is good—it is a comfort to me—to know I do one thing well."

"I think you do many things well, *pireni.*" His mouth closed over hers, nipping at her lips. Instinctively, she opened to him, sighing as his tongue caressed her lower lip, stroking the inside of her mouth. One of his hands cradled her face, the other slipping between them, fingertips dancing feather-light down her throat, cupping her breast. She gasped with pleasure. Valkin deepened his kiss, the demands of his mouth hot on hers, his touch holding her to him, exploring her mouth with a deliberation and exquisite skill that left her breathless.

The pleasure of his lips moving over hers was unbearable. Lydia responded with her own desire, opening farther, pressing nearer as he claimed her kiss. The rising wave of passion whispered that she wanted more of this, more of her skin thrilling against his mouth, her breasts pressing up against him, more of him holding her, tasting her, tempting her; more of *him… More.*

Tight, hard nipples pushed sharply into his torso, her tongue sliding over his, stroking him as intimately as he caressed her. Lydia nestled closer, her hips meeting his hot hardness shifting against her belly as he cupped her bottom, lifting her to him, squeezing gently, his hips moving against hers in a rhythm as old as time, as sensuous as sin. Valkin slid his hands across her back to tangle in her hair, her heart thudding against his. Urgent fire quickened through her veins with a wild need so powerful, her arms tightened around him… while she told herself to stop now, to draw back, he deepened his kiss further, palming her hips as his lips traced a warm, wet path down her throat. He ran his tongue over her collarbone. Lydia tensed at the increased sensations.

He drew back suddenly, loosening his hold, and she wanted to cry out, to pull him closer, but Valkin moved hastily away, leaning against a tree trunk as though he could barely stand.

"I beg your pardon, Miss Dale." His voice was so deep, it came out a growl. "I should not have—"

"I assure you there is no need to apologise, sir." The stiffness in her voice cut the air. "I am perfectly aware that I cannot please—"

"What?" He cut her off with a shout. "Stop *saying* that."

"But isn't it true?" Lydia slumped back against the woodpile.

"Of course it's not true." He muttered several Romany words that might be epithets. "Do you doubt that I want you, *pireni?*"

"Why would you?" she countered with barefaced candour, lifting her chin like a shield.

"Why? *Why?*" He squeezed his eyes shut, banging his fist against his own forehead. "*Mi Dubblesky.* For God's sake, girl, do you need me to spell it out for you?"

Lydia stared. She'd heard the Lord Brishen was controlled and restrained—except when it came to women. Apparently, the rumour mill of the ton had this part right.

Valkin let out a slow breath. "What do I have to do to convince you that you're a desirable woman?" He leaned forward, locking his gaze to hers. "Let me be perfectly clear. I want you, *pireni.* I wake up wanting you. I go to sleep wanting you. And so you cannot mistake me, I want to take you beneath me, make love to you until you beg me for more, cry out my name, and give yourself to me so completely that no other man will ever be able to satisfy you." He hardly seemed to notice he'd moved closer, his lips hovering above hers. "*Not* taking you is just about killing me," Valkin whispered, moving rapidly away as though she burned him. *Or tempted him?*

Lydia shook her head slowly, attempting to dislodge this dreamlike sensation. Valkin stared blackly back at her, the look on his face changing from frustration and exasperation to heat and raw primal need, his charm more potent and magnetic than ever. Ton rumour said his charm was irresistible. *I believe it.*

"You do want m-me? That's why you kissed m-me?" she whispered. "Then—then why d-did you stop? I thought perhaps I didn't have the skill—"

He cut her off with a Romany word she was certain was a curse. "Believe me, you have more skill in one kiss than all the ladies of the ton have in their entire bodies," he said tightly. "If you had any idea…. *Tatchipen si.* Depend upon it, *pireni*, I know what I'm talking about. You have everything in you to drive a man wild. I wish to be this man. I wish—" He stopped speaking, his face pained.

She stared back at him, breath halted in her chest. He wanted *her?* Really, truly, actually *wanted* her? He believed she was—Lydia swallowed—too tempting for his sanity? She dizzied with shock that someone would say such things. That *he* should say them, the man who'd fuelled her dreams of love all these years... A wicked thrill shot through her. But—

"You—you stopped. If you want m-me—" She swallowed again, restless hands twisting over themselves. "Why d-did you stop?" She struggled to keep her voice level.

"I am not such a hound that I will take advantage of a woman who is ill-circumstanced." His tone tightened. "Your—situation. You are frightened and uncertain of me, yes?" He didn't wait for her response. "I will do nothing to jeopardise you or my own honour. This is proving more difficult than I anticipated."

His gaze met hers. Wicked, enticing... *Shockingly tempting.* Lydia shrank back against the woodpile.

"I said I would *not*—" Valkin muttered, clearly annoyed with himself now.

"You h-have not taken your payment because I'm b-betrothed?" she asked in amazement.

"Yes. I mean no. I'll have no more talk about payment. You must realise that you are in no position to be seduced." He seemed to have calmed, though his voice remained low. He gazed at her again, the full force of those blazing black eyes boring into her.

"I thought I h-had d-done something wrong."

"There is nothing you can do that could make me not want you, *pireni*." He released a deep sigh. "It is truly time you stopped doubting yourself. Besides—" Valkin cleared his throat. "You did not think my kiss the kiss of a man who desires you?"

"I-I've not kissed anyone b-before," Lydia explained. "And I thought—" She stopped, blushed crimson, took a breath, and was silent.

"Yes?" he pressed patiently. "You thought—?"

"I d-do not know h-how to say it." She spoke with her eyes screwed tightly shut, her face scorching.

"*Pireni*?" he said quietly. "What did you think?"

"That—your kiss—it's what you always d-do." She kept her eyes screwed shut as though the darkness was the only safe space in her world, then flinched as Valkin slammed his fist against something—an ancient trunk she supposed. Lydia opened her eyes to see him stomping into the woods with an oath.

She'd gone too far. Her brothers always said her mouth would be her undoing. She'd called Lord Brishen a rake to his face. No doubt he'd left before his anger overcame him. He'd told her—her body shivered with warmth—he wanted her. He was going mad with wanting her. Did she dare believe him? *You are frightened and uncertain...* He wished her to be certain—of what, exactly? Lydia tried to remember the last time any man of her acquaintance had considered her at all.

Eight years ago, when the House of Brishen came together to make an Easter egg roll for her at Clifton Hall. When Prince Valkin (as he was then) carved palettes and painted eggs in a room with his sister and herself—and she'd felt completely, entirely happy. The memory faded as quickly as it came. Emptiness flowed in around her, that distance between her and the rest of the world. Experience taught her this was all she could expect.

What if it wasn't? A small voice spoke inside her, barely loud and brave enough to penetrate her furiously whirling thoughts. Was it fair to place Valkin's careful protection in the same place as the indifference of the other men in her life? He'd done more to aid her over the past week than her entire family in the last eight years; since Wil left, in fact.

"*Sarishan*, Miss Dale."

Lydia turned to Narilla as she approached with a bushel basket. "We gather pippins in the forest today and my brother bid me await you."

"Did he?" Lydia's brows rose in surprise, but Narilla had other priorities.

"You do not know the paths here as well as Brishen. I wish to eat first. Will you join me?"

"I thank you." Lydia accompanied her to the fireside, where Narilla commandeered a plate of small buns with honey.

"It is called *marikli* bread," she said, tearing a bun in half. "Try some?"

"Thank you." The bread was sweet and soft. Lydia could tell the honey was from the woods. She ate in silence, wondering if she dared ask Narilla how to go about mending fences with her eldest brother. Before she could remind herself it mustn't matter anyway (she was leaving his camp, wasn't she?), Reyna arrived at her elbow with cups of coffee.

"Thank you." Lydia accepted hers. "If I could request a further kindness from you b-both?"

"Of course," Reyna replied.

"Would you instruct me in m-mounting a horse as you do? I m-must learn to m-mount without a-a b-block," Lydia explained. "I am healed now and m-must continue towards France as soon as m-may be. I n-need to reach my b-brother before Christmas, you see."

"Your mare is in no condition to be ridden so far." Reyna sighed, the look on her face more worried than stern.

Lydia shrugged, finishing her food. "I m-must m-make a beginning, Reyna." She stood, looking towards the *gry* pens. "Will the *gry-engros* permit me to mount a Romany horse?"

Reyna shook her head, watching her. "Not while the *krallis* is from *ker*," she replied. "He is not here at all today."

"I c-can d-do this." She stared at Reyna and Narilla in turn, anger firing the throbbing at her temples. "I shall," she vowed, clenching her fists by her sides.

Getting back on her horse was more important than anything. The sooner she could ride, the sooner she'd leave the Romany camp and Valkin Brishen. The man who said he wanted her so much it was killing him.

CHAPTER EIGHTEEN

Valkin

Valkin sat up, panting with hard riding and shaken to his core. Did Miss Dale believe he always took women just because he could? Did anyone else think this? His family, perhaps? His sisters? He had a nasty feeling they might. *You will not—?* Reyna had said—and Valkin had not, but the truth remained that he wanted this woman. The way he wanted her was different from the way he'd wanted others. He knew this to the depths of his soul, felt it in the hardness of his bones, in the staccato rhythm of his heart when she looked at him.

What you always do… Miss Dale's words reverberated through his brain, pounding in time with the drumming of Bavol's hooves as he put his mount into another canter. That Miss Dale's fear his desire may only be fleeting was of more concern to the woman than her own safety scored Valkin's dignity as nothing else could have. Was he now so arrogant he assumed every Englishwoman crossing his path desired him? Valkin hoped not because this feeling for his *gadje* wasn't going anywhere, but who would believe it? He barely understood it himself.

He spent the afternoon with his perimeter guard, marking out the campsite particularly carefully. It was the *krallis*'s responsibility to greet the heads of the Romany houses joining Brishen for Christmas. It was also his duty to see to the security of *ker*. He couldn't help feeling additional cause for concern when his thoughts strayed to the girl he wanted so badly to protect.

"The law's about." The *sher-engro* of House Lovell raised concerns as soon as his people arrived at *ker*. The man was older, his house nearly as influential, and he glared at Valkin. "Is this your doing, Brishen?"

"All will be well, Manfri," Valkin assured him. "We've mounted additional guards."

Manfri nodded. "We'll take our part in any extra patrols."

"I thank you."

The other *sher-engro* nodded. "House Beti are arrived as well and will assist." He levelled another assessing glare at Valkin. "You look done in, Brishen. The sunset fire?"

"Among other things."

"This is why the *krallis* requires a wife." Manfri slapped him on the back and Valkin coughed.

"I'll consider it when House Lovell has daughters," he replied smoothly.

Manfri threw his head back, releasing a bellowing laugh. "I've only sons so far, as you know. Come, tell me of your horses."

Manfri's house dealt more in pigs and chickens, but House Lovell wished to spread their risk, like all sensible Romany. Valkin did his best to explain his successes in training, struggling to keep his thoughts from his *gadje*'s soft kisses, her breath on his face, her mouth opening to his... He blinked several times, giving himself a mental shake. Each time he found it harder to regain his focus, but he needed to keep his attention on his duties. He checked on the mare again, noting with satisfaction that Chal's men had done a first-class job. The animal remained unrecognisable. She'd be ready for a long ride soon enough—a truth Valkin shrugged off with a pang.

As for the saddle, Valkin thought the best thing might be to gift it to the Lord of Bowland for Christmas, if his *gadje* agreed. There were many gifts to organise, both for Christmas and for Reyna's wedding. He headed into the trees, seeking appropriate pieces of wood to work. He hoped Miss Dale would remain for Christmas. He'd like to surprise her with a special gift.

Valkin returned to his *tan* to shave before sunset. After tipping hot water from his spare kettle into a bowl, he stripped off his shirt.

He took up his straight razor before missing his strop. *Damn.* Three days' growth was unacceptable. Sighing, he squared his shoulders. It wouldn't do to appear unkempt before House Lovell or the other Romany leaders. There was nothing for it. He'd have to see her.

When he received no response to his knock, Valkin eased his *covo* door open and looked in. His *gadje* was absent, though a notebook and drawing materials lay on his table. Exhaling loudly, Valkin opened his drawer to find his leather by the light from the stove. If he was quick, he could be in and out before she returned. Why he felt covert about undertaking such activity in his own home, he refused to consider. He swore under his breath as he mixed his receipt.

Standing before his glass, Valkin covered his face with minted soap. He stropped his straight razor and began efficiently removing the past few days' stubble. So intent was he on his task that he didn't notice the squeak of his *covo* door. Miss Dale's gasp startled him.

"*Bengako*," he cursed as bright red blood flowed from his hand. Glancing back at her, he wrenched open his herb cupboard.

"It's all right," he said. "I'm not mortally wounded." He found the correct poultice and took it, shrugging. "I beg your pardon, Miss Dale. I did not intend to intrude but I required my strop. The blade is blunt." He indicated his razor.

"I'm afraid I must beg your pardon once more," she said softly, draping her rope-tie over a chair. "Is it very painful?"

"The herbs will soothe it and speed the healing." He waved the injured hand at her. "Please, do not trouble yourself. And it is *I* who should beg *your* pardon, *pireni*." A flush moved steadily over his face. His *gadje* must have noticed because she blinked.

"What on earth could embarrass the Lord Brishen?" Only then did she seem to realise she'd spoken her thoughts aloud.

"You'd be surprised," he replied, meeting her gaze. "I had no right to speak to you as I did earlier."

She flinched, regarding him with frosty green eyes before focusing on her rope coil.

"I meant what I said," he hastened on, wishing he could turn her to face him, cup her chin so she had no choice but to keep her gaze locked to his. "I do desire you, *pireni*. I still should not have said it. And I did not mean what you thought I meant. I am aware I have a reputation to live down. I do not consider you another—" *Damn this is difficult.*

"Another what?" She dropped her rope and faced him, her question slamming into him like a fist. "Whore? Trollope?" She answered his shock before he voiced it. "I've heard such words before."

From the earl, no doubt. Surely not from her father?

"W-woman," Valkin stammered as she turned from him again.

Miss Dale resumed coiling her makeshift bridle. Planning her departure, no doubt. *She can't leave.* Not yet.

"Miss Dale, I-I did not mean—" The heat of her glare gave him pause.

"I've not heard your speech falter so before." She stepped towards him, her gaze so hot, sharp, and pointed, he feared it more than any blade. Green eyes dilated as she inhaled, drawing herself up though she barely reached his shoulder. In truth, she stood level with his heart, which thudded so loudly he feared she'd hear it, hear *him*. He ought not to be here, ought not to want to. Did he want to? *Dear God, yes.*

Gathering what remained of his pride, Valkin pushed his poultice firmly against his wound, doing his best not to flinch at the sting of nettle juice on an open cut. Bowing to Miss Dale, he turned to leave.

CHAPTER NINETEEN

Valkin

Valkin reached abruptly for the door handle—and stopped, listening. Desire retreated as he cocked his head. Miss Dale seemed to catch his tension.

"Valkin, what—"

He held a hand up for silence. She obliged, listening intently to the ruction. It sounded as though all of Brishen were banging ladles against kettles, and there was much shouting besides.

Valkin glanced at the window. The banging grew more insistent, moving towards his *tan*, his *covo*—and his *gadje*.

"*Sher-engro. Rak tute.* Valkin, *muscro.*"

Chal's voice, calling in barely restrained panic. Valkin fisted his hand before collecting himself. *Muscro* meant the law was here. The rest of Chal's words were an old Romany warning.

"Chal," he yelled out the window. "My *sherro dukkers.*" Claiming a hangover was always credible to the English and it would buy them a few moments.

"*Ja.*" Chal's final shout came before a tense, unsettled silence as the Romany ceased their noise. Taking a steadying breath, Valkin dragged a hand through his hair. *There's no need for this to get out of hand.*

Locating a fresh shirt, he crept quietly towards the door of his *covo*. Opening it a crack, he glimpsed a private constable arguing with Chal. He glanced back at Miss Dale, his heart wrenching at her terror. Sighing, he pulled out a chair.

"Here. Sit."

"They are h-here for m-me, aren't they?" she whispered.

"We do not know that. I must meet with the law and find out what I can. You will please stay here." He knelt to add wood to the stove. Then he took up a woollen blanket and settled it over her shoulders before taking up his tinder box.

"Leave it," his *gadje* objected. "Please, Valkin."

"Miss Dale, you are far too cold."

"It looks odd to have smoke coming from your *covo* roof if you're not within," she pointed out. "Do not risk more than you have already." The dismay in her eyes cut him like glass.

Valkin's lit taper burned down like time running out. Before flame reached his skin, Miss Dale leaned in, blowing out his fire.

"Do not risk your Romany," she whispered.

Valkin gazed into those great eyes of hers. "It shall be as you wish, Miss Dale. You have no objection to my bedclothes, I take it?"

Her face barely flickered in response as she huddled into his blankets. It seemed as though all the warmth between them cooled. As if to underscore this, the water jug held only frigid refreshment and thinning ice. Cupping his hand, Valkin splashed a little over himself, drying his face with a linen cloth. Locating his warmest vest, he added his ceremonial purple sash and tied it smoothly around his hips.

Buttoning his jacket, he glanced at the woman in his bed. She stared mutely back, fear haunting her face. One pale hand crept out from the covers as she handed him her uncocked pistol. Shaking his head, Valkin curved her fingers back over the handle, pressing the weapon more firmly in her grip.

"Keep it by you, *pireni*." He stroked her knuckles with his thumb, ignoring the urge to trace her lips, taste them again and hold her until the tension eased in her eyes. "I promised you would be safe here," he whispered. "You can trust me. Do you not know this yet?"

"I-I d-do, V-Valkin."

He clenched his fists as he turned from her, anxiety leaden in his gut. Taking his last jar of *levinor* with him, Valkin returned to his *tan*. Once he'd tied the canvas flaps to give himself as much privacy as possible, he brought his palms together and closed his eyes. Taking three steadying breaths, he attempted to dispel the tension across his shoulders. Footsteps sounded outside, moving closer to his quarters.

"The *krallis* may be asleep." Chal drew closer, speaking in hesitant English. Valkin was relieved his brother no longer sounded alarmed. He broke open the *levinor* and tipped a little over himself before returning to sprawl across the steps of his *covo*. He pushed his hair out of his eyes as the other men arrived, attempting a bleary-eyed grin.

"*Sarishan*, my *prala*, my brother." Valkin brandished the wine jar in the air. "Need more *levinor*?" Rising to a mock-bow, he let out a drunken laugh. He made sure to hardly register the official-looking *muscro* standing beside Chal. "Good morning, sir." He leaned into the side of his *covo* as if achieving vertical balance were difficult. A little knot of men stood nearby, keeping a cautious eye. Chore circled them all, growling deeply in his throat.

"Chore, *besht.*" The animal sat, whining and watching the constable as closely as his masters. The *muscro* eyed the dog warily. Valkin took this chance to peer stealthily at him, squinting in the pale winter sun.

The constable had a solid, honest air about him, hair greying under his hat, and the solemn face of a *muscro* who took his work seriously. Out of the corner of his eye, Valkin saw Reyna ride off into the woods astride the mare. She'd not had time to change into her riding habit. He released a slow breath. The horse had been his biggest concern—the animal had been expertly dyed, but any layman could see she wasn't a Romany horse. Even if they did not connect the animal with the disappearance of the *gadje*, he had no wish to see Brishen accused of horse stealing.

"*Boshta?*" He looked at Chal, inquiring as to the whereabouts of the saddle.

"*Gare,*" Chal replied.

Valkin exhaled again. His brother had kept his wits and hidden it. They were safe, if the constable didn't take it into his head to search the camp. This he would not do without Valkin's leave. Or at least, Valkin acknowledged, not easily. He eyed his perimeter guard. All were armed with sticks and rifles. Reminding himself that this *muscro* was merely making inquiries, Valkin sharpened his focus.

"*Muscro*, I see." He straightened his stance, rubbing his face. "How may we assist you, sir?"

"I seek a girl gone missing from a house party," he snapped. "It's been several days now, nearer a week, and we've no news of her."

"I assured him no *gadje* passes our guard unnoticed," Chal broke in, glaring at the constable. "But he is not content to take my word, in spite of our honour being vouchsafed by the Lord of Bowland."

"As his lordship is unwell, I'm unable to confirm this." The constable glanced uncertainly at Valkin, then back at Chal, as if he'd rather question the more sober Romany. "I insisted on speaking to the gypsy king. I understand you attended the house party yourself?" He looked expectantly at Valkin.

Valkin rubbed his hand over his face. "I beg your pardon," he said slowly, pretending to sober up. "You are correct, sir. I'm recently returned from Davenport Manor. I saw no English girl leave her ladyship's gathering. I was occupied with other attentions." He cleared his throat meaningfully, winking at Chal. His brother hardly twitched his mouth.

"We Romany have heard no rumour of an English girl travelling in these woods," Valkin lied, drawing a long, sobering breath before asking the question he'd been avoiding for too long. "Whom is it you seek, sir?"

The constable's gaze shifted uncomfortably. "All I'm permitted to say is that her betrothed, a gentleman of quality, is concerned by the lady's absence. He fears she went out riding and became lost. As far as we know, yes, she went out alone. Her name is concealed to prevent a scandal."

"If her family permit her to stray so far unchaperoned, then they are bound to lose her," Valkin replied. "Excepting Slaidburn, it's a fair ride from any English estate to the Forest of Bowland. In the frost and winter winds, it is not a likely path for a young girl to choose. She'd need to be an expert horsewoman, and you will pardon me sir, but I've not heard your Englishwomen were capable of riding so far. Perhaps she broke her journey earlier or gave up altogether and is now on her road home. Quality these days, as I'm sure you're aware, is more a matter of birth than of brains, sir." He thought he saw the man smile.

"And how the gentleman expects you to find her with such imprecise details as that, Heaven only knows." He smiled sympathetically, and the *muscro* relaxed, nodding back at him.

"I can't disagree with you there, sir," he replied. "And I'm terribly sorry for disturbing your—er—rest." The constable grinned. "I take it you've been busy?"

"The company at her ladyship's is always satisfactory." Valkin shrugged with deliberate casualness. "Since you are here, sir, will you not take some rest and refreshment? I'm sure we can find you a hot meal." He signalled Cato with his eyes. His cousin walked towards them, stooping to pat Chore. "It is a cold morning, and your work is thirsty business, is it not?"

The *muscro* smiled. "It is indeed, sir. A rest and something to eat will be very welcome." He stepped towards the *covo,* but Valkin stood up quickly, barring his way.

"My cousin will show you our fireside, where the food is kept hot. If you'll forgive me, I shall join you both in a few moments." Looking down at his wine-sticky linen, he feigned a rueful expression. "I must dress. I do beg your pardon again, sir, for not receiving you as our head of house should."

"Young men have not changed any since I was one myself, sir." The *muscro* smiled, allowing himself to be drawn away by Cato, whose tense walk indicated he was far from relaxed about these proceedings. Only once they'd passed behind another collection of tents did Valkin unclench his jaw. Beside him, his brother cleared his throat twice.

"Say what it is you wish to say, Chal."

"Taking a missing English girl under your protection endangers us all," he said hurriedly. "We trust in you, *sher-engro*. I just—"

Valkin swallowed. "Her presence here is temporary until she and her mare may travel in safety."

"There is nothing wrong with her horse," Chal pointed out. "Once the *gadjos* are gone, will you ensure she returns home?"

Valkin shifted in place under his brother's stern gaze. To his great relief, Narilla ran up from beneath her *tan*.

"There you are, *sher-engro*."

"What is it?"

Chal's gaze burned into him.

"The *kris* awaits you, and—" She stared from one brother to the other. "Valkin? Chal? What is wrong?"

"Nothing that cannot wait," Valkin replied.

"I beg to differ," Chal added fiercely.

Valkin rubbed his neck, sighing wearily. "Your concerns shall be addressed, Chal. We will speak more about this soon."

"The sooner the better, *sher-engro*."

"Understood." Valkin turned again to Narilla. "The *kris* must wait until the law has left *ker*. I am to sup with the *muscro*. Ensure he has plenty of wine with his meal." With a last glance at Chal's dissatisfaction, Valkin strode to the fireside with an assurance that was entirely feigned. He spent a good deal of time with the constable, fed the man a hot meal, and noticed he enjoyed his drink.

As he suspected, the *gadjo* knew nothing of Miss Dale's name. Basingstoke appeared to be working hard to prevent any rumour of his betrothed's flight. Valkin's knowledge of ton manners was not extensive, but he could guess how such news, on the heels of the former countess's death, might taint the earl's precarious reputation. This boded well for Miss Dale but it didn't explain who she was.

Nor did it clarify why he felt compelled to harbour this woman at such risk. *She's not* that *pretty.* Liar.

An hour or so later, he walked the *muscro* to his horse and bid him good day. "If I or any of my Romany should hear anything, I shall find you." Valkin smiled up at him, holding the horse's head as the man mounted up.

"I'm most exceedingly obliged, *sher-engro.*" The Englishman set off with a friendly wave.

Well, that could have been worse. Valkin watched the *gadjo* out of sight of *ker* before making his way back to his *tan.* His gaze caught Reyna penning the mare back in with their other horses, stroking the animal's soft nose as she chatted to his men. Sacki detached himself from the other *gry-engros* to join his betrothed as they made their way towards him. Chal approached again from the other direction, determination in his eyes. Valkin tightened his shoulders. He considered escaping into the *kris*, or to Slaidburn, or hurrying to join the day's hunt, but when his family had something to say, it was the *sher-engro*'s duty to listen.

Valkin addressed Reyna first, eyeing the distant mare. "*Paracrow tute,*" he said quietly. "I thank you. She is a good horse."

Reyna nodded, waving Sacki away before joining Chal in fixing Valkin with an identical glare. "This cannot continue, my *prala*, my brother," she said bluntly. "I too am fond of the *gadje*, but can you deny she is the missing girl for whom the law seek?"

Valkin gazed across the campsite towards the river. "On the contrary," he answered. "I am certain she *is* the girl whom the *gadjos* seek. I wish to consult Wil. He knows more about the *gadjos* than anyone else and will know how to assist her."

"Is it our business to assist in this, though? Think of your people. Of what an angry *gadjo* lord means to us all," Chal pointed out.

"You are right." The words hurt Valkin's mouth. "She has no escort," he said quietly. "She is a woman alone."

Reyna rested one firm hand at Valkin's back. "I know this, *sher-engro*, but what of the risk to Brishen?"

"The risk for all my Romany is too great," he agreed. *And the risk to yourself?* A merciless voice prodded, *if you let her go?* Valkin pushed this truth away, closing his eyes against a pain that had nothing to do with unquenched desire. *I wish her to stay.*

This was true too, but he needed to lessen the danger to them all. Either he must find a solution for keeping Miss Dale safe or leave to travel with her. A leaden heaviness clanged through him. *Leave? How can I leave?*

He shook his head hard, clearing his throat until it hurt. "How long until Wil and Syeira arrive to *ker*?"

"Janfri sent word they'll be here within two days," Reyna replied. "Syeira's new babe is a girl. You will sing the naming?" Her solemn look returned.

"Of course." Valkin spoke too loudly, desperate for her not to guess the range of his thoughts. "Who else?" Catching the quizzical look on his sister's face, he saw a similar expression in Chal's eyes. "What did you two think?"

"We thought perhaps, that is—" Reyna glanced at Chal before looking again at Valkin, flushing darkly. "Do you not wish to go with your *gadje*?"

Valkin tensed like a drawn bow. He wanted to crawl back to bed and sleep for a week, not face questions for which he had no answers.

"Wil will know what to do." Valkin hoped this was true, because for better or worse he couldn't let his *gadje* go.

CHAPTER TWENTY

Lydia

Gripping her pistol, Lydia listened at the door, fear shuddering through her. *Taking a missing English girl under your protection endangers us all.* Chal's voice. Reyna's too: *This cannot continue.* Lydia listened for Valkin's opinion, not daring to release her breath. He agreed with his siblings, it seemed—and did they mention Wil was coming? Her brother's wife and children, harassed by the law because of her. Lydia's nausea returned. She gulped, swallowing bitter bile. *I won't do this to my family.*

Drawing out her belongings, she packed a swag as she'd seen the Romany do. If one of her new friends showed her the path, she thought she'd a chance. Anything was better than sitting here, frightened out of her wits by the earl and the duke.

Do not cry, she ordered herself firmly as an icy lump wedged at the base of her throat. A small, harsh sound escaped her, then another, and another. Holding a silken cushion to her breast, Lydia let the heaving sobs rack her body. She let the pain out, let it all pour forth, because nothing in this world could be worse than having to flee from all that you want—the man you want—knowing how much you hurt him. *Oh.* His hands moving over her, her skin warming beneath his gaze, his tongue teasing her pulse as though he were a part of her and she of him. Couldn't she stay with Valkin, her *krallis*? The man she wanted to love forever.

"No," she said aloud to the carved wooden walls, to tear-sodden linen, to herself and her heart. "*No.*" Closing her eyes, she took a deep breath, chest shaking with the weight of loss.

She'd leave at sunrise, while Valkin attended *kris*. There was nothing here for her in any case. *Nothing except this...* She clawed at one hand with the other, as if to tear the pain from her skin, then turned back to her possessions, making a mental list of what else she might require. Staring at her boots, she frowned at their four neat rows of buckles. Two were merely decorative. Buckles had value for the Romany. Lydia fumbled for her embroidery scissors and detached the buckles from the leather stitching. Next, she snipped at her petticoats until the lace trim came away in her hand. Selecting several of her best sketches, she reckoned their value and made ready her trades. Her decision was made, her plans in place. Now she must inform Valkin.

The very next time she saw him.

Strangely, though, she didn't see him at all that afternoon. She managed to exchange two of her buckles for bread and goat's cheese, and gained a spare gown. She would take only this dress and the one she'd traded for Reyna's wedding petticoats. She'd leave the others behind. So far as she knew they were loans, not gifts, and she'd traded Reyna nothing in exchange.

"The trade is fair." Sacki's sister was an excellent riding tutor. The woman smiled at Lydia as she accepted the sketch of her children grouped charmingly beside their *tan*. She patted her horse's flank and waved the animal back towards the *gry* pens.

"*Zen?*" Lydia tried the word that seemed to mean "saddle." She managed to mime the rest of her request by pointing indistinctly towards the horses and proffering her last sketch—a study of the *gry-engros* at their work.

The other woman shook her head, shrugging her apologies.

Lydia shrugged in return. Rope ties it would have to be. At least she could mount a horse without aid now. Glancing at the lowering sun, she curtsied and hurried back to the *covo* to prepare for the sunset fire and her last night surrounded by the warmth and safety of Brishen.

Clutching her new belongings, she opened the door with her elbow—and jumped a foot in the air at Valkin's deep drawl.

"Leaving us so soon, Miss Dale." It wasn't a question so much as an accusation. He sat in his usual chair, radiating glower.

"What makes you think so?" Her hedging was unmistakeable.

Valkin's scowl became a glare. "This is my *ker*. Nothing happens here without my hearing of it." He knelt to retrieve her parcels. "You've been riding Sacki's horse. You've traded for provisions. You are making a journey." He stood, dumping her preciously gained parcels onto his table.

"I was unaware my activities were under observation, *sher-engro*." Lydia lifted her chin a touch, tension aching across her back. An image of her father flashed before her. She shuddered. *Valkin is not like that.*

"There are no secrets in a Romany camp," Valkin replied impatiently. "There is another Romany I wish to consult for you. He may be able to assist your situation." He shifted his gaze from her face. "You will stay at *ker* until he arrives."

You will stay...

Anger sparked. "You will force me to remain?"

His eyes widened. "Force you?"

She'd shocked him. *Was it possible?*

Valkin stared determinedly into her eyes but said nothing further, looking as if dozens of words remained pent-up behind closed lips...*his lips.* She licked her suddenly dry mouth.

"It's not sensible for me to remain here," Lydia said at last. "You cannot wish it." She looked away, not wanting to read the truth in his eyes.

"We must consult—"

"There is no 'we.'" Lydia pretended to misunderstand his muttered curse. *There is only me and the long dark road to Paris, Roger, and leaving England behind.* England, and Valkin. Valkin, and this. *What is this?*

"You are running away."

Definitely an accusation, his clipped speech at odds with the way he looked at her, like a touch she wanted. Like his kiss...*his kiss.* She wished she had the sense to look away. *Sense? That's long gone.*

"You are running away and this time your action is foolish. The man I wish to consult—my Romany brother—will be here in less than two days."

Two days? Lydia barcly restrained her gasp. He could only mean Wil. Revealing their relationship would not help Brishen. Her new friends would only become more determined to aid her, placing them more firmly in danger.

Valkin's puzzled frown drew her focus. "My brother is not terribly formidable, *pireni.* You will like to meet an adopted son of Brishen, I think. He was English once."

I know. Oh, I know he was.

"It is not easy to find a way around the *gadjo* laws in your situation."

No, it isn't, but not for the reasons Valkin might think. Panic whirred through her. *I must be gone before Wil arrives.* The thought took root, anchoring the sense therein. She swallowed, steadying her resolve in silence.

"*Pireni*, will you not stay two more days?" he said at last, his voice unsteady.

"I c-cannot." The words thickened in her throat, unwilling to make her refusal into truth. "I m-must leave your c-camp as soon as possible."

"Must you?" His voice, so soft and determined at the same time. "Must you really?"

"I b-believe s-so." She could barely speak.

"You believe...?" He lifted his brows as his blazing black gaze pinned her in place. "I do not understand this, *pireni.* What are you not telling me?"

Lydia stared back in silence as though the answers to her predicament might be found in Valkin's eyes. The knock on the door came as relief.

"Come in," she called, forcing a smile for Reyna and Narilla as they entered.

Reyna added a wrapped bundle to the collection on the table, glancing between Lydia and her brother. Without looking at his sisters, Valkin issued what sounded like a Romany directive.

"I shall see you all at the sunset fire." His gaze didn't falter as he backed out of his *covo*, slamming the door as he turned.

"Miss Dale, are you unwell?" Reyna offered a small smile.

"I am quite well." Lydia straightened her shoulders. *This cannot continue.*

"You do not look it," Reyna pointed out.

Lydia could barely focus her attention. "If I may request your assistance tomorrow?" She glanced uneasily at Narilla.

At a word from Reyna, her sister left them alone. "What is it you require, Miss Dale?"

"To leave." Lydia held herself erect and immovable, burning Reyna's gaze with a determined one of her own. "I must depart your camp as soon as may be. Will you help me?"

Reyna took a breath. "Valkin—"

"I-I h-heard y-you s-say I needed to go y-yourself." Redness flowed into her cheeks at the look on Reyna's face. "D-do not apologise for b-being right, Reyna." She spoke loudly to forestall her friend's objections. "The d-danger I bring to Brishen m-must end n-now." She thought of Roger, her mama, and Clifton Hall. Most of all, she reminded herself that she'd made it this far.

"I do not know the whereabouts of your saddle."

Lydia shrugged. "Then I must find another, or use a rope-tie."

Reyna gaped as if she'd grown another head. "You know this skill?"

"I know it well enough." Lydia smiled without amusement, suspicion seizing her. "I do not require much. Simply a direction and my mare. I believe she may be ridden now?"

Reyna's gaze fell to her feet when she nodded.

Lydia shrugged again. "I shall look out for you tomorrow, at sunrise." She didn't need to add "when Valkin is at *kris*."

Reyna looked up, offering her hand to Lydia.

It is a trade.

Placing her hand in Reyna's, Lydia was surprised when the girl pulled her into a warm embrace, farewells already shimmering in her friend's eyes.

"You are right to go, for Brishen." Reyna rubbed her hands over Lydia's back. "But how I shall miss you."

Lydia's heart was too full for words. Squeezing her friend's waist, she let go a sigh drawn from every part of her.

Reyna released her, looking seriously into Lydia's face with her kind brown eyes. "We shall all miss you, Miss Dale."

Neither of them mentioned Valkin. Lydia stood in his home. His camp. Among his family. Her gaze lit on the carved stallion mounting his mare. *I will not bring this family to harm.*

*** *

Lydia sighed as she carefully snipped at the seam of her Romany gown. With a few quick alterations and a length of ribbon, she created a linen pocket pouch with a concealed slit. Satisfied her pistol could now be worn within easy reach no matter her costume, she ensured mama's gems remained securely seamed into her bonnet. Leafing through newer sketches, she wished she might leave these good people more than prettied-up petticoats and a few likenesses. Dismissing these regrets with another sigh, Lydia continued her preparations for leaving. *Leaving.* She steeled herself. By tomorrow, she'd be gone and that was that.

She stepped to the little stove, glancing at the open page in her sketchbook. When the kettle boiled, she set her Romany tea to steep, trying not to think about her last night at the sunset fire. Taking a deep breath, she closed her eyes, clasping her palms together as she recalled the goodness of her time among the Romany.

Kneeling on the bed a moment later, she peered out of the little window. Slow tears spilled over her cheeks as a stumbling youngster was helped to her feet by her brothers. An older woman showed one of Narilla's friends how to season their meal. Nearby, two men engaged in a trade. Lydia took in each small grouping, each activity, soaking up the sensation of family, drawing it inward to hold in her heart forever. A memory, a source of warmth to sustain her as she rode towards she knew-not-what. *Remember this…* This warmth she must turn from, for the sake of these people she admired. *You are right to go.*

"Does love always hurt this much?" she whispered to her favourite equine carving. *I wish to kiss the Romany king again…* This was foolish. Valkin's kisses were dangerous, and she couldn't risk—what? *What can you not risk? What do you truly have left?* Would it be so wrong to be held by the man she loved one last time? To gift herself a single, warm moment before she left this haven behind? *Do I dare?*

***

At the sunset fire, Valkin carried the same determined shine to his eyes that Lydia saw before they kissed. This accounted for the catch of her breath, the jolt of heat moving through her as he left his seat, striding towards her. *It is his duty; it is his role.*

"May I have this dance, Miss Dale?" His bow, his smile, and his dangerous charm surrounded her.

Lydia attempted to force such thoughts away as she rose, suppressing a moan at the scent of him: leather, coffee, and forest herbs. He swayed closer, drawing her to him as they danced. Leaving this man was harder than she'd anticipated. She blushed for the sudden spike of desire shooting through her body.

*Focus on something else…*like his alluring aura of masculinity and solicitude? Surely this shimmering heat would subside when he stepped back in their dance. Valkin did no such thing, and Lydia's wild thoughts didn't abate at all, as though determined to undermine her resolve. Fearing further well-argued reasons to remain, she tried for distraction.

"W-will y-you t-translate your s-song f-for m-me?"

Warm breath spilled over her as he chanted the words first in Romany, then English. Her pulse pounded a rhythm she ruthlessly ignored.

"This one is a love song about the *krallis*," her host said quietly.

Of course it was, because Lydia's last night was cursed with desires she couldn't fulfil and feelings she dared not credit. Straightening in Valkin's arms, Lydia leaned back, away. *Out of danger.*

"Yes, you are out of danger, Miss Dale." Valkin's words seemed strained. He didn't pull her closer and he did not smile.

"Did I speak so aloud?"

He nodded, staring implacably down at her as though trying to read her thoughts. *Remember this. Remember the man you love.* Warm tones limned his profile in the firelight. Reds, oranges, yellow and pale gold...the colours of her underskirts, his shirts, reminding her of sunsets, horizons, and the utter impossibility of loving this man. But if she could, if he loved her back... Looking away at last, she withheld her sigh. *He truly is shockingly handsome.* She halted her wild thoughts in place, listening to the soft singing.

Oprey the rukh adrey the wesh
Are chiriclo and chiricli;
Tuley the rukh adrey the wesh
Are pireno and pireni.

CHAPTER TWENTY-ONE

Valkin

"Is this song about love as well?" Miss Dale looked up at Valkin.

Valkin watched her face, her eyes, her lips... He longed to teach her more of songs of music, of pleasure, desire, and love. "Many Romany songs are about love." He forced a smile. "The love of family, of our houses. For our *ker* and our people." He stifled an absurd urge to declare himself then and there, actually biting down his tongue to hold back.

"This song is about the love between lovers," she murmured.

He nodded, hoping Miss Dale didn't notice the tremor in his hands as he held her, heart racing like a runaway horse. He slowed his dance, his breath, the whirring of his mind. Their rhythm grew languid as the *levinor* took effect. Singing became humming, dancers swaying closer around them. This only served to prolong his time with his *gadje*, tantalising his body with the press of hers. It didn't help his head at all, nor did the darting curiosity in her gaze. She seemed as nervous as he. Hope rushed through him. Hope and silent, foolish joy.

Valkin held her at the farthest possible distance dictated by courtesy, avoiding her stare.

"Are you afraid of entrapment, Lord Brishen?"

Valkin shook his head roughly, offering another tight smile. Miss Dale smiled back, just as brief and tense. He'd put her on her guard again. Sighing inwardly, Valkin wished she understood how desirable she truly was, and how much he wanted to do for her. More than anything, he wanted her to know how much she was coming to mean to him. Valkin didn't know how to say any of these things, or how to convince her he was in earnest. It wasn't wise in any case, to desire more than this. *In this moment alone...* Moments could be powerful.

He leaned in at last, glorying in her hesitant shiver as his breath tickled the sensitive skin of her neck, the stumble in her step as she swayed against him. Valkin resisted the urge to press her closer, but when the dance ended, she stepped back, curtsying and smiling up at him in a way that made him wish everyone around them gone.

"Thank you for the d-dance." As soon as the song closed, his *gadje* seemed in a hurry to leave.

A sense of foreboding shot through Valkin. He caught her up at the edge of the fireside. "Miss Dale, you're unwell?"

"I am perfectly well, thank you. I wish to retire, if this is acceptable?"

"Of course. Allow me to escort you to the *covo*, where I may rest as well."

She stared at him. "I beg your pardon?"

Valkin smiled. "I shall rest in my *tan* before taking my place on guard again."

"Oh, I see." Her soft smile warmed her eyes, the curve of her lips in firelight more lovely than the dawn.

Once they reached the *covo*, she allowed him to enter behind her.

"If you are troubled in your sleep, I shall prepare more tea," he offered.

"Thank you, I have my notes." So saying, she flipped open her notebook to a page headed "Bedtime Tea," proceeding to follow the detailed receipt as competently as any woman of Brishen. "May I offer you a cup?"

"You have mastered our secrets already?" He raised a brow at her.

She laughed gently. "It is not difficult. It is the least I'm able to offer you, after all you have done for me."

Why does this sound like farewell? Valkin shook off his languor as her deft hands steeped, tested, and finally poured out her concoction. Her actions were sure and confident, but she wasn't at ease and she did not meet his eyes. Miss Dale placed a steaming cup by his elbow and stepped back as if drawing some kind of magic line between them. *Hmmm...*

"Thank you, *pireni*," he said. "How are your nights lately?"

"Much better, I thank you."

"I am glad. Reyna wishes to know if you like her gift, by the way." Valkin indicated the bundle his sister had left on the table earlier.

Seating herself on the bed, his *gadje* opened the parcel, exclaiming in delight at the ornaments and ribbons it contained. Reaching for her oiled brush, she twisted it through her hair, attempting to fit a Romany comb into her curls. There was a clatter as it tumbled to the floor. Valkin knelt to retrieve it for her. He held it out. She smiled, extending the brush.

"Perhaps you know more of Romany ornaments than I?"

Valkin stared at the brush, then shifted his gaze to those eyes of hers, glowing with some inner tension. Her fear was not absent. Nor was her fervent desire for warmth. His body's response heated so violently, he gripped the nearest chair to steady himself, doing his best to look away from the fierce longing in her face. It reminded him of a certain bedside carving, and his parents dancing by firelight. He should do something to dispel these taut sensations filling his *covo*. He should leave. Now. At once. Or summon one of his sisters to help the girl, but it was not in the nature of a Romany man to ignore the power of the moment. Valkin was no exception. *Pretend lover? Hardly.*

Drawing the brush from warm fingers, he sank behind her on the bed, settling her just in front of his chest. His *gadje* didn't resist as he pulled the brush through her hair with long, firm strokes. She didn't relax against him either. *What is she up to?*

"Thank you, Valkin," she said softly.

"It is no trouble," he answered, though this wasn't strictly true. May, in fact, be an outright lie.

Valkin held his breath, aware of the silence widening between them like distance, the only sound his swift movement of hard bristles through soft hair. His hands stilled their movement, cushioning tension. He thought he understood.

"If you truly wish to leave, I will not prevent you." His words seemed to add to the silence.

He thought she swallowed, clamping her mouth closed as though sealing something precious behind her lips. *Her lips...* Valkin nearly groaned aloud. That she did not want to remain at *ker*—that she did not want *him*—he could almost credit, but that she intended to put herself at such risk when there were people willing to aid her, to keep her safe...?

Travel all the way to Paris unescorted indeed. If anything happened to her...something clenched in his chest.

"But I cannot allow you to leave *ker* in so unsafe a manner," he said tightly. "You will stay here until I find you a suitable escort."

"Valkin, no—I—you c-cannot take such risk. I will g-go as soon as I'm able."

"Then you will be here a very long time, *pireni*. You cannot ride all the way to Morecambe Bay in that abomination of a saddle, on worsening roads as the snows close in." He barely prevented himself from shouting.

"Your Romany tell me the roads near the coast are not so bad," she replied. "And I must reach my brother." Her back stiffened.

Valkin smiled despite himself, tightening his grip on the brush.

"I am not your responsibility," she continued. "It is not your duty to protect me, and I will not bring your camp to harm."

Valkin released a frustrated sigh. "You have placed yourself under my protection. I may not be an angel, but I will not flout my own honour." His words rang in the ensuing pause, brushstrokes coming harder into tensile silence. "This is my *ker*. You are my guest. Right here and now, this makes you mine."

His.

"Why?" she whispered.

"I am the *krallis*." Valkin ran a restless hand through his hair. "It is my duty to preside over our Christmas and the harshness of winter. I cannot assist you to Paris until the thaw."

His *gadje* shook her head. "You misunderstand me. I mean why trouble yourself on my account?" Her voice stayed quiet. "I will not stay, and I am not—" Her voice rose. "Not Brishen. *Not* yours. Not in any respect." She gazed down at her hands, taking a breath. "There is n-nothing b-between us."

Everything within him rose up in protest, but he gentled his tone. "Not even when we dance, *pireni*?"

His *gadje* wrenched away and stood, turning to face him, her entire body quivering with tension. "Not then," she said clearly, green eyes flashing as though daring him to gainsay her. "Not at all."

"Very well." Valkin stood before her just as firmly. "Allow me one last dance to be certain, Miss Dale?" He bowed, offering his hand.

For a moment she appeared utterly stricken—the look of any creature before it learns to trust. She exhaled, offering a small nod.

"I—I w-will dance with you one l-last t-time." She seemed to steel herself into a curtsey. "Then y-you will l-let me g-go."

Valkin rose from his bow. His proffered hand remained in place. "It is a trade."

"Y-yes." She nodded once, the tension visible in every line of her body. She stepped forward, but he moved behind her with the brush, drawing her down to sit.

"Allow me to lead," he murmured, drawing the bristles through her curls, aware this was his last chance to persuade her to stay. Aware, too, that he ought not to want this, or her. His mama's voice came back to him. *What of love, my son? What of you?*

His fingers shook as he stroked the smooth curve of her neck, drawing the brush with his other hand. He slowed his touch a fraction, his *gadje* tilting her head, shifting muscle beneath his hand. His eyes widened at her sigh of pleasure.

Every nerve in his body tingled and buzzed. Frissons ran through him, tiny charges, small, but powerful. Valkin continued his soft stroking with one hand, the other drawing on her curls. The flickering pulse in her neck beat faster.

Her nipples tightened. His brush stopped mid-stroke. Valkin laid it aside, breathing audibly behind her. He rose, drawing her with him until she stood before his cupboard. Leaning past her, he flicked open the wooden door, revealing the mirror. He continued teasing the sensitive curves of her neck and shoulder, watching her reflection in his mirror as his made short work of her buttoned bodice with his free hand.

"Close your eyes. Dance with me. Feel, do not think." He slid a palm around her waist, drawing her closer. Her gown fell to her hips, revealing her shift. He exhaled, awakening goose bumps along her exposed skin. Sighing, she closed her eyes, nestling against him, her silks caressing his chest too easily as he held her tight.

He caressed the soft skin of her back through her shift, moving slowly across her front to touch the sensitive hollow below her throat. While his mouth feathered kisses over her hair, he danced his fingertips across her cleavage, sliding his palms over the tender swells of her breasts. He stared at their reflected lovemaking, smiling when she shifted closer with each touch of his hands on her body, her ragged breaths all the encouragement he needed.

Valkin drew these sounds from her lips, fingers circling each nipple before lightly pinching the very tips. Without pausing his touch, he drew off her shift. Lifting his head briefly, he reached for the lavender oil. Returning to nuzzle her neck again, he tipped the oil over her shoulders, and the scented liquid ran slowly over her skin, between her breasts. He smoothed the oil over her supple flesh as his mouth moved to her jaw, her chin, tracing an achingly tender path down her glowing throat. His fingers moved lower, rubbing, soothing, easing away the last of her tension and fears. She shuddered as his knowing fingers brushed ever-so-lightly across her centre.

Shifting her thighs, she gasped again when he cupped her gently, stroking her soft folds. Her legs quivered until she had no choice but to lean backwards, allowing Valkin to support her fully, teasing her with sensual fingers, tasting her pulse with his lips. She almost fell against him, and he paused, smiling at her sweet cry of protest. Turning her to face him now, he pulled her close, groaning aloud as her breasts pressed softly against his chest.

Taking her mouth, he began a slow, soft exploration of her lower lip, filling his mouth with the taste of her. Arms around her, cupping her bottom, he kneaded the soft flesh of her lower back, pressing her closely against his own rigid heat, her hips shifting against his as he lifted her. He laid her down among the silken pillows and drew one tender breast into his mouth. He bit lightly, laving her with his tongue, bathing her sweetness with hot breath.

He nipped over her delicate skin until she whimpered with longing. He tongued her breast, teasing gentle kisses over her belly until she moaned, shifting into his hardness. He kissed around her navel, nipping it with his teeth, and she cried out, gasping with pleasure. She threaded her fingers through his hair, gripping hard as he lavished kisses over her thighs, his warm breath bathing her wetness as he moved closer, closer to her tight, ready core. When his mouth reached her centre, she came entirely apart.

"*Valkin*," she screamed, and all his remaining reason fled before a rising tide of white-hot desire. Her hands fisted in his hair as she cried out again. Twisting beneath the demands of his silken caress, she called his name over and over again, begging him never, ever to stop. She arched against his mouth, desperate for more. He stroked her breasts, smoothing the remains of the oil over hardened nipples and warm, round curves. His hard, questing fingers teased her skin as he pressed his mouth against her, as though her taste were life to him and the only thing that mattered was taking his fill.

She pulsed, hard, against his hungry mouth and he groaned, taking all of her into him, before sliding back up her body, holding her tightly as her release shivered through her in waves.

Valkin held her close, groaning when she wriggled closer, hiding herself inside his arms. She was quivering, pressing her lips to his neck, his collarbone, any and every part of him she could reach, pausing only when her tremors ceased.

"*Pireni*," Valkin murmured, lips beside her ear, voice tight with restraint. "Whatever *this* is, whatever is between us, this is *not* nothing."

CHAPTER TWENTY-TWO

Lydia

Lydia's eyes filled with tears. She shook again as Valkin held her, burrowing her face into his shoulder.

He leaned back, looking alarmed. "I did not mean to frighten you. I—"

"I'm not frightened." She gasped, her voice as unsteady as Valkin's breaths. Lydia touched his face. "I—I do not know what just happened. It is t-too good. For me, I mean. T-to feel like this. I-I didn't know."

He kissed her once before taking her hand again. "Do you still not understand? Do you truly not see yourself as I do? Magnificent. Desirable. Beautiful. I have shown you how the Romany make love. It cannot be too good for you. You are truly worthy of being loved the Romany way."

Lydia furrowed her brow. "But we did not—that is…" Despite the darkness, he must know she blushed. "You d-did not t-take me," she whispered, heat coiling deep within.

"*Apasavello,* remember? You gave me your trust, *pireni*. I will not break it." He kissed the inside of her wrist, then her palm. "In any case, Romany love is not about taking." He lifted her chin, gazing steadily into her eyes. "It is about giving. This is what I wish to show you."

"G-giving?" Her body relaxed. All her fears, all her tension distanced in this moment: forgotten in this breathless aftermath of swirled longing as she leaned into the delicious sensation of Valkin's large, warm body stretched beside her own. She trusted him to love her. A memory created in this single moment. *In this moment alone.*

Could one moment with this man be enough? Lydia wanted more, she wanted all of him. She wanted a memory to last the rest of her life. *I will have this.* She leaned towards him, smiling.

"You have never smiled at me like that before." Valkin kissed her too briefly, closing his eyes with a grunt as he drew back. "I do not know what you are up to, but you are not making it easy for me to return to *tan*." He sighed, shifting away to draw back the covers. "I must take my place on guard soon."

His voice had a tightness to it, the restraint she wished miles away. Lydia didn't want him withholding himself. She didn't want him to leave either, and she did not want to lose the incredible sensation of his skin touching hers. Grasping his hand, she drew him back, nestling her head into his chest, stroking his coarse, springy curls. He shuddered.

"I should not—" His breaths came harder, and Valkin grew very still, closing his eyes as his jaw tightened perceptibly. "What are you—" He didn't finish that sentence either.

Lydia continued stroking his chest, saw his control slipping, disappearing, receding to a distance beyond both of them. She couldn't recollect sensible thought at all. The only thing she knew was that she wanted Valkin, wanted to give him the warmth he'd shown her—and she wanted all of him.

"I shouldn't be doing this," he whispered as he cupped her breasts. Lydia groaned softly as he slid his chin over her hair, kissing her neck with warm, wet kisses and drawing forth shudders of pleasure from her body and whimpers of delight from her throat. She wriggled back against his chest, revelling in his deep groan.

"*Pireni, pireni,*" he murmured, sliding his tongue down the back of her neck. Lydia relished the quiver of her skin, the catch of his breath, passion rising between them as she lifted her head, turning her lips to his, opening to his urgent, seeking tongue. She slid a palm up to caress his face and deepened her kiss, tasting him, claiming him, losing herself entirely in the demanding fire between their mouths.

Then she straddled his hips, welcoming the demanding possession of his hot, ardent mouth, her hands behind his head, holding him to her, holding them together, building their desire to a fever.

He knelt up, removing his breeches before surging rapidly over her, pulling her down onto her back and catching her mouth once more. Her lips opened to him easily, her whole body pliant and yielding. His weight settled above her, surrounding her gently as she lay beneath the warm cradle of him, his hardness pressing eagerly against the softness of her centre, promising more, tempting her with moist, melting pleasure.

Lydia tensed at the size of him against her. Valkin paused, lifting his lips from hers. "*Pireni*, do you want me to stop?" His voice was a growl, each muscle beneath her hands tightening at his patient request. Lydia said nothing, lifting herself, rubbing her wetness against him. The very tip of his urgent, heavy heat slipped inside her. She moaned, waves of warmth shimmering through her until she cried out, shifting her hips. She thought he swore as he reached down, stroking her, caressing her, chanting a steady stream of Romany against her lips.

"Oh, oh," she whispered, slipping closer to his hardness, her pleasure. He pressed a little farther, sliding deeper, teasing her, teaching her, loving her as she cried her ecstatic response into his mouth. He kissed her neck, biting lightly, tonguing her with his passion, marking her with his love. Lydia gloried in the rippling pleasure from his knowing mouth, closing her eyes, giving herself up to the passionate sensation burning between them.

"Valkin," she whispered.

"*Miro pireni*," he murmured. "*Shan miro pireni cana*."

Her heart shook against his chest as the softest part of her surrounded his hardness. Something shifted, altering the depths of her soul. Her eyes opened as he stilled a moment, barely breathing above her. Valkin raised an unsteady palm to her cheek.

"*Pireni,*" he whispered. "Do you have any idea what you do to me?" A soft smile crept across her face. He groaned, sheathing himself completely, tilting her hips towards his, grinning at her cry of pleasure. Valkin moved slowly, deeply, powerfully, claiming her body with his passion and her soul with his tenderness. She cried out again, and he took her breath into him, joining with her more intimately than Lydia thought possible, his tongue echoing the rhythm of his body until he slowed, leaning in to kiss her, as though determined to give her all the pleasure she never knew she could have.

"No," she gasped as their rhythm changed. "Don't stop now. Please, Valkin, don't stop." Locking her knees around his hips, drawing herself up, she pressed him deeply into her. Shifting his weight, moving faster, his thrusts grew wild, savage—and her breaths came shallow, hard and fast, full of her cries, her screams, her rising tide of pleasure as he filled her completely, took her absolutely, loved her undeniably.

She trembled hard as he moved her to shatter against him again, and again and then once more, until it seemed Valkin could hold himself back no longer. All restraint gone, her king brought her to the edge, taking her with him as they cried out to each other, tumbling together in one final, pulsating rush.

***

Valkin

Valkin sighed, revelling in the warm weight nestling against his chest. *Reyna's going to kill me.* But Valkin couldn't bring himself to care. He stared down at his *gadje*, her arms lying across him as though he was all she wanted in this world. *God.* He wanted her still. Not again, he realised. *Still.* Never had he experienced anything like this intimate connection he felt down to his bones. It was as though he'd known her long before he'd met her.

"*Apasavello*," he whispered, rising to dress. He pressed his lips to her chestnut curls, heart hammering as he slipped out of the *covo*. There was no denying it. He was in love. In love with a woman whose name he didn't even know. He must find a way to protect her, and quickly. He'd need to trace this brother of hers. There were many Romany in France, and while his people did not traditionally travel over the sea, he could doubtless get a message to Paris.

Standing in place with the rest of the night patrol, his *gadje*'s taste on his tongue, Valkin hardly noticed the chill. All he could think of was returning to her side. After his shift, he jogged to his *covo* as though drawn by the scent of lavender oil. Looking in, Valkin tucked the bedclothes firmly around his *gadje* to keep the warmth in and stared around his home. His bedclothes lay strewn everywhere and silken cushions scattered across his floor. He flexed his shoulders, feeling the scratches she'd left in his back.

She'd said she trusted him, she believed in him. She'd spoken this in his language where words were timeless and not tossed about lightly. He wanted her with him. Here, now, from this moment on. He wanted her, always. Valkin quickened his pace to *kris* as though outrunning the jarring truth that loving his *gadje* was the easy part. Protecting her would not be simple, but there needed to be a way. She was his. *His.* The Romany took care of their own. Their friends. Their lovers. Their family...*family.* He'd find Wil as soon as *kris* completed, if he had to ride out and meet him on the road. *There must be a way.*

CHAPTER TWENTY-THREE

Lydia

Lydia couldn't remember having slept so soundly in her life before. What had Valkin said? *Like a Romany*. She gave herself no time to enjoy the memory of his warm, large body next to hers. She'd not the courage to face such regret. *Regret?* She didn't regret sharing Valkin's bed, nor did she regret gifting herself such reminiscence. *How could I?*

Valkin had shown her so much warmth. If only she could stay... Lydia shook her head, snapping to attention. Staying would bring trouble for Brishen. For Wil, Syeira, and so many of the Romany she loved. *Including Valkin.*

She arranged her linen and donned her riding habit, mindful of her newly torn flesh. Then she checked her swag. Swift, efficient, sensible activity that was necessary. That was required. *That is doing nothing to keep this ripping pain at bay.*

Her spirit shuddered as she stared around the *covo* for the final time, forcing herself to remember the shared moments in this place. The chessboard, the kettle, the pile of kindling stacked neatly beside the stove. Gazing finally at the bed, she sketched Valkin's slumbering shape in her mind's eye, recalling his mouth, the line of his jaw, the way his brow furrowed in sleep...the feel of his hair between her fingers, his lips moulded to hers, and his flesh buried deeply inside her, reshaping her understanding of pleasure, of love, of what she deserved.

"Oh." She gasped, closing her eyes a moment to keep the pain inside. *Remember this. Remember* him.

Taking a breath, she headed towards the dye tent to meet Reyna.

"I half-hoped you might change your mind, Miss Dale." Her friend handed her a warm drink, fussing with Lydia's travelling cloak and pulling it more firmly around her. "Chal awaits us behind the *gry* pens."

Lydia followed her to a clearing at the edge of the woods.

"*Sarishan*, Miss Dale." Chal held the mare by an old-fashioned bridle that looked recently cleaned. "I do not have your saddle, but I am willing to escort you to the coast if you wish it."

"Thank you, Chal, but I shall manage." Lydia drew her seal ring from her swag and turned to Reyna. "Will you accept this?"

Her friend shook her head. "I cannot, Miss Dale."

Shrugging, Lydia offered it to Chal. "Please, Chal. It m-may assist you at some m-moment in the future. I have little else to offer."

"Your choice to leave *ker* at this time is gift enough, Miss Dale." He fielded a dark look from his sister. "Um, that is, I mean, I do not *wish* you to go, but I believe it is best. Do you understand it?"

Pressing fingertips to her forehead, Lydia pushed away the sting of tears. "Of c-course. It is b-best for Brishen. I am sorry m-my presence here has caused trouble."

Chal bowed. "None of us would have you leave otherwise, Miss Dale." He leaned in, placing a kiss on her cheek, then cupped his palms to assist her mount.

With a shake of her head, Lydia finally managed a smile. "I am used to doing this alone now." She took advantage of a nearby log to mount herself astride. Drawing a parcel from her swag, Lydia slipped the ring into a fold of paper. Leaning down, she handed it to Chal.

"Please see this gets to your *krallis*."

Chal stared at her in surprise. "Of course."

"*Sarishan*, Miss Dale." Tears dampened Reyna's cheeks.

Lydia swallowed past the lump in her throat. Every part of her demanded she turn around and ride back to Valkin's arms. To safety, warmth, and love... *My safety is not Brishen's.*

Forcing a smile, she straightened her seat as Chal tied on her swag. "Which way?"

He pointed down the path. "A day's ride, if you take this path to Morecambe Bay. I ought to warn you—"

"Thank you." If she didn't turn away now, she'd lose all courage to leave. Digging her knees in to her mount's sides, Lydia shot forward abruptly. Nudging the mare into a canter, she focused on pounding hoofbeats as though the sound might drum this thudding heaviness from her heart.

***

Valkin

If kris *completes early, I'll visit the* covo *before Wil arrives.* Valkin was equally torn between wanting to spend time with his *pireni* among his family, and ignoring them all while shutting himself up with her for the rest of the day. He sighed, accepting more coffee from *Bebee* Cin and giving his attention to his cousins. Another of Chore's litters to distribute, and there were two disputes over bride prices.

By the time Valkin exited the *kris-tan*, his travelling family were already riding into *ker*. He headed towards the river, splashing water over his face and running wet fingers through his hair, determined to greet his people properly. He was anxious to find a few moments alone with Wil, but only Janfri and his family squinted into the winter sun as he rode up with his wife, Nan, and Fenella, their young daughter. Valkin assisted their dismount, smiling despite his impatience. He embraced his brother.

"What news? How were our races?"

Janfri grinned, shaking his head. "Always the first question you ask me, my *prala*, my brother. I am very well, thank you." He handed over a small ledger. "These are our takings."

Valkin glanced over the figures and frowned. "Not so good as last month. Is something amiss?"

"A new filly has the touts in a frenzy. Blitzed our young starters at *Boronashemeskrutan.*" Janfri sighed, beginning his full rundown on the derby and the journey to *ker.* "Have you seen Baker?"

"Thank you, I have. We've more to discuss on this. Did Besnik arrive with you?"

"They are setting up their *tan,*" Janfri replied. "*Bebee* Cin is organising the women."

"At her age?" Valkin scowled. "Does she require assistance?"

Janfri shook his head. "Chal's men are there."

Valkin's scowl became a glare. "Chal is not with his men?"

"His betrothed arrived with us. He is pleased to see her after so many weeks. I left Wil as chaperon, along with her brothers." Janfri grinned.

Valkin's glare fell away and he grinned back. Besnik was a house with many beautiful women, from which the men of Brishen were encouraged to find their brides. Valkin's brothers had done Brishen proud, not that they seem to have minded. He kissed Nan's cheek politely. Janfri pulled his wife close, kissing her more fervently on her mouth. She was heavily pregnant with their second child.

A tug at his knee caused Valkin to look down. Fenella peered shyly up at him. Valkin grinned and bent down before lifting her high into the air. She squealed and giggled, her dark eyes full of laughter.

"And how is little Fenella? I believe you are taller than the last time we met." He kissed her chubby little cheek and handed her back to her father, who tucked the child neatly into the crook of his arm.

"She gets prettier every day, just like her mama." Valkin bowed his head at Nan's blush. Janfri was a lucky man. He resisted the urge to tell his brother he'd soon share in such happiness. There was much to discuss beforehand, and with Wil Brishen as well. Valkin ran his hand through his hair.

"You are pale, my *prala*, my brother." Janfri shifted his daughter to his other arm. "And you look tired. Are you not sleeping?"

"It is nothing, Janfri. I'm glad you've come back." Memories from last night whirled through his mind. Valkin looked forward to creating more. *There must be a way.* "Did you say Wil was chaperoning Chal?"

"They're this way." Janfri changed direction towards the fireside. "Wil is keen for you to make a new acquaintance."

Valkin caught his brother up. He was just as keen to meet his brand-new niece and to consult the Consort to the Princess Brishen.

"We met up with them about a day ago," Janfri explained. "It's been slow going. The *muscros* are stopping everyone on the road. Something about a missing girl. They're being very close about it." He shook his head, frowning deeply. "Have you heard anything?"

Valkin looked away, shrugging, and Janfri stopped mid-stride to lay a hand on his sleeve.

"You do know something. I thought so." He looked carefully around, lowering his voice. "I heard a rumour about you and a—a *gadje* mistress. I did not believe it, but Chal didn't meet my eyes when I asked him, and now you—"

"I need to speak with Wil." Valkin strode away so his brother wouldn't accompany him. The concerned look on his face was too much to bear.

Syeira and Wil stood in the midst of a crowd of admiring onlookers while three small children capered round their feet. Valkin nodded to Chal, who hardly noticed him, so engrossed was he by the curvaceous girl resting her head on his shoulder.

"Wil." He near-shouted with relief as he offered his hand. He hugged Wil hard then clasped his sister fondly around her waist. When Syeira recovered from the enthusiasm of his greeting, she handed him the bundle she'd cradled against her, smiling proudly down at her week-old daughter.

"She is anxious to meet her uncle."

The babe in his arms was fairer by far than Wil and Syeira's other children, who seemed to take rather more after their Romany mother than their English father. Valkin stroked the sleeping child's tiny pink cheek. She opened her eyes, staring up at him.

Valkin caught his breath. He looked into wide eyes that seemed somehow familiar, as if he stared into a future from which he may forever be debarred. Struggling with a sharp pricking behind his eyes, he looked away, over the crowd until he found the roof of his *covo*. He swallowed and something warmly solid slid down his throat, taking up residence behind his rib cage. It felt like resolve.

"Valkin?" Syeira recalled his attention, looking from him to her child, then holding out her arms as though he'd been ignoring her for several moments.

"I beg your pardon." He smiled with an effort, thrusting the child back at her. "She is beautiful. What shall we call her?" He finally remembered his duty, his position, his awareness that many Romany eyes were upon him.

"We wish you to name her," Syeira announced to the crowd. "When you perform the ceremony." She smiled at Wil, who grinned at Valkin.

"Do you approve, *sher-engro*?" Wil asked in Romany. "We would be very much obliged."

Valkin stared at them, stunned. Selecting a child's name was usually the province of the parents. Occasionally it was an honour bestowed on the *sher-engro* when the couple formally requested it in front of witnesses. It was said to bring luck to the *sher-engro*'s own family. A bemused smile creased his face. Only Syeira could offer so subtle a hint. The resolution forming within firmed. *My family...* He sobered as his thoughts returned to his *covo*, his *gadje*. *I will find a way.*

"*Sher-engro*? You will do this for us?" Wil prompted.

"I will," he murmured, shaking Wil's hand again. "I'd be glad of a word, my *prala,* my brother, as soon as may be."

Wil looked at him in surprise. Nodding, he made to step aside, but Chal and Janfri caught them up, insisting on discussing the recent turf news. Shrugging, Wil fell in with his other brothers.

It was back to business, and the tension never left Valkin alone.

CHAPTER TWENTY-FOUR

Valkin

Valkin waited by Wil's *covo* with no small show of impatience for the news and chat to quiet. Wil shot several curious glances towards him, and Janfri looked downright disturbed. The *sher-engro* usually led these conversations. Valkin had been entirely silent.

"We were stopped by the *muscro* too," Janfri said to Wil. "Chal tells me they came right into *ker*."

"It is so." Valkin did not meet his brothers' gazes—especially Janfri's.

"Did they question Besnik about the missing girl?" Wil wanted to know.

Janfri nodded, his focus on Valkin. "You've heard the rumours?"

Wil snorted. "Indeed, my *prala*, my brother, I've heard many. The stories about the charming *krallis* and the English ladies grow wilder every Season."

"This story says she is a girl from the ton," Janfri added.

Wil laughed out loud. "Ha. A girl from the ton, mistress to the Lord Brishen? Impossible." He spoke in jest but frowned at Valkin's glare. "I beg your pardon, *sher-engro*."

"Is your sister out this Season?" Janfri spoke into the confusing silence between the two men, as work and conversation went on around them.

Wil shrugged. "Last Season, I believe. I've not heard from the Hall in some time, and their world is such a long way from my own these days. Since the peace, Roger spends so long on the continent he begins to sound like a Frenchman."

Valkin stared at the notes from recent race meets without comprehending the details. He watched Wil smile and look to Syeira. Not that he ever focused very long on anything else. The Romany princess looked up, smiling back at her husband. The way Wil and Syeira looked at each other was beautiful. After eight years and four children, they still enjoyed each other in a way that Valkin had always envied, until today. The thought burned through him, his gaze shifting over tented dwellings, family activities, and parked *covos*, resting only when he beheld the roof of his own home. His home that housed such love he could hardly bear the distance between himself and her, though it wasn't far. *I will find a way.*

He cleared his throat, avoiding the looks of all present except Wil. "Wil? A word, if you please."

Before he could respond, Cato came panting up. "*Sher-engro, sher-engro.*" He leaned up against Wil's *covo*, bent double. When he raised his head, his eyes were wide, afraid. "The English mare—she is gone."

"How have we gained an English mare?" Wil cocked a brow.

"Gone?" Valkin froze. "Chal?"

"The mare is gone with the *gadje*." Chal stared at his boots. "She did what you could not, *sher-engro.*"

Dimly aware of his clenched fists, Valkin levelled his voice, which was more than could be said for his temper. "You let her leave." He slammed his fist into his other palm. "*Alone.*"

"Chal did not *let her leave.*" Reyna arrived behind Cato. "Your *gadje* refused his escort. She *asked* us to help her go."

"She asked you...?" Valkin's anger faded like a blown flame, pain behind his rib cage twisting cruelly. A sound took his ears, a rushing wind or water, as though he dived a river too deeply, or rode too fast into a steep ravine. He stared at Reyna.

"Th-this is truly her choice?"

Reyna nodded, avoiding his eyes but his sister did not lie. "I am truly sorry, my brother, my *prala*." Her voice shook.

Valkin swayed where he stood, clasping a tree bough, barely aware of the people and noise surrounding him. *She can't be gone.*

"She didn't say good-bye," he whispered, and only Reyna heard him.

"She wished you to have this." Reyna indicated the parcel. "Well, this and her stays."

Valkin hardly heard her. Going after the girl seemed pointless and yet... *I must find a way.* Grabbing up the package, he wrenched the wrappings apart, revealing a sketch, and a note:

Valkin,

Please do not fall out with Chal and Reyna over their assistance. I am determined to go, with or without aid. I enclose my seal ring as proof of the full truth of all of it. I beg your pardon for deceiving you.

    You knew my true name long ago, so you will understand why I cannot remain with Brishen. The duke's indifference will not outlast the earl's rage. I'll not endanger Brishen further. I could not forgive myself if anything happened to your family, or Wil's, because of my connections.

    This poor sketch is my gift to you. No trade is needed because Brishen have already given me so much: you, most of all, Valkin. I thank you for your trouble, and for keeping me safe these many days.

    You have gifted me a warm memory to carry over the sea. Do not concern yourself further regarding my journey. I am quite able to manage.

Lydia

Lydia?

Her handling of her pistol, her chess play, her strategic mind—all spoke of a girl from a military family. Valkin shook his head, refusing to believe the certainty of truth breaking over him. She knew him too well. *She* knew *him*, and the image of her at twelve years old came easily. They'd been acquainted at Clifton Hall. Not very well, not nearly as intimately as he knew her now: as a woman, as his lover, as his *pireni*.

Valkin's gut lurched. *I thank you for your trouble...* as though he'd performed a service and loving her had been a chore. The memory of last night throbbed beneath his ribs. She'd tricked him, used his desire against him in order to leave. Bile rose in his throat as the precious paper slipped from his hands. He barely saw the silver object tumbling out. Janfri caught it, squinting at the seal.

"Is this not the duchess of Carston's mark?" Janfri handed it to Wil.

Wil studied the ring, then levelled a deadly glare at Valkin. "What is my sister's seal ring doing here?"

Valkin stared at Wil, stricken. She'd learned chess from her brother, she said. *Her brother.* Lord Major Roger Clifton, one of the heroes of Waterloo. *Brothers*, there were two, of course: two Clifton brothers. Roger Clifton and—

"Wil, no—"

Valkin swivelled his head as Syeira called out.

Wil. God. Shock slammed into him, shock and—

Pain exploded against his face. He glimpsed furious green eyes before crashing to the ground as Wil Brishen struck him full on the jaw.

***

When Valkin opened his eyes, Sacki stood over him with a stick, warning the others to give the royal family a wide berth. Someone—it could only be Syeira—pressed a cool green compress to his jawbone. She glared furiously at Wil, speaking at top speed about the stupidity of men and the foolishness of her husband and brothers in particular. Valkin blinked up at her and silently agreed. Gingerly, he flexed his jaw, wincing. He was better off keeping his mouth shut. Syeira must have felt him move because she looked down and said something similar, if more colourful.

His brothers fought to hold Wil back, the consort scrambling to get closer to the *krallis* at the same time as several of Chal's men pushed their way through the crowd, sticks and rifles in hand.

"Chal. Ah." The men on guard called out to their patrol leader, Valkin's cousins shouting loudly at each other in Romany. Adopted man of Brishen or not, and despite his status as Consort to the Princess Syeira, Wil had just assaulted the *krallis*. The Romany were not inclined to let such insult stand.

Reyna stood silently by, shaking her head at the lot of them. She held the new baby close, prudently gathering all her nieces and nephews out of the danger zone, as far from the pungent phrases and graphic language of her brothers as possible. She shot Syeira an exasperated look before noticing Valkin.

He caught her gaze and sat up with an effort. Waving Syeira's hand away, he took her poultice and held it against his face. Sacki offered him a hand and Valkin accepted, rising slowly to his feet. He took a deep breath.

"*Dosta,*" he shouted, his voice slightly hoarse. *Enough.*

Quiet fell over *ker* as some of the men turned, staring in confusion. Chal directed urgent words towards Wil in a muttering undertone. Wil's eyes widened as he stared at Chal, listening intently. Training his glare on Valkin, accusation blended with simmering anger, but Wil seemed to have mastered himself.

Valkin addressed Chal, moderating his tone with an effort. "She left while I was at *kris*?"

He nodded. "She mounted without any help from me and rode off as fast as she could."

"Where?" Wil broke in.

"She's taken the shortest path to Morecambe Bay," Reyna replied.

"Does she know about the tides?" Syeira asked, but Valkin was already racing to the *gry* pens by the time the others caught him up.

The bay's tidal flats were treacherous at the best of times, but in winter, with poor light and an uncertain rider? The tides came in faster than a Romany horse could run, and if a horse became trapped by quicksands, there was nothing anyone could do to prevent the most appalling catastrophe.

"Steeplechase through the darkest part of Bowland." Valkin eyed the late afternoon sun. "We may outride her by dusk." He spoke with confidence, but horror and dismay condensed inside him. For the first time in his life, Valkin knew a fear that froze him to the depths of his soul.

CHAPTER TWENTY-FIVE

Lydia

Lydia leaned forward, petting her mare. "Good girl," she murmured, receiving a subdued whinny in response.

Tugging the animal's mane, she spurred her little horse onwards, glancing down at the smooth sands of the bay. Despite the looming dark, her mare could manage a clear run across the narrow beach and she'd save time. She may reach Morecambe village in time for a light meal. Her stomach grumbled, and Lydia made up her mind, directing her mount towards the beachward path. She'd put up at the nearest inn tonight and inquire for passage to France at first light. Blinking hard, she tugged firmly on the reins, hardly noticing when her horse's hoofbeats became soft splashing.

The distance to the village seemed more than twice that of her ride out. Lydia stared in horror at the encroaching tide, moonlight glinting cruelly as rising waters swirled across her mare's fetlocks. In a few moments they'd be completely cut off, and she'd not survive this freezing water. Jerking tightly on the reins, Lydia brought the mare to a complete halt. The horse tossed her head and snorted, throwing up plenty of spray as the little thoroughbred continued stamping and trying to walk on. Lydia turned into the fading light, first one way, then the other, staring wildly from the dark path behind her to the twinkling lights of the village in front. In the darkness, rushing waters soaked her horse's frame, drawing frightened whinnies that matched the terrified echoes of her own heartbeat.

Her throat closed as the water kept rising. With mere seconds to make her decision, she'd no idea which shoreline was nearest. Sea spray doused her face as a large wave rolled in, crashing against the mare, and sending the horse into a spasm of frightened pawing. Lydia grabbed desperately for the reins, but it was no use. The terrified animal stamped and snorted, tossing her head. Lydia gripped the mane as best she could, but she started to slip from her seat, screaming as wave after wave rolled in, goading her poor mare to increasing frenzy.

In the distance—she wasn't certain which direction now—a light burned steady. A shout came over the waves, a man calling words she couldn't make out, but the mare took a wild step towards his voice. It seemed their only chance. Bending low over the animal's neck, Lydia stuck her fingers under the crownpiece and squeezed with her knees. The horse reared as wilder waves rolled in, now three-fourths of the way up the mare's legs.

Lydia coaxed her mount towards the light, refusing to look down at the rising waters. She struggled to breathe, her lungs constricting with panic and sheer, cold terror. If she fell, if they didn't make the shore, this would be the end of her. She forced herself to breathe, to keep moving, the leather bridle biting deep into her fingers. Her legs grew numb as icy sea spray swirled over her, the tide rushing in with lethal speed. She leaned forward, tears spilling over her cheeks to mix with the salt spray all around her until she thought the sea must be crying too.

They weren't going to make it. Already the mare slowed through the surging waters. Soon she'd be swallowed up by the sea and they were too far from shore.

"It'll be over soon," she whispered with an absurd sense of relief, but she cried harder. Cried for herself and the brothers she'd never see again. For Valkin and all that he meant to her. She closed her eyes as the chilly water dampened her skirts and didn't bother drawing up her legs, head dropping onto her horse's neck in despair. *At least I'm free of the earl.*

Freezing sea water splashed deliberately into her face. Lydia jerked her head up as a man's large hand slipped under her mare's cheekpiece, turning the animal at right angles to the disappearing beach.

"Listen to me, Lydia," Valkin commanded, his voice unerringly calm as he pulled her mare in close. "Turn your horse and follow me." He bent to the mare, whispering soothing words into the horse's ears. The frightened animal calmed slightly beneath her. In the freezing darkness and fear, a slow warmth took hold.

He'd come after her. Valkin knew who she was, and he'd still come to make sure she was safe. A bead of hope formed, and Lydia drew strength from this. Allowing Valkin to lead them closer to the vanished shoreline, she saw the wisdom of doing so. Shallower water meant her horse moved more freely, but there was little time. Valkin turned them again towards the distant light.

"Do you see it, *pireni*?" he said in that calm, low voice. "We are on a sandbar, but it won't last long. Go now, as fast as you can towards Wil's lantern." Gripping her arm, he pressed the reins into her shivering hands. "Do you understand?"

Lydia didn't move. "What about you?"

"The sandbar may not hold. Go now. I will follow you." His voice had lost its calm. "This is no time for your stubbornness," he said through clenched teeth. "*Go.*"

Lydia dug her heels into her mare's flanks and the animal rushed forward. "I love you," she whispered, glancing back. "*Apasavallo.*"

With hooves flying and waves rushing in all around her, Lydia forced her little horse forwards. Freezing water flooded over her legs. She'd hardly the strength to reach the shore. Looking back towards the sea, all was black as pitch. The wind screeched round her until she couldn't tell wild wind from human voice. Tears flowed afresh as she prayed Valkin was right at her back. Had he heard her say she loved him?

Shaking her head, she carried on, taking as deep a breath as she was able. The ice-cold air in her lungs braced her. Summoning every ounce of courage she possessed, Lydia urged her little horse to one final try.

"*Go.*"

The mare hurled herself towards the embankment. As the horse reached the safety of the lantern-bearer, someone tore Lydia's frozen fingers loose from the bridle and she fell, finally, caught up in strong arms.

"Lydie?"

Wil...

Shouts carried on the wind from a commotion by the shifting shoreline. Struggling to pull herself free of Wil's cloak, Lydia faced him.

"W-what is it?" she asked through chattering teeth.

"Valkin's come off his horse." Wil stared worriedly towards the other men as he set her on her feet. "His brothers will find him. Lydie, come back here." He draped a blanket over her shoulders as she wrapped her arms around herself and started towards the beach.

"*Lydia.*" Wil's shout hardly gave her pause. "The sands are unstable."

"I need to know he's safe." She couldn't explain but held out a hand to her brother.

Wil clasped it firmly in his, guiding her towards the little knot of men. They halted as the group turned back towards the woods, Valkin leaning heavily between Chal and Janfri. Dela led a soaking, snorting Bavol close behind. Wil called to them in Romany.

"He has a head wound but he's conscious," he reported. "He'll be all right, Lydia. Now, *please* will you return with me?"

Lydia nodded, hesitating at the top of the embankment until the others caught them up. Valkin's eyes were open, but his stare was glassy, and paleness bit into drawn cheeks. A vicious bruise bloodied his temple. Once within the wood, they mounted their horses. Wil lifted her up before mounting behind her.

Lydia opened her mouth to object, but soon saw Janfri performed the same service for Valkin. Chal took charge of Bavol and assigned one of his men to walk the English mare back along the forest path.

"Thank you," she said, grateful for Wil's firm presence at her back. She feared she'd fall from weariness before reaching the camp. Her brother held her upright until their party dismounted at the western boundary. Syeira and Reyna awaited them beside a brazier. They handed round hot tea and many helpings of *levinor* before Syeira took charge of the *krallis*.

Lydia's legs shivered beneath her waterlogged skirts, but she shook her head at the proffered cup, struggling to catch up to Valkin.

"Lydia, no. Leave him be," Wil called in alarm, grabbing his tea. He caught her arm and placed the hot drink into her hand. "Get warm." He tugged at her until she had to stop or fall over.

She wasn't at all steady. "Wil, I—" She stopped, clutching his arm for balance. "I m-must h-help. P-please." She sipped her tea, staring at her brother. "I must."

"Syeira will know what to do," Wil replied, but he walked beside her to Valkin's *covo* and knocked lightly. Janfri opened the door.

"May I see him?"

Janfri hesitated and Lydia didn't miss the assessing glance passing between Valkin's brother and her own. Shaking her head at both men, she made a noise in her throat and ducked beneath Janfri's arm.

"For Heaven's sake," she muttered, falling silent at the sight of Valkin lying so still. His eyes remained closed as Syeira bathed the cut at the side of his head with hot water and spirits.

"H-how is he?" Lydia whispered.

Syeira glanced up briefly. "*Sarishan*, Lydie. It is a deep cut, but he will heal. He is mostly worn out and too cold from the seawater. I have given him my strongest poppy tea. This is why he sleeps." She placed a poultice against the gash at her brother's temple. "When the bleeding slows, I will pack his wound."

Lydia took up the linen cloth. "May I assist?"

"If you wish it."

Beside her, Wil cleared his throat as though he wished to speak. A glance from his princess kept him silent. Though her limbs shook with cold, Lydia wrapped the bandage tight enough to hold the poultice in place. Valkin's breathing grew more relaxed and regular.

"He'll not wake tonight, Lydie." Syeira watched Lydia attempt to ready more tea, shaking Wil off as he offered another blanket.

"I can manage alone," she told him, but her legs were weaker than her arms and her feet were too warm and cold again by turns. Struggling in vain to remain upright, Lydia collapsed into a chair with a cry.

"It is from the cold water," Syeira explained. "You are not fit for anything but rest now. It's but a few hours to dawn. I will stay with Valkin. Wil will stay with you. You will please *rest*." Her expression brooked no argument. *Stubbornness is not unique to the Cliftons.*

Lydia sighed, slumping in her seat. "When your Brishen guard first found me, he—V-valkin—sat with m-me most of m-my first night here," she mumbled. "I wanted to—that is, he was so kind. You are all so kind." She inched uncertain fingers towards Valkin's.

"We are your family, Lydie." Syeira rested a gentle hand on Lydia's shoulder. "Kindness is not the word. We look after each other. This is what families are for."

Lydia flinched as though her words were cursed. She hardly dared look at Wil, but this didn't dampen her resolve.

"I will sit with him," she repeated.

"For a while, if you insist." Syeira shrugged, addressing Wil. "The stove is lit and the *covo* is warm enough. I must see to our children, in any case."

***

Lydia had no clue what the hour was when Wil shook her gently awake.

"Lydia," he whispered. "Lydie, come to our *covo* now. There's no more you can do here, my sister, my *pen*."

Raising her head, she wriggled her shoulders, glancing blearily around. The sight of Valkin slumbering nearby was enough to shake her head at Wil.

"I shall remain here."

"You need rest and looking after," he persisted.

"I've managed well enough so far." Lydia sat up properly and opened a drawer to find her notebook. Getting to her feet, she measured a powder into the relief tea, according to the receipts she'd recorded. When she'd set the tea to steep and checked Valkin's dressings, she resumed her seat, laying a pillow on the little table and placing her head upon it.

"Do you see? I am resting," she said, closing her eyes.

"Lydia."

She opened one eye and peered at him. "If you insist upon it, Wil, you might find another blanket." She looked at Valkin. "I'll not leave him."

"Lydie, what is this all about?" Wil's tone tightened, and Lydia recognised his fear for the first time. He located the blankets and wrapped another over her shoulders.

She sighed, more weary than she'd been in her life before. "Family, Wil. This is about family." She tried offering a smile. Her lips were too tired to turn upward. "G'night," she mumbled, threading her fingers through Valkin's.

CHAPTER TWENTY-SIX

Lydia

Tiny needles of heat plunged alternately into Lydia's skin and withdrew. It was something like falling in love, and she formed a smile. Murmuring sounded nearby. Something herbal scented the air and she smiled again, dreaming she was back in Valkin's home. Warm. Safe. His blankets wrapped round her like his arms, his hands, his voice in her ear calling her his *pireni*. A dream and nothing more, because her eyes were closed. Something warm and wet moved over her brow. She remembered the water, the night, the freezing wind. The terrified whinnies of her little horse. Crying out, she jerked awake—and fell onto a wooden floor.

Ouf.

"Lydie." Wil was beside her in an instant, lifting her up and placing her firmly back into her seat. The memory seemed so far away, and she was so tired. Surely Wil's voice would go away and let her dream.

"Lydia."

She blinked her eyes to focus on Wil's pale, anxious features and stared mutely for a moment before her throat seized and bitter, scalding tears spilled over.

"Oh Wil, how I've missed you," she whispered, surprised at the croak that was her voice. Her shoulders shook as Wil hugged her tight. She thought his shoulders shook too. Wiping her eyes, she pulled away and stood, ignoring his protests. She checked her notes and peered beneath Valkin's bandage. "His swelling reduces. Fetch Syeira."

"In a moment." Her brother shook his head, attempting to wrap her in yet more blankets and plant a kiss on her hair. "Please, Lydie, you must not risk yourself further."

"Wil—"

Before Lydia could argue her point, Syeira opened the door, her new daughter in her arms. Smiling, Wil continued addressing Lydia.

"I've written to Roger in France, and to Sir Geoffrey in London. I'll have the latter's reply just as soon as Sacki can bring it. You do know Sir Geoffrey?"

Lydia furrowed her brow, trying to remember. "Has he been to the Hall at all?" A dim memory surfaced as Wil nodded. She recalled a portly figure, closeted for some time with her brothers in the Hall library. Once, when Roger attained majority, and again when Wil came of age. "Is he—uh—a large man?"

Wil laughed. "He is. He was also Mama's lawyer. He may be able to assist us."

"Will he not feel the need to protect the duke's interests?" Syeira squeezed Lydia's hand reassuringly.

"Mama and the duke had separate counsel." Wil exchanged a thoroughly Clifton-esque expression with Lydia, full of shared pain and embarrassment. The duchess's humiliations at the duke's hands were an open secret.

Wil cleared his throat. "In any case, Mama was the Baroness Bristol in her own right before she wed His Grace. That estate is created in succession only of our maternal grandfather's line. The baronetcy has been divested by Sir Geoffrey's people for generations. I take it you've not met with Sir Geoffrey lately, Lydie?"

Lydia shook her head and Wil let out a breath.

"I beg your pardon, Wil. I do not understand what difference his information may make."

"You've nothing to apologise for." Wil sounded both frustrated and angry. "The duke ought to have seen to your meeting as soon as you came out. The culpability here is his. And Roger's. And my own, as well." He spoke with a self-disgust she could not bear.

"Please, Wil. This is not your fault. Your Romany are barred from the duchy, and you have your family to consider. A wonderful new life with Syeira—"

"I have *you too*." Wil went on doggedly and Syeira nodded. "You are my family, and we will sort this mess out together." He gave her a determined look that silenced further protest. His silence stretched, like tree-hung silk. Wil stood, pacing uncomfortably to the opposite end of the caravan and back. He looked unhappily towards his wife.

Syeira clicked her tongue impatiently before seating herself on the bed beside Lydia.

"Lydie," she said softly. "I understand you stayed with Valkin?" Her cheeks blushed a dark rose as Wil sat down on his chair, grasping an empty cup as though it were best he employ his hands away from anyone's throat.

Lydia braved the scorching heat in her cheeks, forcing herself to stare into Syeira's face—and nothing but unaffected concern came her way. Syeira flicked a glance at Wil, speaking a few words in rapid Romany. Wil nodded, leaving so quickly he nearly stirred a breeze. Syeira smiled at Lydia again, chuckling softly.

"Sometimes your brother forgets he is Romany now." Clasping Lydia's hands in her own, she spoke briskly. "You must understand, Lydie. These things are not the same as you are used to. Romany girls receive instruction about this sort of thing when we come of age. At thirteen we are taught *camello*, or lovemaking, as you would learn pianoforte. It is all theory of course. It is to prepare us for marriage." Syeira nodded at Lydia. "The subject is not an embarrassment for Romany women. Although—" Syeira looked at her solemnly. "It is not one to be taken lightly either. Now, how long were you with Valkin?"

Determined not to look away, Lydia held her gaze. "I was w-with h-him only the last n-night," she replied stiffly. "He stayed in h-his tent m-most of the time. He was v-very kind."

Syeira nodded. "Only the one night. I see." She swallowed. "Are you aware that a woman who stays the night with a Romany man in his home is considered his wife?"

Lydia's heart slammed into her rib cage so hard she'd surely bruise. For one dizzying moment, happiness flooded through her. Then air constricted in her lungs, the colours of painted wooden carvings swirling oddly before her eyes. She choked on nothing. *Wife?*

"Syeira, this c-can't be right. I c-cannot b-be Valkin's w-wife. I am sure he did not intend it—" Lydia shook her head vehemently, barely breathing. Syeira let go of Lydia's hands and drew her palms together, nodding as Lydia followed her lead. Closing her eyes, she drew three breaths in, three out, her heart rate steadying and her nerves settling. She opened her eyes as Syeira continued.

"What transpires in that time is irrelevant. The *camello* is assumed. It is not an English law," Syeira hastened to explain, eyeing Lydia closely. "But this is the Romany way. And Valkin is our *krallis*."

"He is a good leader, and a good man," Lydia replied quietly, glancing at the unconscious *krallis*. Truly, Valkin Brishen was the best man she'd ever known, and he'd told her what he wanted in his marriage. *I seek a certain kind of love...* She finally understood. He didn't wish to marry someone he did not love, but what had Syeira said? *This is the Romany way.* So Valkin was surely aware of it.

"Does this apply to m-me? I mean, a *gadje* woman?"

Syeira shrugged, her brow furrowing. "There is no tradition for a *gadje* woman staying the night in a Romany man's home," she acknowledged. "Such a thing does not happen often." Looking carefully at Lydia again, she was silent for a long moment. "You do not wish to stay with us?"

Lydia didn't answer. How could she explain that she wanted this more than anything, but had no wish to trap the *krallis* into an arrangement he must despise? She was the one who instigated the loss of her innocence. Who'd wanted to give of herself so badly that she'd begged him to— But how could Valkin have allowed her— How could he have allowed *himself*? Lydia shut her thoughts off in a hurry as colour flooded her cheeks.

Syeira repeated her inquiry, studying Lydia with the same patient gaze she gave her young children. Unable to stop her eyes filling with tears, Lydia sat very still.

"I do not know," she said finally. *I do know Valkin deserves to marry for love.*

Syeira handed her another cup of tea and sighed.

Lydia sipped her drink in fraught silence. "Is Wil very angry with me for—for what I did?"

Syeira raised her eyebrows. "He is angry with himself for failing to protect you properly." Her baby cried out in sleep and Syeira rocked her gently before continuing. "You did what was necessary to safeguard yourself, Lydia. There is nothing you need to apologise for in that."

"I do not mean my running away," Lydia whispered. "I mean Valkin."

Syeira settled her child in Lydia's arms. "I think he is angrier with Valkin," she replied at last. "And he does not understand it." She took up the kettle, studying Lydia as though she didn't fully understand her motivations either. Their silence seemed to grow louder.

"What does '*pireni*' mean?" Lydia looked down at her tea.

Syeira refilled their cups. "Where did you hear that?"

"It is what Valkin calls me. He didn't believe my name was Martha."

"I'm not surprised. You do not look like a Martha." Syeira smiled gently. "Valkin called you *pireni*? You're certain?"

Nodding grimly, Lydia met the princess's gaze with a shudder. "Is it not the Romany word for m-mistress? Like the French, you know, *maîtresse*?"

Syeira laughed, sobering at Lydia's frown. "I beg your pardon. You should know that there is no Romany word for mistress. *Pireni* is our word for 'sweetheart.' A betrothal endearment." She squeezed Lydia's hand and kissed her cheek. "Finish your tea. I shall speak with Valkin when he wakes."

"May I assist in his care? I will beg if you insist upon it, Syeira."

"Begging is unnecessary. Wil always said you were a determined girl. You will return to our *covo* with the babe. Rest there while I gather the herbs for my paste to mend the skin. Perhaps you'd ask Narilla to fetch my children their dinner?"

"But—"

Syeira raised her hand. "I give you my word I shall fetch you the moment my herbs are ready. Will you find your brother and my sister?"

Lydia sighed, already feeling the effects of the tea in her limbs. She nodded, leaving Valkin to Syeira's care.

CHAPTER TWENTY-SEVEN

Valkin

Valkin woke feeling like the very devil. He hated the weakness in his arms and legs, the pounding at his temples. Reyna piled on another blanket because he couldn't stop shivering. He was in no mood for Syeira's fierce glare as she entered his *covo* with food for them all.

"In polished society, it's considered polite to knock," he joked weakly through chattering teeth. "Is Bavol all right?"

"Knock?" Syeira retorted, nodding to Reyna. "You are lucky I do not let Wil call you out again, my *prala*, my brother. Your horse will recover." She frowned at Valkin before smiling at Reyna. "You are becoming so accomplished, my sister, my *pen*, soon you will have no need of me."

Reyna blushed with pleasure but stood anxiously by until Syeira concluded her examination.

Valkin had to ask. "Reyna says Lydia is resting, but how is she?"

"Like you, she is very cold," Syeira replied, more gently. "She would take no rest until she'd seen you out of danger."

"She is stubborn."

"Hmmm," Syeira agreed. "Wil calls it determination." She examined him for signs of fever and frostbite as Reyna added more wood to the stove. "You are aware that half our *ker* regards her as your wife?"

Do they indeed? Valkin knew this Romany tradition, of course: another of the many reasons why he'd not taken a woman to his *covo*. Even his arrogance didn't extend to insolence. No doubt both sisters held expectations of him leaping from the bedclothes and making straight for the door. That was before he fell in love, wondering daily whether the woman he desired loved him back.

"I will not make assumptions on Lydia's behalf," he replied finally. "Not even to placate her brother." Diffidence was no poor part of a man's character, after all.

"Our Romany traditions make no provision for *gadjes*, as you know," Reyna said, unexpectedly supporting him. She handed him a green leaf to chew.

Valkin waited a few moments with his eyes shut tight. As his headache receded, he opened his eyes, favouring both of them with his firmest glare.

"Despite appearances to the contrary, I am aware of my duty and of my responsibilities." He took another breath. "There can be no talk of marriage until we are certain of Lydia's own position."

"And if she is free to wed?" Syeira persisted.

Valkin's discomfort increased under the combined gaze of two pairs of fierce feminine eyes. Clearly, Syeira and Reyna knew what they thought he should do. He wished one of his brothers were present. He was outnumbered and out-glared.

"I will not make myself into another trap she is forced into. You may tell Wil it is so."

"What, pray, is she to do if you do not marry her, Valkin?" Syeira asked baldly. "She cannot return to the ton. No Englishman will have her now, should one dare to gainsay the duke."

Resisting the urge to raise his chin, Valkin remained adamant. "Lydia must make her own choice."

"If she stays with us—" Syeira raised her hand to cut off his insistent demand. "—which I have every intention of requesting she shall, Lydie cannot hope to find a husband among the Romany. You know this." She stared levelly at Valkin, her face stern.

He nodded slowly. "I know this."

"Then why—?" Syeira snapped in exasperation. "Why in the name of all that is holy did you—do what you did?"

"*Mi Dubblesky*," Reyna broke in. "Syeira, look at him. Can you not see?"

Valkin bit back an epithet as Syeira studied him anew.

"Our brother looks terrible," she agreed, smiling. "*Kosko*. Good." Kissing him on the cheek, she shrugged at Reyna. "Wil will be pleased."

"Thank him for me," Valkin replied drily. His pride may have taken a battering in recent days, but it was still *there*, damn it. Despite himself, he smiled back at his sisters. "Thank you both for your healing. Can you find Chal or Janfri? I want to know about my horses."

"They will attend you here after the hunt. Now, you must rest." The sharp lines around Reyna's mouth told Valkin he'd better not argue. He sank back into his pillows and let it pass. He was exhausted in any case, his limbs shaking. Sisters, he decided, were a special kind of torture.

***

Lydia

Lydia knocked quietly on Valkin's *covo* door, flanked by Syeira and Wil. The flanking was unnecessary, in Lydia's opinion. She was here to treat Valkin's head wound, not indulge in wild nights of passion. Chal answered the door.

"How is your *sher-engro?*"

Chal stood back to allow their party entry. He offered Lydia a small smile, which she managed to return.

"His temper is evidence enough he's well." He opened the door wider to admit Janfri.

"I heard that." Though Valkin's irritation was obvious, Syeira snorted.

Lydia checked her elation. The firm looks from Valkin's brothers were enough to sober them all. Chal and Janfri took care to place themselves on either side of Wil. Lydia had already heard of his assault on the *krallis*.

"*Sarishan*," Valkin greeted them all from beneath his bedclothes, wincing as he turned his head.

Perhaps it occurred to Valkin that his acquaintance with the Cliftons might be hazardous to his health. He hardly glanced at Lydia, and she dared not meet his gaze. Guilt trebled in her belly at the dark stain seeping through his dressings. She busied herself at the stove setting the relief tea to steep, before seating herself beside Wil and leafing silently through her notebook for healing receipts. Syeira took up station at Valkin's bedside, undressing his wound.

"You must stop moving about," she scolded.

"Cannot this wait, my sister, my *pen*?" Valkin flinched as she tilted his head to bathe his temple.

"If this could wait, I would wait." Syeira tutted impatiently, ignoring the tension between him and her husband. Handing her mortar bowl and materials to Lydia, she turned back to examine Valkin's cut. "Your dressing is well done, Lydie. The wound hardly bleeds. We must make up the paste now, yes?"

Grateful to busy herself with medicinal preparations, Lydia took up the bowl, grinding coarse salt into an alcohol and iodine solution.

Chal stood to his brother's left, head bowed as Valkin stared at him. The *krallis* seemed to deflate suddenly, offering his hand. "It is forgiven, Chal. Brishen has matters of greater weight to discuss."

"Indeed." Wil broke in, looking as dangerous as Lydia had ever seen him. "The *sher-engro* can hardly maintain his anger towards one brother when he's so grievously offended another."

"Wil," Lydia spoke warningly as Syeira shot him a steely glare. "We're not here to—"

"I beg your pardon, my *prala*, my brother." Valkin glanced at Syeira before meeting Wil's gaze. "I had no idea she was Lydia."

Indignation bubbled in Lydia's gut.

"*No idea??*" Wil burst out fiercely, eyes blazing. "How the hell can you say you had no idea?" His effort to rise was firmly checked on either side by Chal and Janfri. They nodded sympathetically at all parties, neither of them easing their death grip in the slightest.

Lydia glared at her brother. *I'm right here.*

Valkin ran a hand through his dark hair, all but pulling it out in consternation. Syeira slapped his arm impatiently.

"Do not be foolish."

"*Both* of you." Lydia scowled at Wil before darting a glance at Valkin. Paleness gone, his cheeks darkened, those black eyes fixed on her brother. He didn't turn to her at all. Then again, Wil was the one stating a grievance. Lydia's chin rose.

"I'm right here, Wil," she spoke levelly. "And this is not your concern."

Both men ignored her. Syeira nudged Lydia, muttering a Romany epithet.

Quite.

"But you know my sister, Valkin. You've met her, for God's sake."

"As a child, Wil. Not as…" he hesitated. "As she is now."

Lydia didn't need to ask what he meant. It seemed she was not required to speak at all. Syeira paused her work to murmur in Lydia's ear.

"Romany men and Englishmen are not so very different, you see, Lydia. Each as foolish as the other. A firm hand is best." She glanced into the mortar, nodding. "*Kosko.* Keep at it."

"Wil." Lydia stood, rapping her knuckles on the table. Her brother jumped. *Good.* "This is *not* your concern."

He turned slowly towards her as though he'd forgotten she was there. "How can you say so, sister?"

Lydia ignored the heat flooding her cheeks as she stared him down. "My primary concern in this moment is to assist Syeira in preparing this remedy." She placed the mortar on the table to emphasise her point. "Is it all right?"

Syeira glanced into the bowl and took it up, patting her shoulder.

"Good." Lydia resumed her seat, expelling a long breath. "I-I l-lied, Wil. I u-used a f-false n-name," she said heavily. "T-telling Chal's men I t-travelled as V-valkin's m-mistress—"

"His *what*?" Wil shook his head, briefly shutting his eyes and making a visible effort to unclench his fist.

"I must protect myself as best I can."

"From what?" her brother asked, truly listening for the first time. He took a long, audible breath, shifting his stare from Valkin to Lydia. "Where did you think you were going, Lydie? And *why*?"

Dear Lord, how to explain it all? Old bruises on Lydia's back ached suddenly and she suppressed a cry, remembering heavy shoves against her shoulders, hands at her throat, and stinging slaps across her face.

"There is so much you do not know, my brother."

CHAPTER TWENTY-EIGHT

Lydia

Lydia took a deep, steadying breath, then another, and one more. Three breaths, three drawings of strength learned from the Romany. She opened her eyes and faced them all, speaking in a low, flat voice.

"Have you heard of the Earl of Basingstoke?"

Her brother's expression darkened as Lydia outlined her reasons for the desperate plan to find Roger and beg Lord Clifton's assistance. Wil looked as though he might actually be sick at one point. Lydia didn't omit the incident in the garden, causing Wil to fist his hands as a curse so foul escaped his lips, it made Valkin start. His eyes blazed when Lydia told of the rumour the earl had spread.

"Oh, I wish I'd known," Wil snarled. "The old earl would have seen the end of his days at twenty paces past my strike."

Valkin raised a quelling palm towards him. "This will not help your sister."

Wil buried his face in his hands. "So, what can I do?"

"Can you not guess the duke's game?" Valkin said. "There must be something you can think of."

Wil massaged his forehead. "Basingstoke is a crony of the duke's," he said haltingly. "I recall Mama taking pity on a ruined scullery maid, turned off without a reference. The poor woman ended up in a sanatorium after her child died." He shuddered, looking at Lydia. "The idea of the duke forcing you to wed such a man...?" Wil appeared nauseous again. "I beg your pardon, Lydie," he said softly. "Can you ever forgive me?"

Lydia's gaze met his. "Forgive *you*? I—I'm the one who—it was I who…" She couldn't finish, could not list her sins before her brother. She shook her head vigorously. Wil reached out and grabbed her wringing hands, forcing them apart.

"Stop it, Lydie. Listen to me." He seemed to be fighting the emotion in his voice. "I should have taken better care of you. You are my sister. I should have protected you. I was complacent. I placed too much faith in Roger and—and the duke. I did not think he would—" He stopped, apparently unwilling to put into words what was all too obvious.

Her brother shook his head. "I know what His Grace is, how little he thinks of me—of us, but I didn't want to believe he could be so—so—" He struggled for the words.

"Indifferent?" Lydia suggested, failing to keep the bitterness from her voice. "Uncaring? You are mistaken, Wil. In regards to his self-interest, His Grace shows all the energy and solicitude you could ever wish to see him display." She closed her mouth to stop the words threatening to burst forth. Years of pent-up anger and pain washed through her.

"What could you have done in any case?" she asked quietly, easing her hands from his. She doubted he was aware of the dangerous expression flashing across his face. "I am not of age and the duke is my legal guardian."

"Lydie, I would have done *something*." He sat stiffly, flexing his shoulders. "He cannot treat you like this. And—and I wish you had come to me," he said, his voice very low. "I understand why you did not. You thought, I am sure you did, that if you found me, I wouldn't help. Can—can you forgive me at all?" Taking her hands again, Wil embraced her. "I will take better care of you now. You are my family, and I should never, ever have let you forget it."

The lump in her throat threatened to rise again. Pushing her brother gently back, Lydia took a large gulp of tea to steady herself.

"I do not want your family to suffer because of me. This is why I left the camp. The duke will not allow me to stay here, and he won't sit back and let you take me from him. My only chance is to find Roger. You see that, don't you?"

Wil tightened his jaw. "I will not let our father do to you what he did to our mother." He looked round at Brishen, clearing his throat thickly. "Is there anything to drink?"

Before Valkin could respond, Reyna found his *levinor* and divided it up between several cups. She placed the largest one beside Lydia.

Lydia shook her head and sniffed, staring at a certain wood carving as though she hadn't memorised every raised ridge. "Thank you, Reyna. Your *krallis* needs this more than I."

***

Valkin

Valkin barely smiled as he accepted his cup, watching his *pireni* face her brother, her lover, and his family. Her shaken voice uttered aloud the horrors she'd endured at her father's hands, perhaps for the first time in her life. He'd never seen a more impressive feat. To face such pain alone... Her courage was greater than any of them had understood. *She did what you could not.* He was proud to love her, and he wouldn't apologise for it.

"What I don't understand—" Wil's voice shook as he spoke. "—is why you didn't tell Brishen who you were, Lydie." He glanced at Valkin. "You'd have sent for me. I know you would. I'd have found Roger myself and dragged him back bodily to face the damn duke down if I'd had to." He sat silently for a long while, staring at his hands before meeting his sister's gaze. "You're right, you know," he said hopelessly. "Roger is the only one who can help you now. No wonder you didn't come looking for me."

"That is not the reason, Wil." She sighed. "Your Romany are already barred from the duchy. I did not—*do not*—wish to endanger your family, including my nieces and nephews, any further."

"Your sister offered to leave *ker* for the same reason," Valkin broke in. "Your father's reach is powerful. Once he hears Brishen are here, he may guess where she is, and the law is on his side. Am I right in assuming the earl may pursue the duke through the courts if Lydia does not fulfil the engagement?"

Wil nodded. "If Basingstoke doesn't marry Lydie soon, her devised inheritances will settle upon her regardless." He looked to his sister. "You gain independent access to Mama's trust in January. Roger told me so when last I saw him."

"When was that?" Valkin asked sharply.

"About a year ago, after Lydia's coming out," Wil answered him but continued addressing his sister. "It's why I was so sure you'd be besieged with offers from handsome, eligible young men." He shook his head. "You've plenty to recommend you, dear Lydia. Whyever did the duke allow Basingstoke to press his detestable suit?"

"His Grace believes m-my speech impediment m-makes an eligible m-match impossible."

Wil shrugged back at her. "You've a slight stammer, is all. You did not used to stumble so in your speech."

"It began not long after you wed," was all she said, green gaze tumbling to her lap.

Valkin repressed a shudder as he recalled the older bruises he'd seen on Lydia's back.

"You're a duke's daughter and your dowry is substantial." Her brother reached for her hand. "You are also beautiful, intelligent, and determined. I assure you, His Grace's argument is preposterous."

Lydia straightened in her chair, offering a faint smile. "I have missed you so, my brother." She turned back to the others. "It must have something to do with money, though why His Grace is in need of it, I cannot guess. Perhaps Basingstoke holds something over the duke's head. I wouldn't put it past either of them."

"Leaving aside the earl's poisonous reputation and that he is practically the same age as your father, Basingstoke is not rich, nor does he own much in the way of estates. He's gambled away most or all of what he stole from his last two wives. He seems an odd match for Lydia." Valkin bit back an epithet as an image of the earl with his *pireni* skittered through his mind. "Even granting your father's disinterest in her."

Wil shifted uncomfortably in his seat. "I fear the true answer is unlikely to redeem the Cliftons in this matter. Quite the reverse." He sat back, pursing his lips. "My inquiries to Sir Geoffrey deal with the late duchess's estate," he explained. "I will try to remember what I can, but I was only a boy when she died." He fell silent again, then rose abruptly. "Perhaps I ought to be in London."

"You ought not leave your sister." Valkin indicated the small bundle in Syeira's arms as well. "This is no time to leave Brishen, my *prala*, my brother." He locked his gaze on Wil's, only breaking it when the new father nodded and resumed his seat, turning back to Lydia.

"I wish you'd have come to me. I'd have—"

"What?" Syeira broke in. "What could you, Valkin, or any of us really have done?"

"I don't know," Wil burst out. "But I would have done *something*, even if I'd had to hide her."

"And if the duke threatened your family?" Chal spoke up from the *krallis*'s bedside, looking miserable.

"Please," Lydia begged, staring desperately between Wil and his adopted family.

"Chal. *Dosta*," Valkin commanded, keeping his focus on Wil who was clearly struggling with himself. "I understand, Wil. Lydia is your family too."

"You are," Wil addressed Lydia first. "She is," he said finally, looking at his Brishen relations.

"Then we agree." Valkin brought his palms together, leading his family in the three breaths. When he was done, he eyed each family member in the *covo*, managing to avoid Lydia's troubled gaze. "We stand together or not at all, yes?"

"Yes, *sher-engro*," Janfri replied from his place at Valkin's bedside.

"Chal?"

His brother nodded, looking as tortured as Wil, who rose quietly to stand by the door.

"If Brishen will excuse us, Valkin, I believe we must speak. Shall I meet you outside?"

"Wil." Lydia's voice sounded as exhausted as Valkin felt.

Syeira gazed at both men with concern. "I will not stand for more bruises."

Valkin nodded heavily. "There will be none, Syeira. A Romany man who does not ensure the safety of his family is not judged well. This includes his daughters and his sisters in particular. You have a debt of honour to your sister, Wil, and to Brishen." He raised his hand as Syeira opened her mouth to protest. "As do I," he affirmed, shooting her a look that silenced her at once.

"If you will all leave me in peace a moment, I shall dress, and *no* thank you. I do not require assistance." He managed to hold his weak glare in place until his visitors filed out, pretending not to notice Lydia running her thumb over a certain equine carving. His glare died the moment she looked into his face.

"Valkin, I—"

"It is I who—" He'd not let her apologise to him, or for him.

"Lydia." Wil's voice came from the *covo* steps.

She flinched. "Yes?"

Wil could sound commanding too, when he wished. "You ought to be at rest in our *covo*." He may as well have ordered Valkin to keep his distance. *With good reason.*

Dropping her gaze, Lydia offered him a short curtsey. "Th-thank you," she said simply, hurrying out with the others before he could respond.

"Lydia," Valkin whispered in his empty home, sighing as he drew on fresh breeches and found his jacket. *I'm in love with Lydia.* He felt foolish and strong and horribly uncertain all at once. Lydia's true name made no difference to his heart, but for the first time in his life Valkin couldn't easily determine a woman's desires. He knew every curve of her body, each secret place inside her…and yet he couldn't read her heart at all. It was maddening.

Drawing in a deep breath, he gave his *levinor* a considered stare. Tipping his cup back, he swallowed the remaining wine in a single gulp. The liquid burned like the devil, all the way down his throat to his gut. He felt it there, a Romany fire.

Once outside, Valkin led the way to the riverbank, ignoring the shouts and waves from his many cousins and friends.

"How's the jaw?" Wil's mouth twitched.

Valkin glanced at him and grinned, wincing nearly immediately. "I'll live."

"Is this mess what you needed to speak with me about earlier?"

Valkin slowed his steps, staring at the river. "I wanted to know if you could—if there was some way to—*damn* it." He faced Wil, voice cracking. "You know more about the *gadjo* laws than I. Perhaps something may be parlayed…" His voice trailed off.

"Are you trying to tell me Lydia is betrothed to you?" Wil's face was a study in puzzled astonishment.

Valkin gazed back at him. "Betrothed…er, not exactly."

That dangerous look crossed Wil's face again.

"There is no legal ceremony in the Romany tradition," Valkin hastened to remind him. "A man and woman residing together is enough to complete a Romany marriage, once the bride price is paid."

Wil nodded. "Of course. You know Syeira and I didn't hold a Romany wedding, but Lydie is not a Romany girl, and if she is to wed the *krallis*…." His tone hardened. "I will not let my sister be outcast, *sher-engro*."

"I wish her to stay at *ker*." Valkin met Wil's unflinching glare. He didn't want to wed Lydia by default. To have her accept him only because he wasn't Basingstoke. He wanted her—God, how he wanted her—but he wanted all of her: heart, soul, and the sweetly passionate depth of love that was simply *her*. The woman he loved. His *pireni*.

"I want Lydia to stay with Brishen, Wil. I do not wish to limit her choices. We—we do not have to marry if she is unwilling. I haven't spoken to her of marriage because I do not know—"

"I do." Wil eyed him sternly. "Just what are your intentions, Valkin? Do you wish to wed my sister?"

"Of course," Valkin said so quickly that Wil seemed appeased.

He sighed heavily, rubbing his face. "Another English marriage contract may be all that can stop the earl and the duke. Still, we cannot have the law pursue Brishen for bride kidnapping. That is a serious charge."

Valkin blinked. "I did not—"

Wil made a sound in the back of his throat. "Of course not. Do you think the English law will hear it?"

Valkin shook his head as a leaden weight landed low in his gut and stayed there.

CHAPTER TWENTY-NINE

Lydia

Lydia knelt to cut nettles below the prickles. She checked her harvest for brown spots before carefully gathering the spiked leaves into her bushel basket. Once she had as many of the precious winter plants as deemed safe, she drew out her notebook and worked out a quick sketch. She recalled the information Syeira had imparted: *fertility aid. Crush to soothe the skin.* Adding these notes, she made her way back to the camp, pausing to claim the plants she recognised, though many were browned by winter. Her resolve to remain busy and avoid thinking of her predicament proved fruitless.

"I see you've found some stores." Syeira made her way from the birthing tent. "Wil is returned from Slaidburn already."

"Is there no word from London?" Lydia posed the same question she'd asked at breakfast.

Syeira shook her head, looking solemn. "Reyna is most anxious for her betrothed."

Guilt stabbed low in Lydia's belly. "D-do you believe he's met with accident?"

Syeira tutted. "Sacki is a skilled and clever rider but a Romany among so many *gadjos* is always at risk, Lydie."

"Of course. I have much to understand."

Syeira took her arm. "Life is about learning, my sister."

Lydia gestured to her basket and sat. "Will you assist me?"

The princess smiled and sat beside her. "You wish me to list these healing properties again?"

"If you'd be so kind as to run through your various methods of preparation, I shall complete my notes this morning. They must be accurate."

"I may sit with you a short while," Syeira replied. "Then Reyna may assist you. Cato's child will be born today or tomorrow, I think."

"This is good news." Lydia smiled. "My notes may wait a little. I shall find Reyna once I've completed my sketches."

"She is working in the dye tent today." Syeira patted Lydia's arm and hurried away.

A moment later rustles from the wood alerted her to Valkin, a brace of hare slung casually across his shoulder. With the sun behind him, Lydia couldn't read his expression. She scrambled to her feet.

"I-I b-beg your pardon, V-valkin," she stammered. "H-how is your head t-today?"

"Improving, I thank you." He jerked his head towards her work. "May I?" He placed his meat on the ground.

She nodded, handing over her notebook, wondering if this might be a good time to beg his pardon. A busy forest path seemed an inconvenient position from which to assert that she didn't wish to force him to the altar. Valkin deserved to marry a woman he loved, which could not be her. *Obviously.* Who can love a woman who lies about who she is? Who behaves like a mistress—and whose connections bring such threats upon his people? She almost choked this thought into words as he turned over her pages, his focus seemingly absolute.

"Where did you learn to do this?"

"At school, and at home. Mostly with governesses to oversee me. I'm afraid I was a very poor student." She tried a half-smile. "I was always running off doing something I shouldn't."

"Nothing's changed there, then." Wil appeared from the direction of the *gry* pens, his gaze trained on Valkin. "Reyna requires your needlework, Lydie." Her brother held out his arm, fixing her with his most imposing stare. "Your niece and nephew are asking for you as well." He nodded at the notebook. "Shall I take that, *sher-engro?*"

Valkin didn't meet Wil's eyes as he handed back her work. "You have been to Slaidburn?"

"No news yet." Wil drew Lydia's arm through his, leading her away from the Romany king.

As she glanced back, Valkin grunted, hefting his hares with a curse. He had a right to be angry with the woman who'd tricked him and imperilled his camp, and now Reyna's betrothed. Wil seemed to sense this.

"Until we understand your situation more clearly, it's best to remain close to our *covo*, Lydie. Do you understand?" He placed his free hand over hers.

Lydia grimaced, despite her flickering remorse. Then she recalled how Valkin could barely look at her. Fledgling ire died like a blown taper.

"I understand, Wil." Lydia straightened as they approached the dye tent. She was suddenly grateful for the exclusive company of women and soothing sewcraft.

***

The entire camp seemed to exhale when Sir Geoffrey's carriage arrived that evening, with Sacki reining in his horse so as not to outpace the lawyer's equipage. The driver managed his team well, bringing a steaming four to halt outside the eastern boundary. Sir Geoffrey stepped down without aid, clutching a leather sheaf to his chest. He seemed to collect himself before including them all in a sweeping bow, addressing Wil.

"Captain Clifton, how do you do, sir?"

"I resigned my commission on the occasion of my marriage," Wil corrected him quietly, returning the bow. "Sir Geoffrey, may I present my wife, the Princess Brishen?"

Sir Geoffrey took Syeira's offered hand, kissing it gallantly.

She smiled. "You are most welcome, Sir Geoffrey."

He gazed about with evident delight and the genuine curiosity of a well-bred man. "So, this is a Romany camp," he announced to no one in particular, beaming at Lydia before bowing again.

"Lady Lydia," he said. "You have grown up, my dear. I never would have recognised you in that charming Romany costume. I'd hoped to meet with you before now, but I was not summoned." He smiled kindly at her, and Lydia found herself smiling back. She remembered him a little better now and curtsied in her turn.

"I thank you for your prompt attention, but surely a written response to my inquiries would have sufficed?" Wil said. "I assure you I had no expectation of causing you to travel so far."

Sir Geoffrey shook his head vehemently. "I think not, sir, I think not. Your inquiries were brief and to the point, but I am afraid the resolution is less than simple." He handed Wil a copy of *The Times*, the page folded to display Lydia's betrothal announcement.

She couldn't restrain her shocked gasp. No longer was the idea merely a detestable thought in the back of her mind. Lydia quivered, but Syeira's firm hand on her arm gave her strength. A steadying breath revived her. She straightened her stance.

"As yet, no banns are posted," Sir Geoffrey added. "We must proceed as best we can, and with haste." He nodded solemnly before looking around, a little smile playing at the corner of his lips. "In any case, I should not have missed an opportunity to visit the House of Brishen." He inclined his head towards Sycira and Janfri, who stood beside her. "Have I the honour of addressing the Lord Brishen?"

Janfri shook his head. "The *krallis* attends *kris*. That is Romany business, sir."

Sir Geoffrey nodded, studying the Romany about him. Janfri called some of Chal's men across from the perimeter, requesting they take care of the English horses.

"You drive them hard," Chal said to the driver.

The older Englishman grinned, jerking his head towards Sacki. "I was doing my best, sir, to keep up with 'im."

Sacki laughed, offering to show the man where he could find rest and a meal. Dismissing his servant with a wave of his hand, Sir Geoffrey turned back to Wil.

"Allow me to offer some refreshment." Wil led the way to his *covo*, where Reyna and Narilla were putting the finishing touches to a light repast. Lydia hurried to assist with pouring tea for all. Sir Geoffrey seemed most interested in the caravan's clever contrivances.

"Marvellous," he cried as Lydia demonstrated the baby's cradle folding in flat against the wall. "Ingenious."

When he'd eaten his fill (which took some time, Lydia noted with amusement) and tasted his wine, Sir Geoffrey folded his hands and looked steadily at Wil, Lydia, and Syeira.

"I understand these matters are to be discussed openly among your family?" Sir Geoffrey responded to their affirmative nods with another one of his infectious grins. "Excellent, excellent. Then let us get on with business." He turned his head as a light tapping at the door became louder.

"I beg your pardon." Wil rose and opened the door to admit Valkin, attired in his full regal dress.

"You are very welcome, Sir Geoffrey." He bowed, looking from Wil to Lydia. "Is it permitted to join you?"

Lydia stared at Valkin, wishing he might read her apology in her eyes. Before she could speak, Sir Geoffrey rose, offering up his own seat.

"Please," he urged. "It is useful to have as many adroit minds focused on this matter as possible." He waited while Valkin sat.

"First things first." Sir Geoffrey turned to Lydia, taking her hand briefly. "You cannot be *forced* to marry anybody, my dear. It is, in point of fact, a crime." He sighed. "Admittedly, this crime is rarely brought before the courts, for the simple reason that the ensuing scandal becomes highly prejudicial to both the plaintiff and the defendant. It is an unfortunate truth of society, my dear, that it's usually the woman's reputation that suffers, materially damaging her chances of making another match. Do we all understand this so far?" He paused, sipping the tea Syeira passed round.

They all nodded.

"Now, I understand your father has promised you to the Earl of Basingstoke?"

"Yes." Lydia forced herself to exhale.

Wil's hand rested lightly over her own. *You are not alone anymore. Wil is here. Syeira is here. And Valkin.* She worked to dispel further thoughts about Valkin. What had Wil said? *One atrocious mess at a time.*

"You are concerned as to where you stand legally if you refuse to proceed with the engagement?"

Lydia nodded, and Valkin covered her trembling fingers on her other side, squeezing gently. She held her breath.

"Can Basingstoke prosecute the duke for breach of promise?" Wil asked.

Sir Geoffrey laughed. "Technically, yes, sir, he can, but a man who sues a *woman* for breach of promise? Such a case has never yet been decided in the complainant's favour. He would damage his already unpleasant reputation in the process. As your sister is not known to be connected to any other suitor, the assumption made would be that she simply finds the earl detestable. No man willingly places such information on the public record," Sir Geoffrey said confidently.

Turning to Lydia, he said, "It is not for me to criticise His Grace, but I represent your late mother's interests in this matter. I can assure you, my dear, she would not approve of the earl."

Lydia exhaled as though another set of stays were loosened, the relief flooding through her a physical lifting of weights off her chest. She breathed more deeply.

"So—so, if I refuse, absolutely refuse h-him, the duke can *not* compel m-me to the altar?" She looked steadily at Sir Geoffrey, who shifted in his seat.

"He cannot, my lady. The social implications for you, however—
"

"I do not consider maintaining my standing in society reason enough to marry a man like—like that." Lydia was glad of the pressure of Valkin's touch over her fingers.

Sir Geoffrey nodded. "Quite right, my dear. Quite right. I hope you understand it is my duty to make you fully aware of all consequences. Your mother would be proud—and so, I might add, would your grandfather. Baron Eliot was a military hero in his own right, as I'm sure you know. He always appreciated a little spirit." He smiled at her.

"In any c-case," Lydia went on, "I understand that I've little reputation left to protect. About th-the rumour, Sir Geoffrey. C-can anything be done?"

Sir Geoffrey reddened and his voice grew indignant. "It is a despicable trick to play on an innocent young girl," he began, unable to contain his hubris. "Despicable." He took a breath and a sip of tea. When he next spoke, his tone was calmer. "He has done his best to ruin you, my dear. The news *is* all over town, and I am afraid to say it is generally believed. His Grace spoke for the earl, you know." Sir Geoffrey coughed a little, looking away from Lydia's anguish.

"It's not true, Sir Geoffrey," Valkin spoke up. "This being the case, can the Lady Lydia not bring suit against the earl for slander? If Basingstoke insists the allegation is true, would this not make him guilty of rape?" He looked expectantly at the lawyer.

Sir Geoffrey beamed at him. "Wonderful, Lord Brishen, wonderful. I see you have a strong natural turn for this sort of thing. You are certain you've never studied the English law?"

Valkin shook his head and shrugged, his expression ironic. Lydia guessed his thoughts were likewise. *The law and the Romany.*

"Is there anyone who'll stand for the Lady Lydia if we press a suit for slander?" Sir Geoffrey asked.

"Certainly," Wil said. "I believe I speak for Roger as well. His word carries no little weight. You're aware he is a particular acquaintance of His Grace the Duke of Wellington?"

Sir Geoffrey nodded, making a note on one of his papers. "Good, good." He looked up. "Have you heard from Lord Clifton? Is he en route from France?"

"I sent him a letter before I left the Davenports'," Lydia replied. "I do not expect he'll arrive before Christmas."

"I, too, have sent for him," Wil said. "Though I fear my sister is right."

Sir Geoffrey looked at him seriously. "This is a shame. However, it is my duty to look after all that has been placed in my care. As a result, I keep rather a close eye on the Cliftons. The late duchess was—er—very clear-sighted about His Grace, and consequently very specific about her wishes. I shall see them carried out." He turned back to Lydia. "The precariousness of your situation would be very much lessened if you were to marry elsewhere."

Valkin released her hand abruptly, startling them all with the severity of his tone. "Marriage for the sake of it is no marriage at all."

It was as though he'd declared himself. Or rather, undeclared himself. This pain wasn't unexpected. *All Romany marry for love*, Valkin had told her, and as open as he'd been about bedding Miss Dale, he clearly didn't want Lydia Clifton. Releasing a sigh that drew air from her toes to her crown, Lydia nodded silently, her insides freezing to ice.

Sir Geoffrey stared at Valkin before clearing his throat. "Regardless of your opinion on these matters, Lord Brishen, this is how these things are done, sir." He turned to Lydia. "I understand this is your second Season, my dear. Is it correct that you have no other suitors?"

"There is no other suit, Sir Geoffrey." Lydia stared down at her lap, humiliation scorching her cheeks. "There has never been any other suit."

"As I thought." Sir Geoffrey didn't sound at all surprised.

"How is this possible?" Wil asked in genuine astonishment. "And how are you aware of this, Sir Geoffrey?"

Lydia's head snapped up. "Yes, how?"

Sir Geoffrey hesitated. "My information is that you have no other suits because the duke curtailed them before they amounted to anything. I've discovered this recently, by which time there was little I could do."

Even Wil looked shocked. Lydia had never felt so cold in her life. Her father had gone out of his way—had done everything in his power—to ensure her misery. She caught the warning prickling behind her eyes and set her jaw like a snapped trap. She would not cry. She *wouldn't*.

"Are you all right, Lydie?" Wil watched her with growing concern, and Syeira took up station behind her chair to wrap her shoulders in a heavy shawl. Lydia's fingers grasped the thick wool. She stilled, swallowed, and nodded.

"G-go on please, Sir Geoffrey." She struggled to keep her voice steady.

"I should explain myself at this point," Sir Geoffrey began, nodding his thanks as Syeira refilled his cup. "When I heard a year ago that the Lady Lydia was out, and I'd not been sent for, I wrote to His Grace." He drew a paper from his leather sheaf and handed it to Wil. He glanced at it and nodded, passing it to Lydia.

"His response was brief." Sir Geoffrey handed that note round as well. "His Grace informed me that he'd taken it upon himself to apprise his daughter of her rights, under the terms of the late duchess's estates."

Sir Geoffrey looked apologetically at Lydia. "Until you are of legal age, I cannot approach you without the consent of your guardian. As I've now been consulted by your brother, I took that as permission to come hither. However, you should know that I have been conducting an investigation of my own into this matter, since I didn't hear from you. I take it the duke has not informed you of your rights when you come of age?"

Lydia shook her head, mouth open.

"As I thought." Sir Geoffrey's mouth set into a very determined line.

CHAPTER THIRTY

Valkin

"You can tell us why, Sir Geoffrey?" Wil's voice sounded as dangerous as Valkin was beginning to feel, his hands curling into fists as he gazed at the paperwork strewn over his table. Sir Geoffrey rummaged in his pile of papers, coming up with a deed of ownership and several other documents.

"As you know, the earnings from Her Grace's trust are shared equally between your sister and yourself, sir. The real property holdings consist, in the main, of a smallish estate in Dorset and a landholding on the outskirts of Tavistock. Are you at all aware of Her Grace's personal property devises?"

Wil shook his head. "I'd no idea Mama's estate included personal property devises."

"It's not unusual to leave personal property to younger children. Family jewellery, for example, is often left to a daughter," Sir Geoffrey explained.

"You cannot seriously tell us the duke and the earl have gone to all this trouble over the late duchess's jewels," Valkin stated.

"I am already in possession of Mama's jewellery," Lydia hastened to add. "The duke gave me Mama's jewel case when I came out."

Sir Geoffrey waved his hand in the air, proffering his sheaf of papers. "Yes, yes, of course, but it is not of jewellery that I speak in this case. The personal property left to you outright, Lady Lydia, is housed on the Tavistock land. It's an equine bloodline."

"*A what?*"

For a moment Sir Geoffrey didn't seem to know to whom he should respond.

"I've heard nothing of this," Wil spoke first.

Sir Geoffrey shrugged. "The enterprise leases the land on which the breeding program takes place, hence the income that is shared between the late duchess's younger children."

"I am aware of the income," Wil replied, "and I am aware of the horses. Why was I not told they belonged to us?"

"Yes, why were we not both told?" Lydia echoed.

Valkin could think of only one answer: *the duke.*

Sir Geoffrey shrugged again, sighing deeply. "The late duchess's personal property devises are willed only to her daughter, who remains under the legal guardianship of His Grace. Until the Lady Lydia is of age, I am not at liberty to divulge the details of her inheritances to either herself, or anyone else, without His Grace's agreement." Sir Geoffrey paused to sip his tea, lowering his voice. "Addressing the Lady Lydia directly about estate matters without her guardian's permission is unsound. However, there is no specific prohibition against answering a direct inquiry from any family member who's reached the age of majority. This is why I chose to attend you immediately." His volume increased with his pomposity. "It is also why I committed no response to paper." He eyed Wil levelly.

"Our father will be displeased," Lydia guessed.

Sir Geoffrey shifted in his seat, sighing again. "This is likely, but I am not engaged by His Grace." He smiled at Lydia.

She smiled back. "It appears you risk something here tonight, Sir Geoffrey." She cleared her throat. "I thank you."

"I'd rather risk the duke's wrath than the earnest trust the late baron places in my family." Sir Geoffrey proffered more papers at both of them. "Shall we continue?"

Wil took up the first of the ownership papers, raising his brows. He passed it to Lydia.

"I do not understand," Lydia said quietly, staring at it.

Her brother spoke over her head to Valkin.

"Out of Annette, sired by Volunteer."

Valkin caught his breath. He knew—every horseman knew—that these horses were direct descendants of Eclipse, the most famous thoroughbred in England. He glanced over a detailed listing of equine names, dates, and valuations.

"I'm afraid I do not quite follow it myself," Sir Geoffrey said. "I understood all racing horses to be of thoroughbred bloodlines these days. Racing does not come within my province."

"But it does mine, sir," Valkin interjected. "If the late duchess's estate owns a pure Eclipse bloodline, it possesses an unparalleled asset. Eclipse's provenance traces back to the Godolphin Arabian, one of the founding stallions of the thoroughbred breed itself. Eclipse remains unbeaten at track." He narrowed his eyes, searching his memory for details before continuing.

"In his last few years, Eclipse remained entirely unchallenged. He was retired to stud in 1771, due to the impossibility of shortening his odds." Valkin looked inquiringly at Lydia, doing his best not to stare at her lips. He blinked, reminding himself she was under Wil's protection now. *Not mine.* He cleared his throat, clenching his jaw as though this aided his focus. "May I?"

Shrugging, she nodded back at him as he studied her documents in more detail. He expelled a low breath, leafing as rapidly as possible through two decades of General Stud paperwork, while the others waited in silence. It appeared the late baron bred only from horses foaled from Eclipse's direct descendants on both sides. The bloodline was undoubtedly valuable.

"You are quite right, Sir Geoffrey. Most thoroughbreds have some Eclipse blood in them these days. However, from the papers before me," he glanced down, "it appears Her Grace, or the baron at least, sought to preserve a pure Eclipse bloodline. If you'll allow me a few more moments?"

Valkin read through the rest of the ownership slips and glanced again at Sir Geoffrey. "These are all foaled from Eclipse, in as near a line as possible. Is it only the one horse the Lady Lydia inherits?"

"It is a *pair* of horses, sir. A breeding pair and a breeding programme, including all offspring foaled in service to the bloodline itself. The integrity of the line was maintained by Her Grace's careful management of all equine antecedents and descendants." He smiled again at Lydia, who seemed frozen in surprise.

Valkin continued his examination of the paperwork. "This is a pure bloodline." He found it less distracting to address Wil. "At stud, the stallion will bring thirty to forty guineas per service. At auction, each foal could fetch between fifteen hundred and three thousand pounds, should they be sold at all. At gate, well, there are no guarantees in horse racing, but given the pedigree..." Valkin gestured to the registration slips littering the table. He shrugged, flipping Sir Geoffrey's newspaper to the racing form before making hasty notes on a corner of the masthead. His attention restored, he looked up.

"At gate, a horse might stand to bring in one thousand pounds in purses, per year. Each. Not taking into account winnings from wagers. I am being conservative, you understand, as a racehorse's ability to win depends on a great variety of factors." He raised his eyebrows at Sir Geoffrey. "If His Grace is running these horses, Brishen will have heard of it. It cannot possibly be hidden. Eclipse's form is too well known. I fail to see what the duke is about."

"I confess I did at first," Sir Geoffrey acknowledged. "What you have said clears up a great deal, Lord Brishen. The duke is in the habit of selling or gifting these foals all over the country. I believe some are racing on the continent. No doubt he retains a portion of the monies. He is not running them under any colours anyone would notice. This way the purses don't appear concentrated, do you see?"

"I do," Valkin replied.

***

Lydia

Lydia caught the muscle jump in Valkin's jaw. His furious expression matched her own. How dare His Grace? He was her *father,* for Heaven's sake. He was supposed to safeguard her interests. She bit her lip for fear of uttering aloud several fierce epithets.

Sir Geoffrey surveyed them all. "Quite. It will be difficult to trace all the progeny and impossible to prove ownership in every case since Her Grace's passing. However, the duke is required to manage Her Grace's personal property to the benefit of the trust, not the trustee. Yet he saw fit to gift at least one of your foals to—well, have you heard of Madam's Queen? I believe she has been causing quite a stir?"

Valkin nodded. "She won the Epsom Derby this year and is favoured for our Lancashire Cup. I did not attend the owner, but it was not the Duke of Carston."

"I know the owner." Wil leaned forward as if spoiling for a fight. "Miss Charlotte Hayes. The duke's latest—well, she is…" He let his sentence finish itself.

Sir Geoffrey proffered another paper for them to examine.

"This is a sworn statement by the duke's groom that he walked the horse from Tavistock to London before handing care of it over to Miss Hayes and her stepbrother. It states that they know the provenance of the animal. I have it on good authority that Miss Hayes may be prevailed upon to give us her statement in time. When the duke tires—that is, ahem, in time." Sir Geoffrey coughed, looking down at his papers.

It wasn't possible for such a ruddy man to flush deeply, but Lydia thought Sir Geoffrey appeared embarrassed. *She* certainly blushed, having no wish to be reminded of her father's reprehensible reputation. The duke had stolen from her, had actually given part of her inheritance away to his mistresses. She wondered what she'd ever done to make him hate her so much. Taking another deep breath, she straightened in her seat.

"But why does the duke wish me to marry the earl, giving up his own claim over the bloodline?" Lydia frowned in puzzlement.

"His Grace necessarily loses control of your assets when you come of age. It is not the ownership of your asset that matters here, my lady. It's your father's actionable behaviour as trustee. He is in breach of the law. The earl is likely aware of this and uses the information to press for his suit. I believe His Grace's intent in allying you to his friend is to neutralise the earl's threats of blackmail, to protect himself from a prosecution any other husband might pursue, and possibly to retain some claim on the income the asset generates. These are formidable motives. He could not hope to influence any part of the running of the real property. Your brother here would object to such undertaking, I am sure."

"You are correct on that score, Sir Geoffrey," said Wil, the dangerous tone to his voice not entirely absent. "Mama intended those assets to care for Lydia and myself, and I have every intention that they shall. In point of fact, I would suggest our shared landholdings are kept in a better state than Clifton Hall itself. Hudson is a most capable steward."

Lydia smiled tightly at her brother as Sir Geoffrey turned to him.

"Sir, if you empower me to act on behalf of your sister, I believe I see a way to clearing this up."

"Thank you, Sir Geoffrey," Wil replied. "Outline your intentions by all means, but my sister shall speak for herself."

Sir Geoffrey clapped his hands together. "Oh, you wish to do business in the Romany way? I am honoured, sir. *Honoured.*" He bowed his head to Syeira, Wil, and Valkin, all but bouncing in his seat. Lydia looked at Wil in surprise. He smiled encouragingly, placing his hand on her shoulder.

"I'm here if you need me, Lydie," he said firmly. "But this is about you and should be decided by no one else. It's mere weeks until you're of age. I trust you to behave in the manner that best serves your interests."

Syeira nodded reassuringly and Wil took up her hand. Lydia laced her fingers through his, exhaling as the coldness inside her thawed. She took a breath.

"What strategy do you recommend, Sir Geoffrey?"

Her lawyer grew serious. "It's my advice that we keep as much of this out of the courts as possible. It is not the usual recommendation of a lawyer to say so." He permitted himself a cynical smile. "But it can do you no good to feature your name on the scandal sheets."

"But—" Lydia began, hearing everyone take a breath to interject as well. Sir Geoffrey raised his hand.

"Allow me a hearing." He could be commanding when he chose. "What we have here is leverage, my dear. I suggest that I see the duke, letting him know we have evidence of his activities. I understand His Grace has a horror of family scandal. If he fails to support his daughter in refusing the earl and bringing a slander suit if necessary, we shall prosecute him for mismanagement of his duties as an estate trustee. We shall also insist on the return of any traceable equine stock, given no proceeds of either sale or winnings were returned to Her Grace's personal estates."

Lydia nodded. "I understand."

"In regards to the earl, we will suggest he drop his suit or face a charge of slander." Sir Geoffrey looked solemnly at Lydia. "The charge, in a case like this one, would leave his lordship vulnerable to a substantial claim for damages, as he's materially harmed your chance of making a successful marriage. He will know this and be aware of his inability to fund a defence. It ought not to be necessary to have you examined—"

"Examined?" Lydia stiffened.

Wil and Valkin seemed frozen in place. Syeira uttered a small gasp.

"In order to prove slander, the court may deem it necessary for you to be examined. There is a panel of matrons. It is an unpleasant business, and my hope is that the threat of suit is enough to deter the earl from further machinations. Well, that is my advice, my dear. How do you wish me to act?"

Lydia thought carefully over what she'd just been told. A part of her—a large part, she was willing to admit—wanted to see her father get his comeuppance, not to mention Basingstoke. But if this meant submitting to an examination... she tensed, and Valkin seized her hand with a pressure that was nearly painful. Slowly, she turned her head—and caught her breath.

Valkin looked pained, his face pale beneath bronzed cheeks. Lydia tried to meet his gaze, but he blinked, turning away as though her presence offended him. She could hardly blame him. She'd lied to him and tricked him. Yet he'd still ridden after her, saved her, nearly destroying himself in the process, and then sat beside her as she learned the true depths of her father's betrayal—because the *krallis* took care of his own. *Wil's sister. Syeira's sister-in-law.* Not his *pireni.*

Swallowing bitter bile, she focussed on Sir Geoffrey. Surely, the best thing to do was free herself as quickly and painlessly as possible from her father, the earl, and all attendant "unpleasant business," as Sir Geoffrey so tactfully described her circumstances. Lydia wasn't certain there was a way to free herself from feeling like an unwanted responsibility, but perhaps distance was the cure for this too. Breathing past the jagged-glass sensation in her chest, she forced her lips into a polite smile.

"Very well, Sir Geoffrey. I engage you to act on my behalf in these matters."

He nodded back at her. "Very well, Lady Lydia, consider me engaged. I can reach you here?" He stood, gathering his papers.

"For the time being." Lydia flinched as Wil's gaze snapped her way, followed a moment later by Syeira's and Valkin's dark stares. *Now* he looked at her, sure enough—glaring and clearly irritated. She gritted her teeth, fixing her attention on Sir Geoffrey.

"Any direction to Slaidburn will reach us," Wil added. "The hour is late, Sir Geoffrey. Allow me to arrange lodging for you with Bowland. I very much appreciate all you are doing for us."

"Not at all," he replied briskly. "I'll ask you not to trouble about lodging my horses at Slaidburn Castle. His lordship returns from Bath tomorrow. I shall reside there once he is in residence. In any case, I am perfectly satisfied to spend a night in your company, if there is a spare place to sleep?" He turned to Valkin, bowing again. "I may not look it, but I'm an old campaigner, Lord Brishen. I am honoured to be here and wish to observe your traditions. My late father, Sir George Rathburne, is known to the House of Brishen."

Valkin smiled and bowed his response. "Sir George assisted Brishen some years ago. He gathered a company of legal lords to protect us from trumped-up charges of horse stealing. Your family have my gratitude, Sir Geoffrey. I would be honoured to have you accept the hospitality of my own *covo*." He gestured outside.

"I am guarding the perimeter tonight in any case, but if you'll permit me, I shall see my home is readied for a guest. First, I shall accompany you to our fireside, where you'll find a hot meal." He bowed to Syeira and Lydia before escorting Sir Geoffrey out.

***

"What do you mean you still intend to travel to France?" Wil and Syeira had not moved from the table since Sir Geoffrey's departure. Both seemed determined to argue Lydia into submission.

"I do not think it suitable to remain with Brishen. I don't want the *gadjos* to bring trouble here. When I find Roger—"

"You mean *if* you find Roger," Wil broke in. "He's not been at the address you have for months. Lord knows what he's up to."

Lydia's eyes moistened in spite of herself. Did he not understand? She blinked back a wave of memory, wishing she could forget the look she'd just seen on Valkin's face. *Marriage for the sake of it is no marriage at all.* She'd no wish to escape a loveless marriage, only to see Valkin forced into another—with her. Besides, her future ought to rest with Lord Clifton. She sighed as Wil's objections grew louder, just as when they were children.

"You cannot travel all that way unescorted, Lydia. It simply isn't safe."

"Th-then you would not be permitted to accompany m-me?" Lydia's choices narrowed again in a frighteningly familiar manner.

"You misunderstand us, Lydie," Syeira said gently. "We would not dream of placing you in such peril. It is just..." She glanced at the cradle holding her precious new daughter. "The baby naming takes place in a very few days. Wil must be present. Will you at least agree to stay until then?"

They would consent to her leaving after the naming ceremony. She could find work in the dye tent until it was over. Besides, the child was her niece, and Valkin had much to do with his family and his horses. He was hardly likely to seek her out. In any case, Wil made it clear they ought to keep their distance.

Lydia sighed, nodding and slumping in her chair as exhaustion overcame her. Syeira hurried to help her to bed while Wil shook his head at both of them, muttering about the hard heads of the women in his family.

CHAPTER THIRTY-ONE

Valkin

Syeira ordered Valkin to rest after guard duty, but he couldn't sleep. It didn't take a genius to work out why: *Lydia*. When Wil and Syeira brought his morning meal after seeing Sir Geoffrey on the path to Slaidburn, Valkin tried hard to pretend he'd been sleeping—not studying his great-grandfather's woodwork.

"Lydia agrees to remain until the naming only?" Valkin stared at Wil across his breakfast tray, resisting the urge to leap from his sickbed and demand she stay. "This is in less than a week. *Mi Dubblesky*, why?"

"She says it is to spare Brishen," Syeira replied, making them coffee. "My *gadje* sister is brave enough, but I do not believe this is her only reason for leaving us." She eyed him shrewdly. "Do you?"

Valkin shook his head, avoiding her gaze as well as Wil's. He turned the subject abruptly. "Send Janfri in to me after breakfast. We have much to discuss."

"We have *this* to discuss," Wil asserted.

"We can do nothing at present," Valkin reminded them tersely. "I shall see you both at tonight's sunset fire."

"Valkin—" Syeira began.

He raised an unsteady hand to stop her protests, willing them to accept his hint. "Our people expect it."

"They also expect you to marry," she persisted.

"I will not be rumoured into marriage." He managed a glare as the shivering came upon him again. *Nor will I allow it to happen to Lydia—again.* He would have stood, but his head ached, and his limbs remained heavy. *Damn.* "I will take my place on guard this evening, as usual."

"Then you are as foolish with your health as you are with your heart, my *prala*, my brother."

"I beg your pardon?"

"If that was an apology, you'd best save it for your *pireni*." Syeira's glare trumped Valkin's for indignation.

"This choice is not only yours," Wil added.

"I am aware," Valkin said loudly. "This is the point, after all."

Syeira made an exasperated noise in the back of her throat, shaking her head as she and Wil left him alone.

Valkin felt no less annoyed at himself. After all his assurances of protection and his avowal to keep his *pireni* safe, he'd thoroughly compromised her. If Sir Geoffrey's attempt at leverage failed and Lydia was forced to submit to an examination—*what then?* He sighed, pushing his food away. He had no appetite at all.

Drawing back the curtain above his bed, Valkin watched Lydia's embroidered flowers waving in the wind. A reminder of the woman he'd charmed into making love with him… *I love her, and she prefers to leave.*

The memory of their lovemaking sped through him, heart shuddering at the idea such a night might not have been to Lydia what it was to him. Valkin blinked at his body's response. He couldn't bring himself to regret it but if remaining with Brishen— with *him*—was something she might do from obligation… He shook his head.

Lydia must know he loved her, and if she truly wished to return to Roger and the world she'd run from in despair, Valkin must allow her choice. Unreasoning rage rose through him. He slammed his fist against the *covo* wall until it throbbed. Roger had done nothing to safeguard his sister—and she chose him over Brishen. *Over the man who ruined her.* He flinched.

The French were less rigid regarding virtue. Lady Lydia Clifton was beautiful, of valuable dowry, and she was charming, quick-witted, and accomplished. Not to mention her kiss, which Valkin could only describe as unrestrained. As soon as Roger presented her, all manner of potential suitors would fall over themselves to propose. Valkin didn't doubt that Lord Clifton would secure some pompous fop to wed her and that would be that. Problem solved, scandal averted, sister saved—from Basingstoke, and from the rakehell Romany king.

His gut sickened with jealousy. The idea of another man laying hands on the woman he loved filled him with fury. She was *his,* damn it. He felt it, knew it in his heart, and there wasn't a damn thing on earth or in heaven he could do about it—because she wasn't his at all if she didn't choose it. Valkin swore, shoving his bruised hand into a jug of icy water.

This was what he'd wanted, wasn't it? To show his *gadje* she had choices now, releasing her from the awful thoughts she'd been taught to believe. Appalling opinions reinforced year upon year by a family refusing to value her as anything but a pawn. *Any man of sense can see she is a queen.*

He dried his hands, then reached for the wood carving he'd been working on. Taking up his knife, Valkin sat up, heedless of the wood chips littering his bed as he completed his rendition of the Romany queen. When he was done, he stood the figurine on his palm, gazing at the tiny mouth.

"What will it take to have you stay?" he murmured.

"*Sher-engro?*"

He turned on hearing Janfri's knock outside his door. "Come," he demanded, aware of his curt tone. "What reports from Dunsop Bridge?"

***

Lydia

Lydia stood awkwardly by the entrance to the dye tent. All of Brishen must know how she'd deceived them. Both Wil and Syeira assured her no one was angry, but Lydia squirmed with guilt when the old woman beckoned her inside again, without smiling.

She straightened. There was work to do here and she need not be idle. It was better than counting the moments until she heard from Sir Geoffrey. Two days since his departure, and no news. Her niece's naming was but three days away. Taking a deep breath, Lydia called across the tent.

"*Sarishan*, I am in need of a plain silk." Holding her last shoe buckle aloft, she offered her trade. "I-I wish to sew something for Syeira's new babe."

Narilla turned from her work beside the vats and smiled. "Very good, Lady Lydia." "We shall find this for you among our newer bolts of silk. You have not much time."

Lydia dropped her shoulders at Narilla's benign expression, shrugging away the remains of her anxiety. "I know my pattern by heart. A day or so will see it complete." She smiled again as an image of the little child returned to her memory. A prettily stitched gown would be just the thing to gift her niece. Something by which to remember her absent aunt, if she left.

And if I stay… Lydia shook herself, turning her attention to business.

One of Narilla's cousins proffered her merchandise with a curtsey. Lydia curtsied in her turn, accepting the fabric. It was finely woven and light enough. Exactly what she required. She surrendered her buckle and opened her work box.

Lydia resumed her place at the foot of the great oak, sliding her needle through the silk as silently as she imagined Valkin's anger undercut his pride. Shoving this thought aside, she tied off her leaf design before beginning the lavender stalks. It wasn't difficult to avoid the glances of the other women, or the whispers moving through the tent. Once or twice, Lydia felt Narilla's gaze on her or detected a sharply voiced rebuke, but she held her focus as long as she could until she was surprised to note the dimming light outside.

She jumped up, her muscles aching in protest. Gritting her teeth in response, she turned to Narilla. "I must return to my brother's *covo*. Syeira will be wondering where I am."

"Of course, my friend." Narilla took her arm. "I seek Reyna. Allow me to walk with you to your family."

My family... Tears threatened but Lydia shook them away. "You're all truly determined to look after me, aren't you?"

"You are one of us now." Narilla laughed lightly, eyeing the sliver of moon and seeming not to notice Lydia's lack of response. "We've missed your English stories at our fireside these past evenings. Will you join us again?" Her tone was so beguiling, Lydia wondered if she took charm lessons from her eldest brother.

"I am e-expected?" She couldn't keep the surprise from her voice. After everything she'd done?

"Of course." Her friend repeated. "It will please our princess and her consort."

But not Valkin.

"I will attend if it pleases Brishen." Lydia followed Narilla into the tent she shared with Reyna, but only emptiness and shadows greeted them.

"I shall await my sister." Narilla curtsied carefully and sat. "Will you find your way from here?"

"Thank you, yes."

"If in doubt, think like a Romany." Narilla smiled. "Your heart will lead you home."

Lydia made her way into the gathering dusk. On her own in the night, finding her way to Wil's *covo* wasn't as easy as she'd thought. She hesitated—was it left? The faint odour of the *gry* pens reached her and she gathered her bearings. If the horses were straight ahead, then Wil's *covo* must be behind it. This must be how the Romany do it, by listening to their senses. *Your heart will lead you home.* Since when did her English heart exhibit any sense at all?

CHAPTER THIRTY-TWO

Lydia

"Lydie, it is wonderful." Syeira unrolled the finely worked ivory gown the following evening. "However did you manage it?"

Lydia glowed with pleasure. Her lavender flower design with small herbal leaves had consumed two days. The work kept her closeted in the dye tent and out of everyone's way. With such an effective distraction, she'd hardly considered Valkin. *Only every other moment*, her heart whispered. Perhaps one simply became accustomed to heartache as if it were a speech impediment.

"I do wish I'd found a little lace for trimming. Ayrshire lace would suit, I think."

"It is lovely work," Syeira insisted. "I need no lace to admire this. Lavender, in memory of your duchess, and mint grasses. Do I have this correct?"

Lydia nodded, delighted. "It is not too small for her?"

Syeira held out the gown above her daughter as she slept in her cradle. "It is a little large, I think."

"Oh. I beg your pardon."

"What for?" Syeira laughed, laying the gown aside and taking her hands. "My daughter will grow, my sister, my *pen*, just as you have done."

Lydia ducked her head, uncertain how to respond to that.

"You are not used to receiving compliments, I see. We shall work to repair this." She led Lydia over to the little table where she poured tea for them both.

"We still do not know her name," Lydia mused, smiling at the baby.

Syeira sat beside her. "Her name is chosen by the *krallis* at tomorrow's ceremony."

"Tomorrow?" Lydia echoed, cheeks flushing despite herself. "I-I thought we had more time."

"Valkin is prepared," Syeira replied, rising. "Come, I have a gift for you as well. That is, it is a gift from Wil and me, in truth."

"For m-me?" Lydia opened the wrappings, marvelling at the full Romany gown, with skirts and ruffles in place. The cloth was exquisite: a unique Brishen silk tint, the colour of a winter-blue sky. Silver threads woven through the garment gave it a glimmer.

"Oh, how lovely. May I wear it to the naming tomorrow?"

Syeira smiled incredulously. "It is yours to do with as you wish, Lydie. You may wear it wherever you choose. My cousin assisted in making it over. Her figure is the most like your own I have seen at *ker*. She will be pleased you approve of it."

Lydia couldn't stop smiling. "I do, very much. Where is my brother? I wish to thank him as well."

"Wil rode to Slaidburn to deliver Brishen's remedies and seek your correspondence. He returns shortly, and he'd best be punctual," Syeira said smilingly. "He's promised Renie and Culvato a breakfast picnic tomorrow."

"Who has promised you this?" Wil spoke in a mock-boom as he opened the door, piling in behind Culvato and Renie, Little Wil drowsing in his arms. "It cannot be me." He grinned at his son.

"It *is* you, Papa. You gave us your word." Culvato frowned uncertainly at his father.

"You've not forgotten, Papa?" Renie's eyes were wide as she stared pleadingly at Lydia. "He hasn't, has he, *Bebee* Lydia?"

Lydia smiled. "It's not like my brother to break his word."

"Of course I've not forgotten," Wil assured them all. "But, children, you've not greeted your aunt and mama properly."

Culvato bowed towards Lydia and his mama, while his younger sister attempted a curtsey.

"Shall you accompany us then, *Bebee* Lydia?" Culvato asked as he rose from his bow.

"Oh. Yes, do," shouted Renie, clapping her hands before catching Syeira's glance. The girl lowered her voice, but it was too late. Little Wil's startled wail could have woken the dead. Syeira sighed and sat, gathering her youngest son into her lap.

Lydia stood, holding out her hands to the other two. "Shall we eat our dinner with your cousins?" She smiled as the children slipped a hand into each of hers. Syeira shot her a weary look so full of gratitude that Lydia glowed.

"Before you go, Lydie." Wil drew a sealed letter from his watch pocket. "This awaited you at Slaidburn."

Her heart gave a funny sort of jump. The familiar urge to wring her hands was foiled by her nephew and niece tugging her determinedly towards the door.

"I-it is addressed to you, not me," Lydia pointed out as Renie pulled at her.

Wil offered a one-shouldered shrug. "Banished from the duchy or not, I am of legal age and you are not. Sir Geoffrey is very proper."

"Well, my hands are full," Lydia replied, negotiating the *covo* steps without releasing either child. "Open it, please, Wil. Shall you read it as we walk?"

Her brother broke the seal and scanned the page as he exited the *covo*. "It's brief," he reported. "Sir Geoffrey met with Basingstoke in person and is in correspondence with the duke. Both parties are—" He glanced up with a tight nod. "'Unhappy with developments'— hah—but His Grace has agreed not to call the banns. This is good news, Lydie."

Grateful for the distraction of the two children attached to her, Lydia stumbled onward in dizzy relief. She was glad of a chance to sit beside the fire while the children fetched their food.

"Oh Wil," she whispered. "I'm free."

Wil hugged her close, kissing her brow. "You may stay with us in safety now. We must find Valkin." He looked around and made to rise.

Lydia tugged him back to his seat. "M-must we find h-him immediately?" She stared at her brother, willing him to understand that she couldn't remain if Valkin were obligated to marry her. *Marriage for the sake of it is no marriage at all.* Each syllable stabbed deeply into her fragile heart. "I mean, need he know our business?"

Wil gazed back at her with raised brows. "This is his business, Lydie. Brishen's safety is a matter none of us take lightly." He sat back in his seat. "What is it you're afraid of?"

Lydia shook her head, sighing into the chill night air.

"Do you prefer I fetch Syeira?" Wil persisted.

"Your children are coming. D-does Sir Geoffrey say anything else?" Grateful it was too dark for Wil to read her expression, Lydia leaned over the page, studying Sir Geoffrey's spidery scrawl by firelight.

"Hmmm," Wil muttered, returning to his letter. "Basingstoke is particularly vicious in his remarks. No surprises there, but Sir Geoffrey says the threat of scandal has made the duke see reason. His Grace departs for France shortly, while Sir Geoffrey expects the earl's signed agreement at Slaidburn tomorrow. There is more to discuss regarding your horses, but the largest hurdle is behind you." He gave her shoulder another squeeze. "If that's not reason for a breakfast picnic, I don't know what is. You will join us, won't you?"

"I believe I shall." A morning outside camp with her family seemed an excellent way to avoid Valkin's ire, but Lydia couldn't help smiling at the cheers from her nephew and niece. The children handed round stew for them all, setting one aside for their mama.

"*Bebee* Lydia will picnic with us," Renie announced as Syeira arrived, taking her seat beside Wil.

"Thank you, Lydie." Syeira grinned as she ate. "The children cannot easily get into trouble with both their *bebee* and papa presiding."

"Though I am sure you will both try." Wil grinned at his children's protests before turning to Lydia. "Reyna and Sacki may join us, if they can be spared. It will be a fine thing to wander the woods with you again, Lydie. I understand you are keeping notes for our herbs?"

The pride in Wil's face lifted Lydia's heart. So this was family, togetherness, connection. *I do not want to leave this.* Her heart throbbed with a dull pain.

"I must thank you, Wil, for my gown. Such a lovely surprise." And given to her with no expectation other than her own delight. "Thank you both. It is too lovely."

"Nonsense," Syeira responded with vigour. "How are you feeling now? No more of the numbness in your fingers and toes?"

"Not often." Lydia chewed her lip. "I shall be very well for the naming."

"This is excellent news. The paternal aunt usually performs a service, if she is present." Syeira seemed not to notice the clang of words into sudden silence. "Your lot is to bear the babe while the naming takes place. Will you hold our daughter before the *krallis*?"

"Bear the babe?" Lydia repeated faintly.

Holding her niece and standing close beside Valkin. Steadfastness would be required, and a calm visage. Lydia thought of her niece gurgling in sleep, clutching her pillowed sachet of dried lavender and chamomile. She glanced down at her gown, a gift from her family. *My family.*

"It is my honour, truly." She struggled to smile.

"Thank you." Syeira handed her a small bag. "Take six of these seeds each day. You have the dried herbs for your nerves as usual. Both will assist your nausea."

Wil started. "Nausea?"

"Thank you," Lydia tucked the herbs into her pocket-pouch. "Breathe, Wil. I'm not pregnant." *At least, I don't think so.*

"Nausea may be a reaction to near-drowning and the freezing seawater," Syeira said. "It is not possible to know so soon afterwards."

"But—it is, er, possible?" Wil stammered. "He did—you both did, er—" He reddened. Clearly the idea of his sister in bed with his brother-in-law still rankled. Lydia hardly knew where to look.

"Lydie?" Syeira spoke gently. "It is all right." Her tone softened and the gaze that met Lydia's showed understanding. She kept her eyes on Lydia as she addressed her husband.

"A beautiful *gadje*, claiming to be Valkin's mistress, in his *covo* for days, with her stays too tight?" Syeira sounded nearly amused. She looked Wil squarely in the eye. "If it were you, Wil, and a pretty girl was in your home without stays, what would you do?"

Wil lifted his princess's hand to his lips, his eyes warm. "What I did do. Love her. Marry her, make her mine," he murmured, pulling his wife close, brushing his lips over hers. "Every day."

Lydia exhaled, smiling. "I am so glad, Wil, that you chose Syeira."

Her brother's gaze was both pained and powerful.

"Lydie, I never meant—"

"I know," she whispered. "I don't blame you, Wil. Syeira spoke truly. My situation is not your doing." She held out her hand and he took it. "I'll not be able to return to Clifton Hall. Not now." This prospect was no longer as frightening as it once seemed. *I seek a certain kind of love.* Taking another deep breath, Lydia straightened in her seat, meeting her brother's gaze. "I understand why you left, Wil. I do not wish to return, b-but I am not certain remaining h-here is right for m-me, either."

Marriage for the sake of it is no marriage at all.

"Because of Valkin?" Syeira asked.

"Because of me," Lydia whispered, turning to face Syeira's dark eyes. *Eyes like his.*

Syeira took up Lydia's other hand. "It will be Christmas soon. You come of age shortly after and will be mistress of your own fortune. You need not decide everything at once." She expelled a breath. "There are many Romany between here and Paris, Lydia. If you truly wish it, we will find a way to get you to Roger. Agreed, Wil?"

Wil said nothing for a long time. "I believe it is best for Lydie to stay with Brishen." He caught Syeira's sharp glare, flinching visibly.

"It is your sister's decision, no?" Syeira's glance didn't falter but her tone gentled as she squeezed his hand.

Wil blinked hard and nodded, kissing Syeira's wrist. "As you wish."

"Mama. Dance with us." Shrill voices called from the circle of firelight. Syeira rose with a smile and a curtsey, leaving Lydia with her brother.

Wil sighed, settling himself in his chair. "Brishen will make this right, my sister, my *pen*."

Lydia said nothing, her gaze shifting from the lively children to the musicians where the mandolin player appeared absent. She nodded to several women from the dye tent, smiled at one or two of the *gry-engros*, and waved at a group of children. She certainly wasn't looking for anyone in particular. She found him anyway.

The *krallis*, seated in his wooden chair, surrounded by his brothers, Reyna, Narilla, and a Romany woman Lydia didn't recognise. She stared at the striking woman seated to Valkin's right. Darkly attractive, the girl leaned in to whisper something in his ear. He laughed, kissing her cheek. A flash of heat speared. Lydia's muttered oath must have caught Wil's ear.

"It is not like the ton here," he said gently. "The Romany—well, Brishen at least—do not behave like the duke."

Who is she, then?

"She is our sister, Daiena. She wed the *sher-engro* of House Camlo last spring. They travel from Derbyshire for our Romany

Christmas and to share in the joy of our daughter and Reyna's wedding."

Lydia turned her head. "His sister?"

"His sister." Wil sighed, eyes glistening in a manner similar to her own. "And Syeira's, and Reyna's, and Narilla's, and Janfri's, Chal's, and mine. She is your sister too, Lydie, if you wish it."

"W-what i-if…" Her voice shuddered to a halt as she squared her shoulders, balancing the queasiness in her gut. "I-I d-do n-not th-think h-he w-wishes t-to b-be w-with m-me."

To her surprise, Wil laughed softly. "I do not pretend to know another man's heart, Lydia, but I've known Valkin Brishen one-third of my life. Never have I seen him so moved by anyone as he seems to be by you." Leaning in, Wil kissed her cheek. "Valkin appears as much in love with my sister as I am with his."

His tender postscript hung between them, warmly weighted with affection. She took his hand, and Wil gave her fingers a firm squeeze. "It is truly very different here, Lydie. Allow yourself some time to know this."

Lydia searched his face in the firelight, finding nothing but gentle sincerity. They sat there a few moments longer, until the musicians began a series of energetic reels. Her brother rose with a smile, drawing her up beside him. "As I was unable to attend your first ball, my sister, my *pen*, may I now make amends?" He bowed.

Lydia curtsied, smiling. "Thank you, my brother, my *prala*. I would like this very much."

She was free of the earl and of Clifton Hall. This was good news, she knew it was: Roger would assist her once they located him, and most importantly, Lydia no longer faced a life alone. Paris remained her best possible course. She'd have her horses and Roger, who was her family too. *My family.* Lydia sighed heavily, remembering Narilla. *You are one of us now.*

Wil tucked her arm in his, leading her towards the haphazard gathering of children and adults. He claimed his wife as soon as he could, speaking with Lydia whenever the dance allowed. She twirled

Culvato for the most part, who described the morrow's activities as well as his father or mother might have done. Lydia found herself looking forward to her role in the naming of her niece. A single moment in honour of her brother and his family seemed a fitting way to farewell Brishen. *After tomorrow I may go, if I wish.*

***

"What is this one called in English?" Renie deposited yet another leaf among Lydia's skirts while Wil and Sacki shadow-fenced with small boughs, the little boys mimicking the grown men charmingly.

Lydia looked up from her sketch of Reyna and Chore, examining the foliage. "It appears to be an oak leaf. This means there must be acorns. Shall we look?" She stood and placed their botanical collection beside the rifles and the leather bag that held their breakfast. She handed her work to Reyna, who studied the image for a moment, then the slumbering Chore, and laughed.

"Is it like?" Lydia asked.

"It is quite wonderful," Sacki said from behind them, panting hard and grinning at the dog's stillness. "Allow me to trade for this rare illustration."

"Rare?" Reyna smiled, lifting her brows at him.

"Chore only poses for pretty women." Sacki shook his head, tossing his stick aside. "Your hobbies do not weary me as your brother's do."

"Do not mistake my sister's demeanour," Wil called, fending off the parries of both his sons one-handed. "Lydia is a crack shot, though I've not seen her hunt."

Reyna looked up curiously from stowing her sketch. "Is this so?"

Lydia laughed. "My aim has always been keen." Smiling at her brother, she offered a brief curtsey.

No longer able to resist Renie's pleading gaze, she clicked her tongue at the lurcher. Taking her niece's hand, she allowed herself to be tugged past Sacki's grazing mount towards a hidden copse where, presumably, they'd find oak trees aplenty. Wil paused from fending off his sons.

"Renie, show your *bebee* how we find the way back. Culvato, attend your sister." Culvato bowed for Lydia before taking up his musket with an obedient nod. Renie released Lydia's hand, dropping to her knees at the edge of the clearing. Arranging what appeared to be small patterns of leaves and sticks, she jumped up with a smile.

"This is how we make a *patrin, Bebee* Lydia," she called, running rapidly out of sight, Chore at her heels. Lydia hurried to catch them, wondering how Wil and Syeira managed to wrangle three of these seemingly endlessly energetic beings. Then she recalled that the entire camp assisted them. Brishen were more than a family by blood. They were a community, and for a moment the pull to remain at *ker* seemed unshakeable. An image of Valkin flashed before her. *Do I have the courage to stay if he does not forgive me?*

"*Bebee* Lydia, look." Culvato pointed out a withered patch of leaves. "It is the dropsy plant."

Lydia didn't need her notebook to know he was right. "Well done." She smiled and knelt. "Your mama will be proud of you. I'll gather the freshest leaves to take back with us. You'd best keep up with your sister." She jerked her head towards the path ahead.

A second later, Renie's scream jolted like a slap.

Lydia shot to her feet. "Renie. Get up against a tree," she shouted, hitching her skirts and running. She arrived in the clearing to a torrent of Romany from her little niece, who bore a large mark across her cheek.

Blind rage burst through Lydia as she raced towards the little girl. "Chore. Guard. *Rak,*" she ordered, fumbling against her skirts for her pistol.

"*Bebee.*" Renie screamed an alarm and Chore's barking grew frenzied. Loudly drumming hooves were the only other warning. Horses thundered towards them through the trees as the rider sought his target: her.

"Wil," she called behind her, but it was too late.

A footpad grabbed her roughly by the shoulders. "His lordship said yer'd stick out here. And yer know what...? Yer do."

The rider leaned down, dragging her across his mounted seat.

"Got you," shouted a coarse voice as she fought against them.

"Let me go." Lydia wriggled, catching the brute's thumb in her teeth. The man swore, slapping her face.

Crack.

Lydia shrieked as smoke rose somewhere above her head. Culvato moved in front of his sister, one eye on Lydia as he half-raised his rifle again.

Chore's growls grew more menacing.

"Get the brats." The footpad mounted his horse, levelling a weapon at Renie.

The other faced off against Culvato. "Try it, lad, and we'll have the law."

The law and the Romany. Lydia's body went limp. Sheer willpower held her voice steady.

"Leave it, children." Forcing her gaze rapidly over her nephew, she lingered on Renie. "I'll go with these men."

Her captors swung back towards their path. Lydia glimpsed Wil's horror as he ran towards them, Reyna and Sacki at his heels. The last thing she saw was Reyna holding a handful of grasses to Renie's swollen cheek. Years of practise kept her from despair.

He's won.

CHAPTER THIRTY-THREE

Valkin

"You will not offer me a hint of my daughter's name?" Syeira aimed a mock-glare at Valkin across her *covo*.

"No hints." He grinned, tickling his new niece beneath her chin. Her mama hung bundles of winter herbs by the eave for drying. The morning's *kris* had been mercifully brief, and he'd missed Syeira. The babe gurgled up at him, blinking in the sunlight. "Where is your family today?"

"If you mean to ask after Lydia, she is with Wil and Reyna picnicking in the woods. This assists us all. Our sons require arms training and I require a moment's peace."

"I asked after your family." Valkin's face warmed under Syeira's incredulous gaze. "I did not mention Lydia, though I'm glad to hear she assists with your children."

"Lydia assists Brishen with many things," Syeira responded, smiling at her tiny daughter. "Her sewcraft is excellent, her record-keeping is first rate, her knowledge of dyeing grows daily, and she trades as well as Narilla now. She also rides astride nearly as well as Reyna. This is quite apart from the joy she brings to Wil and me."

"And she dances like a queen." Valkin said the words aloud before he could stop himself. The heat in his face intensified.

Syeira snorted a laugh. "Valkin Brishen, you are blushing."

"I-I am not," he stammered.

Syeira folded her arms and fixed him with her stare. "Either you're blushing, or you shaved with nettle juice this morning." Her face softened. "You've heard the news from Slaidburn?"

Valkin pressed a kiss to his niece's brow, hoping his expression remained hidden. "The duke no longer insists on Lydia's betrothal. The earl's acquiescence is less certain." He forced the hope from his voice.

"She will not marry him." Syeira's certainty nearly gave his hope back. "It does not follow that Lydia will stay." Her death-stare collided with his.

Valkin adjusted his glare. "Relying on Roger makes no sense at all. Is she so determined to leave us?" *To run away from this, again.* He kept this last part to himself, but Syeira seemed to hear his thoughts.

She sighed, shaking her head at him. "Lydia has loved you since she was a child, Valkin. No woman of sense and spirit stays where she believes she's unwanted. Especially if she remains unasked."

Valkin nearly dropped his niece. "Syeira, you are not making sense."

"No?" she replied, taking back the babe. "Why else would she attempt to pass herself off as your *gadje* mistress? She chose you. *You.*"

"She chose me," Valkin echoed, blinking in shock. "I suppose… it isn't a terribly plausible ruse." He dared to voice his truest concern. "Syeira, she's barely spoken a word to me since we—" He blushed again, shrugging as his stare caught the forest path he guessed they'd taken.

Syeira drew out a chair and Valkin sat.

"Do you love her?" The gentle question knocked the breath from his body.

Attraction, desire, lust—all these sensations were there, but the need to aid and protect, to be with Lydia because he *had* to, was compelled, had no choice in this obeisance to his own driving necessity… Valkin had seen it many times when a Romany man met a woman he needed beside him no matter what. *So, this is love.*

"Do I love her?" He turned from the forest to his *ker*, seeking the most ridiculously decorated *tan* he'd ever seen. A slow smile creased his face. He looked at Syeira, nodding as his smile faded. "Yet she wishes to leave."

"Love is not easy to recognise when you've not met it before." Syeira rocked her fussing babe in her arms.

Valkin shifted in his seat. "How can she not know I love her, when we—?"

"Did you love Lady Davenport, too?" His sister eyed him shrewdly.

"This is different." He sighed, shaking his head as he pulled the cradle out from the wall. "*She* is different."

"Lydia has cause to doubt those she trusted most, Valkin." Syeira placed her child on her shoulder and rubbed her tiny back, smiling at the small sound. "Loving a Clifton means starting from the beginning." She placed the babe in her cradle and turned to make up poultices with the remaining herbs.

Valkin drew the finished wooden chess piece from his vest, studying the tiny face.

Syeira examined his figurine. "Your queen is complete?"

"Not quite." *What will it take to have you stay?*

Valkin sighed. "Love?"

"Love, Valkin."

He pocketed his queen and stood, bowing himself out of his sister's *covo*.

He determined to find Lydia, but when he approached the woods, he met Wil, Renie huddled miserably in his arms.

"They took her, *sher-engro*," Wil said flatly.

Renie dropped her leaf-filled hand from her face, revealing the bruise. The *krallis* grabbed Sacki's weapon in his fist. "Who?" Steel laced his voice.

Only when Renie wailed did he remember his tone.

"Basingstoke's men." Wil's voice was grim. He jerked his head towards his *covo* and kept walking. "Renie needs her mama."

Valkin hefted his rifle, striding beside them.

Syeira gathered her daughter into her arms, taking charge of her sons from Reyna and Sacki. She examined Renie's face, kissing her daughter's brow. "She will heal." Issuing a command to Culvato, she shut all four children firmly inside their *covo* and joined the others.

"You're certain Basingstoke has her?" Syeira asked. "Your father—"

"Appears to have washed his hands of the whole business," Wil replied, his gaze on Valkin. "In any case, he's left the country."

Valkin swung himself atop Bavol. "Basingstoke will not remain at Slaidburn long."

"It'll be long enough." Wil moved to mount his horse.

"No, Wil," Valkin ordered.

"*Sher-engro*, I must—"

"You and Syeira must remain here." Valkin stared into Wil's furious face. "If the *gadjos* return for any reason, Brishen will require an advocate. One the English recognise."

"Your family needs you," Syeira added quietly, staring across the *ker* at her *covo*.

"I cannot fail my sister again."

"Brishen will not let this happen," Valkin declared.

Wil tightened his jaw, lifting his chin. *So like Lydia.* "She is my responsibility."

"Not anymore." Valkin faced the fierce ire of his adopted brother. "Lydia is my responsibility now, as *krallis*, as *sher-engro*, and as the man who loved—*loves*—her."

"Does she know that?" Wil's voice rose as he shrugged off his wife's touch.

She will.

"I cannot protect Lydia and Brishen at the same time, Wil." Valkin leaned forward atop his horse. "We're losing time."

"But—" Wil stopped at Valkin's raised palm.

"I'm asking you to trust me with your sister." Valkin glanced at Syeira before locking his gaze on Wil's troubled face. "As I once trusted you with mine."

Wil drew his wife close. "Go then, and do not fail her. Or me."

"*Ja.*" Valkin dug his heels into Bavol's sides.

***

Lydia

Lydia's heart beat with dull horror. Her captor's stench was nausea-inducing enough, but the thought of the earl awaiting her at the end of it all had her retching. *The end of it all...* She couldn't bear to think of it. After everything she'd done to keep herself safe, she was back where she began. Memories of her family raced through her mind. Dancing with Culvato last evening, Renie determined to learn English, and Little Wil sobbing on her shoulder at the least provocation. Wil and Syeira, Reyna and Sacki, Janfri and all the Romany who'd risked so much to aid her; and Valkin. She didn't know if she'd ever see him again, but the memories of his *ker* felt like strength.

Then the image of her niece's bruised face…

Lydia bit back a sob.

She had a family again, bonds worth preserving. As the horse's hooves drummed away beneath her, she set her jaw. *I am not alone. I will not be a pawn.*

The horse's pace shifted. A moment later they raced up a steeply paved road, halting just past a pair of immense iron gateposts. Lydia recognised Slaidburn's heraldry. The ancient castle fort sat atop a bald rise of land about a half-mile distant. Her captor halted at the old Lodge, long known as uninhabited. Despite this, candles flickered in the lower windows.

Lydia swallowed, before inhaling as deeply as possible. Exhaling seemed a sort of surrender and she was determined not to give in. Besides, she'd only breathe the scent of the earl's man again. Then she really would be sick. The fellow dismounted, attempting to drag her down.

"You will not touch me," she snapped, though her voice shook.

The brute removed a pistol from a pouch at his hip, covering her inelegant dismount. Lydia stumbled and stood, scowling. She looked for an avenue of escape, but her captor jerked his head towards the doorway of the Lodge.

"Ye'll go inside if ye know what's good for ye."

Her odds of reaching her own weapon before being shot weren't good. Lydia straightened and swept towards the entrance, reassured by the weight of Wil's pistol beneath her gown. Without acknowledging the barrel at her back, she lifted the iron door knocker, letting it thud loudly back in place.

A butler dressed in Basingstoke's livery answered with a pistol levelled at her chest. When he beckoned her inside, Lydia had no choice but to obey.

Her captor pocketed his pistol and snatched a linen bag from the butler. He returned to his horse, snorting as he hefted his blunt.

"She bites," he called, galloping away.

Lydia glared at the butler. "He does not refer to his horse."

The man firmed his grip on the weapon. "His lordship will see you now." His discomfort calmed her considerably, especially when he seemed to baulk at her glare. He showed her into a dim parlour.

The setting was entirely foreign for a moment. Lydia blinked, wishing for the certainty of dirt beneath her boots and the warmth of the great central fire at her back. Turning to the window, she stared down into the Forest of Bowland, needing the sun moving through the trees, yellowing light matching shades of foliage.

The door behind her opened and shut. Bile rose in her throat as an oily laugh echoed in the silence. The clink of crystal and scent of liquor reached her, and still she did not turn.

"I have your contract here," the earl sneered. "Your fop of a lawyer dropped it by my rooms at the castle."

Lydia swivelled reluctantly from the window. *Ugh.*

Brandishing a paper as though intending a duel, Basingstoke slammed it onto an end table with a roar. "Lies."

Lydia jumped an involuntary step back. The broad sill against her buttocks indicated she'd nowhere else to go.

Basingstoke leaned over the table, perusing his contract. Part way through another tumbler of drink, he lifted an ink bottle, emptying it deliberately across Sir Geoffrey's neatly covered foolscap.

"What do you think of that, girl?"

"A-about as much as I th-think of you," Lydia shot back, resting both hands on the stone sill to steady herself. Glancing down at the gown gifted her by the Romany, she recalled a chess manoeuvre taught by her brothers. *I hope you're ready for me, my lord.* Sliding one palm along her skirts, she traced the outline of her pistol.

Basingstoke glowered, veins in his neck bulging with rage, his glare raking over her with undisguised fury. Lydia doubted she'd last the requisite three months if they wed. The earl looked ready to murder her where she stood. He raised his tumbler of brandy in a mock-toast, taking a long swallow.

"You've led us a bloody dance." His address fell heavy with innuendo. "All for nought, it turns out." His gaze strayed to her hand, teasing her skirt. Lydia froze; had he guessed what was hidden beneath her petticoats? *May he remain ignorant.*

"That costume is an abomination," he scoffed, finishing his drink. Slamming the glass down on a table with a loud crack, he advanced towards her.

Swallowing hard, Lydia remembered all that'd transpired between this man and her father. A powerful fury built deep within. Recalling the bruise on Renie's face, she faced Basingstoke with her own deadly determination.

"You will not sign Sir Geoffrey's agreement?" Her voice sounded clearly in the sudden quiet.

"I did *not* slander you," the earl muttered, shifting his bleary gaze as though cheating at cards. "I didn't," he repeated sulkily. "I said you're a whore. That is not a slander."

Dear Heaven, the man was mad. Like some rabid, cornered beast. Should she scream? Would anyone hear? She prayed Sir Geoffrey remained at the castle nearby.

"And I said—" Basingstoke closed in on her. "—that costume is an *abomination*." He moved faster than Lydia expected, hulking over her. She slid her hand across the front of her skirt.

"Think you can tempt me now?" he breathed. "Defective whore."

She found the slit she'd sewn into her gown.

"You bloody tease." Basingstoke grabbed for her skirts. "I'll take my dues." He shoved his knee beneath her petticoats, one hand yanking at her hair. "Beg me," he demanded. "Beg me not to hurt you."

Roaring flooded Lydia's ears. She drew her weapon.

CHAPTER THIRTY-FOUR

Lydia

"Get back." Willpower alone held Lydia's hands steady.

The parlour door crashed open.

"My lord." Sir Geoffrey rushed in, his gasp of horror not breaking her focus. Basingstoke ignored him. Lydia levelled her pistol.

"Get away from my wife."

Valkin.

A pause, a beat, a heart-stopping second. Mind whirring wildly in the gathering silence.

The earl choked. "What the Hell are you on about, Brishen?"

Lydia uttered a sound—something between a gasp and denial— then flexed her fingers on her gun handle.

"You've been outplayed, my lord," she said quietly. "Accept it with good grace, and—"

"*The hell I will.*" Basingstoke grabbed her pistol by the barrel and whirled round, aiming at Valkin.

"Don't you *dare.*" Lydia yanked off her bonnet, slamming the full weight of the Clifton family jewels into the earl's skull.

Basingstoke staggered backwards, shaking his head. Lydia struck him again and a third time, grabbing back her pistol as he fell heavily against the stone sill.

She trained her pistol on him again. Renie's hurt face seared her memory. She could kill, she realised with a strange little beat of awareness. Murder without pause if Basingstoke so much as shifted his weight towards any of them.

Kneeling, she shoved her pistol barrel against his chest. "You will *not* hurt me or my family again." She pressed the weapon harder into his skin. A thin trail of blood marked the earl's temple, his bruised face purpling up nicely.

"Get up."

Valkin hauled Basingstoke to his feet.

"Sir Geoffrey, do furnish his lordship with a fresh contract. I'm afraid your earlier work met with accident." Lydia jerked her head towards the quill-laden table, without taking her eyes off Basingstoke.

Sir Geoffrey scoffed down at his precious paperwork. "Ah." He extracted the copied foolscap. "I request his lordship abstain from further brandies this morning," he said tightly. "I have the agreement we discussed earlier, absolving you from a charge of slander, in return for releasing His Grace from prosecution in the matter of your betroth—"

"I will not sign." Basingstoke sniffed, looking at Sir Geoffrey as though he'd encountered a cowpat.

Lydia tilted her head. "You will sign," she said calmly. "You will sign, or face scandal, ruin, and the ire of my friends and family."

Valkin offered a slight smile. "This includes the duke—"

"His Grace is *my*—"

"Of *Wellington*," he finished as though Basingstoke hadn't spoken.

"Hm. Lord Clifton's commander, who is in far greater favour with His Majesty than my sire," Lydia added. "How many duels can you fight in one morning, my lord?"

Valkin shoved Basingstoke over to a clear table and loaded a quill with ink. "You heard the lady."

The earl glared at him, and Lydia lowered her pistol. "Find some grace to do it without any threat."

"Bah." Basingstoke scribbled so hard the paper tore through. "You'll not get away with this, any of you." He spat at them all.

"Lawful impediment. Breach of promise. Bride kidnapping. Underage betrothal. Unlawful guardianship."

"Slander. Intriguing an innocent. Fraud. Criminal negligence. Assault. Attempted murder. Kidnapping." Matching her steps to her words, Lydia advanced towards him, pistol held steadily before her. By the time Basingstoke backed against the oaken panels, Lydia's breath brushed his face, her weapon pressing into his gut. She shoved it hard enough to bruise. "If one word of your accusations reaches London, I'll prosecute my case for slander and send an account of our *betrothal* to every scandal sheet in the capital," she said firmly.

Basingstoke's snarl became a grimace, then nothing more than a dim little whimper. "You little wh—"

"I've not finished." She raised her chin, just an inch. "Should any harm befall my friends as a consequence of your actions, you'll find the same fate awaits you."

"You'll be ruined. Society won't—"

"Thanks to you, I'm already ruined," she replied. "But I take it you've not played chess before, my lord?"

"Chess?" Basingstoke snarled.

"If you had, you'd know there's none so dangerous as a player with nothing to lose." She lifted her pistol barrel to Basingstoke's forehead. "Remember the chill of this metal," she warned.

"You can't shoot an *earl*," Basingstoke shouted.

Lydia glared at him, taking several steps back. She pressed her index finger into the trigger. The snick of her fully cocked shot sent a jolt through her spine. Valkin moved to her side.

"Remember, you are Romany now," came her *krallis*'s quiet murmur. He brushed the back of her hand with a light feathering of fingers.

"You do not wish me to shoot him?" Lydia arched a brow.

"I didn't say that." Valkin responded. "I only suggested it may be unwise."

"I'm afraid I must concur." Sir Geoffrey tutted. "I must also bear legal witness."

Lydia considered the earl, before nodding towards the door. "Go," she ordered. "Take your horse and get out."

"You'd best heed her advice," Valkin added.

"I need no help from you."

Crack!

Ancient panelling splintered from her well-planted blast. Basingstoke jumped a foot in the air, turned on his heel, and stumbled out. A slamming from the main hall indicated his lordship had flown at last.

A Lodge servant peered cautiously into the room. "Do your guests wish to dine at the castle, Sir Geoffrey?" The man eyed the damaged door. "Is everything in order?"

Lydia glanced at him, trying to hold on to relief. "I take it the earl's left us?"

"He has, my lady."

"Then everything is in order." Lydia sank into a nearby armchair.

Sir Geoffrey turned from mixing up three brandies and waved at too many splinters littering the rich rug. "This mess may wait a little. I'll call at the castle when you're wanted."

The servant bowed and left them.

"I must beg your pardon sincerely, my lady." Sir Geoffrey handed Lydia a snifter. "As my letter explained, I awaited the earl at the castle. I'd no idea he planned anything so desperate until the Lord Brishen alerted me. We deduced the Lodge directly."

"I thank you for your ready assistance, Sir Geoffrey." Valkin took up his drink. "An English lawyer makes an excellent witness when the Romany face a peer of the realm."

Lydia barely heard them. "*Gone*," she whispered, as though speaking it aloud made it more credible. "The earl is truly gone." She stared numbly at the bullet-battered wall of the Lodge. *He is gone.*

"Er…and did I hear right?" Sir Geoffrey addressed Valkin politely. "Is the Lady Lydia now your bride?"

"So my Romany believe." Valkin smiled, setting aside his glass. "The rumours regarding the *krallis* and the *gadjes* are quite wild this Season. It's time I put an end to them all." He knelt before Lydia, taking her free hand in his.

"*Pireni*, will you?"

"Oh. Yes. *Yes*—I—" She stopped, waiting for the stumble in her speech that never came. "I will," she mouthed this last part because her voice stopped working entirely. Possibly this was her lungs ceasing to function, because instead of kissing her hand, Valkin rose, taking her with him and drawing her to his side.

"I should have said so before now, *pireni*." His gaze locked with hers.

Lydia's eyes glistened. "Are you certain?"

"Y-yes." His voice came low but barely steady as he kissed her, just once, softening the heat between them to something more sensual than urgent, more gentle than wild.

His gaze tingled over Lydia's skin. She took another gulp of brandy. *You are Romany now.* Her cheeks burned as Valkin stared at her, fanning her newly signed agreement. The ink was still too wet.

"As you are betrothed, I can have no scruple… My sand box is in the castle library." Sir Geoffrey gathered in his paperwork as though he held the original *Magna Carta*. "The ink may dry more rapidly with sand and—ah—I have correspondence that cannot remain neglected." He left the Lodge at a scurry, though Lydia hardly noticed.

CHAPTER THIRTY-FIVE

Lydia

Valkin fingered the damage to the ancient panelling and shook his head. "It's rather a shame though."

"What is?" Lydia looked up from fixing another brandy. She was in no mood to apologise.

"You've quite relieved me of the need to call the brute out." The pride and admiration in Valkin's voice set her cheeks aglow.

"I may like to undertake such myself." She smiled faintly.

"You are not the first Romany wife to say so, *pireni*." His gaze travelled over her with a searing heat Lydia felt in every part of her, like lightning, like love. *Like him.*

"This is the second time you've referred to me so." She studied the bullet-blasted door as though it mattered.

"Perhaps I enjoy the way it sounds."

Lydia's head whipped around, dazed relief forgotten.

His gaze met hers, stable and warm. That charm again, dangerously intent. Desire flared low in her body. She reminded herself this wasn't over, holding on to her good sense by the thinnest of threads.

"I beg your pardon," she murmured. "I'm grateful for your assistance with the earl, b-but there has not been any wedding. Not even a betrothal, until now."

"Brishen do not require one." Valkin's voice warmed, his gaze heating further, lingering on her mouth. "We may be betrothed under English law, but we are nearly wed in the Romany way. We require only your bride price, and that we've loved—"

"Loved?"

He didn't blink. "That we love each other."

Lydia's heart slammed against her rib cage. Her chest heaved as she stared at him, barely managing a whisper.

"Th-then you were not maintaining form b-before Sir Geoffrey?"

"I was not." It seemed he held his breath. "I am not."

Lydia tried summoning both her wits and her courage.

Valkin got there first. "You avoided me at *ker*, Lydia. You wished to run away again. From this. From us. F-from m-me."

Her gaze plummeted to the ground so quickly she imagined a moment of vertigo. Placing her drink safely on a table, she knotted her hands in her lap. "N-no. I mean..." She swallowed, wishing she knew more curse words. "I understand you must be terribly angry with me."

"Why should I be angry?"

"How can you ask?" She stood, heat burning through her. Shame. Fear. All twined through with her fierce desire for Valkin. She wasn't ready for the rising heat between them as his gaze intensified. *Oh God, that look of his.* Closing her eyes, Lydia heard nothing but his breathing and her own. It sounded remarkably like being in bed together.

"Valkin, I l-lied to you. Endangered your Romany. T-tricked you...I—I..." She breathed deep and ragged, past the knife-like pain beneath her breast. "This is not the moment to beg your pardon, but I must." She twisted her fingers in and out of knots. Valkin drew a sharp exhalation before he clasped her hands, and slowly, Lydia opened her eyes.

"Please," she said. "Forgive me?"

"There is no need." Valkin brushed gently at her knuckles, at the fight she'd just gone through. "I understand why you concealed your true name, and why you felt you had to leave my *ker*. You need not beg my pardon for anything. Though it was never my intent to trap you, it is I who ruined you."

Lydia could have sworn fear laced his voice.

She shut her eyes again. In no possible way could she look at him while asking this question. "Is this how you think of me? R-ruined?"

"Don't *you*?" His deep voice lifted a notch in surprise. He released her, and she wanted him back. His sureness. His certainty. The warmth of his touch.

"I did not accept you b-because we—" she whispered, opening her eyes and finding nothing but desire in his soft smile. Relief rushed through her like a bracing wind. "I don't feel ruined."

"Don't you?" He wore the strangest expression.

She leaned closer, her heart beating a tattoo on her ribs. "I know I ought to." Silence hung between them like a veil. Lydia swallowed, breathing through serrated stillness. "I am not sorry for it." The words slipped out stealthily, emboldening her. "For me, it was…beautiful. Tender. Like coming home." Her voice broke on the word.

Silence once more: warm with another inheld breath this time. Valkin nodded, sighing, a soft sound that might have been beautiful. Her heart shifted in response. His smile warmed his eyes and the air they breathed. She allowed it into her heart, leaving an indelible impression. Like his kiss.

Lydia smiled back as he claimed her lips, his knowing fingers caressing the sensitive flesh of her neck. He stopped, despite her whimpering protest.

"You did not answer my question." He lifted her chin so their gazes met. "I need to be certain that—you are certain." His voice fell so low, Lydia strained to catch his words.

"I'm certain, Valkin." She took his hand, and it was as if a physical flame leaped between them. "I *wanted* to be with you."

"And I with you," Valkin replied with a smile so devastating Lydia blushed anew. "I still do, *pireni*. I love you."

She stroked gently at his jaw as the memory of his flesh buried deeply inside her echoed into her heart, forcing harder, faster beats. The rise and fall of her chest drew his gaze, his lips, his tongue, until his touch brushed her neck and shoulders as she lost herself in intimate reverie.

"Come here." Uttering a low growl, Valkin pressed her body against his. *The power of him. The heat.* His lips took hers in a soundless rush, her mouth opening in helpless surrender. His tongue slipped over hers, possessing her lower lip in a sensuous excursion that had her wanting more. Heated wet warmth pooled between her thighs, her nipples hardening at the thought of his mouth moving over her body.

"I want to be yours again, Valkin." Her voice broke on a breath.

"In good time," he replied on a sigh. Threading his fingers through hers, he wrapped her in his arms, holding her tight.

"In—" He kissed her. "—good—" He kissed her again. "—time."

His last kiss seemed to challenge time itself, and Lydia was certain she lost her balance.

"You have a plan for my bride price, then, *pireno*?" She tasted him again.

He smiled against her lips. "You do not make betrothal easy, Lydia." He drew back. "And I always have a plan."

***

Valkin

God, it was good to hold this woman again, especially when she looked at him like this, all hope and love and burning desire—and a distinct absence of fear. It was gone, Valkin noted with satisfaction: entirely absent, seemingly replaced by trust, in him and in herself. He smiled slowly at her. It nearly hurt to do so because he so badly wanted his mouth on hers, her taste on his tongue. Leaning in far closer than was decent in any English parlour, his mouth found her lips again, pressing a soft kiss.

It was all he needed.

They had time. The rest of their lives, and Valkin put his love for Lydia—all his heart and soul—into moulding the shape of her mouth to his, tasting her until she whimpered his name. He stood before her, barely believing she was his. *Hmmm...not quite.*

"This isn't over yet." Offering his arm, he bowed. "We must return you to your brother's *covo*."

Lydia raised a brow. "I cannot stay with you?"

"Not yet." Valkin didn't bother to hide his grin at the earnest desire in her voice. "I've dreamed of nothing else for weeks," he assured her. "Sir Geoffrey may be relied upon to find a license and arrange the banns at St Andrews of Slaidburn, but we must agree a bride price that will satisfy your brothers. Will you reside with Wil and Syeira until then?"

She nodded. "I understand that being wed in both Romany and English protects us all, but—"

Valkin pressed a light kiss to her lips. "I gave your brother my word. He will not excuse me twice." Stepping back, he drew out Wil's watch and frowned. "He may not forgive either of us if we do not return soon. I'll ride ahead and request they hold over our niece's naming. The Lord of Bowland may find a quieter horse for you, and an escort."

Lydia tutted and glanced at his timepiece. Checking her pistol was correctly loaded, she uncocked it and replaced it in her pocket pouch.

Valkin watched her with trepidation. "What are you doing, *pireni*?"

Lydia shot him a look that might have humbled Wellington himself. "I'll not let our family down." She was already partway to the door.

"Bavol is not trained to carry two," Valkin insisted, weary, worried, and wild with desire all at once. "You are far too stubborn, and—and—"

"You'll not convince me otherwise, so you may as well accept it." Lydia headed out.

Valkin quickened his pace to catch up with her. "I must hasten the ride," he cautioned. "Steeplechase."

"Understood."

In the hall, he took her by the arm and kissed her. He couldn't help it. She was infuriating, she was alluring—and she was *his*. "How is it possible you're wed to a Romany for barely a day, and you're already more stubborn than all of my sisters?"

"Some might call it determination." Smiling, Lydia found the courtyard and Bavol. She stroked the stallion's forehead for a moment, his nose already sniffing playfully at her hair. "Hello, sir."

Valkin cupped his hands to assist her mount, but Lydia grasped the animal's mane, lifting herself astride without aid before cocking one saucy brow. "I don't intend to wait long."

"Nor shall you have need." Valkin swung himself behind her, issuing the command that sent his stallion forward. He reached around her several times to firm her hold on Bavol's mane, but there was no need. Lydia kept her seat with relative ease. A surge of pride welled within him as he grinned into the freezing winter wind.

They arrived on the outskirts of *ker* in just over an hour, dismounting as soon as they spied the perimeter guard. Leaving Bavol with one of Chal's men, they hurried to find Wil, though Valkin found it delightful having to pause every few feet and receive the embraces of his many cousins.

"*Sarishan*. All is well." He looked around for his brothers.

"It's good to see you both." Chal stepped forward and embraced him, the lurcher circling their heels. "We thought to hold over the naming. Will you take some rest, my *prala*, my brother?"

Valkin shook his head. "Our niece has gone nameless long enough and our Romany require assurances. Once I have seen to my attire and found coffee, I shall be ready."

"As will I." Lydia stepped up beside Valkin, then clicked her tongue at Chore. "*Rak tute*," she added, smiling at Chal and the other men. She kissed Chal lightly on the cheek. "It's good to be home."

CHAPTER THIRTY-SIX

Lydia

The Romany houses gathered around the central fire. Several of the men tuned fiddles while Lydia walked carefully on Wil's left. Syeira took Wil's other arm, following a prettily laid pathway of coloured leaves created by their older children. The new babe's siblings sat as quietly as they knew how with aunts Reyna, Narilla, and Daiena keeping a close eye. All around them, a humming sounded as the Romany gathered to honour one of the royal House of Brishen.

Valkin approached from the other side of the fire circle, mounted, booted, and as handsome as it was possible for a Romany king to be. Lydia smiled, straightening her shoulders.

Valkin dismounted, nodding to Wil as he received the babe. Placing a blackened cord twined with golden threads around the child's forehead, Valkin turned and handed the babe to Lydia.

She held her breath, swaying with the little girl whose eyes matched her own. A piece of her heart melted as she gazed down, remembering the way of the naming as Culvato had explained it.

Valkin looked them over, and Lydia stifled a sound because she *felt* him: his proximity to her, his scent of coffee, leather, and herbs. Heated breath caressed her earlobe like a touch as he whispered the babe's name while she held a large leaf over the child's opposite ear.

"Caterina," he breathed.

In honour of the late duchess, Catherine. Such consideration flooded Lydia with warmth and love. She shivered, instinctively clutching little Caterina more firmly as she lifted her head, meeting Valkin's steady, dark gaze.

He'd taken her fully and he desired her still. Loved her: *Dear God, Valkin loves me.*

She presented the child to Wil and Syeira and repeated the name to all of Brishen. "Caterina."

The surrounding throng clapped and cheered, then muttered into silence as the musicians struck their first note. Valkin smiled at the crowd and sang for them all.

> *Coin si deya, coin se dado?*
> *Pukker mande drey Romanes*
> *ta mande pukkeravava tute.*

The humming became a low, chanting lullaby as the attendant Romany took up the *krallis*'s song. Dozens of his people stood around them, watching Valkin with pride. His people, following his lead, certain in his care for them, satisfied in his interest and commitment to their families. How many Romany trusted this man with their lives? All of them, it seemed. Valkin held out his arm and Lydia took it, barely registering the stares and whispers from the crowds of people so gathered. There was interest, certainly, and gossip, but no malice. She held this thought close as she accompanied him to the central fire, trying not to react when Valkin placed his other hand over her own. Touching her, again. *I miss his touch.*

"Caterina." She glanced quickly around. "It honours Mama. I—th-thank you."

Valkin nodded. "This is my intent. She is a pretty child."

"She's beautiful," Lydia said loudly, flushing when he turned his jet-black gaze on her. She hadn't meant to sound officious.

"Yes, I suppose she is." He paused, looking at her with open desire. "Beautiful, that is. Like her *bebee.*"

His voice dropped so low, Lydia leaned in to hear him. "Shall we dance?"

"Yes."

His hold enveloped her: warm, safe, reassuringly firm. The musicians serenaded them. Dimly, Lydia registered her brother moving with Syeira, Reyna swaying with Sacki, and Janfri leading his little girl in the dance. Valkin stepped closer. So close now, the dancing couples near them exchanged knowing glances.

Valkin grazed her ear with his lips. Lydia shivered in his arms, swaying against him as she lost herself in the gentle sounds, his quiet humming. A rhythm seemingly created for her alone. The dance ended and she almost groaned, allowing him to guide her a short way along a secluded forest path.

Lydia smiled up at him. "I am glad to hear you have a plan for the bride price, because I miss—"

"I know," he whispered. "I miss you too." Seating himself on a nearby tree stump, he pulled her onto his lap. Tipping her head up to meet his lips, she sighed as he took her mouth beneath his, stroking her lower lip possessively with his tongue, catching her hot, ragged breaths between his lips, giving them back to her until it truly felt as though they shared the same air. He loosened her braid, threading his fingers through her curls, pulling lightly as he deepened his penetration of her soft, wet mouth.

He stroked one tight, hard nipple with his thumb, responding to her moans, her whimpers, her small, soft gasps, with deeper, longer kisses. Lydia kissed him back, her tongue keeping pace with his, her nails scoring his skin beneath his shirt. This was what she loved best about him, about *them*: this untamed passion, this uncaged storm of love and desire that she wanted to be part of—oh, she wanted nothing more. She wanted *nothing* more...

"Lydia." Wil's voice diffused the haze of desire faster than sleet over flame. He stood like a sentinel guarding the path back to *ker*.

"Your brother." Valkin grinned, shaking his head.

"My brother," Lydia agreed, smiling back.

"I, too, have family to appease. Brishen must know their *krallis* is betrothed." He stood to bow, kissing her hand and leaving her to her family. Until the bride price sealed their marriage, she required a chaperon and Wil seemed determined to shadow her.

"I'm not a child, Wil," she pointed out mildly.

"You are my sister, and your bride price remains unresolved." He stared after Valkin. "We ought to return to the others."

Syeira stepped out from between the trees. "Your sister is older now than I was when we wed, Wil."

"Old enough to make my own choices," Lydia added.

"Indeed." Slipping Wil's hand in hers, Syeira tugged him back towards the fireside. Lydia followed them in time to hear a great cheer erupting amid shouts of Romany blessings. Syeira turned around, beaming at Lydia. "You have accepted the *krallis*?"

"Yes, at Slaidburn. How did you—"

Wil grinned. "There are no secrets at *ker*, my sister, my *pen*. Are you truly betrothed?"

"Truly, I am," Lydia whispered, tears springing to her eyes as she accepted embraces and kisses from Wil and his princess, and an intimate smile from Valkin that crossed the distance of the camp.

So, this is family.

This is home.

This is love.

EPILOGUE

Twelfth Night

January 5, 1821

Forest of Bowland, Lancashire

Lydia

Snow clouds swirled above Lydia's head like some sort of otherworldly portent. Blinking flakes from her eyes, she turned at the sound of voices and footsteps. Two pairs of boots approached with another, heavier tread.

"Easy, girl." Valkin's deep drawl sent heat through her belly.

Lydia smiled in anticipation of his kiss. "*Koshti Sarla*, gentlemen."

"Good evening, Lydie." Wil's was the first face she saw through the mist. He bowed, stepping closer, and it was only then that Lydia saw who accompanied him—or rather, what.

The fine-boned head of a high-stepping bay horse followed behind him. Valkin led the animal carefully by the bridle. The mare stamped two hooves in the freezing air, her graceful neck stretching as she began an exploratory sniff of Lydia's hair.

"*Oh.*" Lydia gulped ice-edged air, moving a step closer to the brazier, gaze riveted on the beautiful creature. "Oh, Valkin. Is she—" She swallowed, breathing deeply. "Is she my horse?"

"She is indeed." Valkin smiled, bowed, then took her hand in his and placed a soft kiss at her temple.

Lydia shook her head slowly, releasing his hand. "It is impossible," she whispered, walking round and round the animal. "Utterly impossible."

"Nothing is impossible, *pireni*." Valkin laughed gently. "If you are stubborn enough. "

She grinned. "Some might call it determination."

"Happy birthday, *pireni*." Valkin lifted her fingers to his lips, kissing them before placing the reins in her palm and curling her fingers around the leather strappings.

"Yes, happy birthday," Wil added, kissing her cheek.

"Th-thank you," she stammered, staring at the horse as though the mare were a dream. "How—*how* did you...?" She stroked the animal's velvety nose. "Hello there." She laughed as the mare rubbed hairy lips over her gloved fingers. "What is her name?"

"She is not yet named, nor registered, but she is yours, Lydie." Valkin smiled gently. "Yours, absolutely."

Lydia smiled back. *Yours, absolutely.* Wil cleared his throat, and she returned her attention to the horse.

"His Grace attempted to sell her abroad," her brother explained. "Sir Geoffrey found it out and Roger fetched her back for you. The mare foals in the spring and ought to journey no farther. Her mate is en route to Tavistock. Valkin parlayed for their return. Your bride price is met."

Lydia breathed out quickly, inhaling another gasp of desperately cold air to dilute this delicious tension. *Better.* Definitely better, and she knew now precisely what she wished to do. She soothed her horse with rhythmic pats on her flank, then reached beneath her to unbuckle the girth. The mare shifted and snorted, horsey breath steaming beside Lydia's own.

"What are you up to, Lydie?" Wil asked.

Lydia smiled to herself. "Unlacing her stays." She kept her gaze on her fingers at Valkin's burst of laughter.

"There." She stood upright, removing the bridle as well. Once she'd placed the leather and silver finery on the bare ground, she led her horse by one confident hand beneath the mare's head.

When she reached Valkin, she stopped, curtseying low and deeply. His gaze followed her movement, lingering over the swells of her breasts without a trace of self-consciousness. Desire flared in his eyes, matching the hot tingles in her belly.

"Will you accept this mare's foal into the Brishen stock, *sher-engro*?" Taking his hand, she placed his large palm beneath the animal's chin. "For all you have done for me," she whispered. She couldn't explain why she needed him to accept her gift, to allow her contribution to Brishen. "Surely Brishen have a use for this bloodline?"

"Your thoroughbred foal will make a valuable addition to our racing stock. I'll train him myself." Valkin spoke with an urgency she'd not heard in his voice before, and he reached for her hand, his warm gaze overflowing with love.

Lydia smiled at the sensation bubbling up from the sweet well inside her, flowing outward until she couldn't contain her happiness, chose not to, and released her delight in a peal of infectious laughter. She turned to Wil.

"Does this mean we no longer require a chaperone? Oh—"

They stood alone, just her and Valkin.

"Did you see Wil return to *ker*?"

Valkin grinned, pulling her close. "Your brother is no fool." His lips found hers, possessing, caressing, loving. "Shall we?" He led the horse with one hand, the other moulding Lydia tightly to his side.

"Where are we going?" Lydia stared at his mouth, wanting him again.

"Our *covo*," Valkin replied. "Home."

"Home," Lydia repeated as though the word broke a curse.

"You belong with me, *pireni*." He stopped to face her. "Now, and every day from now."

Lydia drew his mouth to hers, voice breaking against his lips. "I am yours, Valkin."

"As I am yours, *pireni*." He kissed her passionately until she warmed to her core. "Absolutely yours."

ABOUT THE AUTHOR

Clyve is an award-winning author of historical fiction in Australia and the U.S. She has been writing historical romance for the best part of two decades. The first piece she published was a fictional biography of an erotica writer who made a living crafting extremely explicit dating profiles for online chat sites.

These days, she lives fairly simply, sharing her home with a small white demon dog and a budding Amazonian warrior. She believes love is the highest and strongest force known in the world, and that it manifests only when we are our best and truest selves. She'll continue writing about love in all its various, glorious forms, and that one day her epitaph will read "Just one more read-through."

When she isn't writing fiction, she can be found pounding the sand at any of the beautiful beaches near her Australian home. She's addicted to short-haul ocean swims and researching quirky historical fashion trends.

Stay in Touch with Clyve:
website: clyverose.com
FB : /clyve.rose.5
twitter: @ClyveRose
IG: clyverose
TikTok:@authorclyverose

www.BOROUGHSPUBLISHINGGROUP.com

If you enjoyed this book, please write a review. Our authors appreciate the feedback, and it helps future readers find books they love. We welcome your comments and invite you to send them to info@boroughspublishinggroup.com.

Follow us on Facebook, Twitter and Instagram, and be sure to sign up for our newsletter for surprises and new releases from your favorite authors.

Are you an aspiring writer? Check out www.boroughspublishinggroup.com/submit and see if we can help you make your dreams come true.

Love podcasts? Enjoy ours at www.boroughspublishinggroup.com/podcast

www.ingramcontent.com/pod-product-compliance
Lightning Source LLC
Chambersburg PA
CBHW021505240626
47154CB00002B/518